HIGH PLACES

Stephen Bransford

CROSSWAY BOOKS • WHEATON, ILLINOIS
A DIVISION OF GOOD NEWS PUBLISHERS

First printing, 1991

Printed in the United States of America

ISBN 0-89107-616-6

99		98		97		96		95		94		93		92		91
15	14	13	12	11	10	9	8	7	6	5	4	3	2			

*To Amos and Stacie,
the pride and the light
in their Daddy's eye*

ACKNOWLEDGMENTS

My gratitude toward family and friends is beyond measure. First, to Meganne, my wife, for trimming the budget and making the sacrifices necessary to keep me writing. For helping me through the self-doubt, second thoughts and other emotional lows— not to mention the shared celebrations. (There would be no *High Places* without her!) Beyond that, I owe a lifelong debt to Roger Flessing, who first encouraged me to write, and opened doors when no one else believed. I am also grateful to Mark Olsen; young, talented, well-educated and oh, so tenacious. (Thanks for the freewill editing, Mark.) To my brother Tim and his wife Pam for having faith, and for sending money when I ran out. To Dad, Mom, Sandra Fauth and Ruth Glass for reading the early drafts and giving their comments. To my step-daughter Diana Fuller, whose perfect instinct inspired the ending, to Falcon pilot Rick Jackson, and to Leon and Carol for love and support through the years. A special thanks to Jan Dennis for his encouraging two-page letter and for having the vision to develop this kind of fiction at Crossway. To the incomparable agent Sealy Yates, for wise counsel in much more than just the business of writing. And finally, to Glenda Smith, the intercessor who kept her arms of prayer around me through the dark years. May the God who sees in secret reward you openly.

HIGH PLACES

I

THE INTERCESSOR'S DREAM

For God does speak—now one way, now another . . .
In a dream, in a vision of the night . . .

(JOB 33:14-16, NIV)

1
BROWNSVILLE, TEXAS
Grace Ministries Campus
11:59 P.M.

The Prayer Steeple seemed to sway like a tall ship on the surge of a coming storm. Spotlights surrounded it with a radiant haze, glowing through windblown fog. At the spire's pinnacle, fingers of mist rolled past a cross of finely beaten gold. The swaying was an illusion of light and clouds—the Steeple remained firmly anchored in the South Texas soil.

Beneath the belfry, the structure housed a small apartment where an old woman tossed in her sleep. A student-nurse bent anxiously above her, watching. The sleeper's lips parted, forming a scream, but the constricted air in her lungs would only allow a whisper . . . ". . . Nephilim . . . Nephilim . . ."

"What are you saying?" the student-nurse asked, feeling her stomach tighten with apprehension. "What does that mean?" She grabbed the old woman's satin- and lace-covered shoulders. "Wake up, Lydia. Please? Come on, honey, don't do this to me."

As if to answer, the Steeple bell struck the hour. The coed started at the sound, then slowly relaxed as the carillon rolled its familiar tones across the 22,000-acre campus below—university, hospital, television studio, golf course, administration and residential zones—home to Grace Ministries International.

On a work-study assignment, the coed spent three nights a week in the tower watching over retirees who manned a bank of telephones for Dr. Simon Grace's television ministry. On this particular night the phones had been unusually silent and the girl had taken an elevator to Lydia's apartment on the uppermost floor, hoping to catch some sleep. Hearing a disturbance through the wall, she had come to investigate.

As she continued to watch, the friendly wrinkles at the corners of the old woman's mouth twisted in a scowl of pain. *Why would God allow such a nightmare?* the coed puzzled. Of all the retirees who worked the Steeple, she knew Lydia to be truly devout. None of the endless golf, bridge or shuffleboard parties for her—she lived the life of an intercessor, pouring out her remaining years in prayer for Simon Grace—the man of God who had built this faith healing empire. The calluses on her knees testified to her uncommon zeal. *God should at least protect the old woman in her sleep, shouldn't He?*

A whispered scream continued to force itself between the intercessor's lips, twisting the muscles of her mouth like a distasteful medicine. ". . . Nephilim . . . Nephilim . . ."

The mysterious name invaded the girl's mind like the creeping fog, spreading a blanket of fear in its wake. *Who in Heaven can I trust if God brings this kind of terror on Lydia?* she wondered. A shudder dislodged the remains of her composure, and she struck the old woman on the cheek—once! twice! "Wake up, Lydia! I said, 'wake up,'" she cried, her voice strangely distorted.

The old woman did not wake up, and the girl recoiled in shame, watching the red tracks of her own fingerprints spread across the weathered skin. "I'm sorry, honey. Won't you please wake up for me? Please?"

She picked up a damp cloth and began stroking Lydia's face, but even as she did the sleeper's expression contorted in another spasm. "Aaaaa-ah!" the intercessor cried, her frail body arching upward as if in birth pangs.

The girl drew back with fright. "Did you see that?" She whirled toward a security camera hung in an upper corner of the room. "I hope you're watching down there." Running for the door, she paused momentarily to look back. "I'm going for help," she promised.

The scuffling sound of her oversized house slippers faded down the hallway. Near the ceiling, a red light on the security camera continued to blink, scanning the room from above. Its servo-motor made an electronic whir as it rotated back and forth.

Nearly barren, the room was an odd combination of bedroom and religious sanctuary with a cathedral ceiling and large-faceted stained-glass window. It perched high in the structure, where the outer walls of the tower narrowed toward the cross-bearing spire.

An antique prayer station sat at the foot of the bed, hand-quilted cushions sewn to its pedestal. An open Bible and a box of Kleenex lay on its lectern. The wall above the headboard held the picture of a handsome, snowy-haired minister smiling professionally behind a clerical collar. There were other frames of children. Grandchildren. Freckle-faced. Grinning past missing baby teeth.

The intercessor continued to toss on the bed with labored breathing, eyes flickering rapidly behind her tightly closed lids. Sweat formed a glistening film on her forehead and temples. Within her sleeping mind, the old woman was aware of a peculiarly vivid dream. She felt sharp contractions, like those she'd known as a young mother. Six children had passed through her birth canal. With joy she remembered each one. But she had forgotten the pain of childbirth. Now it returned in this dream, and much worse than she had ever remembered. Her body had grown too rigid for such violence. *What sort of dream is this, Lord? Why me?*

Sensing no reply, her sleeping mind began to search for other clues. She reminded herself that she could awaken and end this discomfort if the dream was not from God. Perhaps it was an attack from the kingdom of darkness. This was a familiar search for her, a battle against nameless dread. Something she commonly felt during times of fasting and prayer.

As she opened herself to the meaning of her dream, she experienced dazzling feelings arising from deep within. Complete, complex insights, more brilliant, comprehensive and clear than anything she could have known when fully awake. These were familiar phenomena. She drew courage from them, welcoming the insights as part of the work of the Spirit. Dreams had always informed her understanding of life, both natural and supernatural.

And so, dreaming insights began . . .

. . . First a memory: Over the years she had suffered other nightmares, always during times of fasting and prayer. On three occasions she had awakened with a suffocating blackness hovering above her bed, feeling as if she wrestled an invisible prince of darkness. Half awake, she had heard a strange cry pouring from her throat—a discordant mixture of two voices—one of holy anger, one of terror. Neither resembled her own. On each occasion she had fully awakened, quoting Scriptures into the blackness. Each time the darkness had lifted.

There's nothing to fear in the valley of death, she reminded herself. *"Thou art with me."*

All such night terrors confirmed to her that indeed her prayers were effective weapons of spiritual warfare. Why else would the darkness choose times of fasting and prayer to hover over her bed? In the wake of these disturbances she had easily drifted to sleep again, resting in the words of the boy David when facing Goliath of Gath: "The battle is the Lord's."

A deeper insight emerged: *Contractions.* Oddly, these painful sensations did not signal an enemy attack—at least not directly. They hinted rather of a pregnant event in the spiritual realm. Lydia understood spiritual birth to be a process which paralleled natural childbirth. First the pain, then the joy of birth. Throughout history the agony of travail had been recorded by those who seriously prayed. Time and again men and women had told of being taken by groaning wails, lasting for hours—even days. Following travail, they had testified of something wonderful being "born" from Heaven to earth: a spiritual hunger in the community, a host of conversions, demons cast out, miracles, signs, healings.

This travail is also for a divine purpose, she encouraged herself.

As she continued to toss on her bed, she grew full of excitement, importance, anticipation. Something wonderful waited beyond the pain of this dream.

"Aaah-ah!" Another contraction took her with surprising power. *Travail is a divine gift,* she reminded herself bravely.

The words of the prophet shouted across her sleep: ". . . Be in pain, and labour to bring forth, O daughter of Zion, like a woman in travail . . ."

In her dream-state now, the intercessor sensed herself arriving at a choice. *Of course!* (She understood. The Spirit did nothing by rude force.) She could choose to wake up and avoid the discomfort of further spiritual labor . . . Or she could go wherever the dream took her and see it through. Perhaps because she had lived eighty years without such an opportunity—or perhaps because she had fasted for several days, loosening the grip of her normal appetites— whatever the cause, she released herself and the dream took her . . .

. . . beyond herself . . .

. . . somewhere . . .

. . . where there was music . . . gentle music, stirring nostalgia in her heart—or someone's heart—the heart she now inhabited in this strange dream. Or did the heart possess her? She could not be sure because the awareness of her dream-body seemed more real than her own. The new flesh shivered with a chill, but even the sensation of cold brought a thrill of entering another life. "Is this a dream? Or something more?" she wondered. She could feel her pulse beating feverishly against a heavy atmosphere on her skin. The air pushed against her almost as if the place existed underwater. But that made no sense because at the same moment the air felt cool and dry. The body itself seemed young, distressed, but alive.

So very alive! "This is not my flesh," she realized. "Why have I entered another body? Why not my own?" The new heart pounded wildly in her ears in contrast to the sweetness of the music.

The old woman had never heard the music before nor the sound of the stringed instrument that carried it to her ears. It was melodic, melancholy. In spite of the fact that it was foreign, somehow the tune seemed as familiar as "Moonlight Serenade." Why?

"Naamah," a male voice called softly.

She was not alone. "That voice," she thought, "it is the most enticing male voice I've ever heard. He calls Naamah, not Lydia." She was impressed with the sound of the name—Naamah. "Nay-aah-mah." It rolled from the speaker's tongue as easily as the bleat of a lamb.

"Naamah, stay with me, love," the baritone voice pled.

"Love? Does he love Naamah?" she wondered. Searching outward with her senses she determined that she lay on a cold slab, which seemed to greedily suck the heat from her body. Her bones ached like a fever, perhaps from the force of the contractions. A strong hand cradled her head, providing a welcome warmth at the back of her neck. "The hand of the speaker," she thought.

Willing her eyes to open, at first the old woman saw only indistinguishable shapes, like the blurred images of a slide projector she had once used as a grammar school teacher. Blinking painfully, she began to make out an arched ceiling. "Some kind of temple," she surmised with wonder. In flickering torchlight now, she began to see arches more clearly, made of crudely quarried stone.

"Oh my!" The motion of his eyelids startled her and she jerked involuntarily, nearly upsetting herself from the slab. He had been there all along—close in front of her face, yet as still as a garden statue. "The one with the voice," she thought. "The one who called Naamah. But he is looking at me! I am in her body."

A creature as magnificent as Michelangelo's David, and nearly as massive, bent his sculpted frame above the slab. His bronze skin radiated vitality and heat, punctuated by deep blue pools. She could feel the cool influence of his gaze on her face, and the splash of his tears that followed. But she could not bring herself to look directly into his eyes—those marvelous eyes. Not yet.

She saw that a golden crown of chain mail draped his forehead beneath thick blond locks. The hair had been swept majestically backward and tied behind. Exotic threads of silver held the seams of his tunic. Golden fasteners and jeweled insignia of unknown meaning embellished the fine linen.

"This can only be an angel," she gasped in her mind. No other words could describe him. Knowing that his hand was the hand cradling her head, she was swept by a wave of giddiness. Through her mind raced a phrase from the Song of Solomon: ". . . his left hand is under my head, and his right hand doth embrace me." She flushed with the image, realizing that it was only half true. His left hand was under her head, but his right hand was braced against the altar on which she lay. This was no romantic interlude.

The angel wept. His tears cascaded over her breasts, which, she suddenly noticed with a new sense of fright—and pleasure, were young and more beautifully formed than her own had ever been. "Naamah's breasts," she marveled. "Why am I in this body, Lord?" Seeing the bulge of her belly beneath a white linen drape, she realized that this woman Naamah was pregnant. She had been the source of the contractions she felt. But the child was huge. In the dim temple light she estimated her own children had produced but half the profile of this one.

Self-consciously she looked up, her eyes tracing the olive-smooth skin covering the muscles of the angel's shoulders. The old woman felt stirrings she hadn't known since she had been smitten with love at sixteen. More than that, she knew that this young dream-body of Naamah's had been taken by this angelic son of God. Her womb was full of the fruit of that union. How could she know? Because their passion had been such that the memory of it cried out from every cell of her flesh as the angel bent over her now!

Lydia recalled her beloved Zachary, husband of forty-two years, dead for six years now. She understood the strength of this physical bond. So strong was the yearning of Naamah's body for the angel that Lydia felt herself washed with a wave of guilt. "What of Zach?" she wondered. "The only man who has ever known me. How can I feel this way?" Then, with an annoyed shrug of her mind, she threw off the guilt. "This is a dream," she told herself. "I am not lord of my own dreams. I haven't conjured Naamah's body, nor the angel's. I have been placed here for some purpose. What is it, Lord?"

Sensing no answer, she dared herself look into the angel's eyes. His gaze poured back into her like shafts of knowing light, uncovering her secrets, reading her unsatisfied longings. She swelled with the promise of fulfillment, as if she had become the center of the *universe in his eyes. In that moment she knew that she had never been loved as deeply as she had desired, nor as deeply as she could return it. Not even by Zachary. He had been only a man, imperfect in everything. She suddenly felt empty, mourning that unfulfilled part of herself, and she sensed that it could be otherwise in the arms of this vibrant angel.*

Without restraint, her mind loosed praises to the glory of his eyes: ". . . more blue than the cataracts of Eden, deeper than the mists of the Sides of the North . . . as inexhaustible as the fountains of the Great Deep." Startled by the poetry that spilled so easily from her mind, Lydia searched her own thoughts. She had little concept of Eden, the Sides of the North, the Fountains of the Deep. "Has Naamah seen these places?" she wondered. "If so, then both of us must be sharing every cell of this body, our thoughts colliding in this brain."

The angel's eyes remained fixed on her. He neither hid his feeling, nor seemed ashamed of the tears he shed. What a contradiction—so strong, yet uninhibited—so unlike the men she had known—her own father, even Zachary, who had always made excuses for crying. "I swear I've got something in my eye," he used to say.

For a long moment she simply lay still.

A fragment from the book of Genesis slipped unexpectedly through her mind—a passage she'd read many times with curiosity: ". . . the sons of God saw the daughters of men that they were fair; and they took them wives . . ." Did this explain Naamah? "Is she, or was she, an angel's wife?" Her name seemed familiar, like the temple music Lydia still heard.

Trembling with forbidden emotions, Lydia dared in her dream what she would never do in real life; she looked full in the angel's eyes and reached up to stroke the strong prominence of his cheekbone. Her fingers turned to fire. She allowed the fire to burn the length of her arm and enter her, igniting urges that flew like sparks to every darkened corner of her soul. Perhaps this fire held some power to redeem her lost love, she thought idolatrously. Or perhaps to condemn. She traced his warrior's nose, flaring nostrils, lips.

"Help me, God," she begged, "I would lose myself—"

"Give her the cup!"

Sudden guilt shot down her spine, and she withdrew her hand. A voice had spoken behind her.

"Keep silence, Jubal!" the angel warned.

How quickly he changed. Lydia chilled at the sharp edge to the angel's command. How fearfully! Who was Jubal? Eyes aching with the effort, she strained to see this one who had said, "Give her the cup." It had seemed an urgent suggestion. In the gloom she gradually made out a young man sitting on a stone prominence a dozen yards away. He plucked a stringed instrument of wood and animal gut.

"The music maker," she thought. "Why does he want Naamah to have the cup? What cup?"

Lifting her head again, she strained to look left and right. She saw no one else in the chamber, but her gaze came to rest on a crystalline goblet placed on a stone hearth just beyond her reach. She laid back in the angel's grasp, more exhausted from the effort than she should have been. "Is it a cup of poison?" she wondered. "That would explain the angel's tears. This pregnancy is terminal. But why does Jubal demand that I drink the cup? Does he want to be rid of Naamah before her time?"

"Aaah—!" The thought flew from her mind as another contraction ripped her like a disemboweller's knife. "So I must share Naamah's labor," she thought, aware of the new body now, lost to her own. Still, in a dimly conscious part of her mind she reminded herself that this was just a dream. In spite of the discomfort, she would awaken soon and be herself again. But sadly, Naamah would not—could not. "Why, Lord? Why have You placed me inside this doomed woman?"

Pain was the only reply. She reached up without thinking and dug her nails into the angel's arm, clenching her teeth over a prolonged scream. Her belly stretched. The child within her thrashed as though her body was a hated prison. "Naamah can't live through this," she agonized. "No one could. And the pain will be unimaginable!" She lay panting, trying to relieve the impossible contraction. "The poison is a cup of mercy," she thought. A laugh of realization filtered insanely through her lips.

"What is it, love?" the angel asked, bending closer.

She had no reply. Pain occupied her whole attention. She forced her hands to explore beneath the covering shroud and found her skin to be leathery, dehydrated and torn. Her fingers became sticky with blood. Suddenly the giant child writhed again, and she could feel with sickening horror rope-like muscles and coarse hair rippling against the surface of her skin.

"A monster! A demon!" Her rib cage felt as if it would burst.

"So this is the offspring of angels and women," she lamented. "A price to pay."

Her thoughts raced again to the obscure passage of Genesis, recalling only phrases, fragments: ". . . and when the sons of God came in unto the daughters of men, and they bare children . . . there were giants in the earth . . . of whom legends are told . . . Nephilim—"

"A Nephil . . ." she moaned, bitter saliva flooding her mouth. ". . . Nephilim . . ."

Every romantic urge she had felt for the angel smothered itself beneath a blanket of horror. "This forbidden love has given flesh to a curse," she realized. "It could not go unpunished."

It was more than Naamah's torment, the fetal demigod, the cup of poison, and the angel's tears that Lydia knew. An impossible load of grief played her heartbeat like a maestro conducting the climax to an epic symphony. In its mounting crescendo she heard the weeping of the planet, falling of trees, howling of hurricanes, groaning of continental shelves, roaring of antediluvian giants, crashing of the firmament, hissing rivers of rock erupting from floors of primeval oceans. Though she had known none of these sounds before, they rang true in her ears now, harmonious and full of new significance as she lay dying in the grip of primal tragedy.

2

GRACE MINISTRIES CAMPUS
12:22 A.M.

"Send an ambulance to the Prayer Steeple. We have a code 11 here."

A microwave dish hidden behind a stained-glass window beamed the message to a cluster of communications antennae on the roof of Grace University Hospital. The sleek Steeple and square-shouldered medical building faced each other across the golf course like opposing pieces on a chessboard.

Within two minutes an ambulance responded silently from the hospital, lights flashing, no siren, according to Grace Ministries' private security procedure. The vehicle turned through several blocks of university housing before accelerating westward between the golf links.

A uniformed driver popped her chewing gum and spoke to a hand-held radio. "Confirm your twenty, code 11. Come back?"

"Prayer Steeple."

"The Steeple?" she muttered, glancing across the seat to a yawning black male attendant riding with her. "Barry, wake up. Who'd be up there at this hour?"

"An old woman lives up there."

"Serious?" She leaned forward, squinting up at the glass-and-stucco spire glowing in the Gulf mist. "That's spooky. You couldn't get me to live up there." Pressing the CB button, she replied, "At your door in ninety. Over and out."

The southernmost piece of real estate in Texas, the Grace Ministries campus lay east of Brownsville on Old Highway 4, near the Mexican border. An eighteen-hole golf course divided the property into several zones of development. The southeastern quadrant, near the public entrance, contained a hospital, a television studio, and a university. The southwestern zone, forested with pine and palmetto, concealed retirement trailer parks and condominiums. The northwestern sector had been zoned for private homes, while the northeastern quadrant remained the personal domain of founder and president, Dr. Simon Grace. The family compound, including servant quarters and guest homes, was dominated by "The Good Doctor's" Taliesin West prairie mansion. A private jetport and hangar separated it from the rest of the campus.

From each zone, the Steeple remained visible at the center of the property, a magnificent freestanding tower with no church building beneath. It served primarily as a symbol, reminding all who saw it that prayer was the heart of this faith healing empire.

The tires of the emergency unit squealed on the pavement as it swerved past a street sign labeled *Steeple Place.*

"Another crazy finals week, eh, dude?" the female driver said, trying to keep things light. "Last semester three blue hairs died on my shift. Can you believe it? It's a conspiracy. I swear they're out to ruin my grades."

In the Steeple lobby a uniformed security guard stood at the reception desk as the ambulance drew up. Beams from its red and blue flashers danced across the room. The guard's eyes remained fixed on one of a dozen video monitors behind the desk. The student-nurse in house slippers stood watching over his shoulder, arms protectively folded across her chest.

"I'm glad I installed that camera," the guard mused. "Lydia's getting too old for this sort of thing."

"Yeah, but she doesn't know a camera's in there. I hope it's OK, you know? Her privacy and all."

"Privacy means nothing to her," he muttered.

The two ambulance attendants banged through the doors and slid heavy emergency kits noisily across the polished marble floor to the desk. The girl in house slippers recoiled, as if someone had scraped their fingers along a blackboard.

The security guard continued to watch the monitors. He beckoned the two attendants with his hand, then pointed to a screen. "Let me give you some volume," he said, turning the receiver knob to its maximum.

On the screen, Lydia lay on her bed, writhing, moaning, her long white hair cascading over the pillow. Suddenly her back arched, and her lips grimaced in pain. "Ahhhh-aah," she screamed.

"She's having a baby," blurted the gum-chewing attendant, as if she were the only one with sense enough to see it.

The security guard and coed looked at her. "She's eighty years old," they said.

The attendant swallowed meekly. "What do I know?"

"She's Dr. Grace's intercessor," the student-nurse explained.

"Intercessor?"

"She prays. Her name is Lydia Nation, and she's been around as long as Grace himself. Came from some reservation up in Oklahoma."

"So she's Indian?"

"I think so. At least part Indian. Anyway, she lives in the Steeple so she can pray for Dr. Grace. That's her life."

The attendant stopped chewing. "People actually do that sort of thing?"

Lydia's body arched. She cried out again, and the attendant muttered, "She's some kind of serious about it, too."

"I haven't been able to wake her up," explained the pajama-clad girl. "I've tried for the last hour solid, and I'm not going back up there by myself. It's just too weird."

"Come on, April. Let's see what's shakin'," Barry said to his gum-chewing assistant. He picked up his kit and started for the elevator doors.

April and the pajama-clad nurse hurried after him.

"There's something else you should know," the nurse advised as they crossed the lobby. "She's been fasting for ten days."

"At her age?" Barry asked, glancing over his shoulder. "That's not smart."

"You don't talk the old woman out of fasting, believe me."

They entered the elevator. Barry pushed the door button.

"It's a conspiracy, dude," April repeated, popping her gum and rolling her eyes as she waited. "Blue hairs are out to ruin my grades."

The doors of the elevator slid shut.

3

GRACE MANSION
12:43 A.M.

A woman in a black-and-gray business suit leaned against a display case in the loft of what appeared to be a colossal studio. She was short, of a rather solid, athletic body, with closely cropped salt-and-pepper hair. Arms extended, palms flat, she pressed her cheek firmly against the humidity-controlled glass of a display case, as if coaxing some kind of affection from its surface—or perhaps from the mosaic icon inside the case. Tiny puffs of water vapor appeared next to her nostrils. In and out, in and out, appearing and dissipating as her breath came in rapid, shallow pants.

Behind her, against the wall, sat a modern desk surrounded by bookshelves, with a built-in television set and file drawers. The screen of a personal computer glowed on a retractable arm above the desk.

At the far end of the room, below the loft, a long meeting table with a dozen leather chairs sat between the walls of a picture gallery. Beyond that, a brace of two-story windows rose in a boat-shaped overlook of terraced gardens below. Outside the windows, the gardens were highlighted by green and amber floodlights. The split shake roofs of three ample homes could be seen at the bottom of the rise. And a mile in the distance the Grace Ministries' Steeple glowed against the night sky.

Eyes closed, the woman began to play her fingers gently along the six-foot surface of the glass. Inside, seven figures of inlaid mosaic *tesserae* mutely watched her, heads tilted to one side, crowned with what appeared to be halos of pure leaf-gold. Their overlarge eyes remained fixed in stares of ancient mystic knowledge. A bronze plaque on the antiquity identified the figures as *The Seven Sleepers of Antioch*.

In the dim light the work of art nearly animated itself. The individual *tesserae* composing the faces were made of polished petrified wood, rather than the usual glass or stone. The unique arrangements of agatized grain, pitch and bark destroyed a viewer's normal sense of perspective, inducing vertigo. A few of the mosaic chips had been broken or lost over the centuries, but *The Seven Sleepers* remained vigilant. Each posed with a palm extended, index and thumb united in the *Pantocrator* pose, indicating possession of the "wisdom of God. " This was much more than a work of art—it was a relic of high religious devotion from the early centuries of Christianity.

The woman's eyes fluttered open as a telephone rang in the background, breaking her spell. She turned to a cellular port-a-pack sitting on the desk.

"Dr. Sylvan," she answered with perfect composure.

"Sorry to wake you, doctor," a male voice responded. "This is Barry Malone—first row, anatomy class . . . never mind. I'm working a code 11 in the Steeple."

"What's the problem?"

"Well, she's one of the retirees, eighty years plus. This is very strange, but she's having a nightmare, pretty violent, like she's having a baby or something . . . but obviously she's not."

Dr. Sylvan's brows knit at the mention of this. Her eyes darted as if visualizing something far away.

"Anyway, we can't wake her up," Barry continued. "I've plugged in the EKG, and she's slipping in and out of arrythmia. No sign of infarction yet, but she acts like she wants to fibrillate. Blood pressure's all over the place. Hit one sixty over ninety a minute ago—"

"You were right to call. Transport her and I'll see her in the hospital."

"Another thing . . . She's been fasting for ten days."

Dr. Sylvan frowned. "Fasting? No one in the program is to fast without my personal release."

"Her name is Lydia Nation. She's the one who lives in the Steeple."

Sylvan started with sudden recognition, pulling the receiver from her ear. "You old Cherokee," she murmured. She sat in a chair, drumming her fingers against the desktop for a few seconds. Pulling the phone suddenly to her ear again, she said, "Barry?"

"Yeah."

"Let me get this straight. She's acting like she's giving birth?"

"Right."

"And fasting? That's highly irregular . . ."

"Listen, Neva—Dr. Sylvan—they've installed a system camera over here. Would you like us to send you a picture?"

"Oh, absolutely." Sylvan sprang upright. "I didn't know we had one in the Steeple." She quickly picked up a remote control and switched on a twenty-seven inch TV monitor mounted above the desk. As the image materialized, a handsome, graying minister in a clerical collar appeared on the twenty-four hour closed-circuit satellite feed. The Reverend Doctor Simon Grace. Though he was presently out of the country, the twenty-four hour closed circuit network carried his videotaped omnipresence into the homes and office buildings of the faithful. This was a teaching show. He stood before a blackboard, pointing to a hastily scribbled Scripture reference—". . . to believe for your healing is to put God's word to the test—"

She muted the sound, speaking into the receiver. "Route that signal to terminal . . . terminal . . ." Dr. Sylvan's eyes searched the housing of the remote control unit in her hand until she found an adhesive label. ". . . terminal one."

"Will do." Barry muffled the receiver and picked up a hand-held radio set. "Security, send video to *numero uno*."

At the Steeple lobby desk below, the night security officer reached for his video control panel. "Terminal one? I thought the Old Man was in Israel." Grace security personnel were routinely briefed on the worldwide travels of their leader.

"He is," Barry confirmed. "So?"

"Terminal one is at 'The Good Doctor's' personal desk. Like, I don't know anyone with clearance to be in the mansion while he's away. *Comprende?*"

Barry discreetly muffled the telephone, speaking carefully into the radio set. "It's Neva Sylvan. Does that make a difference?"

"Oh solid. Med Director's the six hundred pound gorilla around here." He hit an electronic switch and sat back. "Still, it's kinda strange. Anyway, tell her to go to med channel one-ninety."

"Right." Barry picked up the telephone. "Go to medical one-nine-oh, doctor."

Dr. Sylvan entered the number on her remote control unit, and the picture materialized on the studio screen in time for her to see Lydia crying out again. The doctor's eyes narrowed and she leaned closer, scanning the EKG strip which traced Lydia's heartbeat across the bottom of the picture. Neva smiled briefly, realizing it had been at her own insistence that this feature had been added to Grace's closed-circuit channels. "Nothing but the best for Simon Grace," she had pitched. Against the televangelist's inflated ego, flattery proved most effective, she recalled with satisfaction. She had grown to enjoy salesmanship as much as the advantages it produced.

Regaining concentration, the doctor studied the screen, noting April in the room as well as the student-nurse holding Lydia's thrashing shoulders. Barry stood at the foot of the bed, telephone to his ear.

"Can you see us, doctor?" he asked.

"I see you." Dr. Sylvan mused, watching in silence for a time. "Let's just monitor that heartbeat. Sit tight while I pull up her chart." She turned to the computer terminal and typed: "*MEDI-CODE = L. Nation,*" and hit "enter." Ignoring the information that assembled on the screen she suddenly said, "Barry, listen, this case is unusual and I don't have time to explain it. Tell your assistant to administer one ampule of epinephrine immediately. Advanced procedure. We don't have much time."

Barry whirled around. "April, give her a cardiac epi, one amp."

April stared back, dumbfounded. She had no experience with such an injection. It meant penetrating a four inch needle straight into the heart. No margin for error.

Barry shrugged and pointed to the telephone receiver. "She's the doctor."

"I said, 'immediately!'" Sylvan exploded.

"Immediately—she says 'now,'" Barry urged.

April leaped to her kit and began to assemble the hypodermic needle with trembling fingers. "I've never done one of these," she rasped between clenched teeth. Her mouth went dry.

"Are you sure, doctor?" Barry asked, looking up at the camera. "She's not arresting."

"We're losing precious seconds here," Sylvan snapped. "Watch your monitor."

Barry shook his head, muttering to himself, "Of course you're sure—you're the doctor."

Across the screen the heart rate fluctuated erratically.

"—but epinephrine?" Barry asked. He swallowed quickly, then urged, "Hurry up. Hurry."

"I am hurrying!" The needle shook violently as April snapped a premeasured ampule into the syringe. Squeezing the air from the plunger, she watched a cc of synthetic adrenaline arch across the room. She stood up, glanced wildly at the TV camera, and hurried to the bed on rubbery knees.

Seeing the large bore of the needle, the pajama-clad night nurse whispered, "Dear Jesus . . ."

April nervously removed her gum and stuck it to the headboard, then tore open Lydia's nightgown, poising the needle above the old woman's chest. After a moment more, she whirled toward Barry. "You do it!" she hissed, holding out the trembling syringe.

Barry dropped the telephone and hurried over. "Disinfect her," he barked.

She ran back to her kit and rummaged for an iodine swatch.

Dr. Sylvan watched the screen. The heart rate was racing now, peaking above the scale in periodic spikes of panic. "Come on, you amateurs . . . " she purred.

". . . Nephilim . . . Nephilim . . ." Lydia moaned.

Barry poised the needle over her chest. April applied iodine to a target area near the solar plexus. She finished and looked up at him expectantly.

He didn't move.

"This can't be right," he whispered hoarsely. "It's too radical."

". . . *too radical* . . ."

". . . *too radical* . . ."

Lydia heard only a garbled echo against the arches of stone above her. The entire temple chamber seemed to spin. Blackness began to pound in her ears and to narrow the blurred tunnel of her vision. She could smell Naamah's death now, taste it on the back of her tongue. Through the flickering torchlight, her eyes mistook the golden chain mail draping the angel's brow for stars in an endless night. She longed to let go, to float away, to be lost forever in that

twinkling sea of stars. "*Please. Oh please, God, let me be gone,*"
she prayed, feeling all of the agony of the angel's wife.

"*Now,*" *she suddenly demanded, reaching toward the stone
hearth beside the altar.* "*The cup.*"

*Lydia was not aware of making the decision to drink the poi-
son. Nor even of thinking to ask for it. It was a doubly strange sensation as the words slipped from her mouth with the full force of
Naamah's personality.* "*She speaks her own thoughts in spite of my
presence here,*" *Lydia wondered.*

*The angel had already snatched the crystal cup from the hearth,
and held it beyond her reach.* "*Stay with me, love,*" *he pled.*

*A scream seemed to come from far away, and yet it tore from
her own throat. The Nephil wedged itself against her hips and with
a violent shove and dull cracking sound dislodged them from their
sockets. Pure, white pain baptized her senses. The torn ligaments
and nerves hammered like hot irons driven to the bone, and she felt
its foot breach her womb.*

"*Give her the cup!*" *screamed the musician named Jubal.
Through a haze she realized that he had lurched to her side from
the stone chair. His scream was so human, so refreshingly human,
she immediately felt drawn to him.*

"*She is my wife,*" *the angel sobbed, pulling back, holding the
goblet in a sculpted pose.*

The musician thrust his face boldly forward. "*She is my sister.
And it is time for you to let her go.*"

"*So,*" *Lydia thought,* "*Jubal is Naamah's brother.*"

The angel's face twisted with grief. "*I would go with you,
love,*" *he cried, looking back at her.* "*But see . . ?*" *He pulled the cup
of poison to his lips and drank deeply.* "*I cannot.*"

*Lydia and Naamah, both women in the same body, were
beyond caring.*

"*Play, Jubal,*" *Naamah said.*

*Lydia recognized that it was purely Naamah who spoke
through her lips this time. Her voice had become a sad whisper.* "*I
knew this day would come. Play for me.*"

Jubal drew his tortured face close. "*I die with you, my sister.*"

*Lydia's perception of Jubal had changed. Unlike the angel, he
possessed human kindness. She watched him with sympathy and
affection.*

"*I hate Tubal-cain,*" *he said, trembling with grief and anger.*

At the mention of Tubal-cain, Lydia started with recognition.

She could almost see the name printed on a page of her Bible. It was there in Genesis. Tubal-cain—an unforgettable name. Naamah and Jubal were written there too. She was almost certain of it. "These people actually lived," she wondered. "In the world before history, before the Flood."

"I will drink the cup after you," Jubal promised.

"You must not," Naamah whispered. "It is forbidden. Play the wedding song."

He waited sadly, then replied, "For you, Naamah." He kissed her forehead with resolve. "Only for you."

He turned slowly and hoisted himself again to his stone perch. Looking away, he raised the instrument and began to strum the nostalgic notes of the song Lydia had first heard upon entering this dream-world. Now she understood. The song had stirred nostalgia because it had been Naamah's wedding song. It was familiar in Naamah's ancient heart—not Lydia's. The music reverberated against the arches of stone above them like the deep sadness she felt for Naamah and Jubal, and in measure, for the angel.

But her feelings seemed trivial under the circumstances. She restrained her own urges, determined to allow this angel's wife free expression in her own death. She wanted to honor the memory of this singular woman who had lived in the shadows of Eden—or she wanted to honor the woman herself—for in Lydia's dream this ancient era had somehow bent through time and space to touch the present again. She wanted to know what Naamah knew, see what she saw, feel what she felt—remember it clearly when she awoke in order to tell it to those who would listen. She wanted to hear the woman's treasured last words, hold the moment—a moment shared across the millennia.

Together, both women in the same body drank once more of the angel's beauty. The open tunic revealed a mat of hair, like soft, golden threads on his chest. How often it had been Naamah's sweet-smelling pillow. How often she had been lost in it. "His glory will never fade . . ." both women thought in unison. "He is an angel."

"I have loved you, Mithrael," Naamah whispered, touching his cheek. "That has been enough for me."

Begging him with her eyes, she placed a frail hand over his, pulling with the scant influence of a sigh. Slowly, hypnotically, the angel allowed his wife to bring the trembling cup of poison to her lips, where she drank as she had learned to drink in the ancient tem-

*ple ritual, deeply, with what had once been courage but now was
only a death wish . . .*

Choking once, she stiffened. *The cup fell from her hand, shattering across the floor with the exquisite sound of a wind chime. She
was set free of pain now, and free of her body. Both women were
free—their spirits rising together on the notes of the wedding song,
higher and higher toward the arches of stone above them.*

*With sudden realization, Lydia found herself in the grip of
panic. She had slipped the pull of gravity and was rising like a ghost,
unattached to physical form.* "My God—"

"—this is not a dream . . ."

Barry heard the words sigh between her lips in a final exhale of
soul and spirit. He remained poised with the needle six inches from
her chest, blinking, listening intently—not to the whisper, which he
ignored, but to something else, which he could *not* ignore. In a
moment his mind registered the warning tone of a flatlining heart
monitor.

"She's fibrillating!" he screamed, dropping the hypodermic
with a sense of relief. Now his emergency training could take over
without Dr. Sylvan's strange advice. He poised the heel of his left
hand carefully above Lydia's breastbone and let it fall with a thump.
Placing the other hand on top of the first, with practiced surety he
began an artificial pumping action. Glancing at the monitor he
shouted, "April, charge the jumper cables! 200 joules—no, make it
250!"

A mile across the campus in Simon Grace's studio, Dr. Neva
Sylvan sat thoughtfully watching the pandemonium on her TV
screen. The EKG continued to run flat across the bottom of the
screen in spite of Barry's chest massage. She picked up the remote
control and contentedly snapped off the picture. Standing to her
feet, she looked out the giant windows toward the Steeple in the distance. She sighed with a deep, sensual groan and spread her arms
wide. Rotating her shoulders in a stress-relieving motion, she
walked slowly, hypnotically back toward the icon case.

The Seven Sleepers of Antioch continued to stare from their
humidity-controlled glass, eyes wide and knowing—as they had
remained for eighteen centuries.

". . . Uhgnh!"

*Lydia felt Barry's precordial thump like a pillowed fist on her
chest. It didn't hurt, but it arrested her upward flight. She felt herself turning in midair, hovering, coming back to the temple cham-*

ber with the pregnant body askew on the altar below. One of Naamah's lifeless arms pointed delicately toward the pieces of crystal goblet shattered across the floor.

The angel she had called Mithrael was gone. Only Jubal remained. The musician cradled his head blindly against the crook of his arm. His fingers continued to strum the lyre. Lydia heard a sudden commotion, and Jubal's hand grew still.

The doorway filled with the torso of a dark, muscular man. He wore a cape of what had once been a beautiful red animal skin, perhaps fox. He flung it aside, revealing a strange instrument of brass held before him. He wore a blood-red leather apron and skirt.

A dozen or so hooded men followed him, swathed in heavy black capes. They appeared to Lydia to be a contingent of priests. Fetishes of bone, feathers and animal parts reeked from their clothing as they filed across the room. They moved briskly, without ceremony. Beneath the mysterious folds of their robes, they seemed to be merely unwashed, unshaven, banal men—excited, anxious, forgetting decorum and piety in their lusty haste. Meanwhile, the giant child writhed and growled inside Naamah's body, eliciting approving grunts and laughter from the lot of them.

"Turn away, my weaker brother," the dark bearded man sneered at Jubal. He tore away Naamah's linen and placed a semicircular brass instrument around her bulging belly. "Look there," he exclaimed, pointing the others to the breached womb. "It must be a son with a will to be born."

The others murmured assent.

Lydia recalled Jubal's words: "I hate Tubal-cain."

"This must be him," she surmised. "Jubal's own brother, and Naamah's too, doing this terrible thing to her. How depraved."

Tubal-cain inserted a curved knife into the arc of brass. Finding a loose fold of skin, he began to whistle lightly, inhumanly, as he forced the knife to follow the brass arc in a crude cesarean opening of the womb. After a grisly moment he lifted a writhing gryphon high above his head. Dark blood trickled down his forearm.

"It is a son!"

The priests chanted in ritual fashion, "A son of god come down to us. Our blessing. A son of god come down to us. Our blessing."

Lydia remembered her first horrified feel of the monster in Naamah's womb. Now she could see the Nephil for what it truly was, a muscular, hunchbacked specimen. Beneath the sheen of amniotic fluid, it appeared to be buck-skinned in color. Its eyes bulged from beneath a wrinkled brow, set with pointed ears, which moved independently toward every sound in the room. A dark stripe ran the length of its backbone to the tip of its broomed tail. Curious webbed folds of black skin hung behind the armpits. "Wings?" she wondered. "Ridiculously small. Surely the thing can't fly."

Tubal-cain set the gryphonic creature back in his sister's womb, and the priests began passing before it, each mumbling a phrase of an incantation:

"Hail to you, lord of heaven come down to us . . . for we know you, and we know your name . . . and the names of the gods who are with you in the pantheon of justice . . ."

The Nephil slavered, dumbly sucking the back of its clawed fingers as it received their homage:

". . . we know the tree of death, which is life . . . and life, which is death . . . behold we know the one tree which will make us as gods . . . we bring you truth . . . we have not deprived the orphan. . . nor have we caused pain . . . we have not made men hungry . . . we have not made women weep . . . we have not killed . . . we have not diminished the land . . . we have not trapped the birds from the Sides of the North . . . we are pure, pure, pure . . . and nothing that is evil shall ever come into being against us—"

At this, Jubal seemed unable to contain himself. He threw his lyre across the chamber floor and leaped from the stone chair. "I will never again sing of the Nephil," he sobbed grievously. "Never."

The priests broke off their mumbled incantations to stare in menacing silence. One snatched a knife from beneath his robe and stepped forward, but Tubal-cain extended a powerful arm and brought the man up short.

Glaring at his brother, the butcher spat, "Jubal has the heart of a woman. We have already purchased his songs. Summon Mithrael. We must give his son a name." He clapped his hands. "Come, come."

A chorus of ecstatic utterances began to fill the temple. It was the sound of a chanted name. Louder and louder, the cacophony rose in Lydia's ears. A name . . . a name . . . She could not quite make it out because in all of the confusion a brilliant explosion in her chest blew her tumbling backward into an impossibly long tun-

*nel, while around her danced the light of a thousand disintegrated
thunderbolts—*

Feeling the pull of gravity once again, she opened her eyes to
see herself rebounding on her own bed as if in slow motion. She also
saw a black man standing over her, holding electronic paddles to
her chest. He wore a medical team jumpsuit. She had never seen
Barry before, but instantly recognized that he was a member of the
Grace Hospital staff and was fighting for her life. Her whole body
tingled from head to foot, as if it had been asleep, like a leg or an
arm without circulation.

"Got a heartbeat . . ." Barry said coaxingly. "Come on, girl,
help me out . . ."

Lydia did not *want* to help him out. She was sorry to be back.
Her flesh had become nothing more than dead weight—limited,
constricted—full of decay compared to the free-floating state of her
spirit. Never before had she conceived of how her body intruded
upon the freedom of her mind and soul. The dull thing of clay clamored for temporal things—water, food, energy, air.

She choked, but try as she might, she could not draw a single
breath of air into her aching lungs. At this realization, her body
pulled her entire consciousness into one harmonious scream for
oxygen. Just one breath of air! Now! Now! Nooooww!!!

She felt a sharp spasm in her chest, then heard an erratic beep
fading away into an engulfing blackness.

"We're losing her," Barry said, stripping sweat from his brow.
"Charge me, April. 300 joules this time."

. . . joules this time . . .

*. . . Lydia passed instantly through a tunnel and found herself
flying a few inches above a parched, cracked, alkali plain.
Embedded in the powdery alkali were the dark trunks of fallen
trees. They flashed beneath her like burnt matchsticks, all lying parallel, as if thrown down by a vulcan blast.*

*She had a body which she recognized as her own, no longer
identified with Naamah's. It was composed of a nebulous mist, free
of the sensation of weight or substance. It didn't really exist in one
sense, because it appeared only when she looked at it. The arms,
hands, legs, flowing hair would form a millisecond after she
thought of them. In that respect she seemed to embody a kind of
"self image" in a realm where her own perception created substance. "So this is death," she thought. "It is wonderful."*

As she continued to fly, she grew to understand that her

thoughts were not free, but were limited to the direction of her flight. She could change position at will, but she could not change direction. Something bigger was in control. Twisting to look behind, she watched her white hair follow her as she flashed forward at the speed of thought. That was how she had always wanted to see her tresses—billowing, free and loose. She smiled and grew comfortable feeling that her thoughts were limited within the framework of a larger, controlling thought. It was just as well. She wouldn't know where to go in this strange land anyway. And in that sense, it suddenly occurred to her that her journey was not entirely different from that on earth—who knew where they were going?— except here she had no flesh to limit her mind.

"Where am I going, Lord? And where am I?"

The questions quickly faded. Against all reason, she felt like a released prisoner as she flew, enjoying the sensations of her new being. She saw that a wasteland stretched for miles in every direction, ending at a rim of cliffs on the horizon. She seemed to be in a huge crater.

Her flight ended abruptly. Out of a shimmering mirage two trees stood suddenly before her, one mysteriously alive, the other dead. She hovered above the heads of Jubal and Tubal-cain as they stood in a procession behind dark-robed priests. The priests in turn waited behind the angel Mithrael, who now held Naamah's mutilated body in his arms before the living tree. It seemed they had brought her to this place after delivering the giant Nephil in the temple chamber.

As the procession waited, it seemed to Lydia that the living tree's succulent leaves whispered in a breeze of its own making. Golden, pear-shaped fruit hung from its branches. It seemed to exude life rather than to draw it from the ground. The hardened clay beneath the trunk showed no evidence of water, nor of the nutrients essential to life. She wondered how it had survived the destructive forces that had ravaged the rest of the forest.

Suddenly there was movement. For the first time Lydia noticed that above the tree's branches hovered a rod of light that turned in midair, pausing now and then as if sensing the intruders, reading their movements, and perhaps their minds. It seemed to possess that kind of intelligence.

She recalled a Biblical passage: ". . . a flaming sword which turned every way, to keep the way of the—'tree of life,'" she exclaimed aloud. "My Lord, it's the Tree of Life!"

As she looked down, no one seemed to hear. Not even Jubal and Tubal-cain, who were close enough to touch. Apparently they now viewed the same scene from separate realities. If she had been any of the carnal men below she would have thrown herself prostrate before the Tree of Life immediately. But the lot of them seemed unaffected by the fact that they stood in the ruined Garden of God.

Next to the living tree a dead one stood starkly against the azure sky. It was hollow, petrified by the passing of untold ages. Yet it too stood as if by some magical power. Its defiant branches twisted from the bowels of the earth like the scaly hand of a dragon.

As Mithrael drew up before the trees, Lydia heard Tubal-cain whisper to Jubal, "Which is the Tree of Life, my weak brother?"

"The miraculous tree, of course," the musician replied.

"They are both miraculous," Tubal-cain snorted with disdain. "The garden has always been a riddle. Watch."

The angel stepped toward the living tree, extending Naamah's body in his arms. He worked his throat nervously, weeping again as he spoke. "God above gods, may she be made whole and come back to me now. I beg for mercy."

"What a fool," Tubal-cain chuckled derisively behind his hand to Jubal. "Watch, watch," he instructed, as if he'd witnessed this event many times.

As the angel advanced, the rod of fire poised suddenly and fell with a sound like a gust of wind. With perfect articulation the flaming rod traced the outline of Naamah's body in his arms. She began to glow like a human lamp. Her head lifted mechanically, eyelids fluttering, causing Jubal to cry out with joy from where he stood. But like a cruel joke, in the next stunned instant she vanished—her body cremated in a puff of charred, gray ash.

A choking cry came from Mithrael's throat. He fell to his knees.

"Praise to Belial!" Tubal-cain exulted behind his back, dancing a private jig.

The priests turned to acknowledge his glee with knowing laughter. "Life is death," they murmured.

"And death is life," he returned.

Tubal-cain slapped Jubal's shoulder. It was more a gesture of threat than excitement. "Do you see, my brother, with the heart of a woman? Do you know the riddle?" His fingers bit into the musician's soft muscle, and he jerked him roughly as he spoke. "Sing. Sing of the tree of death, which is life." He lowered his voice and

spoke in a rapid whisper as if delivering a universal imperative.
"The dark tree, Jubal. The one with the power to make us wiser
than these pitiful angels."

But as Lydia watched from above, it seemed that Jubal heeded
none of this. He stood transfixed, watching the kneeling figure of
Mithrael, the ashes of his sister's body spilling between his fingers
and drifting across Eden on a pitiless breeze.

And before Lydia could make sense of it, she hurtled backward
again, through the long, long tunnel slamming into her body—

And found herself rebounding on the bed in slow motion. The
same strange man held paddles to her chest and side.

"Beat, beat," Barry coaxed. He reached down and shook her
by the jaw, looking intently into her eyes. "Are you in there, Lydia?
Come on, girl. Help me out. Help me or I'm going to have to get
that big, bad needle . . ."

This time she felt her chest heave, and a huge gasp of air
inflated her lungs. She shot upward to a sitting position. Barry's eyes
grew wide.

"She's back," he yelled. "Hello. Take it easy now . . . easy,
honey."

April and the night nurse ran to the bedside. In the background
the heart monitor beeped reassuringly.

. . . beep . . . beep . . . beep . . . beep . . .

"A perfect heartbeat," April breathed. "How can that be?" She
turned to look at Barry with wonder. As she did, the heart stopped
cold.

They whirled again, and Lydia's eyes stared at nothing.

Barry quickly laid her down. "One more time," he said grimly.
"Maximum power this time."

". . . power this time . . ."

". . . power this time . . ."

. . . Emerging from a tunnel, Lydia now soared beneath a
rugged escarpment of basalt that seemed to rise a half-mile above
her. It stretched further in either direction than she could see. The
sheer scale of the wall was like nothing she'd ever seen on earth.
Below the cliffs, a wide shoulder to the mountain descended grad-
ually into a sea of clouds that rolled unbroken to the horizon. The
sun burned low, frosting the cloud tops with gold. The place gave
her the feeling of being an island in the sky. Like the one she had
read of as a child, at the top of Jack's fairy-tale beanstalk.

Once again she was flying at an impossible speed, and not

according to her own direction. As before, she enjoyed the sensation of effortless motion.

The vegetation of the mountain shoulder seemed to be of high-altitude evergreen, tundra, lichens and furze. She could taste the air, a pungent blend of caraway, sage and thyme. Upland quail and partridge fluttered easily from bush to bush as she passed above them.

Near the line of clouds below she made out an astonishing castle of pure dolomite marble. Domes and towers stood one above the other like piles of gleaming pearl. Several miles beyond the first dwelling she saw another, and still another. The sight of each structure nearly took her breath away as she passed, inspiring her highest fantasies of Heaven . . . Elysian castles in the mists of timeless peace . . .

But as she warmed to this fantasy she hurtled toward another more austere structure. It appeared first as a dark hulk in the middle of the upland tundra, but in an instant she was there, hovering before an ancient colosseum. She felt an urge to admire it, to explore the cracks and crevices of its marvelous stonework. But the same thought that carried her unceremoniously plunged her ethereal body through its walls. In an instant she was deposited, like the turning needle of a compass, above a rough pole in the center of the arena.

Now, as her head cleared from the dizzying speed of her journey, she collected her thoughts. She felt a sense of physical freedom, but her mind told her it was just an illusion. She was not really free here at all.

She heard a guttural snort and looked down. Beneath her sat a buck-skinned ape—a huge, hideous, hunchbacked creature chained to the pole. It must have been ten feet tall. The tight tan hair of its body reminded her of a well-groomed horse, though the black stripe running the length of its backbone sported long, coarse, pig-like hairs. The wild bristles gave it a fierce and unpredictable appearance. It had a broomed tail, and behind each arm hung the useless vestige of a wing, bat-like and pitifully short in comparison to the creature's size.

"Naamah's Nephil," she thought with repugnance, recalling the vile nature of its birth. "How it has grown."

The creature turned to look up the pole, its eyes bulging beneath heavy, wrinkled brows. A drool of saliva poured between its canine fangs into the dust near its scimitar-clawed feet. It sniffed the air and turned its ears this way and that as if searching for her.

*Lydia could not be sure whether the creature actually saw her or
merely sensed her presence.*

*She was struck by the contradiction in its eyes. They were
human and brutish at the same time. Large brown irises brimmed
with appealing softness; yet within each orb a vertical slit of yellow
pulsed with blood lust. It was as if the creature knew it had been
born to a cursed end, and in that knowledge its eyes begged compassion—though meaning only to devour anyone foolish enough to
care.*

*"What is my name?" it asked in a voice that was startlingly
clear, like a parrot's.*

*The intelligent sound sent a shiver through the old woman. She
had not expected it to speak.*

*It began to pant and grin as if playing a schoolyard game, curl-
ing its tail in an S curve in front of its knees. "Am I Bel? Rimmon?
Moloch?" Leaping suddenly from its haunches, it placed a clawed
hand delicately on one hip, mincing effeminately in a circle.
"Aphrodite? Nemesis? Astarte?" Laughing uproariously at its own
joke, it stroked the long black bristles on its head with mock van-
ity. "Adonis?"*

*Unexpectedly it transformed from gamesman to madman. Eyes
bulging with swollen blood veins, it roared with rage and leaped to
the pole, climbing in powerful lunges to the very top. Once there it
stood with superior balance and slashed the air at Lydia's belly with
its claws. She hovered in her nebulous form just beyond its frustrated reach, still not sure it had seen her. She was not afraid.*

*Turning above the pole, Lydia's eyes swept the other sections
of the colosseum. She saw a few scattered spectators in the stands.
Curiously, these people were groomed in twentieth-century gar-
ments. They appeared to wear lab jackets, surgical scrubs. "Who
can they be in this timeless place?" she wondered. "Is this Sheol?
The place of the dead? Some passage between Heaven and Hell?"
Her eyes were drawn to the far end of the arena, where for the first
time she recognized the prone form of an angel—and a beautiful
woman attending him. She knew them immediately.*

*By the power of her own wish she flew near and confirmed that
they were Mithrael and Naamah. But their roles were now reversed.
The angel lay bruised and bleeding, while Naamah wept over his
body. His mouth had been bound by some sort of metallic gag,
which fit like a horse's bit. His lips remained hidden behind a plate
of chrome. He could not speak, and his eyes rolled sightlessly in his*

head. By *wound*, or *by atrophy*, they had lost their ability to behold even the exceeding beauty of his wife. Now the eyes could only express pain as she tended his many wounds. The long scars and open gashes on the angel's arms and torso told Lydia he had been in combat with his own evil offspring. She felt tragically linked to Mithrael and Naamah by that bond known only among strangers who have unexpectedly shared a common tragedy.

A paddock directly behind the twosome held a chorus of women—all exceedingly beautiful, like Naamah. They appeared narcissistic, obsessed, murmuring pettily to one another as they eyed the attention Naamah lavished on the wounded angel. "Who can they be?" Lydia wondered.

Without warning, the intercessor felt herself propelled backward, away from the angel and Naamah. Once again she was flying swiftly just above the surface of the arena floor. She turned, passing the Nephil who raced to the end of his leash like a huge, snarling pit bull. She flew on toward the opposite end of the arena, to a place she had not yet inspected. A man waited there, bound by huge links of rusty chain secured by a padlock. He was a modern man, with graying hair, handsome and familiar in his clerical collar. In an instant Lydia found herself face to face with the very man of God for whom she had fasted and prayed—the Reverend Dr. Simon Grace!

Her weightless world shattered. She felt flesh enclosing her free spirit again. Her strange dream-world crashed to an end. Something solid lay against her backside. In that final millisecond, she saw that Dr. Grace wore a metal gag across his mouth too—identical to the angel's. His pale blue eyes were pleading with her. Pleading! She'd never seen him like this. And then, ever so swiftly, the crow's feet at the corners of his eyes and the weathered lines on his high and handsome forehead, beneath that shock of snowy white hair, began to blur. His desperate expression grew smaller and smaller until it became a mere point of light at the end of a long, nearly infinite tunnel.

Another blinding flash hurled the old woman backward and she knew—absolutely knew—

—that she must continue to pray for Simon Grace. Until this moment, her intercession and fasting had been only for his safety while filming in the troubled territory of Israel. An earthly goal. Now she must aim her prayer to a higher level. She had seen him in a place of spirits—in an ancient arena with a Nephil born of

Mithrael and Naamah. And he was bound there with terrible chains. What could it mean?

Three hundred and sixty joules of electricity defibrillated the old woman's heart. She gasped a lung full of air. The heart monitor began emitting regular spikes again.

"We've got a heartbeat," Barry said, wiping more sweat from his forehead. "Come on, Grandma . . . stabilize, baby . . . stabilize . . ."

Barry, April and the coed in the nightshirt watched the monitor breathlessly as it continued to signal the heartbeat.

. . . beep . . . beep . . . beep . . .

"Maybe the third time's a charm, huh?" Barry said.

"I'm not a believer," said the coed. "Not yet."

. . . beep . . . beep . . .

At last April sighed and pulled her chewing gum from the headboard, sticking it emphatically back into her mouth. She began chewing energetically again, pacing beside the bed. "Save a blue hair tonight, flunk chem lab tomorrow, right, dude?" She chuckled nervously, passing her hands over her blood-drained face. "I told you the blue hairs were out to ruin my grades."

The monitor continued to signal Lydia's heartbeat—strong and steady.

. . . beep . . . beep . . . beep . . .

II

HOLY LAND

The pleasant Valley of Hinnom, Tophet thence
And black Gehenna call'd, the Type of Hell.

(JOHN MILTON, *PARADISE LOST*, BOOK I)

4
JERUSALEM
11:21 A.M.

Two riot-equipped military jeeps growled from the parking garage of the Hilton Hotel followed closely by an eighteen-foot windowless step van and two minibuses full of civilians. Each minibus bore the distinctive Grace Ministries logo: a white dove descending on a target of blue, with *GRACE* superimposed in leaf-gold lettering. As they passed the main entrance to the hotel, a sleek limousine nosed in directly behind the second jeep. A troop carrier of army regulars finished out the caravan.

Golden sunlight crowned the Mount of Olives as they neared the Dung Gate of the old city, descending the road beneath the Zion Wall. Breaks in the stonework offered glimpses of small, private gardens, burning like islands of color in frames of granite as they passed. Down the winding Hativat Yerushalayim they proceeded, entering the shadows of Golgotha. At the Place of the Skull a lone skylark sang in the rustling grass and continued to call insistently after them as the sound of their engines died in the early-morning chill.

Snaking left again, the caravan followed the rough pavement of the Derekh Ha-Shiloah, rolling to a stop on a barren spot in the Valley of Hinnom.

Five hours later the sun had risen high. In the intervening time, a crew of ten colorfully dressed young men and women had emerged from the minibuses to set up three TV cameras. The Israeli military patrol had deployed cautiously around their perimeter. The cameras had already sent nine scenes along a 100-foot umbilical cord, a black, heavy, multicore cable which connected each camera to a Sony one-inch video recorder in the entrails of a van.

The scenes had been narrated by a white-haired gentleman in a clerical collar who now stooped beneath a sunsilk filter preparing to read another speech from a teleprompter. His name was Dr.

Simon Grace, president and founder of a multi-million-dollar divine healing ministry with university, med school, and a string of Third-World hospitals. His syndicated television network kept all of the promotable aspects of his operation visible to the public eye.

A young television director watched intently, seated in a shaded folding chair. He called through a bullhorn in a voice frayed with weariness, "Action!"

A trail of dust fell from Dr. Grace's hand as he spoke. "The dust of infants comprise the bones of this Holy Land—" He broke off and tossed the remaining handful to one side. "Alright, I blew it," he said.

"Cut!" the director called. "It's 'bones' of infants, sir, not 'dust.'"

"I can read, Joel," Grace grumbled curtly, wiping his palms clean. He stood stiffly to his feet.

After two weeks of shooting in the Israeli sun, the preacher's face had grown handsomely ruddy. Against his red skin, his eyes were a piercing Galilee blue. He stood five feet eleven inches, a trim one hundred and seventy-eight pounds. Fighting weight, he liked to call it, because he had boxed a few rounds in the U.S. Army at the age of twenty-one. But on this day he was a sixty-four-year-old tel-evangelist, years beyond enjoying the effects of a suntan. Simon Grace preferred television makeup. He also preferred to speak in air-conditioned comfort to an audience of living human beings—a situation he could play like a Stradivarius, laying hands on the sick, evoking decisions for Christ, and motivating freewill offerings in the same masterstroke. In that respect he was supremely tired of talking to faceless cameras. The hurry-up-and-wait syndrome of location shooting had imprisoned his restless mind for ten days too many.

"Let's get on with it," he groused.

"So let it be done," director Joel Lassiter barked, sending a wink and tired smile to his continuity clerk. "Re-rack."

Immediately a crewman in wire-rimmed spectacles and a bright Hawaiian shirt scrolled the teleprompter script backwards in front of the camera. A blonde makeup girl, in antennae hat and hot pink culottes, flitted back and forth in front of the preacher, powdering tiny beads of perspiration from his upper lip. Two muscular grips adjusted the focus of a sun reflector with each degree of the sun's movement through the sky. Camera one's operator, a body builder of gladiator proportions, worked his lens low to the ground for another close-up of the dust falling from the preacher's hand. Two other cameramen prepared complementary angles.

These were the creme of the crew from Grace Ministries television facility in Brownsville. *"They're state-of-the-art,"* the Reverend Grace was fond of boasting, especially in the presence of rival televangelists. *"God's got nothing but the best working for Grace."*

The crewmen shared a private wish that the preacher would let his *money* do the talking. In lieu of a raise, however, they took other liberties. In matters of dress most obviously. Back in Brownsville they were required to work in suit and tie for the approval of a studio audience. But when traveling they dressed with a casual vengeance, occasionally going beyond the limits of good taste.

A video engineer in wrinkled plaid pants, his shirt pocket bristling with miniature screwdrivers, emerged from the step van and hurried to the director's folding chair. He carried three camera registration charts in his hand. "We took a power surge," he explained apologetically.

"And you told me video would replace film," Lassiter replied. He smiled sarcastically and raised a bullhorn to his lips. "Take five to rechart. We lost color balance." As a second thought he added, "And nobody get lost."

Pauline Grace watched the morning's production from near the limousine. Standing with arms crossed, she had been toying impatiently with a pebble in the roadway, pushing it first one way, then the other, back and forth, back and forth, controlling it in the dust with the toe of her fine leather pumps. She was Simon Grace's only daughter. Her every move bore the signature assertiveness which can only come to daughters who are the "apple of Daddy's eye."

A natural blonde in her mid-thirties, she groomed herself to represent her father and his ministry according to the highest standards. On this morning she wore a moss colored suit of raw silk, tailored to fit her thoroughbred figure. Her matching shoes and handbag were of fine Italian leather.

With permanent waves shaped smartly to her oval face, her makeup had been applied with a light touch to play down what otherwise might have been a powerful sexuality. But in spite of the modest approach, her lips betrayed her. When she spoke, they curled provocatively over her teeth, conveying a tempting promise. The occasional salesmen and consultant-away-from-home who pursued the promise found it quite empty.

But if the promise of her lips was a mirage, the threat in her eyes remained real. They were eyes that could easily express disapproval. Not as widely spaced as the classical model's, they presented her face with a more intelligent, aggressive beauty. In direct sunlight the irises glowed more green than blue. Tiny flecks of gold flashed there, like nuggets in a forge when she grew angry. And she was known to become dazzlingly angry.

On this morning she felt uneasy because her father seemed out-of-sorts. She had sensed his impatience and distraction during the filming of the video sequence, and she was determined to get to the bottom of it. This had become her Number One responsibility in life following the death of her mother years ago. She was the only person who could get to the bottom of Dr. Grace anymore.

She noticed with displeasure that Verlin Stiles, ministry vice president, stood behind the cameras, waiting for "The Good Doctor" to acknowledge him. Accompanied by Bud Cheney, a portly courier from the Logos Mail Corporation of San Diego, the pompous-looking vice president needed decisions. And he needed them now. *Always now!*

This is no time for business, she steamed. *Why should Daddy have to do a dozen things at once? Preacher, businessman, lawyer, statesman, actor—who could keep it all straight?* Pauline strongly believed that her father should be allowed to wear each hat in its own time and place. But no, everywhere he went, Stiles put other business in front of him, pulling his attention this way and that. *If only he would just go away.*

She turned her attention toward Lassiter. Perhaps he could shed light on her father's mood. No one else watched him as closely as the TV director.

"Joel," she called.

Lassiter, rumpled master of the complexities of television, turned slowly in his stenciled folding chair and lowered his sunglasses imperiously. Pauline appreciated his competence, but resented his intimidating air. It made her feel like an intruder. She signaled him to approach. He obediently set down his clipboard and walked toward her, reluctance in his bearing.

"What's up?" he half-demanded.

When will he take me seriously? she fumed. "Daddy's not hitting his marks," she said. "He's been missing lines and looking off into space all morning. Or have you noticed?"

"Oh, yeah, I noticed," Joel said with a dismissing air. "He

wants to wrap and head for Rome. How many four-star hotels and restaurants are on your schedule anyway?" He bobbled his eyebrows cutely. "You are going with him, aren't you?"

That was Lassiter's style, pushing the limits of propriety. "I'm not rehearsing punch lines," she returned firmly. "Something's not right with him."

He turned to look again at Dr. Grace who stood with his arms folded, staring at nothing. "Well, seriously now, I think he just wants to wrap. So does everybody."

Like searchlights, her eyes flashed back and forth, counting the Israeli guards. For two weeks they had kept Arafat's *intefadeh* from stoning the camera crew. *Twenty-four soldiers today. Twice the usual number. Maybe Daddy's received a death threat.* "Why does Daddy have to be out here this morning?" she asked.

"Why are we discussing this now?" Joel replied, wearing his irritation openly.

"Because I want to know."

Joel shrugged and chuckled with exasperation. "It's important to the production. That's why."

At this terse reply Pauline allowed herself to unleash anger. "Who's the incompetent who pulled Daddy out of the hotel to this unheard-of location? I don't see anything here. A second unit could have covered it. Besides, look, they've sent twice the military escort today."

Joel glared at her. "I'm the 'incompetent' in question, Pauline. But for some reason I think you knew that." He grew red from more than the sun. "Do you want me to cancel the day here? What are you getting at?"

She knew he was right. This was the wrong time and place to take issue with the decision. *Why am I so off balance?* she wondered. "I want you to submit your brainstorms to me from now on," she muttered, trying to calm down, but couldn't help adding, "before you do something foolish like this again!"

He forced a smile and shook his head slowly.

"That will be all," she said. "Thank you."

"Have a nice day," he replied, moving his sunglasses over his eyes and turning back toward the director's chair.

Pauline did not feel she had won. She had been out of line, and she knew it. Furthermore, she had missed her mark entirely, gaining no insight into her father's mood. She remained uneasy.

Turning toward the limousine she noticed Colonel Gershon

Canaan sitting in his military jeep monitoring a radio transmission in Yiddish or Hebrew or some such code. The sight of an armed Israeli escort would normally inspire her confidence. She imagined Canaan—and all Israeli soldiers for that matter—to be superior warriors. This impression had become fixed in her mind with the phrase, *Six Day War.* Who else could fight the combined Arab armies and win in six days? Who but the people whose God had created the universe in six days? For whom the Red Sea had parted and the sun had stood still in battle? The Jews, of course.

She remained blissfully ignorant of the fact that the question dividing the Israeli Knesset was, just who is a Jew? Is the distinction racial? Religious? Cultural? Who would live in the shelter of Jewish citizenship? What were the ancestral proofs?

To Pauline, Jews were simply *Biblical.* Meaning they were a people chosen by God who kept the only reliable book on the subject. Everything from Genesis to Apocalypse wrapped itself around their history. Regardless of historians—and she put no stock in them, citing her favorite Proverb (21:1): "The king's heart is in the hand of the Lord; he directs it like a watercourse . . ." —as she saw it, the Jews were God's atomic clock for the world, ticking ever nearer to Armageddon. The destinies of every nation on the planet, whether they believed it or not, would rise or fall with the outcome of that final war. The winning side had been prophesied and predestined.

With these unqualified beliefs, the sight of Israeli Colonel Gershon Canaan guarding her crew should *not* have caused her to tremble. But it did. Perhaps "superior warriors" were only comfortable to regard from a distance. In the Valley of Hinnom her easy faith was being field tested.

Why must the Jews always fight for their lives? she wondered. The question had always been there, but it had never seemed as important as now. Her own welfare might be revealed in the answer. *Why had God allowed His chosen to become the slaughterhouse lambs for Hitler? Why the Soviet persecution? Worldwide anti-Semitism? Why have the Israelis become so hopelessly embroiled in the intefadeh, losing support in America? And why is Colonel Canaan's double guard so necessary this morning?*

I'm just having an anxiety attack. Settle down, girl, she coaxed herself. She took a deliberate breath—a practiced measure against her tendency to hyperventilate. Even the air in Hinnom breathed differently. The rest of Jerusalem's air was holy incense, full of evergreen freshness and sunshine. This air tasted like the air of a bomb shelter, stale and lifeless. It had to be dragged into the lungs by force, and expelled the same way. She wished for a wisp of breeze to clean out the canyon.

Looking up for the first time since they'd arrived, she felt the presence of a thousand Palestinian shanties on the hillside above them. The huts crowded over the busy crew with dark windows peering down like the hollow eyes of sandstone skulls. Each wore a TV antenna with which to plug into the public relations victories of the *intefadeh*. The Israeli soldiers fingered their rifles uneasily, eyeing the hovels for suspicious movement.

She turned her attention away, hearing the telephone in the limousine bleep. She watched Ismail, the hotel driver, answer it. He spoke a few words, then turned, putting the receiver out of the window in her direction.

"A call for Dr. Grace," he said.

Pauline took it and brought the receiver immediately to her ear. "Hello?"

"Hello, may I speak with Dr. Grace?" a male voice responded.

"He's very busy."

"Excuse me . . . Who is this?"

"I think I should be the one to ask," she replied sharply.

"Of course. I'm Barry Malone. I'm—this is hard to explain, but I have an emergency patient at the hospital here in Brownsville who demands to get a message to Dr. Grace. The weirdest part is . . . I mean, I can't believe I agreed to this—You see, she had a heart attack a few hours ago and died . . . Three times actually . . . Had to be defibrillated. But she wouldn't let me rest until I called Dr. Grace, and I mean to say—she's been through so much I don't even think she can talk. But . . ."

"Barry, this is Pauline."

"Miss Grace, I'm sorry about calling you there, but—"

"Never mind. Is this a nut case or is she one of our partners?"

"It's Lydia Nation—"

Pauline's body tensed with dread, feeling sudden sympathy.

"Lydia? My goodness, put her on. This is terrible." She climbed through the limousine door and sat down to listen. Normally she didn't spend much time thinking about the intercessor who lived in the Steeple. She took her for granted—in the best possible sense of the word. She loved her—depended on her being there, praying. "You say she had a heart attack?"

"As near as we can tell, yes, ma'am. Anyway, she's been through a lot. She won't be able to say much, but if you'd like, I will relay what she writes down here on this pad. Would that be OK?"

"Please do." Pauline fumbled in her purse for a notepad. Finding it, she removed a pencil and poised to write. "Go ahead." Static began to obscure the cellular line. "I'm sorry, I can't make you out," she said. "You'll have to repeat that, Barry."

". . . She writes real slow," he said. "You would too if you'd been through what she went through . . . OK . . . here it comes . . ." Static obscured the line again. ". . . —ead Luke 22:31 and 32, she—"

Pauline heard a definite *click* followed by a wavering dial tone. Sighing, she quickly scribbled "Luke 22:31, 32" and handed the receiver back to Ismail. "Let me know if she calls back," she said, stuffing the pad and pencil into her purse.

"Quiet on the set," Joel Lassiter shouted, having cleared the registration charts from the cameras, finishing his preparation for the retake.

Pauline turned thoughtfully in the limo seat and watched the production through the window. As she did, the uneasy feeling she had fought all morning slid down to her gut like a slug of mercury in a cooling thermometer. It lay there, promising to rise again in the heat of panic. Something was coming. Something was wrong. The intercessor had died. Three times. *What is it, Lord? What is going on?*

"Roll tape! Slate it," called Lassiter.

"'Grace in the Holy Land,' segment 8, take 11," replied a female assistant, wielding a chalk-inscribed clapboard in front of the preacher's face.

"Slate out," called the cameraman.

She pulled it away.

Dr. Grace drew to his full height, adjusted his clerical collar, and pushed a tuft of steel-gray hair into place above his tanned forehead.

"Action," shouted Lassiter.

Grace addressed the camera in an orator's bass rivaling Cicero of the Roman Senate.

"This is the Valley of Hinnom—garbage yard for the ancient City of David—the dumpster of Jerusalem, the City of God, Zion. You can learn a lot about the Holy City by digging here. It is without a doubt the most abominable site in the Holy Land, for it was here that the children of Israel turned their back on their God, repeatedly. They bowed their knee to an idol-god named Moloch, a Canaanite demon who demanded that those who worshiped his image would toss their firstborn sons, alive, into a ceremonial fire which burned here day and night. In one generation the idolatrous inhabitants of Jerusalem aborted their future captains, kings and mighty men. Here, on this spot, perhaps another Moses, another Samuel, another Elijah, another Samson, another deliverer was burned in the belly of the idol. No doubt the enemies of God hoped to abort the promised Messiah Himself in this manner."

"Ready three . . . take," Lassiter called.

Dr. Grace turned smoothly and walked toward camera three. "In the year 600 B.C. the Lord God Almighty instructed the prophet Jeremiah to come to this very spot and say, '. . . they have filled this valley with the blood of innocents; they have built the high places to burn their sons with fire . . . therefore, I will make this city desolate, I will cause them to fall by the sword . . . the days will come saith the Lord, that this place shall be called the valley of slaughter.' And the prophet Jeremiah lived to see the desolation of Jerusalem. So terrible was the sight of it that he cried out to God in his old age, 'Cursed be the day wherein I was born.' Would to God I had never lived to see it."

A spell had fallen over the crew. The Israeli soldiers turned from their vigilance to watch. Even Colonel Canaan's eyes were riveted to the preacher's face as silence gripped the canyon.

Grace's voice dropped lower, cutting through the air like a whiplash. "Six hundred years later Jesus Christ walked here. There are those who say it was here the children flocked innocently to His knees. Children. He picked them up, one by one, and held them, saying, 'let them come to me . . . let them come.' Can you see it? Can you imagine—?"

Grace faltered, looking away.

"Close up," Lassiter whispered into the headset. It was a moment the director had seen often, and still wondered if the consummate actor really felt this emotion.

Simon Grace turned back to the camera and his eyes glistened. "—You see, the modern name they have given this valley, 'Tophet,' comes from the word for 'drum,' recalling the drums that were beaten here to drown out the screams of dying children. So when Jesus gathered the little ones to Himself in this place, I have no doubt He heard sounds no one else could hear—the cries of a lost generation sacrificed to Moloch. I believe the voices of those children cried out to our Lord from the dust of this place."

He stooped suddenly and scooped up a handful of dust, letting it fall like dry powder.

"Can you hear them today? The voices of the innocent ones? Who will cry out for the children no one can hear? Those sacrificed to the cheap gods of crack cocaine, or aborted to the gods of modern sexual convenience?"

In the limousine Pauline's chin rested spellbound on her knuckles. She never loved her father more than when she heard him like this. Mountains could move. And with a twinge of guilt she realized why Lassiter had brought the preacher here; it was the only place on earth for this sermon.

A disturbance began at the location perimeter. Giggling voices echoed across the set as a group of Palestinian preschoolers appeared and grew brave enough to launch a volley of rocks toward the Israeli soldiers. Then as the soldiers swung their guns around they quickly scattered barefoot among the shanties.

Dr. Grace broke his mood, "Excuse me—" he said, clearing his throat, then turned to Joel. "Edit that out. I will not do another take here. Understand?"

"Got'cha covered." Joel gave him the thumbs up signal and whispered to the headset, "Did anyone get a shot of those kids?" He smiled and signaled Grace smoothly with a circular motion of his fingers, meaning that the cameras were still rolling.

"To those who stood around him—" Grace cleared his throat loudly again. "—OK. Start over. Take two . . ." He paused to lower his emotion to match the previous tearful take. "To those who stood around Him here, Christ gave another name to this place, 'Gehenna.' Where the worm dieth not, neither is the fire quenched. 'Gehenna.' It's a bad word. It means a place of torment—Hell."

Lassiter pointed downward. "And . . . one."

Grace scooped another handful of dust. "The bones of infants comprise the very dust of this place. Because of the idolatry of God's own people, this unholy soil has become part of what we must call today—" he paused for effect, letting the dust fall before the close-up camera, "—the Holy Land."

"Hold your expression," coached Lassiter. "We're still rolling . . . hold . . . cut!" He stood up, calling the crew through the bullhorn. "It's a wrap. Billy Boren's music sequence tapes at the Garden

Tomb at 1:30. Full crew call." Privately he added to "The Good Doctor," now disconnecting his microphone, "Nicely done, sir. As usual."

Grace dusted his hands together and moved toward the limousine. "Thank you, Joel. You guys are the best." He brushed past Vice President Stiles and Bud Cheney, who stood expectantly, briefcases in hand.

"Let's go," Grace barked at the driver.

This is not like him, Pauline thought. *He's normally more considerate.*

Stiles shrugged apologetically to the portly man from Logos Mail as the preacher ducked into the waiting limousine. Pauline quickly shut her door.

"Follow the Yericho," Dr. Grace said impatiently.

Ismail quickly put them in motion. As the limousine sped away, Pauline fell against the seat. "My goodness . . . What's your hurry?"

She regained her equilibrium and reached into a forward cabinet, handing her father a moist towelette.

"Thanks, baby girl," he said, and began to remove the makeup from his face and hands.

Pauline loved it when he called her "baby girl." He called others "honey," "sugar," "dear," but no one else in the world could be his "baby girl." She loved having that special place.

He tossed the soiled wipe into a wastebasket on the floorboard. She waited with another. "You're not yourself today, Daddy."

He didn't reply for a time, but kept moving the cloth across his face. "I'm not myself everyday, sweetheart. I'm not even this color for crying out loud." He examined the makeup on the alcohol-and-cotton swatch.

"Don't be cute. What's wrong? I can read you like a book."

He remained deeply quiet.

"Something's been bothering you all morning. I can see it."

"Pauline . . . Pauline . . ." he murmured, finishing his last wipe. "I love you, honey."

She paused, not liking the serious signal she heard here. "I love you too, Daddy, but you're making me nervous. What is going on with you? Talk to me."

"I'm tired, baby girl."

"Well alright, we can deal with that."

"No. I mean—*I'm tired.*"

The tires spoke a staccató beat to the cobblestones as they bounded over the uneven surface of the Yericho. Pauline watched the muscles work in her father's jaw, and suddenly she knew she didn't want to hear what he would say next. It had not been the location, nor the soldiers, nor the Palestinian shanties that had been amiss. It had been something else.

"All my life," he said, "I've carried this healing torch for God." His tone was bitter. "I've taken hard ridicule for laying hands on the sick. A few people have been healed—not many. I feel shame every time a stand-up comic wants to play a healer for a cheap laugh. Oh, it goes with the territory, I suppose. But I can't help it anymore. I'm supremely tired of it." He forced a long draught of air through his nostrils. "I'm tired mostly because . . . what I've never been able to understand—" He held both of his hands out, and they trembled. "—of *all* the people I ever laid these hands on, why did she have to die?" His voice dropped to an angry rasp, and he snatched another towelette from the cabinet. "What do you suppose He's got against me?"

Pauline knew exactly what he meant. Twenty years ago it had been Ruth, his wife, Pauline's mother, who had succumbed to cancer. Only morphine had eased her pain. Not prayer, not fasting, not all the love in her husband's heart.

"Daddy, He's got nothing against you. You *know* that."

His eyes fought back tears, and Pauline knew she had missed her mark. She grew alarmed. This emotion was more than she had expected. Furthermore, it was out of place. He was temperamental, yes, and had depressions, yes, but not at a time like this. These were thoughts he might confide late at night, at home, in a reflective mood. Not here. Not now. Maybe she didn't know him as well as she thought she did.

"Daddy, stop feeling sorry for yourself," she scolded. "Who knows why she had to die? You feel more compassion for other people now—it made you deeper—I don't know. But you have a ministry to thousands of people who have suffered more than you. They look to you for faith and hope every day. That's what's important here. Don't you see?"

He seemed to ignore her.

Out of frustration she scolded again. "I had no idea you still dwelt on the past like this, for heaven's sake."

He didn't seem to hear or care. He scrolled down the window

and watched the passing street signs. "Pull over here," he ordered suddenly, pointing to a small side street.

She saw that they were in a backward neighborhood. A series of alleyways sloped sideways along a hill between an assortment of Palestinian dwellings. Some were made of brick and straw, others of corrugated metal. A few of the mud walls were inscribed with Arabic graffiti and universal peace signs. The surface of the road glistened with polished clay. The cobblestones had been removed, no doubt, to be used as ammunition in the children's war with the soldiers.

"Daddy, this doesn't look like the kind of place we ought to stop. If you don't mind, I'd like to move on."

Dr. Grace turned to his daughter, taking her face in his hands with sudden earnestness. "Baby girl, I need you to look after things for me. See to it the TV special runs on schedule, no matter what. Just do that. OK?"

"Where are you going?"

Bible in hand, he quickly slid out the door, shutting it behind him. He spoke to her through the open window. "I will be back," he said, handing her a sealed envelope. "Don't follow me. This is a very dangerous place. When you get home, if you find yourself in trouble . . ." He paused. ". . . call Evan."

"What do you mean? I'm not going back without you! And what does Evan have to do with this?" Her older brother was the *last* person she'd call.

"If you get in trouble, just call him," her father repeated firmly. "Blood is thicker—remember that. I'll be fine, darlin'. I love you."

She did not like what she felt. It seemed dark. She didn't know her father this way. He kissed her forehead and turned quickly toward the alley.

Pauline's heart raced crazily. "Where are you going?" she shouted after him, glancing fearfully up and down the Yericho. He continued on. Suddenly she remembered Lydia's call. "Daddy, I forgot to tell you something."

He kept walking.

"Lydia had a heart attack!"

He stopped and whirled around, ashen-faced, teetering. For a moment it appeared as if he might fall. "She what?"

Pauline paused, realizing she had shocked him. But he had shocked her. "Why are you leaving me here, Daddy?"

He hurried back to the open window. "What do you mean?"

he demanded. He seemed almost in a panic. "She's dead?" he rasped.

"No, Daddy, she's fine. I mean she's, she's OK—"

"You spoke to her? You know she's alive?"

"Yes."

His face grew livid, and he bellowed, "Then why are you bringing it up at a time like this?" He turned on his heel, walked a few paces, then stopped himself. He returned to the window. "I'm sorry, baby girl. I didn't mean it like that." He looked fearfully around and backed away from the window. "She's just got to be fine, that's all. Send her my love. Please do that." He turned and trotted away.

Pauline felt empty of all rational thought. She watched as her father paused briefly at the corner of an alleyway, looking back at her. With a final wave of his Bible, he disappeared.

Confusion flooded her mind. Then abruptly it turned to anger. *Of all the stupid things!* she thought. *Leaving me here. And what a remark, recommending that I contact Evan! So what if "blood is thicker"? My brother despised his spiritual birthright—sold it for a cheap sexual fling.*

Furiously she ripped open the envelope. On a single sheet of Hilton stationery in his own handwriting her father had scrawled, "Keep this out of the press!" What was he up to?

She nearly choked with frustration. "This has got to be some kind of joke, right?" She looked around, half-expecting the TV crew to jump out of hiding to surprise her. "Ismail, is this a joke?"

The limo driver's eyes were wide and uncomprehending in the rearview mirror. He shrugged.

❖

In the deserted side street Dr. Grace slowed his walk, growing uncertain. A beat-up, blue Renault sat idling in his path, its doors open. The quiet clatter of the motor reminded him of a ticking bomb. He stopped.

Two armed men stepped from a doorway wearing the black and white signature headgear of Palestinians. One of them held an AK-47 assault rifle on a sling. The other pointed a Luger directly at Grace's head.

"Not to worry, Dr. Grace," said the Palestinian, speaking English in a thick, Middle-eastern accent. He wagged his pistol toward the car. "This is just in case we are seen. Get in."

"Where's Max?" Grace demanded, backing away.

"We don't have *time,*" the Palestinian hissed, his veneer of cordiality vanishing. He roughly shoved Dr. Grace inside the backseat of the car. The other man leaped into the driver's seat and revved its engine. With a squeal of tires the car spun around and lurched the other way.

At that moment Pauline ran into the alley, the envelope still clutched in her fist. She caught a glimpse of the pale blue car as it disappeared.

"Daddy?" she called in a trembling voice. "Daddy!" She started to run after him.

Three male youths leaped a fence into the alley in front of her, their faces completely draped with Palestinian head cloths. Each carried a shepherd's sling, which they swung with deadly intent as they ran.

She felt a thrill of panic as a stone buzzed through the air, just missing her head. It impacted the wall behind her with enough force to have split her skull. In one motion she removed her pumps and ran for her life. But her fine silk skirt trapped her legs and threw her to the polished clay, slapping her elbows against its surface with bone-bruising pain. She drove her knees under her, ripping the skirt from its stylish slit halfway up the back. Now she could run with freedom. Rounding the corner of the alley, she sprinted for the open door of the limousine.

Another rock whizzed past her head, and another one, which slammed full force through the passenger window of the long black car. The driver lurched forward, spinning his tires in panic. She realized that he was not waiting. He was leaving her to this stone-throwing mob.

"Stop, Ismail! Stop," she screamed with all the angry and terrified air in her lungs. But he drove on. The hireling was a Palestinian himself. *Never again,* she seethed. *The driver will be one of our own next time!*

By instinct she dodged to the left and out of the corner of her eye saw several more youths joining the first three, appearing out of nowhere among the shanties. They ran in deadly silence, like wolves sensing easy prey.

Her lungs screamed for more air. Her side cramped like a stab wound. Bending over, she felt her own true frailty for the first time in her life. *No! No! I will fight this,* she screamed to herself. But the footsteps were closing in, and she knew she was no match for these faceless enemies.

A stone clipped her thigh like the bite of a mad dog, crossing her feet and spilling her headlong to the broken pavement. Instinctively she cried out and buried her face on her arms, waiting for the blunt, bruising pain of the next rock.

But it never came. The youths dropped their attack. She could hear their footsteps scattering behind her.

She raised her head, clearing away the screaming confusion in her mind. Two army jeeps roared toward her at high speed. In a moment Colonel Gershon Canaan and his riot-equipped patrol swept into the neighborhood on either side of her prone body, guns at ready, pursuing the youthful attackers.

Pauline tensed with renewed dread as she heard the terrifying, *thump! thump! thump!* of real gunfire behind her. *Stop it! Stop it,* she thought. She desperately didn't want guns to be fired. She didn't want anyone to be hurt, or to die. She only wanted to get out of the Holy Land and back to Texas as fast as she possibly could.

She twisted around and saw that her nylons were shredded, her feet bleeding from the sharp gravel in the street. The skin of her thigh stung bitterly where the rock had found its mark. The flesh around it tightened into a knot of pain. Temporarily out of danger, and out of breath, she lowered her face to her arms again and began to cry. The envelope trembled between her whitened knuckles. What could it mean?

Behind her, Colonel Canaan ran swiftly from an alleyway, bounding on steel-spring legs toward her prone body. His Uzi swung back and forth as he ran, eyes roving the area for any hostile movement.

Pauline jammed her hands over her ears and cried like a demanding child, "Good God in Heaven, what is going on here?"

5
GARDEN TOMB
1:43 P.M.

Canaan's jeep approached a barricade blocking the way to the Garden Tomb. Pauline rode with him. After the trauma of the morning she had returned to the King David Hotel where she had placed a frantic call to Verlin Stiles, telling him that her father had disappeared and asking him to meet her at the music production site. Then she had changed into a khaki-pant outfit, accepting Canaan's offer of a ride in his jeep. Under the circumstances she felt safer in his presence.

A soldier lifted the production barricade, letting the colonel drive through without stopping. They continued past a muffled diesel generator, wheeling to a stop behind a sea-land trailer bearing the logo of Grace Productions.

The sound of music filtered through the trees from the direction of the Garden Tomb as Canaan got out of his seat and came around to assist her.

Pauline's mind remained preoccupied. She felt that for now, at least, it would be important to do as her father had asked and see that the TV special ran on time. She was equally determined to keep the news from the press as he had asked. With the colonel's help she slid gingerly to the ground, testing her stiffened leg and tender feet.

"When Verlin gets here, would you bring him to my trailer?"

Canaan nodded assent.

"Thank you." She paused, asking almost impulsively, "I would like you to be there, if you would, please?"

He raised his eyebrows with surprise. "Of course. Whatever I can do."

She studied him momentarily, realizing that she had not intended to ask for his presence. But it did seem reasonable. After all, he had rescued her once today already. More than that, there was something about him. His bearing seemed noble, exuding personal power and confidence. Behind his strong voice, handsome features and snapping brown eyes—which seemed to hold back

more than they expressed—she sensed a true ally. At least she hoped
so.

She turned and moved with a slight limp toward the garden.
The familiar flamboyance of gospel pianist Billy Boren's keyboard-
dominated the sounds reaching her ears. The majestic strings of the
Jerusalem orchestra sustained a wall of sound behind him. A hundred spectators and a much larger crew than in Hinnom had gathered here. It always amazed her how much excitement attended
musical production, and yet it played a relatively minor role in the
world of evangelism. She had never understood the disparity.

She approached the production set with the idea of taking Billy
Boren aside. She felt a growing need to confide in someone who
shared her faith, and for years Billy had been such a friend. Yearly
he had escorted her to the presidential prayer breakfast and other
"be seen" religious events. Though gossip magazines had linked
them romantically, the two had shared nothing beyond friendship.
In her present state of fear and confusion she thought, *He's a shoulder—a supportive hand to hold—someone to pray with me.* But
those thoughts died the minute she laid eyes on him.

Dressed in a white sequined suit with exaggerated shoulders
crossed by quilted keyboard bandoliers, Billy Boren burnt up the
ivories of a concert grand piano, grinning beyond the limits of his
mouth like a Las Vegas headliner. Staged incredibly at the entrance
to the Garden Tomb, all six Grace studio cameras, two on hand-
held stedicam mounts and one sweeping overhead on a Chapman
crane, were pointed directly at him. The Grace backup singers
belted, ". . . ain't no grave . . . gonna hold my body down, ain't no
graaaaaaaaaaaaaaa-ave . . . gonna hold my body down . . ." They
delivered the bluegrass spiritual with campy delight as the
Jerusalem Symphony Orchestra added what Billy liked to call
"pure *D* class" to the arrangement.

In that moment Pauline knew Billy had gotten what he wanted
from her. She knew him that well. He had remained at her beck-
and-call for years in exchange for this day, when Dr. Grace would
showcase his talents with thousand-dollar-a-minute production
value. With six state-of-the-art cameras panning his diamond-stud-
ded fingers and perfectly bonded teeth, he had found the end of his
personal rainbow. *Payment enough*, she thought, and dropped
every fantasy of confiding in him.

Leaving the noisy production, she turned and limped painfully
toward the motor coach.

The same makeup girl who had earlier attended Dr. Grace sat on the steps. Noticing Pauline, she jumped up. "Ooh, you're limping, sweetie. What happened?"

"A small accident. I'm fine." On other occasions she might have considered the girl syrupy. *She has the heart of a servant,* she thought now, feeling a need for even this shallow expression of concern. "Do you mind letting me rest in the coach for a while?"

"Sure. Can I get you anything?"

"How about a Diet Coke with crushed ice. And when Stiles and the colonel come by, tell them to come on in."

"Sure thing."

Pauline pulled herself through the door and shut it with relief, muting the musical riot outside. A silent TV monitor showed the camera's view of Billy's production. She ignored it, dropped into a chair with a heavy sigh, and sat still for a moment. Only a moment. Her mind whirled like a buzz-saw. She got up again and paced through the motor coach, restless for anything that might make sense, settle her nerves. An almost palpable shelter had fallen in ruins around her, leaving her with the feeling of being dangerously exposed. *Why has Daddy done this to me? Why?*

Through the window she caught a glimpse of Stiles and Canaan hurrying her way. Verlin had quickened his usual oily stride. Pauline thought he moved as if he'd never walked on anything but carpet in all of his life. Beneath his meticulously blow-dried hair, she could see his fleshy look of self importance, and she felt in no mood to endure it. *Why did I tell him?* she agonized. *It was a reflex when I got back to the room. Besides, he's Daddy's VP, he has to be informed.* Still, she wished she had waited. She had never been able to figure out why her father kept Verlin around anyway. He was a small-time evangelist who had agreed to play second fiddle to a big-time success. It *had* to grate on his unfulfilled ego.

As soon as Stiles entered the door a wave of cologne greeted her. *Aramis,* she guessed. *Cheap, pretentious bum.*

As if to confirm her judgment, he launched immediately into his own opinion. "I don't understand why in the world you would want to keep this thing from the authorities, honey."

She resented his use of the term "honey" in this context. Outside, the music came to a dramatic end.

"The authorities know," Pauline returned as firmly as she could. "Colonel Canaan here is an Israeli official. I don't know anyone else who needs to know. Nothing is settled yet. Nothing is sure."

"How about the U.S. Embassy? They ought to be told."

"Well, I don't know . . ." Pauline turned her eyes to the colonel, fishing for help. "What do you think?"

He replied carefully, studying her eyes all the while. "If, as you have told me, you want to keep this out of the press, then you will have no problem. Mine happens to be an intelligence unit, and we know how to keep quiet. We make the usual backdoor contacts at the Embassy. We can do that for you if you want this handled with discretion. Otherwise, it will be world headlines tomorrow."

"That's the last thing I want," Pauline insisted. "Go ahead and make the Embassy contacts, colonel. We don't need press, at least not until we know what to tell them."

Verlin stifled a small groan. "How can you hesitate? What if he's—" He stopped, thinking better of continuing his worst-case scenario. "I say we need all the coverage we can get right now, and I don't know why you would be holding back. You of all people."

Canaan interjected, "If it helps, your father will not be able to leave Israel without our knowledge."

"But if this is a terrorist thing—" Stiles glanced at Pauline, then shrugged helplessly. "Did he give you any clues? Anything to suggest that he might be under a threat?"

Pauline recalled the speeding blue car and her father's strange instructions to her. "Keep this out of the press . . . Make sure the TV special runs on time . . . I'll be back . . . If you get in trouble call Evan." Mixed signals. Wherever he had gone, it seemed obvious it had been part of a planned rendezvous. But why had he cloaked it in secrecy? The whole thing still confused her. "He said he'd be back," she answered at last. "And he asked me to take care of things."

Verlin flushed. "Now why would he say *that*?"

"How should I know?"

"No, no, don't be offended. You misunderstand," Stiles objected. "Why would he say that to you when he knows very well that we *have* procedures for taking care of things when he's gone? Good emergency procedures, approved by the board."

Immediately Pauline fought to control a burst of anger. Stiles couldn't wait to get his hands on her father's power. He reeked with petty ambition. "Verlin, I just want you to understand one thing here," she seethed, her voice trembling slightly. "You hear me now, and hear me good. This is *my father* we're talking about, OK? Not the board. Not procedures of any kind. Do you understand?" Her voice had risen dramatically.

A giggling commotion outside interrupted the tension, and Billy Boren raced through the coach door, followed closely by the makeup girl. Neither of them suspected that serious business was at hand. The makeup girl carried a Diet Coke and a cup of crushed ice, which she obediently handed to Pauline.

"Pauline," Billy enthused, "excuse us, but will that number knock 'em dead, or what? Did you see it? It beats 'Up From the Grave He Arose,' now don't it?" He grinned, proud of himself. "Oh, come on now. You saw it?"

She remained stone—unable to switch emotional gears.

His expression fell. "Did I overdo?" he asked, indicating his outrageous costume. "Too, too much?"

"No, Billy," she said, "it looked like fun. We're just working out a few wrinkles on the business side of things here, if you'll excuse us."

"Ah—of course. Understand," he said, ducking back to the entrance. "I'll leave all you-alls to your misery," he drawled, turning with a grin. He winked at Pauline. "Later, shug?"

She wasn't watching. She didn't move or reply. He cleared his throat nervously and let himself out of the trailer. "Must be something serious in there," he said as he and the makeup artist walked back toward the production.

6

NEAR JERICHO
2:08 P.M.

The magnified circle of desert bloomed yellow in the binoculars' field of vision as a battered blue Renault outraced a plume of dust through the shimmering heat. The watching soldier swung his glass quickly to the right again, just to make sure. *Kehn!* There it sat on a rise in the road, as it had been for the past twenty-three and a half minutes. A white passenger van, diesel vapors muttering darkly from its tailpipe. At first glance it had smelled of a rendezvous, and now here came proof.

"*Baal agala Renault.*" The soldier barked coded signals to a hand-held radio. "*Bet ha-kneset, Yericho.*"

Having alerted his command post, he settled beneath a camouflage canopy, scribbling a brief notation on a pad. He checked the telephoto lens of a camera, preparing to record the event as it unfolded before him.

The Renault sped forward, engine and trans-axle whining until it neared the rise in the road. Then it began to slow, finally lurching to a stop directly behind the van. An armed man stepped from each side of the car. A white-haired minister in clerical collar unfolded himself from the cramped rear seat—all duly recorded by the busily winding camera in the hands of the soldier-in-hiding.

Meanwhile a uniformed chauffeur emerged from the van. No occupants could be seen waiting behind its tinted windows. The chauffeur walked toward the Renault carrying a book-sized package wrapped in brown paper. The first armed man accepted the package and walked quickly to the car, entering the driver's side. The second held the white-haired preacher by the arm. Meanwhile, the first ripped open the package, examining it briefly. He signaled his companion. At this, the second man ducked back into the Renault, leaving the minister standing alone. The car spun around and sped back the way it had come, trans-axle whining up the scale with each manual gear change.

The minister accompanied the chauffeur to the passenger van. Its sliding door opened, and the minister stepped into the air-conditioned interior. The chauffeur secured the door quickly behind him and returned to the driver's seat. The van then cruised away in the opposite direction at a moderate speed.

The sound of the camera's auto-wind mechanism churned in the descending stillness. The soldier reached again for his radio.

7

JERUSALEM
Valley of Hinnom
3:23 P.M.

A circle of soldiers ringed Zion's ancient garbage yard. More than a hundred of them, standing twenty feet apart, guarded a clean-up crew working the Derekh Ha-Shiloah. It was not an ordinary crew. In the middle of the road sat the smoking remains of a pale blue Renault, torn completely apart by a powerful car bomb. Hinnom had once again become Jeremiah's prophesied "valley of slaughter."

The men and women sifting the wreckage wore civilian clothes, identified only by temporary blue plastic bibs bearing the Star of David front and back. They worked with quiet efficiency, as if sorting carnage was a routine assignment for them. Several wore rubber gloves and used tongs to bag human remains. Others collected blood samples and dusted pieces of wreckage for fingerprints. One scraped the still-hot metal for traces of explosive. Another collected bits of paper.

Amid traces of brown wrapper, a bearded old man in wire-rimmed spectacles found a shredded page of what appeared to be a photocopied document. Upon closer examination he noticed marginal notes. He squinted at the handwriting, then with sudden interest placed the scrap in a canvas satchel and began searching for more.

Colonel Canaan's jeep eased slowly toward the twisted wreckage, having already passed through the line of soldiers. Pauline rode beside him. Verlin Stiles peered anxiously over her shoulder.

Twenty yards from the site, Canaan switched off the engine and sat still, watching Pauline carefully. "I thought you might recognize something," he said carefully.

She felt her insides shift into a desperate sort of shock zone. Nothing to be felt. Nothing real. All better judgment suspended. It was a condition that allowed her eyes to roam over the jagged metal, knowing that it might point bloody fingers to her father's violent end. She trembled.

The doors of the car had been torn free and lay twisted in opposite directions as if the inferno had become a potent corkscrew. Most of the remaining frame had been rendered the hues of charcoal by the heat of the blast. The tires flickered with lingering flame. Just above the rear bumper, near the license plate, a patch of pale blue paint remained true to its original color. In her mind Pauline could see the retreating vehicle again, carrying her father down that Palestinian alleyway only hours ago. *Oh, to go back! I would never let him go!*

Her mind replayed a composite image of his special laugh, crinkling the corners of his eyes, filling them with sparkles of magic blue. That had always been her power over him. Only she could make him smile that special smile—just for her. She had not had her fill of it. Not by a long way.

She opened her mouth. "I . . . I don't know," she managed. But the shock zone began to break up inside, and her lips quivered uncontrollably. A sudden twitch tore at her facial muscles, and she pressed her hand tightly against her mouth.

"Don't draw conclusions," Canaan cautioned. He glanced back at Stiles. The evangelist's knuckles had turned white where they gripped the back of the seat. His stare had become fixed and moist with dread.

Canaan fired the jeep engine and gently turned the vehicle around, heading back toward the perimeter of soldiers. "You need to wait for the coroner's report," he said, and he looked at Pauline with eyes that held back more than they revealed. He seemed to be trying to subtly ease her mind, but she had no eyes to see it.

"I'm telling you, don't draw conclusions," he repeated.

8

BROWNSVILLE, TEXAS
Grace Hospital
6:23 A.M.

In the predawn darkness Lydia's eyes stared upward, following the flow of prayer from her heart. *Who is that foul Nephil, Lord? How does he have Dr. Grace in his power? I know You've given me work to do, but what is it?*

Slowly her eyes worked their way around the intensive-care room, taking in the intravenous drip attached to a catheter in her arm, the heart monitor plugged to her chest, and the oxygen line inserted through her nose. Feeling unduly put upon, she began to pull with exasperation at the transparent tape holding the oxygen line in place.

The telephone light signaled an incoming call. Reaching out, her hand fell short. Half rolling to one side she raised herself to an elbow, snatching the receiver from its cradle. It fell to the floor. Falling back on the bed, she fished it up by its cord and answered as if the caller had been responsible for her discomfort. "Hello," she demanded.

"Lydia? Is that you?" Pauline had not expected to hear her voice. She thought perhaps a nurse would answer, or Barry. Evidently the old woman had grown healthy enough to talk since earlier that morning. Of course, time zones put them nine hours apart. At late afternoon Israel time, it would be pre-dawn in Texas. "This is Pauline."

The intercessor's voice immediately softened. "Pauline, honey, I thought you were another doctor come to mess with me or something."

"I can't believe you're talking. I thought—"

"I'm fine. I'm just fine. Would you please make them let me out of here? These doctors have never seen travailing prayer before. They act like I've taken sick or something."

Pauline grew confused. "But you had a heart attack—"

"Nonsense. I've been in a pitched battle in the heavenlies over your father, honey. That's all it's been." With sudden confidentiality she added, "Pauline, sweetie, I've seen him in a dream—or a vision or something. It was so very, very vivid, like a motion picture. I believe he's in some kind of bondage."

In the privacy of her hotel room Pauline felt shocked and comforted in the same moment. For all of the politics and power of the ministry, almost all of it functioned within the limits of natural activity. But in truth the ministry was supposed to be about matters of the spirit. It took this woman of prayer to remind her of that, even in the heart of this crisis. Lydia had somehow been linked to the matter. Her heart attack and Dr. Grace's disappearance shared a spiritual connection, even though they remained thousands of miles apart.

Pauline began to cry. She had been holding too much inside. "Lydia, Daddy's disappeared. He's gone, maybe kidnapped . . . Or dead. Please, I can't tell anybody. He—he got in a blue car this morning and now—the car's been blown up!"

In the hospital Lydia's eyebrows shot up, hearing this. "No, no, no!" she responded. "Don't you believe it. He's not dead. Listen to me. It's something else."

"But how do you *know*?" Pauline insisted, wanting desperately to believe her. She heard a puzzling commotion on the other end of the line.

Dr. Neva Sylvan had entered Lydia's hospital room. She snatched the telephone from the old woman's fingers, scolding into the receiver, "Who told you that you could call this number?"

Pauline wiped her eyes. "Excuse me, who is this?"

"Dr. Sylvan."

"Oh, Neva!" She felt instant relief. "I'm so glad you're there. What in the world has happened to Lydia?"

"My dear, get this straight—she suffered myocardial infarction. It is very serious and delicate, and she needs to stay off the telephone."

"Nonsense!" Lydia sputtered from her bed.

Neva ignored her, continuing smoothly, "You've got to understand, Lydia is not competent to judge her own condition, dear. She may think she feels fine, but without our emergency efforts last night she would not be alive this morning."

"Nonsense," Lydia snorted. "The Lord will tell my heart when to stop beating."

"Neva, I'm sorry," Pauline said, not hearing Lydia's response. "I thought she was fine because she sounded good on the phone.

She told me she was fine. I guess I should have known better." She recalled her father telling her that terminal patients often become deceptively lucid just hours before death. Maybe that explained Lydia's brightness. *Lord, don't let her die*, she begged.

Neva scolded further, "I just hope you weren't speaking about anything stressful. Even a *conversation* could trigger a relapse. I'm *really* not trying to be ugly about this. Do you understand, honey?"

"Of course, Neva," Pauline said, but she felt something strange in the tone of Neva's voice. "I would never have called, it's just—"

Neva waited. "Yes? Is everything alright there?"

"It's nothing." Pauline felt an inner check. Something was not right in Lydia's situation. For some reason Pauline now felt impelled to make sure that Neva understood her father's affection for the intercessor. "Just please take good care of Lydia for us, that's all. Her prayers mean so much to Daddy."

"Of course they do," Neva soothed. "I know that." Changing the subject brightly, she asked, "We'll be seeing you back here in a couple of days, won't we?"

Pauline paused. "The Lord willing." She placed the phone back in its cradle feeling a desperate need to talk more with Lydia. The old intercessor had insisted her father was not dead. Pauline wanted to cling to those words, but a nagging fear told her that Lydia might only be speaking the words of a dying old woman, in which case she was talking crazy, saying things not to be trusted.

In the Grace hospital room, the old intercessor fluffed her sheets several times and muttered, "You're just full of nonsense, Neva Sylvan. And that's *the only Christian thing* I can say about it."

❖

For the next hour Pauline could not bring herself to leave the Jerusalem hotel room. Stiles called. She asked him to stay off the line, not being able to bear the thought of missing the call from Colonel Canaan with the coroner's report from the car bomb investigation. Had her father been in the explosion or not? Until she knew the answer to that, nothing else mattered.

She paced, looking absently out of the window. A bearded old man haunted a park bench in the garden below her second-floor window. The sight of him made her uneasy. She closed the curtains. Later opened them again. Then shut them again. Then opened them again. Twice she dropped to her knees begging, *O God, please, please* . . . But her prayer wouldn't go beyond that. She couldn't bring herself to pray for God's will because she feared that His will might be to take her father. "The Lord giveth and the Lord taketh . . ." she reminded herself. He was God, and His ways were above the condition of her human heart. The Scripture said, "It is appointed unto man once to die." *No!* She resisted God's will. She would not pray for it, but for her own. She prayed for her father's life. If God chose to grant otherwise, He would have a real problem with Pauline thereafter, or so she imagined. She wanted to threaten Him.

For temporary comfort she clung to the intercessor's assurance. "He's not dead. No! No! No!" Pauline added her own "No!" to the list. Lydia lived a devoted life of prayer, she reasoned. Surely God had spoken clearly to her, hadn't He? Unless she was just a dying old woman. Pauline wished Lydia could stand beside her now, to tell her what she knew. How could she know her father was alive?

Suddenly she remembered the Biblical passage Lydia had sent through Barry that morning. She ran to her purse and pulled out the piece of paper. It read, "Luke 22:31, 32."

She pulled a Bible from the bedstand, opened it to the passage and read aloud, "'Simon, Simon, behold Satan has demanded permission to sift you like wheat . . .'" She stopped and murmured to herself, "Lydia, what do you mean? This is written of Simon Peter. Are you referring to Daddy? Is this a code?" Then she read on: "'. . . but I have prayed for you, that your faith may not fail . . .'" It made no sense.

Shutting the Bible she tossed it on the bed. *I've got to see that woman*, she thought. *That's all there is to it.* She wondered if Lydia had joined in some kind of a plot with her father. *No, surely not.* She had told Pauline that she thought Simon Grace was "bound." *But how? By terrorists?* Pauline slumped into a chair. "O God, please . . . please . . ."

9
ISRAEL
Lod Airport
5:03 P.M.

Rick Gresham wore sunglasses as a career investment; he was a jet pilot. Most of the time he wore the shades indoors, and on cloudy days too, trying to squeeze extra years from his prized twenty-twenty vision. It had become a running joke with Dr. Grace to mention that Rick's stepdaughter Jilly thought his eyes were mirrors. As Grace's personal "jet jockey," Rick made no excuses for the obsession. He knew the preacher deeply appreciated it.

Eyes darting agressively behing the shades, he worked his fingers along the skin of the Grace Ministries' Falcon jet parked near a Lod Airport hangar. The Israel sun glared off the tarmac and the fuselage of the ghostly white bird, dubbed "Spirit I." He looked for something called "hangar rash" on the surface of the craft; bumps and bruises caused by the careless handling of ground personnel—something especially critical in foreign ports. At the same time he checked for fuel caps out of place, unsecured hatches, hydraulic leaks, improper tire pressure, maintenance tools inadvertently left in the jet intakes—anything out of the ordinary. He wanted no surprises at 500 knots and 40,000 feet.

As he continued his check, his mind worked through the evening's flight plan: *take off from Lod, negotiate Israeli Air Defense Identification Zones, turn southwest to the Mediterranean, across the "toe of the boot" to the Tyrrhenian Sea, tracking northward from Palermo to a landing in Rome. Two and one-half hours, 8,000 pounds of fuel, no surprises . . .*

At that moment, across the tarmac a white passenger van with tinted windows moved slowly through the security gate toward the row of private aircraft. Rick's head didn't move, but his eyes took full note of it. He had trained himself to observe and catalog everything within his field of vision. Flying near the speed of sound required that hyperactive skill. He filed the mental note: *van, driving slow, secured area, dark windows . . .* , all the while sliding his fingers around the fuselage, seeming not to notice.

Inside the van, Grace and a tourist sat behind a uniformed chauffeur. Dr. Grace seemed nervous, drumming his fingers on the armrest, working his jaw. The other passenger seemed at ease. A man in his fifties with a rounded belly, he wore a tropical shirt, trunks and a straw skimmer. His fine blond hair and twinkling gray eyes gave him a disarming, boyish appearance. He removed his sunglasses to appreciate Grace's sleek aircraft.

"How do you like the Falcon, doc?"

"The Falcon *Mystere*. A sweet bird."

"I swear, it's about the prettiest I've seen. The French do good work."

The van moved past the elegant tri-engined jet and headed for another—a chartered 727, which sat ready for take-off, engines running.

"Yours?" Grace asked.

The man grinned broadly. "In '57 you were *sure* I was just a poor icon smuggler, right, doc? Dirt under my fingernails and all."

Grace acknowledged with a smile, then grew serious. "Maximilian—" He paused, taking an uneasy breath.

"I'm in trouble when you call me '*Maximilian*,'" the blond man replied sheepishly.

"The kidnapping seemed very clumsy to me. And that's about the nicest word I can use."

Max sat quietly grimacing for a moment. "How can I disagree, doc? It *was* clumsy. Pure theatre. Staged for the benefit of Israeli security." He could see that Grace was not consoled.

The van drew to a stop at the steps of the 727. "I guess you realize that kind of clumsiness makes me very nervous when I consider where we're going," Grace added.

Max took it in. "These people are the best in their field," he assured him. "You'll see that. I just have to beg ya to forgive my own enthusiasm. I'm like . . . well, I'm like a kid on holiday." He paused seriously, then brightened. "What's life anyway, if not for a moment like this? Here we are on the threshold of . . ." His eyes grew wistful. ". . . of more than a dream. And if we're successful you'll never have to raise another ministry dollar for as long as you live. Think of that. Nor will your children. Nor your children's children. It's so much bigger than you or me, doc, I can't help getting carried away. Call me unprofessional."

Grace seemed to hold real affection for the man. He nodded perceptively, and his face relaxed somewhat. He knew Max to be unprofessional only when it was to his advantage. Almost resignedly he replied, "If you were a criminal, you'd get away with it."

The chauffeur slid open the passenger door. Grace stared out at nothing for a moment.

Max saw that the preacher remained hesitant, and the easy grin left his face. "With all due respect, doc, I think you were born for this."

Grace moved decisively out of the door. "Only God knows that," he replied.

❖

Rick had not consciously thought about it, but across the tarmac he had removed his mirrored glasses and now stood squinting in the sun. Forget protecting his twenty-twenty vision. The question "why" associated with the slow-moving van had demanded an answer in his checklist mind—and now he saw *Dr. Simon Grace* ascending the stairway into a chartered 727, along with an elfish man wearing a tropical shirt and a straw skimmer!

10
KING DAVID HOTEL
5:12 P.M.

The telephone rang once. Pauline leaped across the room and answered before it had finished. "Hello? Hello?"

"Hey, gorgeous. It's Rick."

She paused, confused. "Rick?" She had fully expected it to be Colonel Canaan. "Oh, Rick!" she said with sudden recognition. "I'm in the middle of something. Can I call you back?"

"Sure, babe, just tell me one small thing. I know flight plans are made to be broken, but are we going to Rome tonight or are we not?"

"Oh, gosh, I—I forgot all about it."

He chuckled incredulously. "Well, that explains it."

"Explains what?"

"The old man. He just blew by here without so much as a 'hello' and climbs on a seven-two-seven—"

"What?" Pauline shrieked, flying upright on the bed. "You saw Daddy?"

"That's what I'm trying to tell you."

"Rick, he's alive! He's alive!"

"Right. There was some doubt?"

She bounced on the bed and cried with relief.

Rick glanced furtively over both shoulders in the charter lounge and lowered his voice. "I don't get it."

"Oh, Rick, I can't even tell you. I'll explain later, but listen to me." Her voice grew intense. "Don't tell anyone anything, OK? There's something strange going on, and I don't know what it is, but I need you to keep this quiet about Daddy. Will you do that?"

"Whatever you say, babe. So let me get this straight. This means scrap the flight to Rome?"

"Yes." She grew thoughtful. "Can you do a little detective work? Can you find out where that plane was going?"

"I'll see what I can do, but I can tell you right now they weren't doing any local sightseeing. They took on enough fuel to go halfway around the world."

A twinge of fear began to eat at her with this bit of intrigue. "You OK?" Rick asked.

She exhaled sharply. "Yeah, thanks. Boy, this has been some rough day. I'll see you tomorrow."

She put down the telephone. "Well, he's alive," she said to herself, wiping her wet cheeks. Slowly she let herself fall back on the bed. She lay very still, feeling the subsiding beat of her heart. Shortly her eyes closed, and when she tried to open them again they resisted, crossing uncontrollably. "I can't sleep yet," she said. "I've got to tell Stiles. Then I can sleep. Everything else can just wait until tomorrow."

11
TEMPORARY MORGUE
8:46 P.M.

They had commandeered a corrugated metal warehouse tucked from view somewhere in the Mehane Yehuda district of the city. Though an abandoned structure, it provided a well-lighted floor beneath thirty-foot steel girders. Across the concrete lay pieces of the pale blue Renault. Each scrap of metal and upholstery had been placed in the approximate position in which it had been recovered from the Derekh Ha-Shiloah that afternoon. The same crew of men and women in *Mogen David* bibs worked quietly among the debris, just as they had earlier on the road.

Colonel Gershon Canaan crossed the room with a purposeful stride. As he drew near an isolated table in a far corner of the room, he donned a pair of reading glasses produced hastily from his shirt pocket. A bearded old man waited for him, sitting patiently on the tabletop. The colonel bent over, squinting at a restored page, one of several being reassembled from scraps. He read in a voice brimming with recognition, sadness and amazement: "Summon the old gods . . . Summon the champions from their thrones invisible . . ."

He fell silent, still bent over the page. Removing his glasses, he looked sideways at the old man. The two of them watched each other, and as the colonel slowly straightened to his full height their lips began to move in unison:

". . . Let them rise and take their kingdoms lest they be forgot!"

Canaan pulled a cotton swatch from his pocket and began wiping his glasses thoughtfully, a current of violent emotion coursing through his body. "Definitely the Mannheim translation, wouldn't you say?"

The old man grunted disgustedly, as if it didn't need saying.

III

EVIL MEDICINE

But now the giants who are born from the
[union of] the spirits and the flesh . . .
Evil spirits have come out of their bodies.

(I ENOCH 15:8, 9, "THE BOOK OF THE WATCHERS")

12

JUBA, SUDAN
Grace Relief Hospital
10:23 A.M.

Until minutes ago, nineteen-year-old Jesse Stiles had worn his faith in Jesus like a bulletproof vest. He had viewed himself as a "born-again" Anglo-Saxon-Protestant "King's kid"—son of the executive vice president of Grace Ministries International. *What could possibly harm him?* Now he was running for his life, wheezing like a locomotive, trying to pump enough oxygen into his blood to drive his cramping legs. Clothing torn, thorn bushes snatching hair from his rock-n-roll locks, the boy lurched desperately along the tangled banks of the African White Nile.

With a surge of adrenaline, he leaped a hissing viper, broad-backed and powerful, coiled like a pile of deadly leaves in his path. Several crocodiles slithered away through the tall reeds. Still, he ran. His natural fear of such creatures paled next to the human evil he had just seen.

Even as he ran he wanted to deny it all. Had he really walked in on a mass murder? Had the doctors really been giving lethal injections, or just powerful sedatives? Had they intended to kill all of the patients, or had they miscalculated? *Ridiculous questions!* Behind him the angry growl of a jumbo helicopter reminded him that even now they were stowing the last of the life-saving equipment, preparing their getaway.

His mind replayed it. He had arrived three days ahead of schedule to take up his student internship at the Grace cancer unit. Apparently he had not been expected. He had walked into Terminal Ward Three, with the intention of announcing his arrival, in time to see a strange female doctor release an injection into the IV tubes of six terribly emaciated patients. The patients had the haunted look he had seen on the faces of victims in pictures of World War II concentration camps. The woman doctor had seemed to enter a kind of ecstasy as she released the injection.

The whole scene appeared unreal, bizarre. He had hollered, "Hey there! What is this?" And the woman had seemed startled, shrieking, eyes wide, as if she had recognized him or something. Then she had fallen into a dead faint. He had seized the moment to check the pulses of the six patients and found them lifeless. Incredibly, she had been killing them as he had walked in! No doubt about it.

In Ward Two he also found the patients all dead, apparently by similar injection. In Ward One he found them alive, but strapped to their beds with hemp belts, howling and clawing the air like victims of extreme Parkinsonism. The ward had become bedlam.

Seeing the approach of a second doctor across the yard, he had run into a back room to hide and watch, only to encounter a third doctor there, whistling cheerily and wiring some kind of charge into the ceiling. This doctor had turned and smiled insanely at him. "Good morning," he had greeted, as if nothing were amiss.

A world upside down! Jesse thought, and ran for the Nile marshes. *Who were these weird doctors? What were they doing? Where were Beulah Samms and the Grace missionary staff? Had they been killed too?* So much for using his father's ministry position to enter the Sudan three days early. He wished he'd never pulled those strings.

He ran to a lone gum tree and pulled himself to a lower branch. Anchoring a foot, he began climbing to look back at the hospital compound a half-mile distant. The craziness of it all began to tell him that he had actually arrived at the wrong facility. That would explain everything. Grace had nothing to do with it.

A few pounds overweight, he struggled slowly against fatigue as he climbed, yet continued, powered by panic. Perspiration stuck strands of hair to his forehead. Looking back over his aching shoulder, at first he could see only a cloud of dust kicked up by the helicopter at the edge of the compound. Then as he drew himself to a higher branch, grunting and wheezing from the effort, he saw three figures crossing the open ground between the buildings. He assumed they were the doctors he had seen earlier—a woman and two men. Beyond that, he had no idea who they were. From his perch he clearly identified the descending dove of the Grace logo atop the administration building. Incredibly, he *was* at the right hospital.

❖

Dr. Karla Osis, pale and trembling from her fainting spell, walked on rubbery legs across the yard, supported between two physician colleagues, Adrian Van Sutphen and Reginald Lester. They crossed the yard toward the helicopter. Osis laughed giddily as they struggled through the churning rotor wash. "I saw him, I saw him," she murmured.

"Who?" Sutphen asked, stopping. He squinted at her through the dust.

"A being of . . . pure, pure light," Karla panted effusively. "Nine feet tall, he must have been, with a . . . a huge . . . starburst on . . . on his chest and . . . he was gorgeous, with . . . with a red band in his beautiful . . . dark, flowing hair and . . . and the fourth sign appearing over his head . . ."

"The crab?" Sutphen coached.

"Yes. He was beautiful. Just as I injected them, he appeared to me . . ."

Sutphen looked at Lester, a knowing smile playing at the corner of his mouth. They quickly hustled Dr. Osis the rest of the way to the open cargo door of the helicopter, hoisting her through it. Following her in, the craft lifted from the ground on a prearranged signal. Karla Osis slumped to the floor with a sigh.

As the helicopter ascended, Sutphen turned to his colleague with an odd light in his eyes. "The fourth sign of the Zodiac? Is that what she saw?" he asked, still panting from the exertion of carrying Karla.

Lester nodded solemnly. "The Crab. Cancer."

"Is it not synchronous?" Sutphen asked laughing, shaking his head with wonder. "Perfectly synchronous? If it is true. If she saw what she thinks she saw and was not hallucinating, then you realize . . . we brought him here, my man. We reached up and *took* hold of an epiphany! Just the way they said we would! I tell you, we are in touch, Reggie. We are with the gods."

Reminded of something, Sutphen suddenly scooted back toward the open door of the helicopter. The mission hospital grew smaller as they continued to rise in the air. "Time to do this," he said, removing a small remote-control box from his belt. He pointed it at the hospital and pressed a button. The various buildings vaporized in a chain reaction of flame.

"Got 'em all," he said, as if examining the satisfactory results of an appendectomy. Turning to gaze at the horizon, he mused, "Of course, we couldn't explain anything publicly about the epiphany now, could we? Who would believe us? Or who would even care?" He looked at Dr. Osis, still slumped on the floor. "We're alone up here, doctor." He turned thoughtfully back to watch the buildings burn. "All alone. It will be decades before the world is ready for the likes of us."

"Oh, don't be too sure," Lester replied. "Who would have believed we'd see democracy in Eastern Europe? The world can change, and rapidly." He remained thoughtful for a moment. "But for the moment I'd say, at least as far as the public goes, what happened to the hospital down there is just another unfortunate statistic in the Sudanese civil war."

Sutphen smiled cynically and nodded. The glow of burning buildings reflected in his eyes, and he caught sight of a running figure nearly a mile beyond the compound. "Even if the kid gets through alive, our story will fly, considering the political climate here in Northern Africa." Then he chuckled, remembering the look on the boy's face as he had greeted him in the back room. "That kid sure got his wake-up call this morning, didn't he?"

13

BROWNSVILLE
Grace Hospital
9:47 A.M.

Lydia Nation slept peacefully, no longer in intensive care. She still wore an intravenous tube, but the oxygen and heart monitor leads had been removed.

Neva Sylvan entered the room and watched her sleeping for a while. Then she picked up the medical chart attached to the foot of her bed and began studying it carefully. Putting it down again, she stole quietly near to Lydia's sleeping face. Taking a small flashlight from her smock, she prepared to lift the old woman's eyelid to check pupil reaction. But just as she reached out, Lydia sat bolt upright, causing Neva to leap backward with a startled cry.

The intercessor pointed a bony index finger into the doctor's face. "You will *not* touch me, Neva," she commanded, her voice quivering with conviction.

"Why you old—" Neva poised to leap like a lion, but checked

herself. She blinked and wiped at her eyes. Impossibly, she seemed to see a tall figure behind Lydia—powerfully built, long dark hair, scarlet ribbon, gold . . . or brass . . . Then he was gone. It had been a fleeting vision, flashing so quickly she could only be left with her rapidly beating heart, and the impression that the figure brandished a sword. Whirling suddenly around, she saw Barry Malone standing silently in the doorway behind her. Watching. *So that was it!* she thought, nearly laughing with relief. *Of course. I sensed Barry in the room and projected his presence in Lydia's direction. A simple psychic error. I must control the powers, not be controlled.* Regaining composure, she stared at Barry with superiority and disapproval. "Is school out early?" she asked, edging her words with sarcasm.

"Uh, no, ma'am. I'm on my way," Barry replied, somewhat shaken. "Is . . . is that chart OK for you, Dr. Sylvan? I saw you checking it."

"As a matter of fact, it is *not* right. But we can discuss that later. I have rounds to complete." She headed toward the door, stopping to press her face closely into his. "Don't you have some homework to do or something?"

"I . . . I don't understand."

Neva smiled broadly, patting his cheek. She enjoyed destroying the natural protective space around any opponent. "You're a *student*, Barry. You have so much to learn."

He sent Lydia a look of concern, then turned and walked quickly down the hall.

14

SAN DIEGO
Mission Bay Yacht Club
10:30 A.M.

Alan Lavalle's fifty-foot pleasure craft might have swept him away on a tide of disgrace if he had functioned in the public eye as a traditional minister. But he considered himself smarter than that. He had custom-designed a special church to avoid the possibility of scandal. His "church," Logos Mail Ministries, Inc., remained invisible, a personal sanctuary from "the assaults of Satan through the media," as he called them. He had no house of worship, no committee or board meetings to attend, no counseling or sick calls to make. Not a single member of his congregation had ever seen "Pastor Alan" in the flesh. Therefore, who would call him to task for his oceangoing yacht, Palm Springs home, Cartegena coffee plantation, or Los Angeles warehouse filled with fifty-three vintage Rolls Royces? Investigative reporters had knocked at his door for years, but he was not about to answer. He answered only to the associates of his generous payroll, defrocked ministers like himself, carefully selected for their deep attachment to material comforts.

The invisible church that Alan had created—over which he ruled as Founding Apostle—was a garishly designed mail-order religion. Its invisible congregation was to be found in rural Southern white communities and black urban ghettos. "Religiously rich soil," he liked to call it. Through his simplified Bible correspondence courses and in-home ordination kits, he had knit together a vast, lucrative and loyal following whose meeting-place was the mailbox. He had envisioned this "church" in the early 1950s and had expanded it with the emergence of zip code demographics in the 60s, long before the giant electronic churches emerged into the American mainstream.

Though Dr. Simon Grace and many other televangelists privately benefited from Alan Lavalle's pioneering genius through the marketing services of Logos Mail, Alan remained blissfully invisible to the general public. Cloistered in his La Jolla cliffside mansion with Dorothy Morgan, his secretary of thirteen years, Alan lusted not for fame, but fortune.

In all of his fantastical mail pieces, designed by Logos Mail, his non-profit corporation, '"Pastor Alan" had himself photographed as a flashy Bible-belt evangelist. For the role, he wore a dark suit with a blow-dried pompadour wig of blond hair. It was a disguise. The real Alan was rather "California-laid-back." A short man of medium build, he retained a few long thinning wisps of auburn hair, which he combed loosely across an emerging dome of baldness. Sun-freckled skin, eyebrows thick and red, bushy sideburns combed over the ears—apart from his mail-order *persona* he looked like the harmless captain of a love boat.

On this fine Mission Bay morning, Alan Lavalle moved across

the polished parquet deck of his Italian yacht with an unusual grimness masking his features. Wearing sailing shorts, deck shoes and a golf shirt, he paused near the rear ladder. There he turned to look back ominously at Dorothy, who lay sunning herself in a tiger-striped bikini. The bleached blonde watched his every move through her tortoise-shell sunglasses, like a brooding *alter ego*.

He turned determinedly and let himself down the ladder, stepping into an idling powerboat with two men who waited in dark silk suits. Immediately the boat roared away from the yacht for about a hundred yards. Then the driver cut the engines, letting the boat idle in the smooth water of the harbor. One of the two men left the controls and made his way aft to speak with Alan.

❖

Dorothy lay still, watching the meeting carefully. In one hand she held an electronic panic button to signal the bodyguards below deck. She never told Alan what to do, never voiced an opinion unless asked, but she knew that the men in the boat were Mafia. From her years as an East Coast call girl she had learned to smell the upside-down morality bred into crime families. They bolstered themselves with a perverse sense of "family" which allowed them to commit mayhem-for-hire at midnight and attend Mass with wife and children in the morning, absolving themselves through crude "confessionals" of macho-religious ritual. In Alan's Protestant world, she thought she had left such men far behind.

❖

The man lounged easily against the gunwale of the powerboat, allowing a 9 mm pistol to show beneath his jacket. He chewed the end of a bent cocktail straw and studied Alan's face.

In return, Alan studied him. He noticed that the man's shoulders held flakes of dandruff. He reeked of an "old world" body odor—musty, careless. His one hundred fifty dollar shirt had been worn for days. This indifferent fashion struck more fear into Alan's heart than the sight of the gun. *A hitter*, he thought, trying to carefully calculate his next response.

"I am just a messenger boy," the man said, smiling past a roman nose. His English was delivered with a charming foreign cadence.

"Why do I get the feeling that your specialty is 'bad news'?" Alan replied, trying to return the smile.

The man laughed, surprised by his nerve. "My clients pay me well, Mr. Lavalle. I do what they want. Understood?"

Alan nodded. "I've known Simon Grace for more than thirty years. This is the first time he has ever used a messenger. I don't particularly like it."

The man's smile vanished. "Not my problem. I'm supposed to ask you if you got the mail package into the Grace operation as requested? It's important."

Alan nodded, looking away toward Dorothy. "But it cost me some real credibility. Your people are messing with the way I do business. They could blow it for me. But yes, it's in there." He turned back to the messenger. "Look, I don't know what you know about fund-raising, but the letter you gave me is completely bogus. Grace will shortfall by half their budget this month, guaranteed. Grace knows that too. So why is he shooting himself in the foot?"

"I'm only the delivery boy," the man replied impassively. "I'll pass your question along." He handed Alan a slip of paper. "Thirteen-two is being transferred to Logos Mail this morning. It is to be transferred to Grace's private account within twelve hours. Understand?"

Alan thrilled inside. He understood that "thirteen-two" meant thirteen million, two hundred thousand U.S. dollars!

"Another third will come when my people receive the icon. The people I work for wanted me to tell you that your commission comes entirely out of the final payment, not this one, nor the next. Is that clear?"

The draft carbon for the amount trembled between the mail-order preacher's appreciative fingers. He had never held such a sum, though it was the stuff of his many dreams. Staring at it, he salivated involuntarily, noting a Swiss account number.

Simon's into something very, very big this time, he thought. Swallowing hard, he nodded, acknowledging his complete acceptance of the terms.

15
MANNHEIM, WEST GERMANY
Dunamis Foundation
9:45 A.M.

The huge acquisitions began in 1871 when Wolfgang Commagene had first emerged as a Black Forest timber baron. His second purchase, a part-interest in the railroad that hauled his lumber to Mannheim, turned out to be monumentally profitable. Before his death "Wolfie" had gone on a buying spree, amassing a fortune in the fundamentals of civilization: iron, rock salt, lignite, grapes, rye, barley, beef, sugar beets and potatoes. His holdings were strongly represented on both sides of what was later to become East and West Germany.

Since the turn of the century, the German war machine had multiplied the Commagene fortune twice, as the iron-willed nation geared up for World Wars I and II. In the process, Wolfgang's son Otto had built a manufacturing trinity on his father's foundation of commodities, with divisions of steel, transportation and medicine.

But son Otto's crowning achievement came during World War II when he established Dunamis, a foundation for the Commagene family wealth. Its charter purported to further the research and development of medicine. Its inner workings were perhaps not so benign, rumored to have once employed personnel from the death-camp laboratory of Dr. Mengele (rumors that had been easily dismissed as postwar hysteria). By inheritance now, the Dunamis Foundation had fallen to Maximilian "Max" Commagene, nephew of Otto, grand-nephew of "Wolfie."

❖

The long, tall Dunamis Board Room had been conceived by a German engineer, or so Simon Grace suspected. It was a cold intellectual sanctuary housed in opaque glass and aluminum. The entire room contained a single meeting table of robust milled oak. The table occupied a carpeted platform, separated by thirty feet of sterile space on every side. Ambient light penetrated the walls around it, suggesting a shrine for the decisions made by committee. *Committees are straitjackets for the mind*, Grace observed. He always felt uncomfortable entering this room, and today was no different. He detested both engineers and committees.

Seven chairs were positioned at ten-foot intervals around the table. Five doctors—four men, one woman—had already taken seats. But he noticed a significant change from his last visit several years ago. A mural photograph of Fortune of Commagene had been mounted against the wall at the head of the table. A photographer had captured the seven-ton head of the Seleucid statue where it lay atop the ruins of Nimrut Dag. Enlarged to twenty feet across, the photo had been hand-painted with a muted technicolor process. The wrinkled mountains of the Turkish wilderness glowed softly beyond the ruined pantheon as the idol's stone eyes gazed toward the distant horizon. It was a stunning juxtaposition of vivid sculpture and vast panorama. The sight of it brought memories to life in the preacher—sensations from his first visit to Nimrut Dag, guided by Max in 1957.

"What's this?" Grace commented as he crossed the room. "You've grown artistic."

"Wolfie would approve," the German replied offhandedly. "Karl Sester discovered Fortune in 1881 and told Wolfie about the Commagene name on the base of the stone there. Of course, Wolfie was well-read on our family ancestry, but had never heard about the idol. Otto spent time there in the First War, and I'm not sure, but I think he funded the more recent expeditions of Waldmann. You've read his book, I'm sure."

Grace nodded. He had read everything he could find on Nimrut Dag. He took one of the two chairs remaining at the head of the table, nodding to the doctors seated down the line. They were all dressed casually, dispensing with the normal concerns of first impressions. Max stood in shirt-sleeves, smiling disarmingly in front of his namesake idol.

"My friends," he began quietly, rubbing his hands together with contained eagerness, "the questions that confront scientific research today are no longer purely scientific, are they?" He laughed intimately, his voice taking on the tone of a spa director. "After the pioneering work of Sigmund Freud, we could no longer treat the sick body without attending the sick soul, though most of modern medicine still fails to bring these streams of knowledge together in practice. But in research, ah!—there's another matter. We're about to go beyond even that dimension of care. The *spirits* of sickness are coming beneath our microscopes, so to speak. But we are humbled, are we not? We find ourselves on the threshold not of a new field of study, but of a new spiritual kingdom—a kingdom in which the lords of disease can be ultimately defeated. And so we *must* come together as we have here today."

He walked around the table and stood behind Grace, placing a hand on his shoulder. "Dr. Grace and I go back further than the rest of you. Since my Uncle Otto first heard him preach in South Africa in 1949, I've learned to consider him a man ahead of his time. He's always seen more to disease than the physical symptoms. But Dr. Grace here feels that this spiritual kingdom we're about to enter will be . . . shall I say, a particularly *Western* kind of kingdom—"

"I *know* it," Grace corrected. "I don't go by feeling on this. I am here because you can't go beyond the Kingdom of God. You guys are finding that out."

Max cleared his throat good-naturedly. "Excuse me. Can we say then, for the benefit of the others, that you *believe* this to be so? Even though you may feel that you *know* it, you still operate by faith, if I'm not mistaken?"

Once more, Grace was surprised at the sharp foil of Max's reasoning. It had always kept him reexamining his words. "Touché." Grace smiled.

"Oh no. We totally agree." Max glanced around the table. "I just feel that if we operate by the same terminology we will all avoid a good deal of misunderstanding." He turned to the others. "I'll let him go into that more in depth with you at the proper time." He moved back toward the head of the table. "Many of the rest of you think this kingdom will be quite something more *Eastern* in scope." He placed his ample knuckles on the table and bore his weight forward on them until they turned white. "Where we are going, ladies and gentlemen, East and West are no longer relevant. They are as outmoded as the wall between the Germanies. This is an exciting new day. We are after truth. And the truth will heal us, whatever form it may take."

Max smiled reassuringly at Dr. Grace. "So then, Dr. Grace, all of the men and women of science at this table today are here because they agree that your particular faith may be the key to this new kingdom. We are at the door, but at present we have encountered obstacles. Though these colleagues are scientists, and from various belief systems, they stand ready to bow to your faith should it prove correct. I assure you of that."

Grace cleared his throat. "You'll have to excuse me, but after a century of Charles Darwin I retain a clergyman's doubt on that point."

The attempt at humor seemed to fall flat. "Darwin was one of yours," the female doctor objected. "A clergyman."

"So he was," replied Grace. "Touché. I'm outclassed here."

"No, no." Max raised a hand in warning. "'Touché or not touché—excuse the play on Shakespeare, but the answer to that is 'not touché.' We are not opposing each other. We are much more unified than even you may realize. For example, it may please you to learn that each of these doctors has volunteered generously over the years in your Third-World hospitals."

At this, Grace seemed sincerely warmed. "Well, praise God. I seldom get an opportunity to thank the professionals who have helped me around the world, unless I'm visiting on a crusade." He stood and walked respectfully to the nearest doctor, extending a hand.

Max narrated the introduction. "Meet Dr. Alfredo Santesteban of Madrid. His work in viral motivation will revolutionize modern medicine. I'm sure Dr. Neva Sylvan has given you at least a basic understanding of his work."

"She has," Grace responded. "A pleasure, sir."

Santesteban nodded politely.

Grace moved to the next doctor.

Max continued, "Vardan Kassabian, chief of psychiatry for Dunamis. He conducts cross-disciplinary research in—let me get this right—neurophysiology and neurochemistry."

Kassabian nodded. "Well done."

Grace whistled. "Over my head, but nice to meet you."

"Incidentally," Max continued, "Vardan developed the tests and computer charts that are beginning to give us our first look at the spiritual domain of disease. It's a murky area, and his insights are providing an important visual link."

Grace paused, absorbing this. He nodded and moved on.

". . . Dr. Karla Osis, anesthesiologist with a specialty in narcotherapy. Her concoctions have allowed us to take our first honest look into the traumatized memory of resuscitated Near Death patients. Not to mention the Hypnos-3 drug formula itself—her creation."

"We've come a long way since morphine," Grace said, then added with a wink, "No touché."

". . . And next, Dr. Reginald Lester, from Munich. He's seen every kind of cancer on the planet. He lives and breathes to give it the knockout punch."

"I like him already," Grace said, shaking his hand between both of his own.

". . . And last, but certainly not least, Dr. Adrian Van Sutphen, from Johannesburg—specialties in internal medicine and cardio-vascular disease. He has spent fifteen years studying the Near Death Experience particularly. I'm convinced he knows more on the subject than Kubler-Ross. His work is built on Dr. Sabom's scientific approach at Emory University, but he has gone far beyond any of those studies. This is the man who has developed the simulator we use."

"So you can take life and give it back again, doctor," Grace probed. "That must be a frightening responsibility."

"In fact it is too frightening for me, Reverend Grace." Sutphen offered smoothly, playing with a pen on the table. "I'm really hoping you can take the load from my weary shoulders."

Grace continued to study the doctor's face, which had become an impenetrable mask.

IV

SOCIETY OF APOSTATES

Those men . . . are wandering stars,
for whom the [nether] gloom has been reserved forever.

(JUDE 12, 13, NASB)

16

DALLAS, TEXAS
Bachelor's Loft
3:35 A.M.

The answer machine had been engaged, the telephone muted. Soft jazz crooned from the stereo, and the blinking cursor of a word processor punctuated the dark. Above the king-sized waterbed the head of a bull moose watched over the sleeping man like a patient friend, its antlers adorned with boxer shorts, golf clubs, blue jeans, fly rod and fedora hat. Belly down and tangled in his comforter, Evan Grace had descended into the bliss of a four-beer-and-venison-sausage-sleep. Not to be disturbed.

The art of sleeping alone had driven the once married man to strange bedtime habits. By trial and error, he had found that every sixty days or so the right combination of Coors and venison sausage could make a Friday night pass like a Rocky Mountain trout stream, with dreams of trophy-sized cutthroat in the snow melt. Something rank and masculine in this solitary ritual almost made being single seem worthwhile. Almost, but not quite, because Evan had been married for eleven good years and knew what he was missing.

According to his first wife Connie, his emotions had been hot-wired. He was the kind who couldn't function with anything unresolved on his conscience. Grown men ought to be able to at least lie discreetly, Connie used to complain. But Evan seemed incapable. He would erupt whatever bothered him into thin air. Sometimes he would do this while awake, sometimes while asleep, which became part of the reason he slept alone at the virile age of thirty-nine. He had erupted one too many times about his infidelity with Danna Lavalle. This particular sin had not only pricked his conscience, it had cost him his marriage.

On particularly bad nights, plagued by memories of his six-year-old daughter Jilly now calling another man "Daddy," a really foul cigar might help put him to sleep, when beer and venison sausage were in short supply.

The telephone rang, but the muted sound failed to penetrate his fermented sleep. The second, third and fourth rings caused him to stir only slightly. The fifth ring triggered a recorded voice, but it was not Evan's. A female giggled unexpectedly. "Oh, hi there," she said cheerily. "We can't come to the phone right now—"

He jerked upright on the bed, still bewildered. *We? What is this?* He blinked with faint recognition. "Jennifer," he growled.

The girl on the answer machine hiccuped. "Oh! This champagne is just too much!" She giggled again. "Evan would love to return your call, but he's waiting in the hot tub. Leave a message at the sound of the tone."

Evan rolled quickly from the bed realizing someone had switched his answer tape for a prank copy—and it wasn't the least bit funny! Whoever had called him in the middle of the night was now getting an earful of the wrong idea. He didn't even own a hot tub! Scrambling to the far side of the bed, he groped frantically, trying to protect his naked shins in the dark. It all came back to him. This was payback time for Jennifer Bridgeport, his research assistant, who had sworn to get him back for revealing how the twenty-four-hour flu had turned into a day at the mall for her—a secret he had let slip in front of the boss, purely by accident of course. Nevertheless this kind of vengeance seemed totally out of proportion. Especially at 4 A.M.

He found the right side of the bed at last, smashed the answer machine's stop button to squelch the recording, and snatched the receiver from its cradle. "Hello?" He breathed unsteadily and asked again, "Hello?"

He spoke to a full silence. "I'm sorry about—" he began, wanting to explain the prank recording, but a deliberate click terminated the call, followed by a dial tone. He muttered a curse.

❖

Thirty-nine thousand feet above East Texas, "Spirit I" cruised in a westerly path against the jet stream. Inside, Pauline recognized Evan's "Hello" and yanked the sky-phone from her ear with disgust. She had at first hoped she had dialed the wrong number. Hearing her brother's familiar voice, she knew she had not misdialed. Glancing around the jet's passenger cabin she wondered what in heaven's name her father had in mind when he had said to "Call Evan." *He will never change,* she seethed. *He's still a womanizer.*

Stiles, Cheney and Lassiter slept soundly in their reclined seats in the rear of the cabin. She debated the wisdom of calling Evan back and reading him off.

❖

Meanwhile, Evan fumbled through his nightstand, looking for his original answer tape, grumbling about Jennifer's revenge. "Have a few friends over, share my precious venison sausage . . . and this is the thanks I get?"

Noticing a yellow stick-up note plastered to the inside of the answerphone lid, he removed it. "'You deserve this and you know it,'" he read aloud. "Oh ho. I deserve this, do I? What I did was innocent and accidental." He dialed the telephone, glancing briefly at the digital clock. "Three forty. She can dish it out, let's see if she can—"

He heard it ring once, twice.

"Come on, Jen," he prodded. "Answer."

Three rings, four, then he heard the sound of a dropped telephone, and his face broke into a sleepy, satisfied grin. He chuckled low and wickedly, knowing she was disoriented.

A rustling sound followed on the other end of the line. Shortly afterward a female voice squeaked sleepily, "Hello?"

"Hi there!" he said fervently, pausing to savor the moment of triumph. "You deserve *this!*" He hung up emphatically and went back to fumbling through the nightstand.

The phone rang almost immediately. This time he picked it up carefully, not sure if it would be the original caller or Jennifer. "Hello?"

"Just one question," Jennifer said, still cranky with sleep. "Who was calling you at this hour? And don't tell me it was business."

He continued to filter through a bedside reading assortment. "Well, we just don't know now, do we? Whoever it was hung up in the middle of your performance."

She cackled so loudly he had to pull the receiver from his ear. "Revenge is sweet," she laughed. "Now, you be a good sport."

"I'll show you a good sport," he threatened idly as he continued to rummage through the drawer. "Jen, where is my answer tape?"

She paused guiltily. "I recorded over it. We did it last night while you were showing slides of your fishing trip. But don't worry,

I'll buy you another one at lunch today. We've got a deadline on the Walker Railey story, remember?"

"Can't wait," he yawned. "Alright, enough. I've got to get some sleep. Good night."

"Wait a second."

He waited, but she didn't say what was on her mind. Instead, they both heard the signal of an incoming call on his waiting line.

Jennifer sing-songed, "Whoever she is Mr. Evan, she must want you bad."

"Get out of here."

"Yeah. Good night," she said sullenly.

He punched the receiver button for the second call. "Hello?"

"Evan, is that you?"

He stiffened, recognizing her voice like a cold slap. "Pauline?" She *never* called. Instinctively he sensed something tragic and tensed with fear.

"Daddy is missing."

A strange emptiness released inside of him. It was surprising. The feeling should have been *passé* like the rest of his relationship with his famous and powerful father. Still, the emptiness remained strong. "What do you mean, he's missing? That could mean a lot of things. You mean kidnapped?"

"I can't talk right now," she said. "We're in the air. Can you meet me at Addison Airport in half an hour? A place called," she paused to read from a card, "Million Air. That's two words."

"I'll be there." He moved toward his clothes with the phone tucked to his shoulder.

"Who answered when I called earlier, Evan?" Her tone grew cold. "Just curious."

"Oh, that was *you!*" He chuckled nervously, pulling his blue jeans from the moose horn. Of all the people to hear Jennifer's suggestive answer message! "Some crazy friends of mine. Who needs 'em, you know? Had a little get-together here last night and someone messed with my answer machine."

Pauline's silence reeked of disapproval as she tried to picture the guests at his "get-together." Her imagination kept turning up girls in spandex tights and four-inch heels.

Evan sensed it and fumed. It was all so familiar. He reserved a special string of expletives for his sister's pious judgments. "How long have you known about Dad?" he asked, feeling himself slip into the old familiar hostility with her.

"We'll talk. I've gotta go for now," she said, putting the receiver down.

❖

In the pressurized cabin, Verlin Stiles had awakened and now watched Pauline carefully. He leaned across the aisle into her face. "Why in heaven's name did you call *him*?"

She felt offended by his intrusion. "He has every right to know."

"But why bring him in, Pauline? We're talking about someone who was defrocked for *moral* reasons. He's never been penitent about it, either."

"How do you know? Besides, who said I was bringing him in?" She glared back silently as he pressed his point. His entire manner made her want to oppose him just to oppose him. "He's my brother," she said deliberately.

"Pauline, may I remind you that the interest of a one hundred and fifty million dollar ministry is at stake here?" He paused to let his words sink in. "Now I don't know what your brother's motives are, but I am here trying to help you."

She wanted to retch. But Stiles was right about one thing—she *did* need help. Whom could she trust? Now that she faced it squarely, she had begun to fear she wouldn't be able to do what her father had asked her to do. How could she see that the TV special aired on time and keep his disappearance out of the press—and in general, look after so much responsibility? No one had taught her how to do that.

She turned to stare out of the window. She felt like she had been dumped into the deep end of a pool without a swimming lesson. She would talk to Evan—just talk. Her father had said, "Call Evan if you get in trouble. Blood is thicker." With Stiles in her face, at least that much was beginning to make sense.

17
ADDISON AIRPORT
4:56 A.M.

After parking his vintage 3.0si BMW, "the beamer," in the Million Air hangar lot and ringing the security desk, Evan waited at the chain-link fence. Rick approached with a grin to let him in. The sleek Falcon *Mystere* waited in the background, engines screaming.

"Hey, you reprobate," Rick said. He reached into the guard station and triggered the gate. "Where you been keeping yourself?"

An electric motor wound the barrier to one side, and the two spontaneously embraced.

"Hey yourself, Daddy Number Two," Evan replied. "For some strange reason it's always good to see you."

"Same here."

He slapped the pilot's back as they turned toward the terminal. He was reminded that it had not always been so friendly between the two of them. When Rick had first married Evan's ex-wife Connie, they had avoided each other like a social disease, but in the process of protecting Jilly, a little girl who loved her "two daddies" very much, they had gotten over it.

"How's Jilly?" Evan asked.

"She's growing up really fine, Evan. Misses you a lot though. There's no getting around that."

Evan couldn't allow himself to think too much about Jilly missing him. It could destroy the next six years of his life. "I'll sure try to get by and see her more often," he said. "You and Connie OK?"

"Yeah. Thanks."

Evan sensed that Rick understated the case. He knew that his ex-wife and daughter lived very happily with this man. Knowing that, he hurt all over. But it was a good kind of hurt. Good for the people he still loved.

Looking ahead to the terminal he saw Pauline waiting in the Million Air lobby, arms crossed defensively beneath a light wool sweater. He couldn't help suspecting her every motive, and he bristled, as always, at the possibility of being manipulated. "What's Old Bullet Breath want from me, Rick?"

"Easy," Rick cautioned. "Your sister really needs you."

He snorted in disgust at the suggestion. "How long's Dad been missing?"

"Three days."

"See there? She needs me? So why am I the last to know?"

Rick shrugged. "This is a strange deal. She's keeping everything quiet. But Stiles is strong-arming her. He's a snake."

"Yeah. They deserve each other. Pauline doesn't want my help, Rick, she just thinks she needs it to control Stiles now that Dad's out of the picture. That's my bet." They continued walking in silence. "She doesn't have a clue how that's done," he muttered. "Not a clue."

As they neared the door Pauline came out to meet them. Rick went directly inside with the others, leaving brother and sister to face each other in privacy.

As she had waited in the lobby, Pauline had become filled with a new sense of anticipation. She had begun to realize that without her father, Evan would be all the family she had left. *Blood really is thicker,* she had thought. With that, she felt suddenly ready to bury the hatchet between them, at least as brother and sister. Nothing could restore Evan to the ministry. He had burned that bridge through infidelity. But seeing him now as her brother, for the first time in many years she reached out for his embrace.

Evan felt surprised, but allowed it, putting his arms around her tentatively. He didn't trust her—couldn't. He knew that behind every affection—family or religious—his sister hid personal agendas which could turn against him without warning. She couldn't help herself.

"This is so crazy," she said.

"You're telling me?"

"I'm scared, Evan." She pushed back from the embrace, suddenly feeling too vulnerable in his grasp. "I know the Lord has everything under control, that Daddy is fine, but still, I'm scared." She began to walk across the tarmac.

Evan followed, building a guard for his emotional protection. She didn't know God had *anything* under control. The statement merely disguised her private agenda to control him. Knowing that, he couldn't afford to agree with her, no matter how religious she made it sound. He hated religion.

They walked toward the plane in silence as Stiles and Cheney peered after them through the lobby window.

"First I need you to promise me that we are off the record," she began. "I can't afford to read about any of this in *People* or *Texas People* or *The Times Herald* or anything else for that matter."

Evan was an investigative reporter, a professional. "Fine— unless you step on information I've already gotten from other sources."

She sighed, forced to trust him. It was not a position she would have chosen to be in. "Daddy asked me to take charge of things."

Evan stood still. "Wait a minute. Time out. Is Dad missing or not?"

She looked at him helplessly. "Yes and no."

"I don't want to be jerked around here!"

"Evan, this whole thing is jerking *me* around. I'm not doing this to you." She began spilling the story rapidly. "He did give me orders, but then he disappeared. He told me to see that the TV special ran on time. He was very emphatic about it. Why didn't he tell Stiles to take care of it? According to Verlin, that's the emergency procedure. But he told me to do it, then walked away in a dumpy little Palestinian neighborhood. He got into this beat-up little blue car with some scruffy-looking people and disappeared. I'm left there going crazy." She sighed heavily and turned to face him. "There's something terrible about it too, and this is the part that scares me the most—later that day the car was found blown to bits. With bodies inside, OK? Not Daddy's, but that was about my personal limit, if you know what I mean."

She began walking again. "I was waiting for the coroner's report when I got this call from Rick who had just seen Daddy get on a chartered 727 with some guy in a Hawaiian shirt. Talk about jerked around! At least I knew he wasn't in that car. I haven't told Stiles or anyone else, so please, only Rick and I know about him getting on that plane. But anyway, the coroner confirmed that Daddy was not in the car. So Stiles and everyone knows he's alive somewhere. We're pretty sure he left Israel. But what was he doing in a car that was blown up later? Was the bomb intended for him, or . . .? He seems OK, but then, what is he doing with these dangerous people?"

Evan's own suspicions implicated his father directly, except for the car bomb. That didn't seem to fit his style, unless he had fallen even farther than Evan suspected.

"He was supposed to fly with me to Rome that night," Pauline continued. "I had to cancel the flight plans. He didn't bother to say anything to Rick either, and he could have. He left from right there at Lod where our plane was parked." She shrugged helplessly.

"So, is that it?"

"No . . . It's not everything." She stopped and turned toward him, debating whether to tell him more. She reached out and took his arm, a gesture intended to say "let bygones be bygones." "Evan, Daddy told me if I got into trouble to call you."

He winced noticeably. These words uncovered a pain buried deep inside. For many years he had wanted nothing more than to be someone important in his father's eyes—his god-like father. But no more. He knew too much about the human being behind the man-of-God label. So why did it still hurt? Somehow, in spite of the real distance between them, his father's opinion still mattered. Evan couldn't change that.

"So." Evan found it hard to speak. He cleared his throat. "Is that all he had to say?"

Pauline had been watching his reaction. Encouraged by the softening in his face, she pulled an envelope from her pocket and handed it to him.

He opened it, removing and unfolding the note inside. "'Keep this out of the press,'" he read. "What?" He stared at the note with sickening realization. It was unmistakably his father's handwriting. An old familiar anger came rushing back, burying the pain again. *Why would a man set a trap for his own children? Why would he conspire to use them in his money-grubbing schemes? And in the name of God!*

Beside himself with rage, Evan walked away from Pauline for about fifty paces, suddenly fighting tears. He hated everything about religion used this way—for personal power, for money, for control. He was convinced that this was how the "good news" became twisted into "bad news" down through the history of the Church; how the baby of the gospel became lost in a sea of dirty bathwater—men perverting the truth for gain! He knew his father, and he knew that Pauline was no match for his manipulative skill. But, by all hell Dr. Simon Grace would not suck Evan into this deception. "If you get in trouble, call Evan." *The man will use anybody,* he seethed.

In the meantime Pauline had become confused and frightened

by his reaction. She followed him to where he stood and snatched the note from his fist.

He let it go rather than tear the piece of paper. "Sure," he said, "protect the evidence. Your father is counting on that, believe me. If the note finds its way to the FBI or the IRS or the SEC, he goes to prison. Do you hear me?"

"I have no idea what you're talking about."

"Of course you don't. That's exactly why you've been selected to remain in charge. He's counting on you to believe the very best about him. I'm only here in case you get in trouble!" Evan shouted, adding an angry curse.

Pauline's insides convulsed. "Don't *use* that language around me!" she demanded. With shame she looked back and saw Stiles and Cheney watching through the windows of the Million Air lobby. They had probably heard the shouted word. "Evan, please control yourself and say what you mean. Please? This is too important for you to just blow off steam."

He couldn't help despising her attitude. His profanity represented a mild expression of the anger he truly felt. Patiently, he held himself back. "Add it up, Pauline: Number one, Dad said, 'see that the TV special runs on time.' Right? Then he said, 'call Evan'—your brother who happens to be an investigative reporter about to break a story about Grace Ministries and Alan Lavalle—" He looked at her sharply. "Are you following me here? He knew the story was about to come out, Pauline. He wants to neutralize me. Third, he said, 'keep this out of the press.' We're dealing with a very clever man here. He always kills more than one bird with one stone. All you have to do is ask yourself *why* he said all this. Why? Well, let me tell you why; the bottom line is the bottom line. Grace is in deep financial trouble, and somewhere this all adds up to some kind of huge payday."

Pauline hadn't the slightest idea what he was talking about. "I'm lost."

"Conveniently lost," he snapped. "Wake up, sister." He suddenly softened, realizing that it was her love for her father that blinded her. He took her by the shoulders. "Listen to me now, 'cause you can go to prison with Dad if you don't."

She hated the implied superiority in his voice. Wrenching her shoulders free of his grasp, she challenged, "What are you talking about? Prison? He's not going to prison. You're reaching for ridiculous straws."

She still didn't get it, Evan thought. He went to the heart of it. "Dad isn't missing, Pauline. That's why everything seems so strange about this. Don't you see? My guess is, he has engineered his own disappearance."

She had not allowed herself to honestly consider this, even though her father's behavior implied as much.

"Listen to me. Just listen," he entreated. "I'm telling you, no matter what religious project he's using to cover it up, the whole disappearance has been trumped up for money—an ungodly amount of money most likely."

She stared at him incredulously, resisting the impact of his words. *Daddy's not that kind of evil*, she thought. "I—Evan . . ." she fumbled. "I'm sorry, I just can't believe it."

"Of course you can. Hear me out. He's using you by remote control. He knows you, he knows me. He knows what you know, and more importantly, he knows what you *don't* know. He also knows what I know. He knows I was inside the fund-raising loop between him and Alan Lavalle for years. I know too much. I know how the money is raised. Ten, twelve million a month. I once had evidence pointing to a laundry scheme with Alan Lavalle. But that's another story. Listen to me . . . Dad knows that the news about his disappearance will make headlines around the world." He stopped, sighing heavily at her naiveté. "Publicity, Pauline. He's asked you to keep it out of the press. Of course, because when your Daddy is good and ready, the story *will* make the headlines. And I'll guarantee you it will be timed with the arrival of a fund-raising letter that he's already written. He's manipulating the press and the mail, and you and me with them. He and Lavalle have been doing it for years. Only this time it appears they've outdone themselves. If I'm right, he's counting on you to cover his tracks. And who knows?—maybe me too."

Pauline could not receive this—especially not from Evan. He was so obviously bitter. She knew her father. She knew he would not put her through the turmoil of the car bomb, nor the disappearance—not for money or any other reason. Even though Evan presented frightening logic, it came from a polluted mind. He was simply bitter. Yes, that was it. "A root of bitterness" had defiled him. And why not? He was the kind of person who had sold his spiritual birthright for a roll in the hay.

Evan misjudged her thoughtful mood. Believing his point had

gotten through, he said, "Pauline, you know that our father is capable of this, don't you?"

Something uncoiled in her at this statement. "I don't know any such thing! Who do you think you are to suggest it? You haven't even been around since you—" She choked, searching for the word. "—*whored* yourself out of the ministry!" It was a trump card, and she enjoyed playing it. He had it coming, and furthermore she wasn't through.

But Evan was through. He would not subject himself to what he considered to be her ignorant piety. He saw a world of difference between "whoring" and adultery, but to Pauline, who was only interested in judging him, sin was sin. Why argue? He had already turned and walked away.

"Can't take the truth?" Pauline shot the words after him like darts. "Is that it?" She didn't really want to, but she felt compelled to let her anger spill all over him. "I think its time you dealt with *yourself*, Evan. Who are you to accuse your father?"

He stopped dead in his tracks, realizing that his opinion meant absolutely nothing in her world, even though it might be correct. The world of religion was a kingdom, not a democracy. Truth and power were decreed, not voted, wielded by "anointed kings," modern-day men of God. In this case, the word of an ordained preacher easily pulled rank over a defrocked critic of religion. He turned and walked back to her, his anger completely under control. He spoke quietly. "Who am I to say these things? OK, little sister, I'm not much, but I never pretended to be. The real question here is, who is Simon Grace? He's not even a doctor, for heaven's sake. The title is honorary, from one of Alan Lavalle's two-bit mail-order institutions. Check it out." He watched the devastating effect of his words on her. He couldn't afford to show pity just now. She would snap back like a steel trap. "Let me ask you this. Do you want to know what I know? Can *you* take the truth?"

She felt an inner kingdom shaking down to its foundations. *Where is his loyalty?* she wondered frantically. *He'll attack his own father.*

"You don't want to know what I know," Evan challenged relentlessly. "Neither did I. But it's your turn now. Dad has made you responsible whether you like it or not. It's time for you to grow up and face the character of your father. Who knows, maybe you'll do better with it than I did."

Her brother was her enemy, she thought. Anything she could

find—anger, religious conviction, loyalty, decency—she piled it all against the battered door of her mind like furniture. Evan would have to burst through it to get to her.

"You're stalling," she challenged. "You don't know anything. You're just harboring your petty little bitterness for being put out of the ministry." As she said this, she became aware that she desperately wanted to believe her own words. What if Evan really knew something? What then? She attacked in order to distract him—an old tactic with her. "Who are you anymore, Evan? A second-rate writer for a third-rate tabloid. You used to be somebody before you threw it all away. You could have been the heir to a ministry."

It hurt, but Evan seemed unruffled. "When you get back to Brownsville," he said, "get the key to Dad's private lock box from Jann. Go to the Rio Grande Bank and look inside."

She waited. "And what am I supposed to find?"

"Scum files. 'Dirt files.' Call them what you will. Pictures. Dates. Names. It's a little trick Alan Lavalle taught Dad. You'll find a file on me and Danna, and a whole lot more. In case you are missing the point, the files keep our father in control of this ministry." He finished with a shrug. "They can help you do the same. That's what I know."

Pauline felt stunned. She shook her head in denial. Her stomach burned. "I am *not* buying this."

"Just check it out."

It disturbed Pauline to see how completely sure of himself Evan was. She took a deep breath and blew some of her mounting tension into the air. "Please be careful what you say about Daddy." She began to cry. "I love him so."

Evan's face drained, and he nearly screamed at her, "And I *don't*?" He walked in a tight circle, holding his head to regain composure. "Just because I know things about him you don't want to know? That means I don't love him?" He paused, blinking back the feelings. "I think you're afraid that if you know too much, you might not love him at all, sister! That's what I think. But you are through hiding. Your father and mine puts men in power around him with well-documented weaknesses. The kinds of things that would make the scandal page. He's got dirt on everybody, not just me. He does it for control."

Suddenly Pauline really heard her brother. It occurred to her that if Evan believed the files existed, and if he believed they had been used to defrock him in the Danna Lavalle case—and *not* against someone else, perhaps someone like Stiles, still in power— his pain would be unbelievable. She suddenly understood. And she further understood that Evan was a very dangerous "loose can- non." Right or wrong—and she was sure he was wrong—his bit- terness could only explode. There could be no tempering his fury. She could see it like a poison, generating tragedy upon tragedy, making anything bad become something worse. It was imperative that he come under some kind of control, some kind of discipline, regardless of the outcome. He had to forgive. "Evan, please come to Brownsville and help me find Daddy. Will you? We need each other," she pled.

He chuckled cynically. Her personal agendas never ceased to amaze him. "Sure, sis. Bring me to Brownsville and keep me off the record, just the way Dad planned it." He took a deep breath and suddenly felt himself dangling over a chasm of sadness. It yawned beneath his soul all the way to the dark center of the earth. He knew the feeling. It was an overwhelming sense of loss for all of the high dreams of Christian ministry that had once burned in his heart, when indeed he had been heir to the world ministry of Simon Grace. It seemed so long ago—so very long ago. Coming close to Pauline had revived the memory. "No thanks," he said huskily and turned away. "I'm going after Dad my own way."

Something had gone out of his step. She saw it as he walked away. *He is his own worst enemy*, she thought. Still, she wanted to say something, anything to help him avoid the road to destruction he was surely on.

"Evan, you're more than a journalist, you know? Much more than that."

He quickened his pace.

"You're his son."

He continued on without acknowledgment.

She felt more alone than she could ever remember as she turned and walked up the stairs into "Spirit I." The whole scene with Evan had backfired. She was floundering, thrown back into the deep end of the pool without swimming lessons. She wanted to beg Evan to come back with her now, but restrained the urge. She would check out his story first, before she gave him another minute. In her heart she had to believe that her investigation would prove him wrong. He was honestly mistaken about their father, and she would dis- cover the truth that would reconcile the three of them as a family once more. That was her goal—all she desired.

Dropping into the cabin chair she felt suddenly filthy from the discussion with Evan. Her skin seemed alive with an invisible film of dirt. She couldn't wait to get home to Brownsville and to a bath. She also felt a deep need to spend time alone with Lydia Nation— perhaps in a time of cleansing prayer.

18

BROWNSVILLE
Grace Ministries Jetport
6:47 A.M.

As "Spirit I" began its initial descent toward the Texas Delta, Pauline gazed absently at the sunrise. Her head rested on the knuckles of her hand. Her delicately formed fingers and French-manicured nails fidgeted nervously beneath her chin. She chewed her lip while her right foot vibrated like the tail of a rattler. Her thoughts raced ahead to the Rio Grande Bank vault. It was Saturday morning. It would be open from 9 'til noon. Would the lock box reveal her father to be a man of God, or a cynical manipulator? *Oh, God, please*, she sighed in her spirit, but she didn't really want to know the truth if Evan turned out to be right.

Her mind absorbed fragments of Billy Boren's piano music, as Joel Lassiter had awakened to view segments of the Jerusalem production on the cabin TV set. Stiles and Cheney, with opened briefcases at the table opposite her, engaged in business conversation.

"The 'coke baby' thing is a trendy issue," Cheney said as he bounced a plastic packet of sand in his palm. "You got cocaine in the news, you got babies in your hospital, and believe me, one picture is worth a million."

Stiles listened and shuffled pictures of infants—three black children, one white—with life support equipment and medical tubes attached to their tiny, pathetic bodies. "I agree. I don't think we have a stronger issue on tap than this. It'll pull our partners' pockets inside out." He shrugged and tossed the pictures into the briefcase with irritation. "I do *not* understand the Old Man's reaction in Jerusalem. I told him you had flown the package in from San Diego. He knew it was something special. But he walked past us like we don't have a cash flow crisis or something. What's with him—he's seen the books." He shook his head with frustration.

Cheney lowered his voice confidentially and leaned forward. "You got a problem, I got a problem," he said. "If I can't sell a package this good, Alan is gonna ask me what I'm doing to earn my keep." He glanced at Pauline and lowered his voice further. "Why don't we toss it to her? Let her at least send me back to San Diego to develop a mock-up. It'll save my tail—maybe yours too. I know you don't need to be going over the Old Man's head with this . . . but I'll bet he would forgive her." He tilted his head toward Pauline. "In the meantime we do what is best for the ministry." He made this last statement with that strange mixture of conviction and cynicism that is only known among those who merchandise religion.

Stiles watched him, trying to hide his admiration for the young man's shrewdness. He liked the idea of using Pauline, but it was risky, unorthodox, and if it failed he didn't want to be left holding the bag with Dr. Grace. He replied cagily, "We have a cash flow problem that will eat our lunch in the next sixty days. Those are the facts. It's got me hung over a barrel right now." He paused significantly. "With no way out."

Cheney had worked with him long enough to read the implied approval in this answer. He turned to Pauline. "Pauline, honey, can we interrupt for just a minute?"

She had heard snatches of the conversation, but it had only been words to her. Now she tried to assemble the sense of it. *This is about some kind of letter . . . our "coke baby" ward needs money . . . cash flow problems . . .*

"It's simple," Cheney began. "All I need is your approval to go back to Logos Mail and develop this package from concept to design. Then we come back in two weeks for the final decision. Hopefully your dad will be back by then, and you won't even have to mess with it."

She noticed that he had not changed the black suit he had worn every day in Jerusalem, figuring he either had six of them or was very handy with an iron. "How much will that cost?"

"Nothing much. It runs about five thousand."

"Five thousand dollars? That's not much?"

"Not compared to the one hundred and sixty thousand you will spend to generate the actual mailing. This is just a mock-up."

She tried to process this information through her distracted mind. The numbers didn't relate. Looking at Stiles she asked, "We do this sort of thing every month?"

"We do."

"And these costs are in line?"

He nodded. "Pretty close, except the response device is a bit more expensive than normal."

"How much more?"

"About thirty thousand."

"Goodness. Unless I'm mistaken, that's still a lot of money, isn't it?"

"It is."

"If we're in a cash flow crisis, how can you justify it?"

"Only if the concept is strong enough to pull, oh, thirty or forty times that amount in return. In my opinion this concept will do better than that."

"Thanks for the vote of confidence," Cheney said, smiling sweetly. His well-rounded body grew more erect, and his puppy-dog brow wrinkled earnestly. "We at Logos Mail feel the same way. But this is just a demo now, Pauline. It's not the whole decision. That will be made later. It's just that your father was so busy in Jerusalem, he didn't find time to look it over. So we're stuck. But we're trying not to let Dr. Grace down during the current financial crisis, you see?"

As she listened, Evan's recent comments about raising money remained painfully fresh in her mind. "It all adds up to a huge payday," he had said. "Did my dad write this letter?" she asked.

Stiles and Cheney both looked at each other with amazement. Cheney chuckled and waited for Stiles to answer her.

He cleared his throat. "Your dad seldom writes his own letters, Pauline. That's standard procedure."

She had not known this. "Then why is his name on them?"

Stiles glanced at Cheney helplessly, amused at her ignorance. "Uh, Pauline, ministers don't write their own fund-raising letters. There's too much at stake. *How* a letter is written is as important as *what* is written. That's why we hire professionals."

"I disagree," she said, not liking the way this sounded. "If my Dad didn't write the letter his name shouldn't be on it."

"You've got to be kidding," Stiles muttered, unable to disguise his frustration. "I suppose you also feel that if his letters aren't good enough to raise the funds, then he shouldn't have a hundred million dollar budget?"

She pondered for a moment. "That sounds right to me."

"Then you need to get out of this jet, quit TV, sell the mansion, give away the Prayer Steeple and the entire ministry center. Dump the hospitals, the 'coke baby' ward, and all the overseas missions while you're at it." Stiles grew livid, but he spoke with reasoned control. "Where have you been, Pauline? Are you ready to take the ministry back to the size it was in 1957—before someone else started helping him with his letters? Is that what you are proposing?" He felt insulted having to deal with the objections of someone so naive in the fund-raising process. He felt she should have known all of this before now. Condescendingly, he tried another explanation. "You're thinking of what's important in a personal letter—not a letter that goes to a list of millions of people. One word, one sentence in a letter like that can mean the difference between hundreds of thousands of dollars in a ministry's income. Are you ready to carry that responsibility when the payroll for a thousand employees, the mortgages, the education of the university students, the hospital care, and everything down to the maintenance of this jet are at stake? Are you going to have your dad write his own letters and let the chips fall where they may?"

Pauline remained unswayed, but she suddenly realized a bigger opportunity than this decision lay before her just now. Because of his own uncertainties, Stiles offered her the opportunity to make this executive decision about the letter. If she made it, she would exercise a measure of legitimate control during her father's absence—and that with Stiles's own cooperation. A truly important decision about the method of writing letters could be made later. "Let me see the letter," she said, masking her true feelings.

Cheney eagerly reached into his briefcase and began to assemble the pieces of the mail package on the table.

"Buckle up, pigeons." Rick's voice crackled over the intercom. "We're on final approach."

"OK, this is the 'coke baby' package," Cheney explained quickly, pointing to each piece. "Envelope, copy, response device, reply card and return envelope."

As she buckled her seat belt Pauline tried to make sense of what she saw. Crudely rendered, the envelope and letter had been hand-drawn with colored pencils. Spaces for pictures were labeled "pix here." Only a few words were readable; everything else had been represented by squiggly lines. It was a concept. Hardly anything she saw would be recognized as a real letter except the overall design.

"Understand now," Cheney explained, "the final copy will be presented later."

Stiles went further, trying to reassert himself in the decision process. "What we need is your permission to create 'mechanicals,' complete with copy, typesetting, color separations, things like that. In ten days Logos Mail will come back with a full mock-up, copy, detailed budget, everything needed to complete the mailing. If we don't do *this* letter, we will have to come up with a twelve million dollar letter somehow. Got any twelve mil ideas?"

She had none—had never been asked before. "I understand, Verlin," she said without looking at him. She recognized a line from her father's Jerusalem sermon on the envelope: ". . . the bones of infants comprise the dust of this place . . ." She pointed to it, remembering the scene in the Valley of Hinnom. "What is this?"

"Teaser line," Cheney explained. "Curiosity. Gets people to open the envelope. Our response device is this plastic packet of sand from the Valley of Hinnom. We have this peek-a-boo window in the envelope, see—so the sand shows through. That's the thirty thousand dollar piece we were talking about. But when you consider that most of the people who get the letter will have seen the TV show with your father in the Valley of Hinnom—hey, this thing gets hot! We've tested a similar device to our list and I've got to tell you, it has been phenomenal. Almost a 22 percent response, with 19 percent money mail—eighteen dollars average gift. If you know anything about this business, you know this is one of the hottest tickets around."

Stiles jumped in. "The problem with most bulk mail is, it goes straight into the trash can. People are not going to throw this piece away until they at least open it. That gives your 'coke baby' message a chance to be read, and that's the whole idea of the teaser line."

Pauline suddenly understood the envelope concept. She saw her father's partners looking at the packet of sand, recalling the TV images of the sand filtering between his fingers in the Holy Land, reading the line on the envelope, and—the whole thing suddenly sickened her. *Please, God, don't let this be Daddy's idea,* she prayed. "I'm glad you haven't gone to any trouble with this, Verlin," she said. "I will not stand for the teaser line."

"But wait," Cheney objected, "you do understand that this letter will arrive in your partners' homes the day after the TV special airs? That's dynamite in this business. That's credibility and message reinforcement."

She snatched up the packet of sand angrily. "Do we come from different planets, or do you see that people are going to look for baby bones in this thing? It's disgusting. It's worse than morbid."

"Well . . . ah . . ." Cheney faded.

"It's a sick idea!" she continued. "Get rid of it and come up with something creative."

The wheels of the jet squealed on the runway, and Rick engaged the reverse thrusters.

"But wait, wait," Cheney said. "You're right. It is a bit morbid, but this letter is about babies who are born addicted. That's not a pretty sight. They are being cared for in your father's hospital, and that costs money. Where does the money come from?" He held up pictures of the babies for Pauline to see. "Can you afford to look down your nose at crude teaser copy if it means these little ones will be taken care of? Even if, in your opinion, the money comes in for reasons of bad taste?" He remained quite still, holding the pictures of pitiful infants before her eyes.

Pauline felt herself caught in an emotional dilemma. Perhaps she had been thinking too selfishly. How far would she bend her own sense of taste in order to care for "coke babies"? And what was the fine line between taste and decency, ethics and morality? She had never faced anything like this before. "Surely there is a classier way to get the people to open the envelope," she entreated. "There just has to be."

"But is there a more appropriate way?" Cheney replied. "That's the question. Your father's sermon spoke of the children sacrificed to Moloch. That is morbid. We don't like to think about it, but it happened. You might ask, what's the point in bringing it up? We can't do anything about it. I would agree, but we *can* do something about *these* children. See, that's the whole point of the concept, Pauline—not to insult you, but to get results for all of the worthy projects in your father's ministry." He held up a headline. "Look, here's our copy concept. 'We must not allow innocent children to be consumed by the cheap god of crack cocaine. Send a generous gift today.'"

Pauline groaned inwardly. Cheney had no sensitivity for anything but money.

The Falcon taxied toward its hangar where two limousines waited. The Prayer Steeple stood tall against the sky behind the buildings.

"I'm not approving or disapproving," she said. "Just get me some other choices. Then let me see the mock-up when it's ready." She desperately hoped her father would be back to take care of the decision. *Dear God, how can anyone deal with this stuff and remain clean enough to preach the gospel?* she wondered.

19
GRACE MINISTRIES, INTERNATIONAL
7:12 A.M.

J ann Parker had been a Brownsville minister's wife until her husband had died of leukemia nine years ago. He had been an exceptionally fine husband who gave her all her heart desired in marriage. She had no wish to marry again. Now in her fifties, she happily devoted her remaining energies to the intense circle of power surrounding Dr. Simon Grace. Possessing a "just right" combination of motherliness and tight-lipped discretion, for eight years she had served as his executive secretary.

She steered her forest-green Mercedes 190DL from Old Highway 4 through the entry gate at the south end of the ministry property and wound for a mile between the golf links filled with retirees and college students. Everywhere on the property she had to slow for visitor traffic. Some tourists had actually stopped in the road to gawk at the modern buildings and pastoral campus. With the attractive Gulf weather, she had grown to expect such crowds on any weekend of the year.

Beyond the Prayer Steeple she left the traffic behind, entering an unmarked lane leading to the executive office building. It was a seven-story pyramidal building with a central atrium and stood in a grove of pine and palm trees hidden from the normal flow of traffic. Dr. Grace and a dozen secretaries and assistants shared an entire floor beneath the glass apex of the pyramid. The staff normally worked Saturdays, even Sundays, to keep Dr. Grace in touch with the far-flung interests of the ministry.

Jann approached the parking ramp beneath the building. She stopped, inserted a magnetic card into a meter, and waited as the electronic barrier swung upward, allowing her to pass through. Inside the nearly empty garage, she parked in a reserved space near a glass-enclosed elevator lobby which glowed in the dark garage, lighted by the atrium skylight seven stories above. An Hispanic security guard waited inside, arms behind his head, tilted back in a chair before a bank of video monitors. With a subtle motion of his foot he switched off the volume of a football game on a portable TV set on the floor.

Jann noticed his action as she got out of her car with a clutch of files. She reached into her purse and dutifully pinned an ID badge to the lapel of her sweater before walking into the parking lobby.

"Good morning, Ramon," she said cheerily.

He got up to greet her. "Morning, Jann."

"How about them Baylor Bears?" she asked, carefully stepping through a metal detector.

He laughed, realizing she had noticed his hidden television set. "You don't miss much, do you? I'm an Aggie fan myself."

"Didn't know Aggies were playing today," she needled, stepping into the elevator.

She smiled to herself as the doors closed, pleased with the subtle influence she had over Ramon, knowing she commanded his respect primarily because she was Dr. Grace's secretary. She turned to watch the atrium garden drop away as the car climbed. She enjoyed her place in life as a helper. *Women are created to be helpers*, she mused. *They are never happy otherwise.* Her life held privileges that came from serving. Her limited role was a shelter. Grace bore the weight of things. Small influences were quite enough for her.

On the seventh floor the elevator opened and she stepped into the brightly lit walkway, where planters of fern, palm and ivy soaked up the sunlight. Sorting her ring of keys, she walked to a door with *Dr. Simon Grace* inscribed on a copper panel beside it. She unlocked, and pushed it open—and screamed like a schoolgirl.

A man dressed in black, wearing a matching ski mask, was calmly rifling a file drawer.

"What are you doing?" she demanded.

The man paused, then picked up and pointed a pistol with

silencer at her. She screamed again and threw herself to one side, running for the atrium rail. She leaned over and yelled down the seven floors to the garage, "Ramon! Come quick!"

Ramon had heard her first screech and stood in the center of the atrium looking up.

"He's got a gun, Ramon!"

He reached instinctively for his holstered .38 and ran on his toes to the elevator. As he did, he placed his hand-held radio to his mouth. "Code 1, Code 1. Request backup at the Pyramid." He pushed the seventh floor button, gun drawn. The chamber seemed to fill with the sound of his own heartbeat as the door closed and the car began to move upward.

Jann ran to the opposite side of the atrium, watching the open office door carefully in case the burglar emerged. She crouched behind a potted fern and waited. Nothing happened. No one showed. Apparently the burglar felt he could take his time.

The elevator bell sounded, and Ramon emerged silently into the hall. He moved furtively toward the atrium.

Jann stood up and pointed. "He's still in the office," she rasped.

Ramon ran to her side and crouched down, aiming his gun at the door. He whispered breathlessly, "He's got a gun. I've got to wait for backup. Then we'll go in."

Ten minutes later, backed by two shotgun-toting assistants, Ramon called for the burglar to come out. Getting no response he entered the office. Directly above Dr. Grace's desk a ceiling panel remained slightly askew.

"We're going to have to seal the place off and go in after him," he said.

20
DALLAS
Texas People Magazine
8:08 A.M.

Jennifer Bridgeport was busy "feeding chickens" when Evan arrived at his Las Colinas workplace. He called it "feeding chickens" because of the pecking sound her word processor keyboard made as she edited copy for publication. *Cluck-luck-luck-luck-luck-cluck*.

He crossed the word processing pool quietly and stopped to peer over her shoulder at the screen. "That's very good," he said.

She gasped with a start. "Why do you *do* that?"

"I think I'll just leave the job to you and catch up on the sleep you made me lose last night."

"Don't play the martyr with me. Besides, you can't leave. Putnam is waiting to see you. It seems really important. Come on."

She stood and hustled him toward the perimeter of glowing CRTs. He hung back, making her pull him forward, aware of how very much she liked to hustle him *anywhere*. With her brat-bobbed hair and intense brown eyes, Jennifer was young, pushy, demanding, presumptuous—everything he disliked and needed in an investigative assistant.

"Did she let you sleep at all?" she pried. "Your midnight caller, I mean."

"That's not what the call was about, Jen." He decided to mischievously dump on her. "There was a death in the family."

She gasped and stopped in her tracks. "Oh no." She put both hands slowly to her mouth.

"Just kidding."

She grimaced. "Then it *was* a woman, you scum. Just as I thought."

He moved on toward the office. "The woman was my sister. It was a family emergency."

She let her breath out and followed him, only half relieved. "Now you're telling me your *sister* got an earful of my act?"

"That's right."

"I'm not buying that either." The thought struck her funny though, and she suppressed a titter.

"That's right, and it's not funny," he nodded. "You'd better be sorry. You've ruined my reputation with my family. I think as penance you should offer to finish the Railey story while I see what this is all about." He paused and knocked at Putnam's door. "Don't you?"

"Come in," a muffled male voice called from inside.

"OK," Jennifer whispered. "But only if you tell me what *this* is all about. No secrets, OK?"

"But of course," he said evasively, prompting a quick frown from her.

He pushed through the door and crossed an unoccupied receptionist's area. Passing through a second open doorway he entered a corner office with a twelfth-floor view. Charles Putnam, a totally bald, fretting gentleman in his late fifties, sat brooding behind a desk in a multicolored jogging suit. Following his gaze, Evan watched the Carpenter Freeway stretching like twin ribbons toward the heart of Dallas, fifteen miles in the distance. The trademark Reunion tower finished the skyline like an upside-down exclamation point on the southern horizon.

"I've been trying to reach you all morning and I get this dial-a-porn thing," Putnam groused. "Is this some kind of joke?"

"Yeah." Evan flushed. "A practical joke. Jennifer."

"What'd you do to her?" Putnam didn't want an answer. He stood impatiently, dismissing his own question with a wave. He walked to his corner-view window. "Does your father own an icon?"

The question came out of nowhere. *Why should this be on his mind?* he wondered. As far as Evan knew, he was the only person with an interest in the icon. One of only a few people who even knew of its existence.

"Yes," he decided to say.

Putnam seemed unsatisfied with the short answer. Evan knew plenty more about the piece from years of private research. But unless Putnam came up with a good reason to spill it, he wasn't giving his hard-earned information away. "Charles, why don't you help me out? I'm tired. Didn't sleep much last night and my brain is slow. Where are you going with this?"

"*The Seven Sleepers of Antioch*. Is that your father's icon?"

Evan was even more surprised that the publisher knew it by name. "Yes."

"Tell me what makes it so valuable."

Evan didn't know its true value. He had never had it priced. His mind began sorting the possibilities. "Well, its value could come from several sources, Charles. What makes you think it's valuable?"

"I asked you first." Putnam watched him and waited.

Evan was reminded that in his father's ministry he would never have had to put up with this prying question. Here Putnam called the shots.

"Alright. For one thing, the icon is one of five or six mosaics to survive the eighth century. That's when icons were destroyed throughout the Roman and Byzantine Churches. That makes it pretty special."

"OK. Who would buy it?"

"Private collectors, museum curators, black marketeers, I suppose."

"Black marketeers? How much could one get for it these days? Any idea?"

"Maybe."

"Come on. High? Low?"

"The black market in art and relics is a billion dollar a year racket. But the largest single deal I know of was for one point two million for the *Kanakaria Christ*. It's a mosaic like the *Sleepers*. It also survived the eighth century. In a bull market I think *The Sleepers* might go as high as five million. Tops."

Putnam chuckled. "Not even close.

Evan was struck by Putnam's mysterious manner. "How much are we talking here?"

He paced the windowed corner with his hands behind him and said nothing.

"I didn't know my father was selling," Evan prodded.

"What else is so special about this icon?" he asked. "What *is* an icon? I'm not sure I even know."

"The long or short of it?"

Putnam turned. "Just the important."

"That depends."

"Well, that's what I want to know. Depends on what?" Putnam leaned against the wall and waited.

"There are those who believe in icons deeply, like eighty or ninety million Russian and Eastern Orthodox. To them an icon is equal to Scripture. To a good many Roman Catholics too, and Coptics and Armenians. Then there are those who detest icons. Iconoclasts. They believe they are a satanic invasion of the Church. Mostly Protestants believe that way, but some Catholics too. They might try to destroy an icon as an evil device."

"Believe me, that's not what's happening in this case. I have been informed that a . . . shall we say, significant sum is being paid for your father's icon. The sale is being handled through Logos Mail. That's why I've called you in."

"Alan's outfit?" Suddenly Pauline's visit began to cast a shadow on this seemingly unrelated conversation. "How much?"

"First I want to know some things, like what does your father believe about the icon?"

"He's on the Protestant side. Sees it as something of an idol. But I noticed that he started to talk about it more openly in 1984 after reading about Billy Graham accepting an icon from the Russian Orthodox Church. Privately, he was always proud of *The Sleepers*. He knew it was a rare piece. And he had another connection; icons were supposed to have caused miracles of healing down through the centuries."

"A charismatic faith healer with a healing icon? Did he put any stock in its powers?"

"No. But he put stock in faith. I think if someone had faith in the icon, he might try to use their faith to pray for a healing." He added cynically, "Or maybe to take up an offering, I don't know."

"Where did your father come by this icon?"

Evan began to feel uncomfortable. Like a traitor. "Charles, can you tell me where you're going with this?"

"Trust me. It's important."

"The icon was given to him in the 50s when he was in the Middle East somewhere. He didn't really know what it was then. I got curious about it when I was in college and began doing my own research. The piece still fascinates me. As far as I know, I'm the only writer who sees a connection between icons, relics and guys like my father and Alan Lavalle who use trinkets and religious devices to trigger mail in offerings. I see it as sort of a Protestant version of the same old idolatry."

"Idolatry? Now as I recall, that's against one of the Ten Big Commandments, isn't it?"

"The second. Images, idols, other gods."

Putnam nodded, listening intently. "So an icon is an idol? How so?"

"Well, not technically. Or legally, according to Canon Law anyway. The Orthodox Churches make a distinction between the worship of an idol and what they call the 'veneration' of a Holy Image. It's a fine line. Like another 'how-many-angels-can-dance-on-the-head-of-a-pin' question. The sin of idolatry, in general, seems to be in substituting anything in place of the True Invisible God. We all commit idolatry in a life of faith, I'm sure."

Putnam had no time for religious sidelights. "OK, OK. Forget idolatry. What about icons?"

"Some say icons began with the burial shroud of Jesus. Better known as the Shroud of Turin. But really, it was a pagan practice to venerate objects like the Shroud long before Christianity. The problem became extreme in the early centuries of Christianity, when the Armenian nation was converted. The king used the army to bring his entire nation into the Church. This happened a half-century before Constantine converted the Roman Empire, by the way. The Armenians had been lifelong pagans. With the new religion of Christianity they demanded something pagan to go with their faith. Something like the rituals they were used to in their old religion. They happened to be familiar with idols and secret initiation rites.

"So the new Christian Armenian king had a problem. Jesus had ascended from the earth, leaving no permanent record behind—He wrote in the sand once; no one could preserve that. The problem of the king was, 'how do you get a handle on this thing that Christ created?' There was a lot of insecurity. Who was in charge? Where was the authority? By now the apostles had died. They had expected Christ to return in their own lifetime. You have to remember, the Bible had not yet been put together—"

"What's the point?"

"You said you wanted the important stuff. This is important."

"Sorry."

"People were mostly illiterate in those days, and the Bible wouldn't have made the same difference then as it makes today, see? Images were much more important to the illiterate population. As they say, 'a picture is worth a thousand words.' So, the image of the resurrected Jesus that was seen on the Shroud of Turin became very, very important in that early age. Some people wouldn't believe in

Christ until they had seen the Shroud. They pilgrimaged to see it. Pagan ritual, see?

"To the early Christians, the fact that the Shroud showed the face of the resurrected Jesus seemed to give God's approval to the idea of leaving a truly Holy Image behind Him on earth. Something more than the memories of His acts, and His words in the sand. They believed that the face on the Shroud had been made by the power of the resurrection itself; therefore it was called an 'image made without hands.' This became the first holy relic, and the pattern for all later icons."

"That's good, Evan. Makes sense. I'm from Missouri—the 'show me state.' I have no faith for the invisible. Go on."

Evan began to pace his half of the room as he continued, "Not only was the image visible on the Shroud of Turin, but it was said to cause miracles. Pilgrims had blind eyes restored, cripples walked, demons were cast out—and miracles became the second evidence that the face on the Shroud was a Holy Image. People began to adore it. An 'image made without hands.'"

"But icons are made by human hands. They're made by artists, for crying out loud."

"Right. The church grew fast. Pretty soon they had a problem. There was only one Shroud, only so many splinters of the cross, or crucifixion nails, crowns of thorns, 'Holy Grails,' bones of Stephen, skulls of John the Baptist, apostles' robes, prayer cloths of Peter and so on. Christianity grew beyond the reach of most of these relics. So artists were commissioned to create new images, inspired by the original."

"Relics were duplicated?"

Evan chuckled, recalling his own research. "Supply and demand. The first religious black market."

"And icons?"

"Even bigger. Bishops and church leaders conspired to keep this thing under control, so they made a Cult of official rules to canonize icons. Still in effect today. According to Canon Law, no icon can be bought or sold—but Canon Law was frequently broken in that regard. The canonization of icons began with the Second Nicene Council. A strict formula was developed from the original Shroud. Paintings or mosaics of the face of Christ were duplicated by following the church formula to the letter. It was all controlled by the bishops. According to the Cult, an icon of Christ could be adored and venerated in the same way as the Shroud. But only if the formula was strictly kept. Later on that rule was expanded to include images of Mary, the Christ-child, saints by the dozen, martyrs, and so on down the line. The Cult claimed that if the artist was true to the Cult, keeping his own personality out of the picture, then the icon would produce healings and other miraculous signs. To this day in Catholic and Eastern Orthodox churches you hear about works of art with weeping eyes, bleeding wounds, and such. The church investigates the miracles and if they find them legitimate, they are canonized as 'images made without hands.' The seventh Ecumenical Council went so far as to give icons equal status with Scripture."

Putnam remained thoughtful. "You enlighten me. This is fascinating. Really. OK." He shook his head. "So, is your father's icon canonized?"

"Yes." Evan hesitated to say more. "There's a dark side to that."

"A dark side?"

Evan grew disgusted. "This is where the free information stops, Charles." He was speaking to a publisher. He had to protect his material. "Charles, this information is a personal treasure of mine. You've drawn me out a long way here."

"You want to write a book or something?"

"As a matter of fact."

"Is that what you're worried about? I'll publish your book. Guaranteed."

Evan had long been eager to publish his knowledge of the icon. "You're serious?"

Putnam looked dead earnest. "I'll put it in writing today, OK? You name it. A scholarly work? A coffee-table book? Now, tell me about the dark side of *The Seven Sleepers of Antioch*."

Evan felt on equal footing at last. He was eager to share his knowledge with an ally. "The icon is a hoax, Charles."

Putnam's eyebrows arched with surprise. "A hoax?"

"Not a modern hoax. That would make it worthless. If my sleuthing is correct, it's a hoax from the fifth or sixth century. Canonized in the Armenian Church. It was supposed to be an image of seven Christian martyrs killed before the conversion of Armenia. But a Gnostic text found near Nag Hammadi claims that they were actually seven apostates who were killed for refusing to convert to Christianity. The exact reverse of the Orthodox tradition. According to Gnostic records, the icon was created by a secret Society of Apostates who worshiped the ancient Urartian gods of Mount Ararat. Out of spite, they introduced their pagan icon into the Armenian Church through the Cult of Icons. When the church canonized it, the Society claimed the authority of the church to be null and void. The icon then became the rallying symbol for their occult celebrations and rituals, which I'm told continue in some form to this day."

Putnam was nodding eagerly now. "Would any of this make *The Seven Sleepers* worth forty million dollars?"

Evan heard the number but felt nothing at first. Then the realization hit him. Forty million! He nearly choked. A lot of skulduggery could lie behind forty million dollars, not the least of which being the mysterious disappearance of Dr. Simon Grace. Whatever his father had to do with the icon sale, Evan was now sure it had nothing to do with a fund-raising letter. Not for forty million dollars. He had misjudged the whole discussion with Pauline. "I had no idea," he replied hollowly. "Maybe the Eastern Church would pay that much to take it out of circulation? I don't know. Who's the buyer?"

"Ask Alan Lavalle. He's handling the transaction through Logos Mail. Delivery is scheduled tonight."

"Tonight?" Evan's mind began to whirl rapidly. "Where'd you hear about this?"

"From inside Logos Mail. My source."

For the first time Evan smelled real danger in his father's disappearance. "Charles, can we go off the record here?" He waited for a reply before continuing.

Putnam paused disagreeably. "I've funded the Lavalle investigation for three years now, Evan. You owe me. Don't keep me from doing my business, for Chri—" He caught himself. "—for heaven's sake." Putnam knew that Evan cursed, but drew a hard line at profaning the name of Christ.

Evan held steady. "I've got to go off record."

Charles stared, then shrugged reluctantly.

"My father left Jerusalem under suspicious circumstances three days ago. Pauline flew in here last night, desperate about it. I told her Dad had engineered his own disappearance to coincide with a fund-raising letter. You know, the kind of stuff we've been looking into. But now I'm not so sure. If a forty million dollar payday is in motion, the letter is child's play. Something's not right. Whoever can drop that much money for the icon is in a bigger league than my Dad."

"Do you think more than the icon is involved?" Putnam posed. "Something like ransom?"

Evan nodded. "It smells bad."

21

BROWNSVILLE
Grace Family Compound
8:36 A.M.

Daylight sliced between the seams of the master bedroom drapes. Weary pilot Rick Gresham had arrived at his home in the sheltered Grace family compound. It was his first appearance there in weeks. He lay across the canopied bed while Connie sat beside him, holding his hand, stroking his hair. He had not taken time to undress. His pilot's cap had been tossed to the pillow beside his wearied body. Jilly, a blue-eyed child in pigtails and bib overalls, amused herself on the carpet nearby, peeking at the sunlight beams through his discarded dark glasses.

The telephone rang.

"The phone, Mommy," Jilly said, jumping up and reaching for the bedside stand.

"Shhhh," Connie whispered. "Let Daddy sleep. We'll take it in the kitchen."

She took her daughter's hand and walked quietly out of the room.

The little girl took the door handle. "I'll close it so Daddy can sleep," she said, peeking in at Rick one more time as she closed the bedroom door.

In the kitchen Connie, still in housecoat and slippers, ran her fingers through her thick brunette curls as she picked up the phone. "Hello?"

"Hi there."

She recognized her ex-husband's voice in an instant. "Evan. Rick said he saw you this morning." She was immediately brimming with a question. "What in the world is happening with your dad?"

Evan tapped a pencil at his desk. "We don't know, but it's getting thicker by the minute. Any chance I could speak to Rick?"

"He's really exhausted, Evan—"

Jilly's ears pricked up at the sound of his name, and she pulled at Connie's skirt. "Mommy, is that Daddy?"

"Yes, honey." Connie spoke into the receiver. "You've got a little girl here asking to speak to her daddy."

"Tell her that Daddy wants to talk to the prettiest little girl in Texas—not to mention the whole entire universe—in just a minute."

She nodded to Jilly. "Just a minute, honey, your dad wants to talk to 'the prettiest little girl in Texas and the whole, entire universe.' OK?"

Jilly beamed.

"When we're through."

Jilly nodded obediently and waited

"So Rick's crashed?" Evan continued.

"We don't use that word around here—"

He smiled, self-rebukingly. "Of course not."

"But yes," she sighed wearily, "he's dead asleep. I haven't seen him for more than two weeks. We had maybe five minutes of talk. I cooked a big breakfast, and he couldn't even eat it."

"That's crazy. Does he have to fly again or something?"

"Yeah, he's got a flight to San Diego tonight. But it's a short out-and-back."

"When will he get up?"

"In about four hours."

"OK. Four hours?" Evan checked his watch. "Good. Listen, Connie, I need to be on that flight with Rick tonight. Tell Rick to expect me, but keep it quiet. Could you give me Pauline's unlisted number? I think she'll agree that I should go."

"Let me get it from the desk. Why don't you talk to Jilly while I look it up?"

"Great."

She handed the receiver to Jilly, who pressed it to her ear. Her face glowed with pleasure, and she began to swing her legs back and forth, her voice taking on a new sweetness with him. "Hi, Daddy."

"Hi, my sweetheart."

"Daddy? Oh, gosh." She giggled. "You know what? I've got *two* daddies. One in there and one on the phone."

"That's right, baby sweets. But I've only got one little girl, and that's you, Jilly Boo."

She grinned widely. "I love you, Daddy."

"I love you more."

She suddenly grew wistful. "Huh-uh. I love *you* more. Oh,

Daddy, you're the best daddy in the whole wide world, and I miss you so much."

"I miss you too, sweetheart." Evan flushed and swallowed hard, clearing his throat. "But just think how lucky you are to be so smart, and so pretty, and to have two daddies who love you so much. Right?"

She grinned widely. "That's right."

"Yeah. That's my big girl."

"Here's Mommy. Bye. I love you."

"I love you more."

"Oh, Daddy, I do," she scolded, handing the phone back to her mother. "He always says, 'I love you more.'"

"Yeah, I know," Connie said. "What are we ever going to do with that daddy of yours?"

22

DR. GRACE'S MANSION
9:15 A.M.

Pauline walked up the sloping lawn to her father's mansion. Her house sat below the terraced gardens, along with the Greshams' residence and the family guest house. She walked briskly across the lawn toward the mansion's tall rustic doors. An armored car sat parked on the drive.

She'd had every intention of being at the Rio Grande Bank at this moment, but Evan had called informing her of the icon sale. She had taken her shower, dressed, then hurried to check on the icon for herself. Her head was still reeling over the forty million dollar figure. *Why wouldn't Daddy tell me about something this big?* she wondered. Her confidence in him was seriously shaken.

Adding to her distress, she had called Jann Parker and had learned of a masked burglar who had been seen rifling her father's files that same morning. In her mind now, she entertained fears about the reality of the "dirt files" Evan had told her she would find. If they existed, someone with dirt in their past might have hired a professional thief to take the evidence back. If Evan was right, it smelled of a plot to take control of the ministry as well. She could easily believe such a thing of Stiles. Especially if, as Evan had said, Dr. Grace had kept him around because of his well-documented weaknesses. Who could blame him if he grabbed his file while "The Good Doctor" was away? *But what about this icon deal?*

The mansion doors were unlocked, and Pauline entered to the sound of a tapping hammer and workmen's voices. The entry hall was unoccupied. It rose twenty-five feet to the ceiling beams and extended completely to the back of the house. An open second-story loft crossed between two main wings of the structure, but no stairway intruded into the space. The hall sported animal and mounted fish trophies. One wall held only African species, the other North American varieties. Sailfish, marlin, trout, tarpon, plus trophy carnivores and herbivores were amply represented. They testified to her father's lifelong obsession with the Great Outdoors.

She followed the sound of the hammer to her left, passing beneath a large open archway. She descended into a library and sitting area, moving through another archway which led down several more steps to the long meeting table in her father's studio. Descending the steps, she entered the picture gallery beneath the tall windows. Below the windows the terraced gardens led down to hers and the Greshams' residence—formerly belonging to Evan.

Turning to her right she ascended six steps into the loft, where two workmen labored over the icon case as two shotgun-toting security men and a female security guard watched over them. Grace employees. But the two workmen were specialists. They wore pressed gray jumpsuits with *Antiquities Unlimited* sewn in black lettering to the backs.

The female security guard turned and recognized her. "Pauline, welcome back," she said, approaching with a grin and a handshake. "How was the Holy Land?"

"We had quite a time," Pauline replied, watching the workmen with concern. Looking at the security guard again, she couldn't recall seeing her before. But then Grace Ministries employed a thousand people. "What is your name, honey?"

"Camille."

"Camille, could you come with me a minute?"

The girl glanced uncertainly at the workmen. "Sure."

Pauline led her from the loft into the meeting area, out of earshot of the others. She stopped and turned. The wall behind her

held poster-sized black-and-white pictures of her and her father,
standing in various Third-World settings. In each shot, huge crowds
of people stretched as far as the camera lens would allow, while in
the foreground crippled and blind people waited in line for prayer.
Pauline smiled broadly beside her father in nearly every photo.

"Daddy never told me about this icon sale," Pauline said.
"Who told you to do this? To have it packed?"

"Well, I understood it was Dr. Grace's order."

"Who told you that?"

"Ramirez. Security chief."

"Where did he get *his* orders?"

"I think from Neva Sylvan."

Bewildered, Pauline remembered her telephone conversation
with the doctor in Lydia's room. *What would Neva have to do with
the icon?* "OK, Camille. That will be all. Thank you."

"No problem."

As Camille returned to the loft, Pauline pulled open a drawer
beneath the meeting table. Inside was a telephone. Picking it up she
touched a pre-dialed button labeled *Dr. Sylvan* and waited as it
began to ring.

"Dr. Sylvan's office."

"Danna." Pauline recognized Danna Lavalle's voice, who was
Neva's secretary—not to mention the other half of Evan's episode
of infidelity. Dr. Grace had retained her as an employee in a gesture
of Christian restoration. After all, she had always seemed penitent.
"This is Pauline. I'm calling for Neva."

"Welcome back," Danna said, sounding professionally polite
and helpful. "Neva's taken a CareFlight to the Matamoros clinic.
Would you like me to try to locate her for you?"

"Yes, I would. Have her call me as soon as possible."

"Sure. Anything I can do?"

"I don't think so." Pauline paused. "Unless you know something about the icon."

"Aaah ha. In fact it rings a bell. Neva got a call from your dad
about it. That's all I know."

"When? When did he call her?"

"Well, let me check the call record." Danna, a pretty redhead
in her late twenties, flipped a stack of pages on her desk, pretending to search for the call date. "Yes, here it is," she said, stopping
arbitrarily. "He called on . . . Wednesday."

The day he disappeared! Pauline quickly calculated. *Why didn't he tell me?* "Thank you, Danna. Be sure to have Neva call me when she gets in, will you?"

"Sure thing."

Pauline hung up and stood puzzled for a long moment, her eyes wandering aimlessly over the pictures on the wall. *Why would Daddy talk to Neva about this and not to me?* She felt less and less in control of things. "If you get in trouble call Evan." *Well, Daddy, you asked for it. I'm going with Evan on this, but you may not like the outcome.*

She turned and headed purposefully back into the loft. Approaching the uniformed Antiquities Unlimited workmen she asked, "Which one of you is in charge here?"

A young man with long immaculate hair and horn-rimmed glasses turned and answered in a British accent, "I'm Geoffrey, ma'am. What can I do for you?"

"Can you make a decoy shipping crate that will look and weigh exactly the same as this one?"

He paused, calculating in his head. "Yes, ma'am."

"Can you do it by 4 P.M.?"

He stopped and looked at his assistant. They began to nod hesitantly to one another, mentally figuring the time and materials. "It will be expensive."

"Do it." She turned to the security guard. "Camille, I'm giving special orders overriding any that you have already received. Do you understand me?"

"Yes, ma'am."

"I want an identical shipping crate prepared. My brother Evan will tell you what to do with both of them when he arrives here this afternoon. The icon is not to leave this room without him."

"Yes, ma'am."

"No one is to change my order—not even Dr. Sylvan. Is that clear?"

"Yes, ma'am."

"Bill me for the extra cost."

23
GRACE HEADQUARTERS
9:26 A.M.

Verlin Stiles burst through the door of his sixth-story executive office suite followed closely by Bud Cheney and Norm Dole, a young assistant in a salmon-pink golf shirt and plaid Bermuda shorts—Saturday work attire.

"Who does he think he is?" Verlin blustered.

Norm shrugged. "Alan assured me the new letter had been cleared to the top. Of course I assumed that meant you."

"*Never* assume."

"Hey," Cheney protested, "Alan's my boss, but I gotta plead ignorance on this deal here. Before I left San Diego, your letter was still in the mill."

Verlin pounded his desk, spilling papers to the floor. "Bud, would you mind waiting downstairs?"

"Not at all." He gathered his briefcase and walked to the door, pausing. "Uh, I'll get myself over to the hangar. Don't worry about me."

"Close the door after you please," Stiles said, not looking.

"Sure." Cheney closed the door, sending a walking-on-eggs glance in Norm's direction as he did.

"When I left here," Stiles began, containing his anger, "I had committed us to the 'Heaven Help Us' letter. Now I come back and find this 'Reverse the Curse' thing has gone out to the entire list. I've never heard of it. Where does Alan get off going over my head like that?"

"I don't know," Norm said with dutiful sympathy. "It's never happened before. Alan calls me and tells me he's got an executive order to change horses in the middle of the stream. He's got all the material in San Diego. I didn't question. But obviously I should have."

"Have you read the letter?"

"The letter seems . . . good, but—Naaah." He obviously thought it stunk.

"What do you mean, 'Naaah'?"

"The response device is weak. It's not like Alan's work, unless he's got some kind of subliminal persuasion in there I don't know about. I'd say it's going to flop. At best."

"Alan wouldn't do that. Let me see it."

The assistant handed him a fat sand-colored envelope with a tease line printed on the outside in blazing red lettering: "I won't come back until I reverse the curse!"

"This is spooky," Stiles mused, skimming the material. "'I won't come back'? What does he mean?"

"What's spooky?"

"Oh, nothing, nothing." Stiles's mind ran back over the events in Jerusalem. Grace's disappearance. Pauline's grabbing power and keeping the news out of the press. He opened the envelope and examined the overall form of the letter and reply card. "Does the letter say where he has gone?"

"Just the usual, you know, to the desert, the wilderness, like the prophets of old. I assumed he was going to take a walk around Palm Springs or something." Failing to get a humorous rise out of Verlin, he added, "Excuse me."

"No. You may be right. What kind of response device is this?" Stiles held up a sand-colored sheet of paper with lines on it.

"Well, see, that's the part I can't figure. It's *blah*. All it does is tell them to write the curses of their life on the blank lines and return the sheet with this month's gift. It's too much work for most people, plus the only extra motivator is a time factor. You have to return it in time to have the requests sent to the place of prayer in the desert with Dr. Grace so he can pray over them. This kind of thing used to work pretty well back in the 70s. But today it takes more *pizzazz!* You know?"

"The Old Man must have the fulfillment details worked out with Alan. Otherwise who's going to handle the logistics of getting all those prayer requests to him in the desert, right?"

"Right. I called Jann Parker and she doesn't know a thing about a desert prayer trip. Nor an executive order. Nor a 'Reverse the Curse' letter. Nor anything else. As usual."

Stiles shook his head. "If people only knew the inefficiency— the off-the-wall stuff that goes on in a ministry. I'm just *this close* to calling an emergency board meeting right now. It's showdown time." He angrily stuffed his hands in his pockets and stalked around his desk. "That'll be all for now, Norm."

"Sure." Norm made his way to the door. "I'm really sorry about my part in this, sir. I should have checked with you."

Verlin did not reply. With that, the young man crept out, pulling the door closed after him.

Stiles walked back to his desk and slumped down, punching a preset number on his speakerphone.

A phone rang in San Diego. It was mounted to the handle of an exercise bicycle. The cycle, in turn, sat on a redwood deck overlooking the La Jolla coastline in the soft light of morning. Alan pedaled as he read a *Wall Street Journal*, working his cardiovascular system before breakfast. He stopped, wiped his forehead with a towel, and picked up the telephone after the second ring.

"Hello."

"Sorry to catch you at home, but this is important."

"Verlin. How was the Holy Land?"

"A lot of work. Listen, Alan, Norm just told me about the 'Reverse the Curse' letter you inserted into our mailing list. What gives?"

"Orders from headquarters."

"Last time I checked, I *was* headquarters. At least where mail is concerned."

"Ah!" Alan mopped his head again. "All I can tell you is what I told Norm. The Old Man gave me a direct order on this letter. I guess you're going to have to take it up with him."

"Yeah, I'd like to do just that."

"Well, do it, and let me know."

Dorothy, in a boa-trimmed housecoat and slippers, crossed the deck and handed her boss a frosty orange Mimosa. He thanked her with his eyes and took a welcome sip. "Listen, Verlin, don't let this thing get to you. You're a good man. If this means that Simon's cutting you loose, you come talk to me, OK? Don't forget I said that."

"Do you know something I don't know?"

"Not a thing. I just know what it looks like." He paused. "If you know what I mean."

"What it looks like is that you and Grace have gone behind my back for no good reason that I can see. Grace pulls that disappearing stunt in Jerusalem—"

"Wait a minute. Wait a minute." Alan quickly gulped his mixture of champagne and orange juice. "What disappearing stunt are you talking about?"

Verlin paused, wondering if Alan was bluffing this ignorance.

He figured he had to be in collusion with the preacher. He wouldn't dare do something like this out of step. "Oh come on, Alan . . . What's the teaser line on the letter? Huh?"

"'I want to reverse the curse in your life' or some such thing."

"Some such thing? You know what it says: 'I won't come back until I reverse the curse.' Where is he, Alan? Where has he gone?"

Alan's eyes narrowed with curiosity. "To the desert. Palm Springs, right?"

"Thanks a lot," Stiles said glumly. "You guys didn't need to do this to me. Not at all. I'll see you later." He set the receiver down carefully, then picked it up and slammed it a second time for good measure.

24

THE STEEPLE
Intercessor's Apartment
9:35 A.M.

The elevator doors parted like the Red Sea, and Lydia Nation entered her familiar apartment on a rolling hospital bed. The intravenous drip remained attached to her arm, a bag of saline fluid held above her by an aluminum arm. Barry and April, the emergency attendants who had resuscitated her four nights ago, guided the bed toward the sanctuary of her bedroom.

"Here we are," April commented, speaking past a wad of chewing gum. "Do you feel better being back home?"

"You better believe it," Lydia replied.

April rolled her eyes privately at Barry as they glided along. She still felt spooky in the stained-glass tower.

"I told them we could monitor you over here. Your tests are all positive, and there is no reason to hold you at the hospital anymore," Barry said. "But they wouldn't listen to me. It took Pauline's call to shake them loose. That woman's got clout."

"Something about the last name, I think," Lydia commented dryly.

They came to a stop in the bedroom, where the harsh daylight filtered softly through the stained-glass wall.

"See," April explained, "we took your regular bed out, but you'll like this one better. It's got more toys. You've got your electronic motors so you can sit up and down." She switched the motors up and down to demonstrate. "Whee . . . see? A regular carnival ride. Then you've got your own remote control TV." She looked around and saw no television set. "Hey, no TV. No 'Munsters' reruns for you, eh? Alright. Well, let's see . . . You have an emergency button here. See that? Just like the one in the hospital."

"Thank you, honey," Lydia replied with a smile, putting the electronic switches down beside her with finality. She was not really interested in the bells and whistles of her bed.

Barry summed up, "We'll have a nurse here in the apartment around the clock. We'll take care of your food. Everything. I brought the honey and crackers, like you asked."

"I always crave it when I'm coming off a fast."

"Well, you crave it, you've got it—that's our motto. Will there be anything else?"

"No. Just be sure and tell Pauline to get herself over here to see me right away. I've got something burning hot to tell her."

"Will do."

25

MATAMOROS, MEXICO
Remote Cornfield
9:39 A.M.

The Bell Jet Ranger helicopter swung low, scattering dust over two Mexican men digging with shovels in a cornfield. A gold Mercedes Benz with darkly tinted windows waited at the edge of a dirt trail beside a nearby shack. The luxury sedan sat low to the ground with custom air spoilers and polished chrome wheels. The helicopter hovered briefly and touched down between the car and the wooden structure.

Neva Sylvan sat in the copilot's seat. She removed a helmet and communications headset. As she waited, a male technician in a white lab suit let himself out of the cargo door. He wore a surgical mask and rubber gloves and walked briskly toward the shack.

The door was ajar, and he nudged it open with his foot. Stepping inside, he paused, allowing his eyes to adjust to the dim light. A dozen chairs lined the walls of the room. In the center sat a long enclosed table. On either end of the table lay fruits and vegetables, broken and in disarray, having spilled violently out of two wicker cornucopias. Remnants of fresh blood glistened on the table. Some sort of occultic altar. The wall behind the table held a goat's skull mounted with a set of curved nubian horns. These were decorated with a mosaic pattern of obsidian and turquoise. Beneath the skull a large-lettered placard read: "When self-realized masters are drawn together in alignment, the universal vision will manifest itself, Heaven on earth. It will happen organically—no problem. Birth is death is birth." The quote was attributed to "Jesús." On the floor beneath the placard buckets of unrecognizable filth sat between piles of gourds, pumpkins and cornstalks.

The lab technician moved carefully across the dirt floor until he stood behind the table. Even through the surgical mask, he reeled at the stench of rotting flesh that greeted him. Flies buzzed busily about. He quickly bent down, removing a long screwdriver from the pocket of his smock. He used it to pry a metal bracket loose from a stainless steel canister attached beneath the table. The canister was a machined medical fixture in contrast to the trashy workmanship of the altar and the rest of the shack. Carefully the technician removed it from its loosened bracket and set it on the tabletop. He stopped to briefly inspect a greenish culture inside. It appeared to be a thickened, half-set Jello. Taking a lid from his smock, he screwed it over the sample tightly, sealing the contents. Then with gloved hands he carefully picked it up and hurried from the room, holding it at arm's length.

As he emerged from the shack and moved toward the helicopter, a Mexican girl, nearly six feet tall, wearing a blonde wig and sunglasses, emerged from the passenger door of the Mercedes. She moved to the front of the car and leaned against its grill, crossing her arms haughtily.

Dr. Sylvan ignored her, watching instead the returning lab technician until he had entered the aircraft. Only then did the doctor step from the helicopter. She walked directly toward the driver's side of the car.

"Jesús says this one is very powerful," the girl said as Neva waited. The girl spoke in a simple, soft Mexican accent. "More powerful than all the others."

Neva ignored her and tapped impatiently against the driver's window. It scrolled slowly down, revealing a dark-eyed man in his late twenties wearing a black cape. Dr. Sylvan pulled a bundle of cash from her pocket and laid it in his palm. He immediately began counting it.

"This one was powerful," he murmured.

"I will be the one to tell you what is powerful and what is not," Neva replied.

"Will there be more?"

"Perhaps," she hinted. "If you really are powerful, and not just another two-bit fake. It's hard to tell the true from the false these days."

The young man stopped counting, and his eyes blazed fiercely up at her. "I assure you we're the real thing, doctor. I took my time with this one. I followed that old scribble you gave me to the letter. With a few secrets of my own, of course." He smiled to himself. "The place was thick with spirits before I finished, so your little soup there," he nodded toward the helicopter, "should be plenty hot."

She laughed. "Then you can quit trying so hard, guru. We'll know if you have the power when we get back to the lab. It's that simple. By the way," she pointed to the men with shovels, "are they doing what I think they are doing?"

Jesús laughed. "Don't worry. In Cuba where I'm from we call them 'zombies.' They have nothing inside but fear. They've seen me in action." He glared back at her. "They know what real power is."

"I suggest you use it then. These undertakers are simpletons. They could be your undoing if they were captured by the other side. The world is not ready for us!"

She turned and walked to the helicopter, climbing aboard. Its rotors whined with a surge of renewed power, and shortly it lifted into the air.

By then the Mercedes had already traveled a quarter mile across the cornfield, leading a plume of dust toward a distant blacktop. Behind the shack two Mexican men dragged a six-foot bundle toward a fresh hole in the ground.

26
DALLAS
Dallas/Fort Worth Airport
10:02 A.M.

Charles Putnam, still in his jogging suit, and Evan in sport coat and tie, walked through D/FW Airport's crowded terminal 3E.

Evan checked his ticket and glanced at a flight information monitor as they passed. "When I called her, Pauline had no idea about the icon," he commented. "Nor the forty million."

"I'm trying to imagine forty mil myself. That's putting *The Sleepers* up there with Van Gogh's *Sunflowers*. But who would pay that much?"

"Beats me. In ninth-century Rome, in spite of church policy, they actually formed a corporation to sell relics to the wealthy of Europe. They raided the catacombs, trumped up saints' and martyrs' bones, paid kickbacks for ecclesiastical seals and such. They packaged reliquaries. You can still find bogus relics in the cathedrals and castles of Europe, but they're a part of church history now, so who could begin to weed the true from the false?"

He shifted his carry-on bag and lined up at a counter. "If I can find out who these people are, I figure to find Dad. In the process I'll get inside Logos Mail. I'm telling you, we're going to get your Alan Lavalle story one way or the other. You can milk Logos Mail for years and get a Pulitzer for the effort. What a business, huh?"

"That's the business we're both in," Putnam reaffirmed, sensing a subtle distance in his employee's statement.

The gate attendant handed the ticket to Evan. "Thank you, Mr. Grace. You may board now through gate 35."

"Find a fax modem wherever you go," Putnam said as Evan prepared to walk down the jetway. "You owe me one jim-dandy of a story for this."

"Right," Evan replied.

As he walked through the gate he felt a trace of guilt. His motives seemed no longer those of a committed journalist. Between family and career, loyalties had begun to shift.

27
BROWNSVILLE
Bank Vault
10:56 A.M.

Pauline conversed via porta-pak cellular telephone while waiting near the Rio Grande Bank vault. She spoke with Ramon, head of Grace security, concerning the burglar in her father's office that morning. Security had entered the ceiling after him, but had found no trace of the man.

"But if he could just escape into the ceiling, what is secure around there?" Pauline asked.

As she spoke, her father's secretary signed her name in the vault registry. The clerk checked it against an authorized signature book and nodded her approval. She produced a key and handed it to her. "Here you go, Ms. Parker."

"From now on I want an armed guard inside Daddy's office whenever it's unattended." Pauline concluded her telephone conversation hurriedly. "Will you please see to that immediately, Ramon? Thank you. I'll be over there later this morning." She hung up and turned to Jann in a lowered voice. "Start shopping for a new security company out of Houston or San Antonio. Keep it quiet. This is scary."

Jann nodded and handed her the key, making a note to herself on an electronic pocket calendar as they entered the vault.

Once inside, Pauline selected a private viewing booth and handed the key to a male vault attendant. "Let's review," she said, quizzing Jann as the young man searched for her lock box. "Who knows about Daddy being gone?"

"Verlin, Evan, Rick and me."

"Good." She suddenly remembered. "There's one more—an army colonel in Israel named Gershon Canaan. He was good to me. I don't expect him to blab anything. But if anyone else seems to know, tell me immediately. That means we've got a leak."

Jann's eyebrows knit with uncharacteristic worry. "If your father's in some kind of trouble," she said, "I can't help thinking it has something to do with that masked man this morning. It shocked me so, to think that someone could get right in our offices like that."

The vault clerk approached with a large safety deposit box. He placed it on a table in front of Pauline. With all of the new excitement about the burglar and the icon sale, she had not allowed herself to think about to why she had even come here. Now the realization hit her with a bundle of anxiety.

"Jann, are you sure you don't know what's in here?" she asked.

Jann shook her head. "I figured it was his business. I had access if he wanted me to know. But he never did."

Pauline sat down. "I need some privacy then, OK?"

"Absolutely. I'll be in the lobby."

Jann shut the booth door, and Pauline stared at the box. Did it contain the "dirt files"? Were these the files the burglar sought? If so, then a power struggle had begun for control of the ministry. Not to mention what the files would say about the character of her father and those who worked with him. *O Lord, please help me*, she prayed.

She opened the box quickly and felt a cold, numbing wave wash over her face. The box contained files. Just files. Nothing but files. She quickly thumbed the titles, recognizing names. Harlan Harris, board member . . . Rev. Maria Cortez, board member . . . Billy Boren—*What? Billy?* She opened his file and saw a grainy black-and-white picture printed with electronic date and time, as if it had come from a home video camera. It showed a hotel room and two men . . . She slammed the file shut, not sure whether to be more angry with Billy for an act of homosexuality, or with her father for harboring the information. Both seemed impossible to imagine. Her stomach groaned within her.

"What is this about?" Her breath began to come in shallow, painful bursts now. "Please don't do this to me, Daddy," she whispered, trembling all over.

Deliberately, protectively, she engaged the dead zone inside of her. Reaching into the box, she pulled out file after file after file, stuffing them determinedly into her open briefcase. As she did, she noticed Evan's name, Danna's and Verlin Stiles's too. And there were others. Some powerful people, some not. All went into her briefcase. Then she slammed it shut, latching it. The lock box was empty.

She stood and leaned against the door of the booth for a

moment, pulling herself together. The entire room seemed to spin. Her world was coming apart at the seams. She would have to deal with this later. At home. Right now she wanted to see Lydia. Managing to get her breathing under control, she turned, and her hand rattled against the door latch when she touched it. Finally opening the door, she found the attendant waiting outside. She handed him the key and the empty lock box, thanked him, and walked briskly out of the vault.

In the lobby Jann held the cellular phone to her ear. "Verlin's on the line," she announced, seeing Pauline.

"Tell him I'll call him back," she snapped, continuing toward the door.

"Honey," Jann urgently rasped, "he's calling an emergency board meeting right under your nose!"

Pauline stopped. So Verlin was going to take advantage? Make a grab for power? Now? She had no time for his pettiness. Returning to the counter, she took the telephone. "Hello," she said curtly.

After a moment of silence, Verlin unloaded. "Pauline, my conscience will not allow me to hold back a minute more. Too much is at stake." He pontificated with enough conviction in his voice to make her want to throw up. "As a member of the board I have no choice but to insist we call an emergency meeting to appoint interim leadership. Lavalle has made an end-run around me, and it is going to send us several million more into the hole. Wait until you see this 'Reverse the Curse' letter. I never authorized it. He says your father authorized it. I say your father needs to show up and account for himself." He paused and asked rhetorically, "Where is he, Pauline? Either I've been fired without notice or this ministry is without a leader. In the meantime the sharks and the vultures are closing in. We have the interests of a ministry to protect here."

Pauline waited quietly for a moment. "You're right, Verlin. But the name on this ministry is Grace, not Stiles. Remember that." The receiver trembled in her grasp as her mind raced. In her briefcase, evidently, were the files her father had used to control this man, and the entire board. As soon as she got over the shock, maybe she'd use them too. Maybe she would be forced to use them in order to carry out her father's wishes.

"OK then, Verlin. Call a board meeting. Just let me know time and place."

Stiles seemed stunned. "You will not oppose it?"

She paused as if uncertain. "Call the meeting. Just don't tell them about Daddy. I'll do that myself. Can you cut me that kind of deal, Verlin?"

"Of course, Pauline. You've got it."

"Thank you."

28

EASTERN TURKEY
Lake Van Airport
8:07 P.M.

In the distance, the snow-draped shoulders of a massive peak glowed in the moonlight. To the immediate left, the gentle lapping of an inland sea wafted a healthy, mineral influence across the night. The sounds of clanking metal, coiling rope, orders and curses in Arabic gave life to the scene as a crew of men unloaded the belly of a chartered 727. The delicate minaret of a mosque silhouetted itself against the stars, rising above the ruins of an ancient citadel beyond the airstrip.

Dressed casually, with light jackets and sweaters for the desert night, Doctors Sutphen, Lester, Santesteban and Osis descended the passenger stairway, making their way silently toward a large cargo helicopter, similar to the one that had evacuated the hospital in Sudan.

After a few minutes Max Commagene came down the stairs, followed by Simon Grace and the psychiatrist Vardan Kassabian. Commagene and Grace each carried slender graphite tubes and wicker fishing creels.

"We'll let the others fly on ahead," Max said. "They'll need a couple days. In the meantime we'll spend the night here, have a nice breakfast, then take the scenic route for old time's sake."

"Past the old fishing hole," Grace added with a toothy smile, saluting the stars with his fly rod.

At the bottom of the stairway they turned in the opposite direction of the other doctors and walked toward a waiting land rover.

29

SAN DIEGO, CALIFORNIA
Montgomery Field
2:14 P.M.

"Spirit I" taxied to a halt beside a stretch limousine and a waiting Wells Fargo armored car. The jet's stairway door opened and Bud Cheney stepped out in a badly wrinkled suit, having worn it days beyond his original plans. He walked unhappily toward the Logos Mail limousine with Evan Grace hard on his heels. Behind them, two security guards stepped from the jet and positioned themselves to either side of the entrance, poised with sawed-off shotguns. They waved off the Wells Fargo crew, which had arrived to take delivery of *The Seven Sleepers of Antioch* for Alan Lavalle.

Entering the Logos Mail limo, Cheney punched a "hot button" on the telephone. It rang once and was answered. "You can have it only after seeing him in person," Cheney said into the receiver. It was obvious that previous negotiations had taken place via the telephone on the plane. He waited, listening to Alan's reply. "Right," Cheney nodded subserviently. "He's acting like a renegade, I agree." He glanced at Evan. "He says you're acting like a renegade." Evan wagged his head humorlessly. Cheney turned back to the telephone. "He says he'll turn the plane around if you don't talk to him in person, boss." He listened to Alan choke with rage on his end of the line. Then he turned and offered the phone to Evan. "He wants to *parley vouz.*"

Evan refused. "Tell him it's in person or nothing."

Cheney put the phone back to his ear. "Did you hear that? Yeah. Right." He hung up. "He says you're a renegade but come on out to the house. He'll have a drink waiting." Bud seemed surprised at the concession, knowing nothing of the icon or its value. "How do you rate anyway? I've never seen the inside of the home place in twelve years with the man."

"My stock went up suddenly," Evan replied. Secretly he was elated. Everything worked on money with Alan. It was the magic key. He turned and gave Rick a thumbs-up signal. Daddy Number

146

Two waved acknowledgment from the cockpit of the jet, and Evan slid into the limo. It pulled away from the idling Falcon, leaving an uneasy standoff between the Wells Fargo armored crew and the Grace security guards.

30

BROWNSVILLE
The Steeple
4:18 P.M.

"Excuse me," Pauline asked, "would you mind giving us some time alone?"

"Not at all," Barry replied. He stood up from the stool beside Lydia's bed where he had been feeding her a bowl of chicken broth, a diet easy on her stomach following the fast. As he walked toward the door, he paused. "Pauline, I'm Barry Malone." He held out his hand in a by-the-way introduction.

"Oh hi, Barry," she said absently, clutching a black briefcase across her chest.

"I called you in Jerusalem, remember?" He could sense her troubled feelings.

"Oh . . . yes." She paused, her mind racing like a computer. "Oh, yes . . . The phone call. Thank you." She reached out and shook his hand briefly.

"Well, as you can see," Barry replied, nodding toward Lydia, "her recovery is remarkable. No trace of scar tissue from the heart attack, or whatever it was. We're all amazed."

"Yes, you told me that."

Barry could see that her thoughts remained troubled. He nodded and smiled to Lydia, continuing out the door.

As soon as the door shut, Pauline moved toward the old woman like a dark cloud. "Don't lie to me, Lydia," she warned.

Lydia was taken completely aback. She had expected to tell Pauline about her supernatural dream, hoping to explore a solution to the riddle of her father's whereabouts. But this—? "Whatever in the world are you talking about?"

"I don't want you to say anything to make me feel good, that's what. I don't want to feel good. I want the truth."

"I don't know what you mean."

Pauline paused, forcing herself to go on. "Is my father a true believer?"

Lydia could see instantly that Pauline was sitting on some disturbing news. Her heart hurt for the girl, but she had no hesitation. "Yes, he is, my dear. Don't you doubt it. He is."

"How *can* he be?" Pauline lamented, tossing her briefcase on the foot of the bed. She turned on her heel and paced with her arms angrily crossed. She wanted to believe that Lydia's faith was real. Needed to believe it. But if her life of prayer gave her no more discernment than this—if she had given her life in prayer for a man who operated in treachery and deceit—how could her faith be credible before God or man?

Lydia watched her, sensing the storm of doubts and fears assailing the young woman, praying inside. *Show me Lord. What is it You want me to say?* She reached out with the first thought to enter her mind. "I don't have to know what you know, Pauline. I always knew your father had feet of clay."

"We're not talking feet of clay here!" Pauline felt her anger exploding. Her face flushed hotly.

The intercessor waited for the emotion to subside, then asked patiently, "Did you expect him to be perfect?"

"I expect him to be a man of God!" Pauline's face now twisted with inner pain. "I expect him to act godly." She choked and whirled away from her. "And apparently he doesn't do that, Lydia. He doesn't do that!"

Lydia answered calmly. "If this is true, then he'll be corrected."

Pauline had no patience for pat answers. "When? What I'm talking about didn't start yesterday. Where is God's correction?"

Lydia held patiently to her own train of thought. "God loves your father, dear. He doesn't let the men He loves get away with sin. I don't know how long it will take, but God is at work." She picked up the electronic controls and powered her bed into a higher position, praying silently for wisdom. "You've learned something terrible, and now you're afraid. Your father may have gone astray. That may be."

Pauline wiped her cheeks angrily.

Lydia pressed on. "Abraham fathered Ishmael out of wedlock, and yet he is called the father of faith. Isaac was a coward, letting his wife go into a harem rather than claim her publicly. Was he a man of God? Jacob lay with a prostitute. The children of Israel sold their own brother Joseph into slavery. Gideon became an idolater. David ordered the murder of Uriah in order to take his wife. Moses had a temper. Peter denied the Lord. Thomas doubted." The old woman looked imploringly at Pauline. "Now, what has your father done?"

Pauline remained silent. She had listened to Lydia's litany of Biblical characters, but had never read this much humanity between the lines of Scripture herself. Hearing it like this seemed strange, and she was in no mood to placate her feelings with such talk. But the old woman *had* reminded her that these things were part of the Biblical record. How did they reflect on her father's manipulations? Did they justify them? *No! Then how did they apply?* "You make it sound as though God goes around looking for jerks to do His work."

Lydia shrugged. "I never thought of it that way." A small, knowing smile crept across her face as she watched the young woman struggle with an element of truth in this statement.

It did not amuse Pauline. She loved her father, and felt resentment growing against God or anyone else who would elevate moral weakness. Or leave it unpunished. *Why does the old woman act so superior?* she wondered. *This is repulsive.* "We are talking about my father," she said. "I never wanted to think of him as one of God's . . . *jerks.* At least I didn't think of him that way until . . . I never wanted to . . ." Her thoughts circled hopelessly, trapped, with no decent exit from her knowledge of the "dirt files." How could she vindicate her father's motives ever again? How could she salvage the pride she had once felt for the man?

Lydia sensed this loss immediately and fed the vacuum from her own understanding, speaking sarcastically. "When Jesus walked the earth, honey, He said, 'I have only chosen the people who are good enough to serve me.' Right?"

Pauline sent a sharp look in her direction for this obvious misquote.

"Why have you never understood?" Lydia went on. "Christ said, 'I came not to call the righteous but sinners to repentance.' What kind of disciples did He choose, Pauline? Listen to me. Did He pick from the educated? The scribes and Pharisees? The theologians of his day? Or the Sanhedrin? The rich? The powerful? If he had done that, He would never have been crucified. He would have acknowledged the systems of religion and government and found a home in them. But no. He chose fishermen, tax collectors, doubters . . . a fanatical zealot, a traitor. Somewhere the Bible says, 'He has chosen the things that are not, to bring to naught the things that are.' God makes no peace with the world, dear, even when it offers Him its very best. What did the apostle say? 'When I am weak, then I am strong.' God's strength is made perfect in weakness, Pauline."

These thoughts did not set well under the circumstances. She had not come to Lydia to learn that her father's treachery was OK. And yet, that was not exactly what the old woman was saying. "I'm sorry, Lydia, I don't think I even *like* God tonight." Immediately she felt shocked at what had come out of her mouth.

"That's alright," Lydia responded. "He likes you. But be careful what you say in your heart, honey." The smile was gone from her face now. "Young lady, one day you are going to look in the mirror and see your*self* for the very first time. And on that day, believe me, you are going to need a God who favors weakness."

The air in the room seemed to grow icy. Pauline could almost feel the disapproval of the Almighty, cutting her off from the warmth of His Presence. God suddenly seemed like a stranger to her. It was a strong feeling. She had never in her life entered such a moment. In response to its cold threat, she shivered and felt a fountain of feeling welling up deep in her soul. She was not even sure the feeling belonged to her. It surged powerfully upward. She didn't understand it, but felt herself breaking in response to Lydia's words—against her own desire to do so. The emotions twisted at her face and filled her eyes with stinging tears. She fought them.

"I've seen your father, Pauline. I've seen him in a dream sent by the Spirit of God. Something like I've never known. I don't know why, but I've seen him bound by something in spiritual places, honey. He needs our help. Our prayers. I don't know what binds him, but he's terribly bound. In some sense it's demonic."

Pauline wiped furiously at her eyes. "He's bound alright." Her mind raced ahead to the pressing demands of the coming board meeting even now being summoned by Verlin Stiles. And to the stack of files that would soon tell her their dirty secrets. She retrieved her briefcase from the foot of the bed and started for the door. "I'm afraid he's more than bound." She paused in the middle of the floor, choking on still-hot emotion. "I can't pray, Lydia. Not now." She moved toward the door again with her load of "dirt files." "Will you pray for me? Please?" She opened the door and whispered, "Pray like you've never prayed."

"I will pray, honey," Lydia promised.

But Pauline had already gone.

31

SAN DIEGO
La Jolla Heights
3:42 P.M.

Escorted by two deceptively short men who moved on either side of him with the reserved step of martial arts experts, Evan entered the home of Alan Lavalle. The bodyguards were not only physically subtle, they dressed deceptively as well, in friendly sport coat and tie. But the nature of their calling could not be called "friendly" and he knew better than to mistake them for gentlemen. He felt his own muscles flexing beneath his stride, and was glad for his regular workouts at the Dallas gym. He was no match for these two, but if it came to a fight he wanted to at least inflict his share of damage.

As they left the entryway behind, the California ranch house seemed to open and deepen like a giant oyster shell reaching down toward the sea. At the lower cliffside, he could see through the windows a lush carpet of clinging ice plants and shrubs. What had appeared to be a modest one-story home from the crest of the road turned out to be two stories of luxury above the aqua-blue breakers of La Jolla Cove.

Alan and Dorothy waited together for him in a skylit den between an arbored breakfast nook and a formal sitting room. An ocean-front deck bordered the entire area. As he entered, Alan and Dorothy projected a casual confidence, appearing tan and successful. Alan wore blue canvas shoes, beachcomber pants and a boat-necked shirt. He sipped a Mai Tai. Dorothy wore a figure-complimenting white cotton dress with turquoise sandals.

"Evangel!" Seeing him, Alan leaped up, opening his arms expansively. He walked forward and hugged him.

For a moment Evan grew distracted by the respectful use of his full name. He and Alan had worked together more than a decade ago, and a reserve of affection remained strangely alive. But it was a loose end Evan knew he must cover. He reminded himself that he was dealing with an evil genius.

Dorothy held forward a tray with a mixed drink.

"No thank you, Dorothy. This won't be a social visit." He turned and glared at Alan. "I came to talk with you alone."

Alan's expression fell.

"Now."

He placed his drink down soberly. "Now, son, you need to polish your approach just a little. You're in my house."

Evan pulled up his watch. "The icon is on the jet. Rick has orders to leave with or without me in ten minutes unless I place a call to a security number in the plane. We don't have time for small talk now, do we?"

Alan sighed and looked at his two muscle men. "You guys take a walk. We're fine here."

They glanced at Dorothy, cross-checking the order. Upon her nod, they stepped tentatively out of the room.

Alan said, "OK, talk."

"Sorry, Dorothy," Evan replied without looking at her.

"She hears everything I hear," Alan protested.

"Not this time."

"I told you, your approach is nasty," he replied. He turned abruptly and crossed to the sliding glass doors, unlatching them. He slid them open and went onto the redwood deck.

Evan followed, knowing that the threatened loss of a commission on a forty million dollar icon sale was all that opened this door. Not goodwill. Not friendship of any stripe.

As the Pacific breeze hit his face, he felt a rush of dangerous anger seethe up in his gut. It raged recklessly, beyond caring about the consequences. The core of it had been building for years. Beginning with his first shocking view of Alan's warehouse full of Rolls Royces. At the time he had naively considered Alan a true minister of the gospel. It had continued with the discovery of the man's manipulative influence over his own father. The anger had been enlarged by seeing the unchecked cocaine use on the Logos staff when he had worked there. Not to mention the accounting irregularities. It had expanded when he had learned how Cheney had cynically recruited Dorothy for Alan from a nationwide inventory of call girls. Yet Alan, the sleaze, had continued to pull off his self-appointed apostleship role to the tune of millions. The topper had been his use of the "dirt files" to get rid of Evan, implicating Danna, his own daughter, in the process. This after Evan had uncovered a suspicious pattern of accounting irregularities. His early naiveté had been more than assaulted by this man. It had been brutalized. And any minute now he would be finding an excuse to let it all come back on Alan's head.

As he crossed the deck, he talked himself into holding the explosion inside just a little longer, until he could lure the vermin into a trap.

At the railing he leaned over. Twenty stories below, the rock-lined shore of the Pacific whispered up to him like a promising storm. He spoke in a deliberately lowered voice. "Alan, where is my dad?"

"I'm sorry?" Alan moved closer, straining to hear. "What?"

"I asked you, 'where is—my dad?"

"Where's your dad?" He paused as if hearing it for the first time. "You mean he's missing?"

Evan smashed his fist against Alan's lips. The blow sent the man sprawling backward, blood running from the corner of his mouth, but Evan didn't pause. With fury he followed the blow by lifting the man by the shirt, twisting and bending him quickly over the edge of the deck railing. He could hear Dorothy calling for help in the house behind him. With blinding fury mounting even higher in his heart, he wedged his leg beneath Alan's own kicking legs, hoisting him over the edge.

Alan screamed with sudden terror, falling free of the railing. Now he dangled over the rocks. Evan held him by the lapels of his thin cotton shirt. The lapels began to rip. Alan struggled for his life, clinging desperately to Evan's wrists. "Don't do this! Please don't!"

"I'll kill you," Evan heard himself growl, his own voice so full of hatred he didn't recognize the sound of it. He panted and strained to hold to the shirt. "Where's my dad?"

"I swear I don't know," Alan pled. His body flopped as his legs sought a foothold in vain. Looking up at Evan, his only link to life, he said, "Please! I didn't know your dad was missing. Nothing. I swear to God!"

Evan heard footsteps running onto the deck behind him. "Tell them to get back."

"Go!" Alan rasped. "Go back in. Just do it!" he screamed.

Evan turned to watch as slowly the two bodyguards stepped backwards off the deck and into the house.

"Shut the door," he barked.

Dorothy came to the door and called in a clear contralto, "Honey, are you sure you want this?"

She's a cool one, Evan thought.

"Yes, baby, I want this," Alan choked, his eyes bulging with terror.

"You drop him, Evan," Dorothy promised, "and I'll drop you."

"Shut the door," Alan screeched. "He means it."

She slowly slid the glass shut and stood inside, watching, waiting.

"Alright, where *is* Dad?" Evan continued.

Alan spilled his guts. "I wish I knew. I thought he was in Jerusalem. Brownsville. I don't even know. We're talking about a friend of mine here, Evan. You know that."

"Four days ago . . ." Evan studied Alan's face as he talked, "he disappeared in Jerusalem."

"OK. I got a strange call this morning from Verlin. The Old Man authorized my letter over his head, and Stiles didn't know about it until this morning. Maybe it has something to do with all this."

"How'd you get the letter authorized?"

"Your dad sent word from Jerusalem."

"How do you know it was him?" Evan's arms burned like fire, but he suddenly pushed the man further over the edge.

"Ahhhh!" Alan screamed. "It had to be him. He paid for the mailing in advance. Three hundred and seventy five thousand dollars. He's never done that before. Don't drop me, Evan, please! Please! Let's talk like normal people. I'll look into it for you," he begged. "I'll trace the money. Whatever you want."

"Who's buying the icon for forty million?"

Alan smiled weakly. "OK. OK. Here's what I know. A Swiss bank account number, and that's it. I'll give it to you."

"You're a funny guy."

He nodded. "I could retire on this deal. I don't know how your dad put it together. It's monstrous."

"I want you to make me a promise."

"You got it."

"It's not what you think. I want you to use everything you've got to find out who's behind that Swiss account and tell me as soon as you learn. Will you?"

"Cross my heart. I'll be on it in an hour."

"If you mess around with me on this, I'll see to it that you go out of business for good. I'm sitting on the exposé about you that no one else can write. And you know it."

"I know it. I know it."

Evan was partly bluffing. His evidence in the *Texas People* story was all circumstantial.

"I won't mess with you," Alan promised.

In that moment Evan learned something new about himself. He learned that he could not kill Alan. As intense as his anger had been, it would be satisfied with justice, not vengeance. He actually pitied the scum. "OK, let's get you up."

Heaving upward, Evan could not budge the man. The muscles of both of his arms had become hopelessly cramped and locked. He strained again but could not move him. He began to laugh crazily. "I can't get you up."

"Sure—of course you can," Alan whined.

"I'm telling you my workout's not working out here."

"Evan!"

Alan slipped farther.

"Help!" Evan hollered, looking back over his shoulder.

The door slammed open, and the two bodyguards rushed to the aid of their boss. Dorothy came close behind. Reaching over the railing they grasped him by each arm.

As soon as they had secured a firm grip, Evan let go and backpedaled toward the house. His hands were cramped half-closed from the effort of holding Alan. "Thanks, guys," he said, sliding the glass doors shut and locking them onto the deck.

"I'll get you, wimp!" screamed one of the bodyguards over his shoulder, still pulling Alan toward the railing top.

Evan sprinted through the giant oyster-shell house, back toward its modest entrance. A yellow cab waited for him there. Rick had timed the cab call perfectly. *Way to go, Daddy Number Two.*

32

BROWNSVILLE
Dr. Grace's Studio
9:01 P.M.

Pauline's eyes stared straight ahead, puffy and red-rimmed. Nothing remained of her makeup. Nor did it matter. Her nose was swollen, her face flushed and chafed from the use of too many tissues. They lay in sodden piles on the table. Others had fallen to the floor around her shoeless feet.

She sat alone in her father's studio at one end of the long meeting table. The floodlit Steeple could be seen through the tall windows, glowing in the distance. To either side of the table, posters of healing crusades watched her. Mocking her in her distress. The truth lay before her on the table. File after file. Pictures, names, dates, innuendo, investigations in progress. Mean trump cards in the game of religious power.

For the past four hours she had learned more about these people than she had ever wanted to know. Why had her father stayed in the faith, knowing what he had known all these years? Evan had said, "He places men in power for their well-documented weaknesses." Now she understood. She could see why Stiles held the vice presidency, why the board consisted of its current members. Weaknesses, well-documented.

She wondered how long her father had used information like this. What had brought him so low? Were all ministry power structures sheltering sicknesses like these? Who could be trusted? *No one!* Especially not Simon Grace, the one man in her life who had stood next to God Himself.

For all of her life she had heard that being "born again" meant "old things passed away, all things became new." Why then did so many sins of the flesh still cling to the private lives of God's people? *Nothing has changed,* she lamented. *Nothing is new. They might as well be honest unbelievers. Faith is only for naive fools like me!*

She knew that true Christianity could be entered only by "new birth." This was a freely offered and freely accepted gift—to become a child of God. So simple, yet impossible to grasp without

156

the illumination of the Spirit. She understood also that most Christian nations, societies and traditions were merely cultural. Not reborn. They remained bereft of the true Spirit of Christ. She knew that so-called "Christian" factions killed each other in Lebanon and Northern Ireland. Armenian terrorists had taken innocent lives in attempts to gain attention for their "Christian" cause. To her evangelical Protestant way of thinking, ecumenical, Catholic, Orthodox, Apostolic and "modernist" bureaucracies, full of pomp and decaying traditions, were religious "clouds without water."

But her own father's ministry had always seemed different to her. She had seen it as part of the "remnant" of true denominations still advocating the "born again" experience plus nothing. No tradition was held above the regenerating work of the Spirit. Now Grace Ministries too took its place among the other hollow religions. With anger she grasped the notion that no organization could contain the real thing. The true Spirit would burst them apart like old wineskins. At their very best, they were never more than what Christ called them: "whitened sepulchres, full of dead men's bones." There was none righteous. No, not one.

Her shoulders began to shake. Slowly she lowered her face to the table for the third time that evening. "Oh, Daddy," she cried, and the sobbing thinned to a whisper. "How could you do this to me?"

33

SAN DIEGO
Montgomery Field
5:24 P.M.

The sun appeared well along on its nightly race to the Pacific horizon as the Wells Fargo armored car pulled away from "Spirit I." The icon crate having been securely exchanged, Evan and Rick shared a seat on the narrow stairway of the jet, quietly watching.

Pulling a longnecked beer from a sixpack under his arm, Evan unscrewed the top. The knuckles of his right hand wore a bandage.

"Excuse me there, Daddy Number Two," he quipped. "I know you can't drink and drive, but I'm going to have one on the way home myself. It's been that kind of a day."

"So who'd you hit?"

Evan laughed. "Someone I've wanted to hit for fifteen years."

"You hit *him*? You actually hit Lavalle and he didn't have your legs broke?"

"Hey, there's still time."

They chuckled, then grew quiet. Rick suddenly looked back at him sideways. "Why do I get the funny feeling . . .?"

Evan stood up, slapping his friend's shoulder. "'Cause Connie's told you too much about me, that's why. What say we go on home before the fireworks start?"

Rick looked at him sharply. "Spill it. What fireworks?"

Evan remained evasive. "I can't trust Alan, the old snake . . . you know? I don't believe a thing he tells me even when his life is hanging by a thread." He took another sip of beer. "You know that armored truck that just pulled out of here?"

Rick nodded ominously.

"There's no icon in that crate."

Rick understood the dire implications in that statement. He stood abruptly. "What do you say we haul on outa here?"

"Sounds about right to me," Evan grinned. They hurried up the steps of the Falcon.

Evan pulled up and secured the air-stair as Rick activated the cockpit. Spooling up the jets to minimum RPM, the pilot added fuel, and the tail-mounted Garretts roared to life. As he shoved forward on the throttle the white bird raxied promptly away from the terminal. He finished a quick-turnaround checklist as they moved toward the runway.

V

THE RESPONSE DEVICE

*. . . handkerchiefs or aprons were even carried
from [Paul's] body to the sick, and
the diseases left them and the evil spirits went out.*

(ACTS 19:12, NASB)

34

EASTERN TURKEY
VAN
Municipal Garden Cafe
6:52 A.M.

The rooftop held a dozen empty tables in the half-light. Grace and Maximilian, wearing khaki fatigues, sat facing northward above the wakening village. The orb of sun broke the horizon to their right, painting the desert with a Midas touch. The glow of dust particles in the air wrapped a golden halo around the ruined citadel of Van Kalesi, its crumbling walls and broken parapets jutting into the sky beside the inland sea.

"Memories," Max said fondly, indicating the Urartian ruin on the shore. He leaned confidentially closer to Grace. "Frankly, I didn't know grave robbing from archaeology in the 50s, but with the Turks in charge, who cared? The stuff I pulled out of this land! Figurines, sphinxes, gryphons by the dozen, huge brass caldrons for the blood of sacrificial bulls. The Urartians took baths in those rituals, you know? Blood showers actually." He pointed to the crumbling earthen walls of the distant fortress. "There's a chamber up there to this day where you can trace the blood channel in the solid stone floor. Ah well," he looked around. "Uncle Otto was here in the First War. He told me I'd find it that way. Said the Young Turks didn't value anything that wasn't Muslim. Until recently he was right." He chuckled imperiously. "Which left a wonderful field of artifacts to me."

Grace thoughtfully sipped a cup of hot tea and boiled goat's milk. "The Western World has forgotten this land. All the churches are in ruins. No Christians."

Max cleared his throat nervously. "Of course, that's the sad story. The Christian Armenians. And a delicate one to tell in these parts. In fact, keeping it quiet is part of the tightrope we walk in the Common Market. It's the same in the good old U.S. of A. You've got twenty-odd military bases here. You have to be careful. Vardan will tell you a million and a half Armenians were exterminated at the turn of the century. Other estimates go as high as two

161

million. The Turks claim that it was merely a wartime deportation. That's why they all disappeared."

Grace snorted with derision. "I've seen the extermination orders. Telegrams from the Triumvirate."

"Now be careful. A lot of people feel that some of those have been manufactured and blown out of proportion."

Grace chuckled. "Yeah. The Holocaust never happened. The Allies made up the stories of Auschwitz, too."

"OK. No one denies that certain unfortunate—"

"—massacres."

"—OK, massacres took place along the evacuation route. It couldn't be helped with the long-standing hostilities between the populations.

"In Vardan's village, he says they herded the children to the city square and hacked off their hands.

"I am aware of this as much as the next man. I know that a certain amount of cover-up happened. Here in Van the locals say the Armenians burned their own section of the city."

"I suppose they deported themselves, too?"

Max's fingers drummed the tabletop. "The atrocities can't be denied. I told you Uncle Otto brought out pictures, didn't I? Pretty disturbing. I've seen an entire wall of decapitations. Rows of gallows."

"Now you're talking." Grace never failed to feel the weight of atrocity when visiting this remote region of Turkey. Once the capital of Christian Armenia, it had become the forgotten genocide of World War I. He also privately reflected on the German alliance in the deed. *So Max's uncle Otto was here,* he noted. That was something to be remembered about the privileged Commagene name.

Max glanced around to see if they had been overheard. "We should change the subject." He said, and pointed to a caved-in shoulder of the fortress wall. "Once, right up there by the mosque, I unearthed two ceremonial bull heads. Urartian. Magnificent things, cast of bronze. They are now in a London Museum."

A waiter wearing a black wool fez approached them with a tray of inlaid tile. He set it down and served bread and goat's cheese for three places at the table. Max quickly peeled a generous wad of *lira* into the man's hand. The waiter's eyes glowed and he thanked him, backing away.

Grace sipped his cup of aromatic tea. "It's been years, Max, but the flavors of this land have never left me. The smells. In every building there's a hint of frankincense. Have you noticed?"

Max chuckled. "And *hashish*. Breakfast of boiled goat's milk and *otlupenynir*? It only tastes this way when you're out here in the land of Urartu."

"True enough," Grace agreed, ladling a piece of spring bread with herbed cheese. "I don't know. It might go over as an appetizer at The Fajita Kitchen in Brownsville." He shuttled the mixture beneath his nose. "Where else on earth can you can taste the caraway of Eden and the dry sage of Ararat in the same mouthful?" He chewed and savored it, leaning back to take in the view in the early-morning air. "In many ways, you know, this is more the land of the Bible than the Holy Land."

Max listened, busying himself with his own breakfast.

"Think about it. It's the land of Genesis, not to mention all seven churches of Revelation. The bookends of time are here. Nothing but ruins now. The source of the Tigris and Euphrates. Eden. The great Flood. The Ark is still locked up there in the snows of Ararat. It's really there. I've heard the stories of those who have seen it. Reliable stories. You've got the ancient Urartian culture and the Armenians tracing their ancestry from Noah. It's a rich, rich land, and we can only hope the Turks learn to appreciate its values for the sake of the whole world."

"I think they have," Max commented, speaking around a mouthful of cheese-laden bread.

Dr. Grace paused before continuing. "Antiochus IV plotted the abomination of the Temple from here." His eyes darted furtively above his cup. "Maybe the Turks can appreciate that."

"Be nice, my friend," Max cautioned with an uneasy smile. "Dunamis has expensively courted this relationship."

"Who can hear?" Grace paused for another sip of tea and crossed his legs, leaning back in the rooftop chair. "To the south, Antioch, where the disciples were first called 'Christians.' The Armenian Patriarch is called the Bishop of Antioch to this day. Credit that to this land. Paul's missionary journeys were here. Bartholomew and Thaddeus were martyred on this soil. This is where the chalice of the Last Supper was found. The Holy Grail. It's the land of *The Seven Sleepers* icon. In fact, the Cult of Icons began here." He leaned forward intensely. "The first and second Nicene Councils took place in this land. The *Nicene Creed*, for heaven's sake! It was born here! This land is part and parcel with

Judeo-Christian history, but there is scarcely a Jew or Christian here today." He looked into the distance. Their history has become merely a distant echo."

"Would you like me to write that down?" Max grinned disarmingly and shook his head. "Look at the up side. Because of the Turks, it's relatively unspoiled by tourism."

"Not for long."

"True enough." Max shifted soberly. "That's the only thing I regret about what we're doing here. If we're successful, there'll be a Hilton Hotel and a golf course on the shores of Lake Van next year. I've already heard the Turks are planning a Hotel Zeus at the foot of Nimrut Dag. The glory days are gone, doc. I guess I should let 'em go."

They both paused, listening to a crier calling the faithful to prayer from the minaret of Van Kalesi. Suddenly remembering something, Max pulled a polished agate cross from his shirt. He handed it to Grace. "By the way, here's that specimen you wanted. A courier brought it to the room this morning."

Grace took the quarter-sized cross and turned it in his palm, showing displeasure. It was a shining Christian charm suitable for a necklace or bracelet. "It's nice, but we want the unpolished version."

Max shrugged. "I liked this one. I had to try."

"My people will go for the *texture* of Eden on this deal," Grace explained, rubbing his fingertips together. "Don't make it fancy. Make it rough."

"You told me that." Max pulled a small carton from his shirt and dumped out several unpolished samples. The crystallized fibers of wood still retained their rough texture.

"That's more like it," Grace said. "What's the cost?"

"Without polish? Pennies."

"That's all you need." He picked out an unpolished version and held it up to the morning sun. "If I know anything at all, this device will bring the greatest single mail response of my life. When I tell my partners what it is, and what we're doing here, well, Katie, bar the door. The numbers get astronomical. They will be praying for me and wearing these things around their necks as a reminder of what we are doing here."

"I thought they'd like the pretty one," Max said, still mystified by the preacher's logic. He gathered the samples apologetically. "Guess I'll have to leave the mail business to you."

The Armenian psychiatrist, Vardan Kassabian, walked nervously across the rooftop to join them, taking the third seat at the table. He was disguised as an Arab, wearing a turban and dark glasses. The preacher did a double take, but then quickly understood. He had almost forgotten the Russian's special problem, the telltale suffix of his name, Kassabian. His ancestors had been easily rounded up and deported by the Turks, identified by the Armenian suffixes of their names, ending in either *i-a-n, j-a-n,* or *y-a-n.*

Max whispered. "*Perestroika* got him out of Yerevan, but it's still death to be Armenian in these hinterlands."

35

BROWNSVILLE
Grace Hospital
7:58 A.M.

The workday had not officially begun, but Danna Lavalle had been at it for hours, working at the computer terminal in Neva's administration office. Soft red tresses fell to her well-postured shoulders. Bangs had been trimmed across the front, giving her a younger appearance than her twenty-nine years. Her eyes were wide and sky-blue, above pretty cheekbones, framing a face that could switch between sweet, girlish innocence and smoldering wit. Except for the red hair, little else identified the young woman as Alan Lavalle's daughter. And at first glance one would never suspect the marriage-wrecking passion that had burned between her and Evan Grace.

At the moment her eyes appeared dark with concentration as she watched the screen of Neva Sylvan's personal computer. Calling up a private window of information, she simultaneously fed an accounting document to a printer across the room. It continued to pour out page after page from its paper guide. But the commotion had only been raised as a smoke screen. Danna ignored it. Her deep concentration focused on the private window, in which she transcribed data to an auxiliary disk-drive sitting near the keyboard:

". . . *Cure Phase I, NDE critical report, date code N: Juba 39 @ home; 16 similarities; 23 anomalies. Juba 39 @ tree; 39 similarities; 2 anomalies. Emotional side effects, total disable. Conclusion: Target similarities, begin Cure Phase II.*"

The office door opened suddenly and Neva entered, dressed in an olive-green suit with black military-style piping. With the deft stroke of a key Danna made the private window vanish from the screen, and a red light indicated the recording activity of the auxiliary disk drive.

"Morning, Neva," she greeted with a lilt to her voice, all sweet-smiling innocence.

"Morning," Neva returned. She seemed preoccupied, but then she stopped short and looked at her again.

Behind Danna's clear blue eyes a curtain dropped. Subtly she lost the easy friendliness, calculating the odds of discovery like a bridge player watching an opposing player's lead. It was a moment of possible revelation to the employer, if she understood what she saw. Or suspected.

"Whatever are you doing here?" Neva asked. "I mean, it's so early."

"Getting you ready for an emergency board meeting," Danna returned, letting her voice work for her now, full of earnestness and believable weariness. She gestured toward the busy printer. "You were out when Stiles called yesterday. They're flying to D/FW day after tomorrow. Thought you might want to look over these status reports before you go."

"Oh. Well, aren't you thoughtful?" Neva remained puzzled. She looked at the printer. "Too bad I won't be able to make it." She picked up her purse and continued into her inner office.

"Oh, I'm sorry. Well, they will need these reports anyway," Danna said. "I hope I did you some good."

"Rest assured, dear, you did. Thank you, really."

Danna's nostrils flared ever so slightly as she slipped the unlabeled floppy disk from its auxiliary drive into her purse. In the same motion she removed a mirrored compact and tube of lipstick, sat down and began to paint her ample lips.

36
STILE'S OFFICE
3:18 P.M.

The intercom buzzed on Verlin's desk. He sheafed through a series of papers, removed his reading glasses and touched the speaker button. "Yes, Myra."

"A call from Pauline," his secretary replied.

"Thank you." He watched the blinking line with weariness for a moment, then aggressively cleared his throat and picked it up. "Pauline, what can I do for you?"

She took a moment to reply, and when she did her voice trembled. "Verlin, I have to ask you something, and you need to be honest with me."

What is this? "Of course." His eyes darted around the work space as his mind raced.

"Did my daddy know something about you that you wouldn't want to see in the newspaper tomorrow?" She said it as if pushing each word reluctantly from her mouth.

Both remained quiet in the wake of it.

She pushed on. "The reason I asked is, well . . . I didn't intend to find it, but I found a file of information. Evan has it now."

An involuntary moan grunted between Stiles's suddenly clenched teeth. His face had drained of color.

"Don't worry. He won't publish anything unless I release him, and I don't have any plans to do that. OK, Verlin?"

"OK. That's good." He wiped beads of perspiration from his forehead. *Game, set, match.*

"I'm sorry, Verlin, but I need to find my father, see? And I really want you with me, helping me all the way. We don't know what Daddy's up to, and I'm not ready to turn it over to the police, or to the board, or anyone else. You can understand that, can't you? He's my father." She was almost pleading with him.

"Yes, of course. Perfectly." His voice had become monotone.

"I need to have the ministry board behind me so I can do that. So I can keep looking for him. I need your help, Verlin. Can I count on it?"

He paused only briefly. "I'm sure you can."

"About the board meeting—I think what would be best is if you would nominate me as interim president of Grace Ministries until Daddy returns from his desert trip."

Verlin's eyes widened, not believing her gall. "The board is going to ask questions. Can you handle them?"

"I don't know. Will you help me, Verlin?" She waited for his answer.

He remained quiet for a while, his mind churning through a thousand ways to scuttle her plan. She was a novice at this game. He was not.

She exploded, "Verlin Stiles, I'm not bluffing! I'll do what I have to do. Are you behind me?"

"Of course," he replied earnestly. "I was just—"

"Thank you so much."

Some novice. Verlin hung up and immediately got up from his chair. Snatching his jacket from a coatrack, he walked out of the office.

"I'm out of touch indefinitely," he said to Myra as he passed her desk.

Her eyes followed him out with a worried expression, knowing something had gone wrong. Beyond that, she hadn't a clue.

37

DR. GRACE'S STUDIO
3:24 P.M.

Hands shoved deep in his pockets, Evan walked slowly past the icon shipping case in the loft of his father's studio. He stepped down into the meeting room and walked along the paper-strewn table toward the tall picture windows. As he did so, his sister gagged and coughed in an adjacent bathroom. He stopped and listened, not sure how much of this kind of stress she could handle. She had always seemed so strong. The straight-shooting member of the family. Now he grew worried that what had seemed to be strength was merely inflexibility. Could she bend now without breaking? As if to answer him, the toilet flushed for the third time in five minutes as her stomach emptied its contents yet again. Obviously she needed her brother to carry this load.

"Let *me* play the bad guy from now on!" he yelled through the wall. "It's just not your style. And there's nothing wrong with that. Do you understand me?"

He waited for a reply but heard none. Knowing she had heard him anyway, he moved on toward the window.

Below the terraced gardens a regular rhythmic movement caught his eye. A flash of blonde, back and forth like a happy streamer in the air. Jilly flew high on her swing set in the latía-enclosed yard he had built himself a decade before. Now the weathered mesquite latía poles hosted a riot of climbing honeysuckle.

Rick stood behind Jilly in the yard, maintaining her momentum on the swing. Evan could almost hear her carefree giggle, ringing like the song of a skylark. Connie stood nearby. Evan was never completely ready for this sight. He lectured himself that it was past time for accepting their happiness together. In a moment he smiled again, feeling a familiar warmth. He was truly happy for the three of them. *In love and divorce, a man really can't ask for more than that*, he mused.

A whispered step on the carpet behind him told him that Pauline had returned to the ugly business at hand. This was no time to indulge his own pain. He turned back to the table. Her face was a mask of determination as she plopped down a glass of water and picked up the legal pad she had been using to make notes.

Inside she ached. Outside her skin crawled for the way she had cornered Stiles with his sordid past. Just as her father had done many times, no doubt. But she had acted from a better motive than he, hadn't she? Then why did she still feel so rotten? All she wanted to do was to get her father back, let him answer for his own ministry. Then she would abandon such tactics forever. She promised herself that she would.

She cleared her throat. Then another time, loudly. Then she took a sip of water. "Alright," she said, looking at a list of eight names on the page, "Stiles is done. That leaves seven. I need at least four more votes."

Evan picked up his own pad, watching her reaction carefully as he spoke. "Forget Sharpey. He'll vote his conscience."

She sighed and dropped her pad. "Dear God, I wish they were all like him."

"Oh, you do?" Evan fought a simmering anger at her indulgence in a stupid wish. It didn't even approach the mark of a true conviction. She probably didn't know the difference. *All these "Holy Joe" types*, he thought disgustedly. *They're self-righteous until they have to get their hands dirty, then they want to check into a "nicer" world.* It made him want to get back to *Texas People* where at least he understood the rules.

He pulled together what remained of his patience and replied, "Any more Chester Sharpeys around here and you and I, and Dad, are history. So why don't we just quit complaining and play with the hand we're dealt?"

She resented his superior tone of voice. "I don't like your card game analogy."

"So what?" He glared at her. "It works. We didn't deal the hand. Now let's just do what we have to do, for heaven's sake." He picked up his checklist. "What do you know about the hospital lady, Neva Sylvan? There's no file on her."

Pauline pictured Neva in her mind. She seemed friendly enough. Competent. Pleasant. "Let me just talk to her, heart to heart. I'll ask her outright for her vote. I need to talk with her anyway about the icon. She heard from Dad on it."

"Good. But to be safe, let's not count on her vote." He hiked a leg into the seat of one of the heavy leather chairs. "Now for the rest of the board. Harlan Harris, the Chevrolet-dealer-from-God, is obviously a prolific adulterer. Maria Cortez is on his list."

"What does she see in him?" Pauline immediately checked herself. "What am I saying? Sin is sin."

"The arrangement works out in our favor—two birds with one stone, so to speak." He checked Harlan Harris and Maria Cortez as votes they could count on. "Now, Peter Avanzini—there is the surprise for me. Building contractor from the blissful resort of Carefree, Arizona. He's the one who set up a money laundering scheme through Logos Mail years ago. Mysterious donors, shall we say, send cash in the form of large donations." He paused. "I smelled *all* this when I worked for Alan." He swallowed disgustedly, remembering that it had been the *real* reason his sin with Danna had been used to defrock him. "So anyway, Avanzini, who owned the printing company for Alan's mail contracts, overcharged to retrieve the 'special donations.'" Evan threw his clipboard to the table. "That, dear sister, is what I couldn't quite prove back in 1979 when Alan and Dad pulled my file. Excuse me, but that's when I lost all respect for Dad."

A solid weight in Pauline's stomach sympathized with the pain in Evan's voice. Somehow, against her better judgment, she began to understand this black-sheep brother of hers. *And* his outrageous behavior. Who could survive the destruction of family and faith in the same blow? She wasn't sure she could. "That's why I'm agreeing to go ahead with this," she explained tiredly. "It just seems purely evil to me."

"Thank you." In that moment Evan realized that he really wanted her approval more than he let himself believe. "You know, what I have always wanted to know is why Dad allowed Alan to pull my file. It made it seem as if Dad had something to hide too."

Pauline honestly searched her own soul. Why *would* her father expose his son? He merely held the files over the heads of the others like a sword of Damocles. Was he a complete user? She tried to imagine his reasoning, but could only come up with her own. "You *did* commit adultery, Evan. You kind of did that to yourself."

A cold fear knifed through his heart. *She can make me feel that she's almost human, and then—bam!*

"What I mean," Pauline continued, sensing his vulnerability, "all these other sinners don't excuse *you*. You have to deal with yourself before God. That much is still true."

"That seems completely beside the point for the moment," he replied coldly. Once again Evan reminded himself, *Beware of her hidden agendas*. He could not trust even her expressions of sympathy. "Moving right along," he continued, "finally, there's Reverend Cecil Dewey, pastor of Kingsway Cathedral, Sturgis, Arkansas. Addicted to uppers and downers. Harlan Harris, with the sensitive nose for sexual misconduct, walked in on him during a homosexual encounter." Evan dropped the legal pad to the table. "He's now in counseling and we wish him all the best." He paused. "Unless, of course, he decides to vote against us. And there is your fourth vote."

He finished and walked to the window again. The yard swing below the gardens moved listlessly in the breeze. Empty. "You know what I think, Pauline? It's easier on Wall Street than it is in the ministry. Out there, money is the bottom line and everyone knows it. You can understand that kind of ambition. But in the ministry you've got the same stinking ambition wearing all these robes of righteousness. I mean, they can believe they're doing God a favor when they cut your legs off. Do you know what I mean?"

She was thoughtful for a time. "Are we any different?"

He turned around to face her. "Yes, we are. We are cutting their legs off with no pretensions of morality whatsoever. We do it simply to gain control of this ministry so we can use the resources to find Dad."

"Feels the same to me," she replied glumly.

"Well, it's not for me." He began to pace. "Now, think about this situation for a minute. Think about Dad, a young preacher who maybe one day really cared about the Christian way of doing things. He gets knifed and undermined by all these self-righteous types quoting the Scripture in order to tie his hands. After a while he sees that they only want to control him. To hold him down. It's jealous ambition masquerading in a pulpit committee."

He looked up at the picture gallery. "So, maybe he sees all their ploys as keeping him from laying hands on the sick, see? They are wasting his energies in mounds of red tape while millions of souls are waiting for the gospel. The committees keep inventing more religious red tape. Then one day he discovers the big hypocrisy factor. He discovers that very few of those who tied his hands had clean hands of their own. He asks himself, 'Why should I go on taking this self-righteous garbage?'"

"He wouldn't say that."

"Maybe not quite like I would." He turned to Pauline. "But just maybe that's exactly what he said. Dad has been ahead of us all along. Maybe he gave the religious power structure what it really deserved."

Pauline stood abruptly. She couldn't stand his line of talk. "I'm afraid you and I are very far apart on that little speech," she said with a sigh. "Ministries should be run with integrity. By men and women of integrity. Nothing less. There's no anchor for the soul in anything less."

"No? What's your anchor for the soul? Dad? The ministry board? The Protestant church? Or should we go all the way back to the Catholic Church and look for a holy Pope?"

She didn't respond. She didn't really have a response at the moment. She just felt dizzy.

"OK, I'm sorry," he said. "Let's agree to disagree." Changing from his philosophical mood, he said, "What we have to do is play the 'good guy, bad guy' routine on this deal. I'll naturally be the bad guy and make the rest of these calls. You rest up and get ready for that board meeting."

Pauline felt herself sinking into her own pain. After a long silence she spoke in a ragged voice. "I still find it hard to believe Daddy operated this way." She looked around at the pictures on the walls. "To me, this has always been God's ministry. Daddy worked directly for God."

Evan looked around the room too, noticing how many times Pauline was pictured with her dad on the gallery walls. Only one small black-and-white frame held an image of Evan. A picture taken with his dad in some foreign land, when Evan had been only eight years old or so. He walked nearer, examining it as she continued to speak.

"You know what I remember?" Her voice grew wistful. "When I was growing up, whenever I caught a cold or the flu, Momma would call Daddy to come lay his hand on me and pray the 'prayer of faith.'" Her face flushed with the memory. "He'd always come in my room and lay his warm hand on my forehead . . . and he'd say, 'How's my baby girl?'" She smiled painfully to herself. "He always said that. 'How's my baby girl?'" She began to choke up. "Whenever . . . whenever he would say that, everything was right with the world, you know? Did you ever feel that way, Evan? Do you remember a time when everything was right with the world?"

Evan reached up to touch the picture before him. "Yeah, I do. It sure is funny the things we remember, though. You know what I remember? Something Dad said when we took this picture."

Pauline turned. She saw the picture of Evan and her father standing in a barren place with a mountain in the background. The mountain had some kind of ruins on each side of it near the top. She had often wondered about the picture, having not been born when the photo was made.

"I remember this day," Evan said. "I remember he said, 'Son, take a lesson from this place . . .'" He turned to Pauline with irony in his voice. "'. . . this is the desert that sin made.'"

He walked slowly back to the table and gathered his papers. "Maybe that's the desert we're in now, huh?"

38

EASTERN TURKEY
Medieval Castle
6:01 P.M.

The land rover's transmission growled like a complaining camel as it rocked gently down a barren ridge in the waning light of evening. Fuel sloshed in its belly as it picked its way between boulders, holding the grade in four-wheel drive. In the distant north, the tip of Ararat glowed pink against a turquoise sky as evening shadows of China-blue crept up its lower slopes.

Max Commagene drove. Grace rode beside him. Kassabian sat in the rear, squinting through a pair of reading glasses at a series of computer printouts. "Everyone has his or her own vision of Heaven," Vardan began in his whimsical Armenian accent. "Did you know that? Listen to these: 'walking on clouds,' 'a road which ended at a golden gate,' 'the world split apart like diamonds,' 'music and brilliantly colored flowers.' Here's one: 'a misty field full of people working on all kinds of arts and crafts.' That's one of my personal favorites. But they're all so different. Truth serum has really been the only way to raise the curtain on this Near Death thing. The subconscious simply buries whatever it wants to forget. The bad stuff."

"Tell him about the Russian experiment," Max prompted.

"Certainly. Well, it's *glasnost* time. Everybody knows we've used amytal for years in the KGB. How short-sighted. But I was able to help them see beyond that limited political use, and in Yerevan we began interviewing resuscitated cardiac patients who had experienced NDE. We found that almost all of those who claimed 'heavenly' experiences during resuscitation had actually suppressed other memories of 'Hell.' It seemed almost as if their conscious minds were running away from this traumatic memory into a fantasy of Heaven."

"Is that what I predicted or is it not?" Grace asked triumphantly, poking a finger at Max.

Commagene nodded in firm agreement.

"I want to know if any of those were 'born again' Christians,"

Grace said. "If they were 'born again' they would not go to Hell. Dr. Rawlings, with the Advanced Life Support Program in Chattanooga first wrote on the Hell experiences. He saw the 'born again' connection."

"Born again?" the Russian psychiatrist asked. "How do you determine such a thing? Scientifically I mean? As a scientist, I try not to prejudice my research."

"It's too late for that," Grace argued. "This whole thing comes down to a matter of prejudice when you enter the spirit realm. The gods have been at war in every culture. Every century. They don't negotiate—they fight for dominion. Read your history books. Every pagan war has been a struggle between demigods. Now, in World War II we looked evil in the face. There was more of God against demons in that one. I think the next big one will be even more vivid. Perhaps against the Prince of Babylon. Finally Armageddon will be an out-and-out war against the God of the Universe. So here, we are looking into the same war inside the human body. The spiritual realities are the same for medicine and disease as they are for Armageddon. It's war. So who is right and wrong is a question of ultimate importance. That *is* the question here."

Kassabian cleared his throat loudly. "My goodness, you are an interesting fellow. So anyway, these 'Hell' descriptions surfaced during our sodium amytal interviews. We had 'dungeons and dragons' and underground caves, fire pits, tar pits, a lot of prehistoric vulcan landscapes, chains, surrealistic wastelands, arenas . . . things of that nature. But the startling discovery we made in 1978 was when two different people describing two different 'Hell' experiences, seemed to encounter exactly the same demonic figure. It so happened that they were both dying of the same rare form of lymphoma."

Max smiled at Grace. "And that, my friend, is exactly what *you* predicted twenty years ago. I keep telling these people you're ahead of your time."

"Actually I was late," Grace mused, looking down at his suddenly trembling hands, recalling the death of Ruth, his wife.

Max did not understand his friend's disturbance. "Look there," he said, distracting him.

Ahead, in a high Turkish *vilayet*, stretched a remarkable earthen wall, built twenty feet high like the serrated teeth of a band saw. It surrounded a stunning medieval castle dominating the mountain pass.

"Hoshap Castle," Max announced with his infectious, boyish enthusiasm. "Built a thousand years ago as the furthest outpost of Edessa, which was then one of the Latin States. Imagine, the Knights of the Kingdom of God out here in their armor, doc, seeking the Holy Grail. Broadswords and Christian standards flying in the breeze. Wouldn't you have loved to have been a fly on the wall back then?"

"This'll do, Max," he replied. "Are we going to be able to find a bath around here?"

39

ADDIS ABABA, ETHIOPIA
U.S. Embassy
9:29 P.M.

Jesse Stiles wiped a filthy hand across his face, mixing dirt with the sweat that had collected and dried there over the past three days. His clothes were torn and splattered with mud from the African road. His trembling fingers dialed an international telephone number as a young Embassy attaché watched over his shoulder.

"God loves you. Grace Ministries," answered a cheerful Grace receptionist.

"Let me talk to my dad."

"Excuse me, young man? Your dad?"

"Oh, yeah, I forgot. Uh, Reverend Stiles."

"Of course. That's extension six-four-two. I'll dial it for you."

He waited as the extension rang. "Verlin Stiles's office," Myra, the secretary, answered.

"Let me talk to my dad."

"Jesse?" She instantly recognized his voice. "This is Myra, honey. What's up?"

"I need to talk to my dad."

"Of course. He's just not in his office right now, sweetie. Can I help?"

He pulled the telephone from his ear, his face twisting with disappointment. The prolonged stress of his ordeal in the bush was beginning to crack all of his normal reserves. "Oh no, he's not there," he lamented as if he had not just survived much worse.

The Embassy staffer prompted, "Isn't there someone else you can tell about this?"

"Yeah. Oh yeah." He focused his mind again. "Dr. Sylvan. She was my assignment supervisor." He looked at the young attaché gratefully. "OK, I'll get transferred." Into the receiver he said, "Myra?"

"Yes."

"Uh, can you transfer me to Neva's office?"

"Sure, Jesse. But are you sure I can't do anything for you?"

"Just tell my dad I'm coming home, alright?"

"You're coming home? Why?"

"Just tell him everything blew up over here."

"Blew up? Jesse, what's wrong?"

"They killed everybody, Myra. OK?"

"What?" She sat stunned, trying to get a grip on what he was saying. "OK. You've got to get on home. Do you hear me? We'll get you back no matter what. I'll transfer you now. They'll know what to do over there, but then you transfer right back as soon as you make some arrangements, OK? In the meantime I'll try to find your dad."

"OK." He waited until the second phone answered. "Dr. Sylvan's office. This is Danna."

"Danna?" Jesse began crying. "Tell Neva they blew up the hospital, and they killed all the patients."

Danna stiffened and lowered her voice. "Jesse, where are you?"

"The Embassy. I'm in Ethiopia."

Danna glanced around and began making notes quickly on a pad. "Tell me that again so I can get it straight."

"They injected the patients. Then they blew the place up. I had to come to Addis Ababa because I couldn't get to Khartoum."

"Why not?"

"Here . . . let me handle it." The Embassy attaché pried the telephone gently from Jesse's fingers with reassuring nods. "Hello?"

"Hello . . . who is this?"

"David Nagle, military attaché, U.S. Embassy. Are we speaking with Grace Ministries?"

"Yes, you are."

"I've been in touch with Khartoum, and it's going to be very difficult to order a check on your facilities in Juba. The rebels have become active in the south again. Things have heated up. Even the Wycliffe Translators are pulling out now, and they're usually the last to go in these situations."

"What about Jesse's report?"

"Like I said, it's going to take some time before we can get anyone credible in there to check it out. Frankly we can't trust a report from either side at this point. We've got the Christians and animists in the south going against the ruling Muslims in the north, and that's a real crock of soup, if you'll excuse my saying so."

"Can you see that Jesse gets on the next possible flight for home?"

"That I can do."

"Grace Hospitals will reimburse you, or we can pay however you like."

"I'll call you back with the particulars."

"Thank you very much. Good-bye."

Dr. Sylvan had entered the outer office, overhearing parts of the conversation. She now picked up Danna's notes and examined them. "What's going on out there?" She read the notes and sighed. "Get his dad on the phone, will you? I'd better talk to him."

"Will do," Danna replied. But from the look on her face it wasn't at all what she *wanted* to do.

40

BROWNSVILLE
The Steeple
9:49 P.M.

Stepping from the elevator toward Lydia's bedroom, this time Pauline labored under the burden of her own sin, not her father's. She felt an overwhelming need to be absolved. What could she do? She had become totally unworthy of asking forgiveness. What she was doing was deliberate. Uncovering her father's evil, she had become part of it in the same hour. Never in her life had she regarded herself as personally guilty before God. Oh, she had made grand confessions of original sin, a theologically worked-out condition she had inherited from Adam. Almost absolving herself in the confession. There had been no glaring errors on her personal record. Nothing specifically horrid. And in some small corner of her virginal heart, she had always felt that she had done God a favor by giving Him her allegiance. All of that was gone now.

As she traveled the darkened hallway she wrestled the regrets of Judas, of Peter. The cock was crowing and she had denied her Lord, committing the harm of blackmail against Verlin Stiles and four other board members. She had done it for votes. For power.

Dressed comfortably in a cotton jumpsuit and jacket, she hesitated at the door before moving into Lydia's bedroom. To her surprise, the old woman was sitting up reading.

"Pauline, come here and listen to this," Lydia said, looking at her over her half lenses.

With some disappointment for the distraction, Pauline nevertheless sensed a change in the old woman. She had hoped to simply pray and confess herself privately to the intercessor, relieving her pent-up feelings. But Lydia seemed out of the prayer mood.

"I told you I had a dream," the old woman said, oblivious to Pauline's troubled thoughts. "When you were in Jerusalem I . . . I guess I sort of shared a . . . I don't know what it was . . . a . . . a sort of dream, or vision. Anyway, there was an angel, Mithrael, a very handsome angel who, I must say, turned my head." She paused, recalling the feelings of attraction she had felt through Naamah's body. "Anyway, he had married a woman named Naamah. Now, when I entered this dream I entered her body, and she was giving birth to a giant. Which was impossible. It was the angel's child. She died in childbirth because the giant was so huge and deformed. I died with her. She had a brother named Jubal. A musician."

"Yoo hoo," Pauline called, thinking, *Too much fasting has unhinged the woman.* "I hate to interrupt this, Lydia, but I've got an emergency board meeting in Dallas, and I was hoping we could pray together before I go. Do you mind?"

"Of course not." The old woman stared back at her blankly, trying to grasp Pauline's situation.

The young woman saw that she had put Lydia completely off track. "I'm sorry," she said, and sat down. "You go ahead and finish first. This will wait."

Lydia nodded gratefully and slowly resumed. "This was the

same dream where, in the end part, I saw your father all bound up in chains."

A connection was suddenly made in Pauline's mind. "So you think this dream has something to do with Daddy?"

"That's the whole point. It does. Let me read you something." She readjusted her glasses and shifted the large-print Bible on her lap. "These are some of the descendants of Cain, who lived before Noah's flood. 'Lamech took to himself two wives: the name of the one was Adah, and the name of the other, Zillah. And Adah gave birth to Jabal; he was the father of those who dwell in tents and have livestock. And his brother's name was Jubal—' This one was in my dream—Jubal. I knew when I heard his name that it sounded familiar. '. . . Jubal; he was the father of all those who play the lyre and pipe.' In my dream Jubal was playing a harp. Don't take this as gospel, I don't understand it myself but it was a very, very, real dream. Right down to the details of the clothing and the instruments and names and such. Well . . ." She sighed and turned back to the page. "'As for Zillah, she also gave birth to Tubal-cain—' Oh, honey, this man was in my dream, and he was evil. More evil than I can tell."

Pauline had trouble concentrating on these arcane ramblings. "Now, he was in your dream?" she repeated.

"Yes. Jubal said he hated Tubal-cain. Well, when I saw what that monster did to his sister—"

"Monster? What monster?"

"I told you, Naamah gave birth to a giant."

Pauline frowned, feeling stupid talking of such fantasies.

"This Tubal-cain delivered the giant by this awful cesarean process right after Naamah died. It was just bloody and awful. I knew he was Tubal-cain. And because of one other reason too. He used this terrible metal tool to do the job, and here in Genesis it says that Tubal-cain was a forger of iron and brass. Now I had never really thought of any of this detail before my dream, you see?"

"No, Lydia. I really don't." Pauline felt she could listen to no more. Her mind demanded that she deal with hard realities. "I don't mean to sound insulting, but I don't see what this has to do with anything. Really."

Lydia looked at her closely, realizing that in all her life she had never heard of such a thing either. She would simply have to be patient. Simply go ahead in faith. "I think you will see," she reassured. "Let me finish." She read, "'Tubal-cain, the forger of all implements of bronze and iron—' See? He *was* in my dream. '. . . and the sister of Tubal-cain was Naamah.'" She closed the Bible and removed her glasses. "Naamah died trying to give birth to that Nephil. OK. It was one of the giants that came from the 'sons of God' marrying 'the daughters of men' in Genesis 6. They were a race before the Flood called Nephilim."

Pauline nodded absently, having only a vague memory of the reference.

"That Nephil has something to do with your father."

At this, Pauline felt her time being totally wasted. One more word from Lydia about this crazy dream could only be a mockery of the real dilemma she faced. Her agitation rose until she feared she might insanely lash out at the old woman just to shut her up. She grabbed her hand. "Lydia, let's just pray. Can we?"

Lydia *connected* in that moment. She sensed a disturbance in Pauline. Perhaps in her spirit. An enemy. She placed both hands on the young woman's hand and felt confirmation of this discernment. Chaos flowed from Pauline like a silent, screaming legion. In the heat of her skin, the trembling of her bones, the shallowness of her breathing. Lydia read the signs. The old woman was not surprised, nor fearful. She simply made the spiritual diagnosis and did what she always did in such cases; she spoke past the disturbance—not to it. She knew that words of faith were predestined seeds from the Spirit of God. They would take root and grow in the young woman in time. They would not return void.

"Young lady, I will pray with you, but you listen to me now . . . I don't know why, but you need to hear this."

Pauline felt love in the gentle rebuke. She closed her eyes and took a deep breath, tossed by the thrashing within. She told her thrashing heart to be still, and to her surprise it obeyed. She opened her eyes again, and Lydia continued.

"This Nephil has something to do with your father. I saw its birth. It was a grotesque . . . *obscenity* worshiped by Tubal-cain and the other children of Cain. Only Jubal sensed the wrong in it. But the demon is on a leash. Do you understand me? It is not powerful beyond the limits God has placed on it. I saw the creature full-grown, tethered to some kind of pole in an arena where your father is bound up. There is some kind of spiritual reality behind this scene. Some key to our prayers. I believe your father has bound himself somehow. The angel in the dream, Mithrael, wrestled that Nephil. His own offspring. For some reason the angel wore a metal gag on his mouth, and he was blind. It reminded me of Jude, where it says, 'the angels who kept not their proper abode, He has kept in eternal bonds under darkness for the judgment . . .' Maybe it is the darkness of blindness. I don't know. Anyway, he was gagged and he was blind. It means something."

Pauline's mind kept going blank as Lydia spoke. "Lydia?" she pleaded. "Can we save this for another time? I'm just not up to it."

The old woman felt no chaos in this simple request. It came from a submissive, respectful heart. "Of course, dear. I will save it. Let's pray."

"Evan should hear about the Nephil," Pauline offered apologetically. "He studies so many things."

Lydia's face immediately brightened at the mention of his name. "Are you telling me Evangel is here?"

"You know him?" Pauline was surprised. She thought Evan had been forgotten among Grace employees.

"Yes. I remember him from his college days. God loves that boy," Lydia said with deep conviction. "There's always been something special about him."

Once more, at this assessment of Evan's character Pauline questioned the old woman's discernment. Sometimes she felt as if the intercessor were nothing more than a religious sideshow. Quirky. A waste of precious time.

41

SAN DIEGO
Mission Bay Yacht Club
SUNSET

The scene nearly duplicated the one of a few days before it. Detail for detail, almost. Except that this time Alan played it with a bulging bruise and a Band-Aid on his upper lip, where Evan's fist had recently landed. As before, he stepped down the ladder of his yacht into a powerboat, where two "messengers" waited. Dorothy watched on deck again. Instead of a tiger-striped bikini, on this day she wore a cool pink cover and sat cross-legged at a table beneath a sunshade. She held the same panic button ready in her palm.

The boat roared away from the yacht for about one hundred yards, then stopped, idling in the water as it had done before. The same "messenger" came aft to speak with Alan, smiling, chewing another cocktail straw, except this one had been twisted into an excruciating series of knots.

"You look funny," the "hitter" began, eyeing Alan's swollen lip.

Alan touched it lightly. "I had some trouble with the little lady," he said.

"She looks lively," the *mafioso* acknowledged with a lecherous grin, then sobered menacingly. "The people I represent are very disappointed with you, little man. You just can't mess with them, see? Like the shell game you pulled with the icon not being found in the shipping crate? It has them very upset. They just can't trust you with their merchandise."

Alan felt the blood drain from his face. In a moment he realized what had happened. "Evan Grace, you son-of-a—" He realized the icon case had been switched, and he could see the commission check of a lifetime flying out of his grasp. He entreated, "Listen, you've got to understand. Not just anybody could do this to me. Simon Grace's own son stung us. Tell Grace it was Evan. He'll understand, believe me. I'll straighten this out."

"Straighten it out?"

"I'll get the icon."

The man laughed. "My clients have already straightened it out. They *have* the icon." He pulled a small electronic switch, similar to a TV remote, from his pocket and pointed it toward Dorothy, who now stood watching from the railing of the yacht. "Your contract's been terminated, Reverend Lavalle."

A band of cold sweat clamped around Alan's scalp, and he suddenly realized what was happening. He lurched toward the man, screaming, "No!"

But too late—

❖

Oddly, Dorothy thinks that the two men have suddenly begun to move in slow motion. She feels transformed. Her eyes record a raging inferno that suddenly engulfs her body. There is no pain in this vision. She watches matter-of-factly as exquisite tongues of flame explode upward from the diesel-laden atmosphere of the engine room. Splinters of deck pierce her body completely through, hot rivets glowing red in the wicked shards of wood. Space is no longer strictly space, and time no longer time. Everything passes before her as if in a dream.

She hears a roar and flies upward past the flames now. In the descending silence, which is no longer completely natural, she steps backwards in time and sees the entire yacht explode once again below her ghostly form. She is like one of the Watchers, watching her own spirit-body fly out of the ball of flame to meet her in the air. The spirit-bodies of Bud Cheney and one of the two bodyguards who are waiting below deck fly upward too.

In the distance a speedboat leads a silent foamy wake toward the open sea. A man remains behind, struggling in the water. It is Alan.

"Good-bye, Alan." The sound of her own thought cascades around her ears as if shouted from behind a pounding waterfall.

Then she hears music. Unexplainable, inexpressible music of surpassing power and beauty, beckoning her irresistibly to turn around. As she turns, her last impression is of a burning hull at the dark water line to mark where Alan's ill-gotten pleasure craft had been anchored. A thousand—no, thousands of feet below . . . and yet she can reach out and touch it like a toy. She has lost all sense of size and distance.

"Enough of earth."

A light, more brilliant than any she has ever seen. It doesn't hurt her eyes but opens them more truly. Drawing her, drawing her into an infinite tunnel. She is swept inside and suddenly is moving with a cloud of diamond-like particles. They dance and shimmer around her, transforming reality, or perception. "Oh," she giggles, "they are one and the same. Perception-reality." She has begun and ended her journey. Eternity has existed hard by her side from the moment of conception. "Yes!" It can only be known from the inside! And she knows it now. She is standing blissfully still at the dazzling speed of light.

But as she enters deeper into the moment, the music changes. Its loveliness begins to decay. She wishes to turn from it with a shudder of helplessness, but she can't. Like the tune of the Pied Piper, she must follow. No choice. The music begins to clash with uncertain sounds which produce in her doubt, nausea, foreboding.

The feelings descend in an ever-increasing vortex. Irreversible, no matter how she fights. Oh! Hot terror pumps her spirit-body, streaming through a network of nerves, until it pours in fountains of terror from her fingertips. She exudes an aura of endless regret. Every nerve—and she is all nerves now!—vibrates to the sound of a perverse, engulfing chant. It is the most ancient chant of all, whispered and screamed in the self-same moment, over and over and over and over and over in her ears. Like the endless, mindless churning of a washing machine that cleans nothing, does nothing, cares nothing. The sound is a refrain of unearthly words, unearthly meanings, vomited between a million sets of gnashing teeth!

VI

NIMRUT DAG

With gay Religions full of Pomp and Gold,
And Devils to adore for Deities:
Then were they known to men by various Names,
And various Idols through the Heathen World.

(JOHN MILTON, *PARADISE LOST*, BOOK I)

42

EASTERN TURKEY
Tigris River
8:30 A.M.

Grace stood his ground as the swirling current tugged at the top of his waders. He studiously launched twenty-five feet of double tapered flyline in a graceful arc, back and forth, finally dropping a hand-tied grasshopper to the surface of the Tigris River. It landed forty-five degrees upstream from his position. Textbook cast. He watched it drift past, retrieving slack through the ferrules of the pole, anticipating the strike of a trout.

Maximilian waded fifty feet downstream, working a black nymph through an eddy behind a submerged rock. As he slogged along, he lugged a wicker creel under one arm and trailed a hand net from his belt. He wore a turned-up fishing derby with a wooly worm and several colorful coachmen patterns stuck in the sweatband. Both men resembled something from an Orvis catalog, transplanted here in this high and exotic land.

"Whoop!" Grace yelled, his rod arching against the weight of a two-pound fish. It thrashed in the brownish water, kicking up a froth on the surface.

"I'll net him," Max offered, moving quickly toward shore.

Grace chuckled as he played the sporty fish in the current, swimming it expertly into Max's waiting net.

With a broad smile, the German industrialist pulled out the trophy, displaying it for Grace, and for Dr. Kassabian who sat reading from a leatherbound volume on the hood of the land rover.

"Bravo," the doctor acknowledged, peering over his rimless glasses.

"There's nothing quite as beautiful in all creation," Grace said, wading closer. "Look at the colors on that fish."

Max examined the trout more closely.

"See the brilliant fluorescent spots there?" Grace pointed to the fish's gleaming side with awe. "And where in this desert do you find those yellows? Greens? And the silver and gold blends?" He gestured to the surrounding hills. "Do these things occur by chance? I scoff at evolution."

Max removed the hook from the fish's jaw and released it back into the water.

"There's nothing quite like fishing in the rivers of Eden," Grace concluded, untangling his line for another cast.

"The trout is beautiful," Kassabian said from the hood of the land rover. He looked up from his reading with preoccupation. He was a man more focused on intellectual pursuits than the simple pleasures of fishing. "What did William Blake ask in 'Tyger, Tyger'? 'Did He who made the Lamb make thee?' Well then, I ask you, 'Did He who made the trout make Jubal's antediluvian brutes?'" He looked down again and read from a tattered manuscript. ". . . Apollyon was possessed of a huge forehead with the tiny eyes of a shrew. Though his body appeared weaker, once he made contact, he wrestled the others with unmatched skill. Dagon hulked into the arena like a human sea lion. His torso dark and hairy, with long, brutish arms, he once slung Bel completely out of the colosseum. Rimmon appeared hairless and sniveling, with a rat-like tail. His naked interest was purely erotic. Winning any contest meant for him the pleasure of sexually humiliating an opponent. A ritual greatly enhanced by the vocal approval of the crowd. Moloch, a gryphon with hungry, hunting eyes, filled the arena with blood. He slowly stalked his opponents, panting a chancrous tongue between canine fangs. Between contests, he was kept constantly in chains.'" Vardan looked up. "Did these mutations evolve by chance? Or are they the deliberate work of the Creator?"

"Neither," Grace replied quickly over his shoulder, casting again upstream. "It's the difference between the original creation and the corruption we find after the Fall, Vardan. Sin brought about these curses." He cast upstream again. "But while we're on the subject, tell me, which of them would you say is connected to the sun?"

"First I'd like to say that if God created everything, He also created sin. I don't see why we should have to suffer for it. That's my view." Kassabian smiled to himself, then paused thoughtfully. "To answer your question, I'd say Rimmon has a connection to the sun."

"Why do you ask?" Max asked, shooting Vardan a cautionary look.

"I have a theory," Grace replied.

"How about Hadad?" Vardan suggested.

"The Syrian sun god, right?"

"Right."

"But he's nowhere mentioned in Jubal's list," Grace said. "I've studied it myself. Of course, I believe there were many more Nephilim than Jubal saw in the contests."

"Ah, but Vardan is right—Hadad is there," Max replied. "He goes by many names. Hadad was the Syrian sun god, known as Sol Invictus in Rome—his day became the Christian Sunday under Constantine—but in Damascus, if my memory serves me, he was worshiped as Rimmon. Right, Vardan? Read about Rimmon again."

Kassabian checked the page. "Let's see . . . 'Rimmon appeared hairless and sniveling, with a rat-like tail. His naked interest was purely erotic.'"

"There you go. Hairless. Maybe he was the first nudist," Max quipped. "They're sun worshipers, aren't they?"

Grace laughed. "You may be 'righter' than we know, Max. Anyway, I'll tell you what—" He became serious. "I want to look into the history of old Hadad-Rimmon there, because we know that a connection exists between the sun and cancer. Right?"

Max nodded. "Especially skin cancer."

"Perhaps all cancer," Kassabian added. "Don't forget the sun creates mutations."

"The sun creates nothing," Grace corrected. "It causes mutations but creates nothing. Cancers are renegade cells." His demeanor had grown stern, angry. He stopped fishing and squinted at the sky. "Perhaps radiation turns them loose. Once they get started, they multiply themselves and grow into renegade organs demanding blood and nutrients. We call them tumors." His voice sounded suddenly distant. "I saw them in Ruth's body. We couldn't medically stop them." Shaking himself free of the memory he began to cast again. "These rebel cells and organs rob the body of its life source and eventually kill it. But in connection with the sun, I've always been fascinated with theories about the firmament. Have you read of it?"

Vardan shrugged and looked over his glasses at Max indulgently.

Grace pressed on. "This is, of course, unscientific, but I believe the Bible to be without error. Genesis says that God originally created a firmament in the sky, dividing the waters above the firmament from those below. I believe that is exactly true. Some scholars believe this was a vapor canopy, and there is good evidence for that. For example, have you ever wondered why the dinosaurs were so big? Their bone structures would hardly stand up against gravity today. The fossil record tells us the plants and trees of the ante-diluvian world were huge compared to those we know today. You even had dragonflies with five-foot wingspans. Why don't we see insects like that anymore? Well, because the firmament is gone, that's why. The atmosphere changed. Under the firmament, see, you had this heavy air that could fly those monster insects." Dr. Grace had grown animated in his explanation. He truly enjoyed the subject. "Not to mention the flying reptiles! Ever see a Pterodactyl skeleton? That sucker had a fifty-one-foot wingspan! Max, that's as big as my eight-passenger jet. A snake that big couldn't get off the ground today, but under the firmament he soared through the heavens. That big old ugly thing must have been a living terror with those reptilian teeth and that huge ugly hammerhead, flying around up there searching for raw meat. But Pterodactyl couldn't fly today. Gravity's the same. It's the firmament that's changed. The atmosphere. The Bible says the firmament fell down and released all of its waters during the Great Flood. I believe it happened just the way the Bible says it happened. It was worldwide. There was a Noah's Ark. The Bible says that the Flood was the first time it had ever rained on the earth. That rain was the falling firmament, and when it fell down, there was a permanent change in the environment."

"I see," Max said slyly. "Without the firmament the earth had more dangerous exposure to the sun's ultraviolet radiation."

"Exactly. Losing the canopy spawned all manner of genetic disorder. I think that's when the lords of disease started their killing spree. Life in general got shorter after the Flood. Think about it. Noah lived nine hundred years, Salah four hundred, Abraham one hundred and seventy-five, and Moses died at one hundred and twenty. Today we get maybe seventy or eighty years if we live right. My theory is, one of these demigods associated with the sun was given power to set disease loose in the earth. He was able to use that power after the Flood."

Max had stopped casting and listened intently. "Listen to the man." He turned to the Russian psychiatrist. "Maybe this is the critter who's been showing up on the transcendental maps? Maybe it's the one the two Russians saw."

"Please," Vardan replied without humor, "don't prejudice my experiments with this emotional drivel."

Grace smiled with satisfaction. From the hostility in the Russian's response, his theory must have hit somewhere close to the data. Like a well placed cast.

43

HOUSTON, TEXAS
Hobby International Airport
8:57 A.M.

Ethiopia to Frankfurt, Frankfurt to New York, New York to Houston. Jesse Stiles was drunk with jet lag when he deplaned at Hobby International. He stumbled through the line with one thing in mind—to get to gate forty-two as quickly as possible for his final connecting flight to Brownsville. Before he could do that, however, he had to endure American customs.

At last he passed through the gauntlet of questions and passport checks and emerged into the main terminal. To his pleasant surprise he was met by a smiling Dr. Neva Sylvan. Seeing her was the next best thing to being home. She had been his foreign assignment advisor and had strongly urged him not to go to the Sudan hospital in the first place. He had gone around her by invoking his father's vice presidential authority. Her welcoming smile told him she was an all-forgiving friend. Like an emotional zombie, he walked into her embrace.

"I'll listen to you next time, Neva," he promised. "What am I saying? I don't know if I want a next time."

"Danna tells me you've been through quite an ordeal, young man," she said. "Why don't you tell me about it?"

"I need to get my luggage."

"Oh no, you don't. Don't worry about a thing. It's all been taken care of."

"Really?"

"Yes," she said, walking beside him with her hand sympathetically on the back of his neck. "It's checked through. I'll have a driver pick it up in Brownsville. In the meantime your next flight is delayed, and I'm here with the hospital helicopter. We'll fly you home."

"The sooner the better," he said with weariness and relief.

She steered him across the busy terminal, then out the passenger entrance to a low-slung gold Mercedes Benz with chrome wheels and tinted windows. "This belongs to a friend of mine," she explained. "Kind of fancy, huh?" She opened the rear door for him and whispered knowingly, "He's a major donor."

With a nod, he got in. She slid in after him, and the car pulled immediately away from the curb.

Behind it, another car pulled out and followed. Inside a man held a telephone to his ear. "She's got him."

A female voice responded, "I know you've got bigger fish in mind, but don't lose sight of that boy. Do you hear? Stay close."

"Quiet on the line," the man in the tailing car corrected sternly. "I won't risk tipping them off. Aerial . . . How's our signal?"

A black Ranger helicopter shadowed a freeway a mile away. A group of armed men huddled around a monitor in the passenger compartment inside, silently watching a signal blinking on a radar screen. A gum-chewing technician in a communications headset spoke with the bored monotone of an expert. "We've got signal."

"OK then," the driver said, "I have them in sight and they're headed for the chopper pad. Everybody stay out of sight and let them run."

"We're gone," replied the helicopter pilot. The chopper veered away from the airport and receded into the distance.

"So help me," the woman's voice on the telephone warned, "if that kid comes up dead, I'm holding you responsible, Benji!"

"This is not Entebbe, Danna," the driver rebuked. "The kid is beside the point."

Danna waited for a moment, then spoke more humbly. "Promise me you'll try."

"That goes without saying," the man named Benji replied.

"No, it doesn't. Promise me," she insisted, waiting for a reply. None came. "I don't care if you have to blow your cover on this! That boy belongs to us—now promise me!"

44
BROWNSVILLE
Grace Ministries Executive Offices
9:13 A.M.

"That's where he went out," Jann said, pointing to the ceiling panel where the masked burglar had made his getaway. "Just as slick as a monkey."

Evan set down the notepad he had been holding and leaned back in his father's chair. Pauline stood across the desk from him.

"I just don't see how he could get away," she complained. "It's a pyramid building, for heaven's sake. The higher you go, the fewer places there are to hide."

Jann pursed her lips with seriousness. "I love Ramon, but it does makes you wonder about our security, doesn't it?"

"Have you contacted a new company?"

"Three of them. Interviews are set for next week."

"Good."

Evan listened impatiently. He sat forward, picking up his checklist. "If this guy is the kind of professional I think he is, you're wasting time. You're not going to find security people who are a match for him. Shall we get back to work here?"

Pauline's face grew red. "Evan, you can have your opinions, but will you please keep them to yourself?"

Jann shifted uncomfortably. "Uh hum, well, what about Jesse and the African hospital? Should we look for a connection there?"

"Don't rule anything out," Evan suggested, cooling his glare at his sister. "But Sylvan spoke with the Embassy, and the civil war has heated up again. We can't get confirmation about anyone still alive out there."

"How's Verlin taking it?" Pauline asked, looking at Jann.

"He's bottomed out. Myra says she's never seen him like this. He and Peggy are picking Jesse up at the airport this afternoon."

"I think all the Sudan stuff is a waste," Evan said, examining his notes. "I'm staying after the icon deal. First, I'll call Alan to see if he's learned anything. Not that I can trust him." He checked his page. "Then I'll go back to the house and see if I can dig up any

more clues in Dad's files on 'who, when and where' about the icon."
Another check on the pad, then he dropped the list to the desk
again. "I've already called the lawyers. The icon was Dad's personal
property, not the ministry's. Positive ID. See? I mean, forty million
dollars would more than pull the ministry out of the financial hole.
But if the forty million is Dad's personal fortune, what's the plan?
Is he going to take the money and run?"

"You've got to be kidding," Pauline snarled. "He's not running."

"She's right," Jann added. "He wouldn't do that."

"For forty million?"

"For nothing," Pauline replied.

"Well, put his forty million dollars together with the fact that,
according to Stiles—and I agree with him—Dad changed the current ministry letter from a winner to a loser. Why would he want
to weaken the ministry on the one hand and make forty million dollars on the other?"

Pauline glanced at Jann, uncomfortable with this line of spec-
ulation.

Evan pressed his point. "Maybe he wants to become the Savior
of his own ministry. Motive is very fuzzy here, but I'm telling you,
money is our best lead when it comes to finding Dad."

Pauline's disapproval showed openly. *Why does he always
look at one side of it?* she wondered. *Daddy's never done anything
purely for money. He also happens to love God. Evan never even
considers that. It's like it doesn't count.*

She glanced down at her own notes. "Jann, you will work in
outward circles from Jerusalem, calling every contact on the
rolodex beginning with our hospitals. Tell them you're . . ."

". . . that I'm Dr. Grace's secretary," Jann picked up the scenario
they had already rehearsed, "and that we have missing personnel
from the Sudanese hospital, and that Dr. Grace has ordered an
immediate head count of every Grace associate they've had contact
with in the last ten days."

"Good," Pauline approved. "I think if anyone's seen Dad,
maybe we can smoke the information out. Keep your ears open."

"Will do, and I'd better get to it," Jann said, walking briskly to
the outer office. She was relieved to get away from the sibling ten-
sions.

Evan stood up, stretched, and walked to a world map. It occupied an entire wall to the left of the desk. Two dozen hospital locations were marked by small, blue pennants bearing the Grace logo.

"I have a theory," he mused aloud.

Pauline couldn't help it—something ugly happened inside at the very sound of his voice. She didn't care if he had a theory or not. *Do I really hate him?* she wondered. *I don't want him to be right about anything.*

He turned from the map, ignorant of her inner conflict. "How about this? Dad is engineering the cash flow problem to keep us from finding him."

"How do you mean?"

"Jet fuel is expensive. Thousands of dollars per hour in the air. In a financial cutback the non-essentials go first. Or they should. He may be trying to keep us grounded."

Pauline doubted it. She saw her dad at work on much bigger motives. "It doesn't matter. I'm making emergency priorities to find him, using the jet. For a while at least, the other bills can wait."

The desk intercom buzzed. Evan answered. "Yes, Jann?"

"Verlin is here to see you."

He looked at Pauline with surprise. She blanched slightly and swayed. "Send him right in," he said.

Pauline fought a wave of guilt as the door swung open. She had to look the other way, pacing to the far end of the room as Stiles entered, not wanting to face what she had done to him.

"I understand Jesse is coming in," Evan offered as the vice president entered. "We're just very glad he's not hurt."

"Thanks," Verlin replied in a subdued voice.

To Evan it seemed that the VP's face had the serene look of a thoroughly defeated man. No more personal agendas burned behind his eyes. The "dirt files" had done their work. And now his son's problems had piled on top of it all. When it rains it pours.

Verlin held a Federal Express package in one hand, pregnant with some kind of importance. He dropped it on the desk in front of Evan. "You need to see this," he said.

Evan opened it and pulled free a letter proposal titled "The Tree of Life." A sample response device fell free of the sheaf of papers. It was a cross made of cut, unpolished agate.

"It's from your dad," Verlin followed. "But it came through Dallas WordSmith. Ever hear of them?"

Evan mentally scanned his firsthand knowledge of direct mail companies in Dallas. "No."

"They're new to me too."

Hearing news of her father, Pauline returned quickly to the desk and picked up the cross. "Where do you get the idea that this package came from Daddy? Anyone could have sent it."

"It's on the work order." Verlin picked up a cover document and pointed to, "By order of: Dr. Simon Grace."

"But where's his signature?"

"Well, there isn't one."

"Then I'm not paying for it."

"You don't have to pay for it," Verlin replied. "According to this document the down payment has already been received."

She looked at Evan. "Let's call these Dallas WordSmith people and put a stop to it right now."

"Wait, *wait*!" He held up a hand for caution. "We have our first real lead here. Before we blow it apart, we need more information." He turned to Stiles. "What's your assessment of the letter. Another loser?"

"This is still just a concept. No copy yet. But it orders the biggest mailing list I've ever seen for a Grace mailing." He pointed to the number on the work order.

Evan leaned over and read it aloud. "Thirteen million seven hundred and fifty thousand names?"

"That's initial. It could go higher. He's including our entire inactive list from ten years back, plus new names purchased from other ministries. In short, he's acting like he expects this letter to be a financial home run with the bases loaded."

"And it's to run next month?"

"Right."

"So last month he does an end-run around you and has Alan switch to a 'loser' letter while you are away in Jerusalem. Next month he's done another end-run around Alan, and orders a grand slam with these people at WordSmith?"

Stiles nodded. "That's how it looks."

Evan looked at Pauline, and his voice became edged with anger. "Do you get the feeling like maybe Dad is pulling *all* the strings around here?"

"We still don't know it's him," she shot back. "Maybe somebody is forging this letter."

"Oh come on. What do you need, a federal indictment?"

"How about a presumption of innocence?" she demanded. "You can get that in a court of law!" She would never understand him. He seemed so eager to tear his father down. *Why, oh why did I let him in?* she wondered as she stormed from the room.

Evan turned to Stiles as he dialed the *Texas People* Dallas office. "Is Dad innocent?" he demanded as he waited for the ring of the phone. "Well, is he?"

Stiles hesitated, then shrugged.

Evan grinned. "Spoken like a true diplomat."

A receptionist answered, "*Texas People.*"

"Jennifer Bridgeport please." He pulled the phone from his ear. "Verlin, I need a minute. I'll get back to you on this, and thanks, really. Thanks a lot."

Verlin held up his hand and shook his head vigorously. "I'm not through. There's something else you need to know. Right now."

Jennifer picked up her line. "Bridgeport here."

"Jen, this is Evan . . . please hold the phone. I'll get right back to you. Please." He punched his hold button and looked at Stiles.

"I got a call from someone who heard it on the local news out there. It seems Alan's yacht blew sky high in Mission Bay last night. It was a bomb."

Evan felt his stomach tighten and grow sour. "Anyone . . . any . . .?"

"Word is, nobody's seen Alan since. I can't raise him or Dorothy, or Bud, or anybody else from Logos Mail."

"O God, help . . ." Messing with the icon had perhaps been more than dangerous. Foolhardy. Evan blew a huge breath of air forcefully between his teeth. "Get me confirmation, will you please? Stay on it."

Stiles nodded and went out, closing the door behind him.

Evan hesitated with the telephone, feeling near to tears. Steeling himself, he punched in the other line. "Jen?"

"Where have you been, for cat's sake? Have you heard about Alan Lavalle?"

"Just now. I mean just this minute. I'm in Brownsville."

"Well, you're a long way out of touch, boy. I was going to call you about it, but nobody knew exactly where you were. Are you still working for us?"

"I think so. Speaking of which, I need some help, and don't ask questions."

She hawked loudly, "You don't want much, do you?"

"Consider it part of the Lavalle investigation. I need you to check out Dallas WordSmith, job number . . ." He read from the work order. "GMI—that's Grace Ministries International, 0719-8776. This is the biggest mailing package we've ever put together, and Dallas WordSmith just replaced Alan Lavalle for the first time in our history. Nobody here knows who they are or what is going on. We don't even know who's paying the bill, but someone has paid in advance. Understand?"

She whistled. "Hey, do you think the same people sunk the competition in San Diego?"

He paused. He hadn't put together the fact that Dallas WordSmith had just replaced Alan—who might at the moment be at the bottom of Mission Bay. That would imply they also shared a connection to the icon deal. "That won't be funny if it turns out to be true," he replied soberly. "I need you to pose as Verlin's assistant and find out everything you can, but especially where the orders came from." He suddenly took Pauline's advice and gave his father a presumption of innocence. "We, uh, suspect someone may have used Dad's name to either ruin us or manipulate our income with this letter. So watch your step."

"Since you've left me here to shuffle all my own schedules, where does this fit in exactly? On a one to ten?"

"Fifteen."

She paused, checking her watch. "Everything's a fifteen with you, Evan. You're manic."

"Not this time. If I don't hear from you today, we'll be at D/FW tomorrow for a board meeting. Airport Hyatt. Meet me."

She made a note.

"And, Jen, if you get by my apartment would you mind changing the telephone answering tape? I forgot to change your gag copy before I left town and it is still out there killing my reputation."

She smiled. "Now there's a big fifteen, huh?"

"Make it an eight." He paused briefly, realizing the diminishing worth of what might be called his reputation. "No, make that a three."

45

MUNICIPAL AIRPORT
11:00 A.M.

Dr. Neva Sylvan had set about to temper Jesse's telephoned reports about what had happened in Juba, Sudan. Verlin's secretary Myra had already sprung a leak about the killings, prompting several hysterical phone calls from other departments. It always looked bad for the hospital program to send young people into dangerous areas of the world, but Neva had everything to her advantage in this instance. She had only to quote the U.S. Embassy and place blame for the violence on the civil war, plus in her call to Verlin, she had simply to remind him that she opposed sending his son to the cancer unit in the first place. With this, Jesse's reports of a mass murder had been tempered by his own father, who further corrected the speculations of his secretary while he was at it.

The beaten evangelist stood now at the Brownsville municipal airport, his arms around his anxious wife, waiting for their son to deplane. He wrestled regret. *Why did I have to throw my weight around and send the boy?* He kept the thoughts to himself. He had not even informed his wife of the extra measures he'd employed on Jesse's assignment. Father and son had been an adventurous twosome about it. It had been a way for them to plan and scheme, man to man, feeling that the reported dangers of the Sudanese civil war were overblown. Jesse had wanted the special credit he would receive from working in the cancer unit to help him gain access to a top medical school. So Dad had pulled the necessary strings. Now Jesse was returning traumatized from some kind of bloodshed.

Fifty-one passengers filed past Reverend and Mrs. Stiles. Verlin became deeply agitated when Jesse did not appear. When the last one had passed, he asked the gate attendant to check the plane register for his son. They were informed that he had been listed, but had failed to board in Houston.

Fear and reason fought for control of Verlin. His first fear was that Jesse had been right. Something murderous *had* happened within the hospital staff and now had caught up to him. But his first rational thought tempered that view with a more likely scenario: his son had temporarily lost his mind in the aftermath of his first violent encounter. Under the circumstances, he'd rather believe the latter.

He called Myra from the airport to see if Jesse had checked in at the office. No word. He ordered a search through the airline and filed a missing persons report with the police.

46

MATAMOROS
2:45 P.M.

The CareFlight helicopter settled to the ground in a Mexican cornfield near a shanty. Dr. Sylvan sat in the copilot's seat. Jesús, the Sanetria priest, remained in the compartment behind her with Jesse Stiles. A lab technician wearing a surgical mask climbed out of the door. He made his way toward the wooden shack carefully carrying another stainless steel canister in rubber-gloved hands.

Jesse sat imprisoned, his hands tied behind his back and a black hood secured over his head by a hangman's noose. Jesús idly played with the other end of the rope. Neva turned in her seat. "Don't wait for the others to come. Do it now." She held up a bundle of bills, waiting for his reply. "Did you hear me?"

He snatched the bundle from her fingers, laughing evilly. "*No comprende.*"

Like a cat, he leaped from the door of the craft, squinting from the rotor wash. Turning around, he took the rope in both hands and jerked the noose tight around Jesse's neck. The boy stumbled forward, choking, blinded by the hood. Hands tied, unable to break his fall, he plunged face first to the ground with a cry of pain and fear. Jesus yanked the noose tight again with a growl, delivering a kick to the boy's lower back.

In the helicopter Neva saw none of this. She listened to her headset and watched her lab employee entering the shack.

Opening the wooden door with his foot, the man in the lab

jacket glanced furtively around in the gloom. Moving quickly, almost blindly, he stole toward the altar. Once there, he quickly placed the medical canister down and fumbled through his smock for a screwdriver. His breathing sluffed unevenly through the filter of the surgical mask.

Near his feet a hand in a black leather glove reached swiftly from beneath the altar cavity. The whites of the attendant's eyes suddenly appeared above his mask as the hand firmly took hold of his ankle. He dropped the screwdriver and screamed, kicking wildly. But the hand held firm. His screams could not be heard outside, above the roar of the helicopter engines.

His thrashing dumped him backward across a five-gallon bucket of filth. The container toppled under his weight, spilling a black oozing fluid which released a vile stench. A half-decomposed human skull rolled from the bucket across the earthen floor. Seeing it, the technician roared with renewed terror and wrenched his body around in the dirt, crawling, rolling, kicking, clawing. Suddenly he was free and scrambling toward the open door.

Instantly a black-clad pursuer threw the altar across the room, emerging from beneath it. Leaping after the young man, he tackled him from behind just as he reached the door. The lab attendant screamed and kicked against him with all his might, breaking the man's grip. In a split-second the young man burst through the door and sprinted across the open area toward the churning helicopter.

Behind him in the shack, a metallic click sounded in the darkness.

Halfway to the chopper he passed Jesús leading Jesse by the rope.

"What is this?" the priest demanded.

The lab assistant neither paused nor bothered to explain. He continued to run for his life, shedding the lab jacket now covered with dirt and liquid filth.

"*Andele!*" Jesús turned and dragged Jesse by the noose toward the tall corn. He looked back in time to see a man dressed in black, wearing a black head mask, standing in the door of the shack. He saw rather than heard the strobe-like flash of an automatic weapon and felt the vibration of bullets passing within inches of his face. Abandoning Jesse, the priest bent low and plunged headlong into the corn, simply running for his life.

Seeing the gunfire, Dr. Sylvan ordered the chopper into the air. The lab assistant didn't quite make it to the door of the craft before it lifted free of the ground. He managed to desperately grab the landing gear, which tilted the craft to one side. As the pilot struggled to stabilize his power, Neva coldly cocked a .45 pistol, preparing to shoot the assistant off the runners.

But a second helicopter had suddenly arrived on the scene amid the confusion. It was an unmarked black jet Ranger. Hovering in front of them, several commandos aimed automatic weapons from the open doorway.

"Get us out of here," Neva screamed to her pilot.

But one of the gunners sent a short burst of fire through the windshield, shattering glass across both of their laps. The pilot set the CareFlight chopper down quickly in spite of Neva's screaming orders to the contrary. The lab assistant dropped free ten feet above the ground, and as the aircraft came to rest, it pinned one of his legs beneath its landing gear. He struggled vainly against it on the ground.

Near the door of the shack the black-clad man with the ski mask headgear waited with a hand-held radio. "Hocus-pocus got away," he said breathing hard. "Do you want me to bring him in?"

"Negative, Benji. No time. We've got Neva red-handed."

"Very well."

47
MINISTRY GOLF COURSE
3:53 P.M.

In the previous four hours, Pauline had paid a visit to the hospital administration offices to find Neva Sylvan, wanting to question her about the icon and about Jesse Stiles. Once again the elusive woman could not be found. Danna had provided no reliable clues. Pauline had left disgusted.

Next she had gone to the television post-production suite where Joel Lassiter was busily editing the "Grace in the Holy Land" TV special. He assured her that he would have it ready ahead of schedule at the rate he was going. He seemed to enjoy his work. His goal was excellence, pure and simple. When he delivered a project, he no doubt went home and slept well, carrying none of the heavy burden Pauline now brought to the viewing. She managed to see various edited clips of her father's sermon from the Valley of Hinnom. The scenes created in her a discomfort more powerful than the sensation she had fought the day she had been there. The discomfort had become more acute and real now, knowing so much more than she had known then.

She requested a look at Billy Boren's music segments. A few clips were available in an off-line editing suite. Lassiter informed her that they were quite rough, requiring much more technical work to get them ready for broadcast. He explained that this was because of the complexities of the sophisticated sound track. She watched the limited clips of his performance through new eyes now, unable to enjoy the music. She hoped never to see him again after the disgusting picture she had found in his file. *Is he repentant?* she wondered. *How can he masquerade with that phony smile?* She ordered his music segments cut from the show.

In frustration she had decided that she needed to speak with Lydia again, and ordered her driver toward the Steeple. Spying the golf driving range nearly deserted as they passed in the limousine, impulsively she signaled her driver to stop. By late afternoon the crowd had thinned to a pair of retired businessmen in baseball caps. The two of them leaned on their irons and chatted amicably, as if they had the rest of their lives to drive their bucket of balls.

Manuel swerved from the roadway and slid the limo to a stop in the gravel parking lot. He enjoyed spontaneous orders. Leaping out, he opened Pauline's door. "Clubs in the trunk?"

"No." She shook the wrinkles from her dress. "I just need to *hit* something. Know what I mean?" She spoke with uncharacteristic venom.

He grinned. "Bad day, huh?"

"I wish I were Mike Tyson."

He paused, then hurried toward the equipment shack after her. "Don't you mean Lee Trevino?"

She thought about it as she carefully selected a one-wood. "No," she smiled grimly. "Mike Tyson." She stepped across the walkway to an open tee.

Imagining each ball to be one of Evan's contrary ideas, or one of her Dad's unpleasant revelations, or one of her own glaring errors, she sent several dozen slices deep into the trees to the right of the fairway. *Who cares about form?* she seethed. *This just feels necessary.*

Whack! She continued to lash away at ball after ball. *Whack!* Everything in her world had turned on her. *Whack!* The things she had always counted on seemed about as stable as quicksand. *Whack!* Every time she turned around there seemed to be a new crisis in her lap. *Whack!* Next she'd probably hear that Billy had AIDS. *Whack!* Jesse Stiles is missing. *Whack!*

Watching the last white ball impale the green orb of a distant tree like a bullet, she tossed the driver aside. "That's all," she said, turning to go. She strode back toward the limo fingering a small blister in the palm of her hand.

Manuel hurried ahead, chuckling and talking to himself. "*Una mujer muy mandona.*"

A banged-up yellow Pinto squealed suddenly from the pavement and pulled in beside the limo. Barry Malone leaped out and approached apologetically. "Pauline, could I just see you a minute?" He glanced about, as if fearful of being followed.

I don't want to hear this, she thought. *I don't care what it is.* She reluctantly waited for his approach.

"I need to tell you something," he said, taking a deep breath to calm himself. "About Dr. Sylvan, just in case—"

Pauline was already suffering from crisis overload. Not only that, she had been used as an unofficial channel of information all of her life and she deeply resented it. It was part of being the daughter of a powerful man.

Barry sensed her reluctance and grew tentative. "I'm sorry. I don't know who else to tell. She—she did something dangerous. It could have killed Lydia that night before I called you in Jerusalem."

At this, Pauline put aside her weariness, figuring he was either a paranoid kid or he knew something she needed to know. In either case, she'd better listen.

Encouraged by the change he saw in her eyes, he went on. "Sylvan ordered April and me to give Lydia a shot of epinephrine before she fibrillated. Before her attack."

Pauline didn't understand what this meant. "You need to take this up with the medical staff, Barry."

"No, listen, I've checked all the manuals, and it's completely radical. Outside of all recommended procedure. I couldn't follow through with it because at her age I was sure it would overload her heart. All of our tests show that Lydia has no heart disease. No enlargement. Nothing requiring that kind of extreme measure. Sylvan knew that. She was looking at the charts that night on the computer. The EKG was on the med channel. Anyway, I didn't know what I was going to do and then suddenly Lydia fibrillated and I had no choice but to start normal CPR. Later on, you know, I wondered if Neva had made a mistake or something. Maybe she had a bad night, or bad information. But I checked the records, and there was nothing to indicate using epinephrine under those circumstances. Today I find that Lydia's medical chart has been altered to remove my notes about the epinephrine order. For one thing, that's criminal. I don't know if Neva changed it, but who else would it be?"

Pauline began to feel a darkening suspicion about Neva. But she didn't want to be governed by her feelings on the matter. She needed hard facts. There was no solid evidence of misconduct yet, and she had not been able to track the woman down in all the chaos. She weakened at the thought of running down the details of Barry's information. She had enough to do. "Whatever you do, you should go through proper channels on this, Barry. There are grievance procedures."

"Grievance? Who do I grieve to? Neva? Or someone who works for her?"

Once again Pauline felt overwhelmed. Too much too fast. "Alright. I don't know." Her mind cross-referenced her own knowledge of the woman. She had been her father's medical director for several years. "Don't spread another word of this, OK? Let me look into the procedures and I'll get back to you. Remember, chain of command is there to protect all of us." It was the pat line she'd always used in these situations.

Barry couldn't believe he'd heard it. He stepped backwards, confused and growing more worried for exposing his suspicions to her. "OK. Yes, ma'am," he said. But he paused as he prepared to enter his Pinto. "Miss Grace?"

Pauline looked back from the door of the limousine.

"Procedures might protect you and me, but what did they do for Lydia that night? She might have been killed." He entered the car and slammed its door, spitting gravel as he sped from the lot.

48
GRACE MANSION
4:15 P.M.

Evan inserted the key Pauline had given him into the lock of the mansion door. Pushing it open, for a minute he just stood there. He had the next half-hour to look through the library for more information on the icon before taking supper at Rick and Connie's house. In the meantime a new emergency had been added to the current crop of mysteries: Jesse Stiles had disappeared between Houston and Brownsville. Verlin was beside himself. Evan had a hunch that the abduction was linked to Dr. Grace's disappearance and the bombing of Alan's yacht. No real evidence, just coincidental catastrophes. But he couldn't rule out the possible link. Something bigger than he could see was going on here.

Moving into the entryway, he shut the door and stood listening to the silence of the house. It revived in him a childhood memory. A feeling of guilt. The sense of guilt he'd felt when sneaking around his parents' bedroom as a boy. He'd searched through bedside stand, mattress, closets and private boxes of jewelry, buttons and keepsakes. He'd never found what he'd found in another bedroom, when he had stayed with a staff minister's son. In that house they had found magazines of pornography. His own bedroom sleuthing at home turned up nothing. This had reaffirmed to the boy that his parents were true Christian believers, practicing what they preached. *Funny to recall it now*, he thought. Once again he felt that "sneaking around" guilt.

A supporting timber settled at the top of the entryway with a creaking sound. He imagined that one of the mounted animal trophies had actually snorted. *It's really a watchdog*, he kidded himself. *Any minute now an elephant or antelope will turn its head and trumpet a warning to the entire house, "Evan's back! Sneaking around again!"*

He smiled as he walked on through the sitting area toward the studio, chuckling at the vivid insanity of his own imagination.

He entered the meeting room at the lower level and stopped, feeling as if someone was staring at him. He glanced around and saw nothing amiss, but felt himself drawn to the gallery of healing crusade photos on the wall. Dr. Grace's sympathy-lined face appeared handsome and credible beneath his gray hair, wearing his ever-present clerical collar. But beside him Pauline's smile lit up each picture like a model's pose, eclipsing the Third-World throngs with their hand-carved canes and leprous litters in the background. His sister's face reflected that single-minded delight of simply being there in Daddy's shadow.

"Hmm," he said with realization, "no wonder I don't belong here. I never felt that way . . ."

He wandered across the gallery to the lone picture of himself. He and his father had stood in a desert place so long ago. Dr. Grace had only gray temples then, not the thinning white crown he wore nowadays. He had been in his late thirties, Evan estimated. In the picture his father's arm rested across his shoulder. Once again Evan could almost feel it. *So this is how Dad chooses to remember me?* he mused. *I was eight. There's no going back.*

As he examined more closely, his eyes were drawn to a penciled date in the lower left corner of the frame. He pulled the picture from the wall and read it to himself. "1957." He turned the picture over and saw a name, "Nimrut Dag." An unusual name. Not one he recognized. He turned back to the picture and studied it more carefully. He noted the ruins of an ancient pantheon on the side of the mountaintop in the background of the picture. *That must be Nimrut Dag.* One demigod figure stood tall above a forest of fallen idols. Their features in the picture were not clear enough to make out, since they appeared out-of-focus. He returned the picture to its nail on the wall and straightened it. But as he walked away toward the loft, it tilted again behind him.

Near the top of the steps his vision was arrested by an empty space on the floor—where the icon case had been! *Please, God! No!* He looked quickly around. Nothing. He felt a helpless feeling. Someone else was pulling all the strings. *No wonder they blew Alan's yacht from the sea,* he thought frantically. *They knew they could get the icon anyway. Anyone who could pay forty million could pay to have it stolen. They could buy the security staff, for crying out loud. And probably have. Those killers have been in here.* He ran down the steps to the table and picked up the telephone, punching a pre-dialed number.

"Dr. Grace's office."

He was out of breath. "Jann, let me talk to Pauline."

Jann checked her watch. "She should be with Lydia about now."

"Thanks. Later," he said, hanging up.

He punched the speakerphone button and hit the one-number code for Alan's La Jolla home. The telephone rang and rang and rang. As it had done all day when he had tried to call. Each unanswered ring accused his conscience of reckless endangerment. He had interrupted the icon deal and had probably cost Alan and the others their lives. He reminded himself that Alan had been an unmitigated con man. But as the phone continued to ring, unanswered, he couldn't bring himself to believe that the man deserved death. Besides, his own life was obviously vulnerable now. And Pauline's. Not to mention his daughter Jilly and ex-wife, living just down the hill.

He disconnected the line and looked up at the wall of crusade pictures. "Alright, Old Man, I need to know if this is your doing or not. OK? Things are getting pretty damn serious around here." He checked his watch and muttered, "Whoever did this had inside help or I don't know anything."

49

THE STEEPLE
4:35 P.M.

"Neva was a lab technician in those days," Lydia recalled, shuffling across the bedroom floor.

Pauline walked beside the old woman as she exercised. In this meeting with the intercessor she had decided to learn whatever Lydia knew about the enigmatic medical director, Neva Sylvan.

Lydia continued. "I was interceding for the cancer research project in Matamoros. That's how I got started with your dad back then." She turned to pace another lap of the room, seeming to gain strength as she went. "This feels good," she commented to the side before continuing. "Your dad built a . . . a prayer loft up there on the wall above the floor of the lab. Did you know about it?"

"No, I didn't know that. I don't know much of anything about the lab."

Lydia stopped to gesture. "We didn't stay in the loft, though. Sometimes we actually came down and laid our hands on cancerous tissue to pray. We had no fear."

"You say 'we.' Who else did this?"

"Well, maybe it was just me. It was such a privilege to pray for—well, it was like praying for the future. We prayed for the cure, you know? Not just sickness. We prayed for the final cure."

"You mean, *you* prayed?"

"Well, sometimes I could get some of the other girls to join me. Most of them had conflicts with their bridge clubs and bake sales and such. But that was a special time for me. I'm not sure what we accomplished in the Spirit, but prayer is never wasted. Well now, let me see, that was . . . 1967. You had Laetrile clinics and a lot of that stuff starting across the border. Other preachers attacked your dad for being a charlatan, a charismatic or whatever they wanted to call him." She stopped and looked Pauline in the eye. "I say your dad was courageous. He didn't rule out anything God didn't rule out, and that's what I always liked about the man." She shuffled on again, muttering. "He let God be God. Not many do these days. They want God all figured out on their charts and graphs. All the loose ends tucked into some brainy position. But oh, you know, we wanted to see a cure so bad back then."

"Mother died." Pauline's mind simply clicked out the comment like a remembered statistic. Once again she saw her father's quaking hands in Jerusalem, trembling while riding in the limousine.

Lydia continued quietly walking. "Yes. Come to think of it, the project sort of ended after that. Your father went into a long period of mourning."

"I'm not sure he's ever come out of it, Lydia. Is that possible? Maybe that's what has him bound?"

She thought about it carefully. "Something sure does. Who is that Nephil I saw in the dream? Maybe that's it. Cancer. I don't know."

"So when did Neva become a doctor?"

"Oh, she disappeared for about ten or twelve years after we stopped the program. Then here she comes back in '81, a full-blown doctor. Next thing, she was medical director. You know, it has never been easy for your father to find doctors willing to give prayer any credit. Most of them want their medicine and prayer in two different worlds. But Neva allows for it. I'm not sure what she believes about it, but she allows for it. You know—" She checked herself. "—but then, I don't want to say anything out of turn."

Pauline waited, but it seemed the old woman was going to let it drop. "What were you going to say? I've heard rumors about Neva. I need to know everything."

Lydia waited quietly, thinking it over. "Well, I'll . . . I'll simply say that I rebuked her. She was going to touch me, and I just up and rebuked her. I don't know *why* I do these things sometimes. I called her by name, I pointed at her, and I said, 'Neva, you will not touch me.'" She looked at Pauline as if amazed at herself. "Can you believe I said that? Back there in that hospital I did that."

Pauline began to see the possibility of a mysterious wisdom at work in Lydia's action. Perhaps a divine protection. Especially if Barry was right about Neva's harmful intent. "You don't know why you rebuked her?"

"No." She began to walk again. "There are times I don't know the 'why' or the 'wherefore.' Only God knows. I just *know* sometimes, or I just do sometimes, and I have to trust God to pick up the pieces. Sometimes I don't have the foggiest."

"Let's rest for a minute," Pauline said, turning the old woman around to sit on the bed.

Lydia's eyes grew distant and serious. "You know, we don't go through anything in this life by accident. There's a great purpose to it. I've found He seldom does things the same way twice. He's always bigger than our eyes to see Him. His ways are always above ours. Always. I think it was Paul who said, 'we know in part.'"

She finished, color invigorating her cheeks. "I'm feeling stronger every day, don't you know it? Praise my Lord for another day. I love Him so." She closed her eyes and rocked quietly back and forth. Pauline felt suddenly like an intruder.

A commotion drew her eyes to the door behind them.

"Excuse me," Evan said, crossing the room on tiptoes. "I'm afraid I've got to break in with some bad news here. The icon—"

"Well, look who's here!" Lydia called happily. "Evangel Grace!" Her face was instantly rapturous.

"The icon's missing," he whispered to Pauline as he tried to acknowledge the superfluous greeting from the intercessor.

Hearing Evan's words, Pauline's mind whirled with fearful new possibilities. She was immediately struck by the arrogance and power of whoever had been able to pluck the fixture from her father's house. She instantly assumed that they had employed inside help. *Now who can we trust?* she thought.

Evan paused, seeing that the old woman stood with arms open to receive him. During his turbulent Grace University years, and the early years of his career, he had known Lydia by sight and reputation. They had talked a few times, he dimly recalled. She had been a friendly fixture on campus, but never a personal friend. He turned partially around, feeling that she must be calling to someone behind him. But no one was there. It was him she meant. It was the same kind of welcome he'd received from Alan Lavalle, but surely this was from a very different source.

He took a step toward her, and she reached forward and hugged him tightly.

He chuckled. "Well, it's good to see you too, Lydia." He patted her back patronizingly. Straining to his right, he caught Pauline's eye for some kind of explanation.

But she only shrugged. She, of all of them, hadn't expected this bond to exist between the intercessor and the black sheep of the Grace family. Once again she questioned Lydia's judgment.

But the incident was not over. Suddenly the old woman's frail arms clutched Evan even more tightly, in a vise-like grip. Surprising him with her strength. Something was going on beyond the obvious. Her grip became so tight it actually hurt his neck. He was more or less stuck, bent awkwardly above her. Afraid to stand and lift her from the floor, afraid to fall forward and land on top of her. So he strained to just hold the old woman steady while she clung to him.

"Oh, Jesus . . ." she whispered.

To his surprise he could feel tears soaking through his shirt. At first the tears felt warm, then they grew quickly cold against his skin. She was reacting as if she'd found a long-lost family member.

"There's an anointing on you, Evangel Grace," she said with such conviction in her voice it sent chills down his spine.

After the delay of a moment, her comment hit home. He felt like he had missed everything God had ever intended for his life. He was beyond any special place in the big religious scheme of things. He had blown it. The "anointing" she spoke of had been lost with his childhood and his naiveté. And to his way of thinking, that's where it properly belonged. How could he have an "anointing" now? Whatever that meant. He was empty of spirit. Full of his own ways. "Anointing" was a religious word for religious people.

"Excuse me." He tried to pry her arms loose from around his

neck so he could explain these things. "What do you mean by anointing?"

She didn't turn loose but held even more tightly, with more strength and determination than he thought she could possibly possess in her aged arms. "The anointing was on you before you were born," she said. "Like Jeremiah, 'before God formed you in your mother's womb He knew you and ordained you.' Your mother knew it. I've always seen it. The anointing of the Lord is without repentance. You belong to Him."

"You're into some deep theological water there," he chuckled, trying to make light of it. He was starting to feel more than a little put-upon. "Thank you very much for the sentiment, Lydia, really, but—" Once again he failed to pull her arms free and looked at Pauline helplessly.

The old woman cried out suddenly, "Your Father loves you, Evan!"

At this he grew quite uncomfortable. By "Father" he knew what she meant. "Heavenly Father," not Simon Grace. For most of his life he had struggled to know the difference between the two, and even now he was not free of confusion about it. What he knew to be ungodly in Simon Grace continued to infect his feelings toward God. He'd given up sorting it out.

"You've forgotten how He loves you," she whispered. "He's never lost you. He never, never, never loses one of His sons."

Evan patted her reassuringly for a moment, hoping to cool whatever passion had come over her. "Thank you for that kind word," he said.

"He never lets go," she continued. "He counts the hairs of your head every day. He weighs the thoughts of your heart. He makes plans you've never even dreamed for yourself. His storehouse is full of good things with your name on them. Your name. Go ahead and run if you will. Make your bed in Hell if you will. He'll be there. That's the love of your Father."

Evan almost laughed aloud—it was something he wanted to do in order to avoid the sudden sensation rushing upward in his heart. He'd never experienced anything so completely crazy in his life. *Has she gone nuts up here in her tower? Or is she simply an old woman too long without a man?*

"He loves you. He loves you so." She held to him with a deep purpose, knowing her words were not enough. The impression of her arms were not enough either. She knew that something inside

Evangel must break. She also knew that it was something she could not do in her own strength.

"Whew!" Lydia let him go and sat back on the bed with a light laugh. She wiped tears from her shining face. "Whew!" she said again, as if she'd just gotten off a carnival ride.

How totally nuts, Evan thought as he self-consciously straightened his wrinkled shirt. Still, he smiled at her like a good sport.

She sat there beaming, looking back and forth from Pauline to Evan. "That wasn't me," she explained.

Evan looked at his sister. His face had grown deeply red.

Pauline remained speechless. Not at all sure of what she had seen.

Peace ruled Lydia's heart. She believed she had delivered a word by the Holy Spirit of God. Let the enemy try to destroy it. That was merely his carnivorous nature—"a roaring lion, seeking whom he may devour." He had already had a field day with this boy. *Peace.* Lydia smiled. Let the birds of doubt pluck at the seed. Let the weeds of Evan's own intellect rage and choke it. *Peace.* Come what may, the Word of the "Prince of Peace" would germinate by the Spirit in due season. Invisibly, it would send down its roots to break Evangel's heart of stone.

50

GRACE FAMILY COMPOUND
Rick Gresham's Residence
5:25 P.M.

A hastily planned dinner at Rick and Connie's house seemed a convenient way for Jilly to spend precious moments with Daddy Number One *and* Two. Pauline had been invited along, to enjoy a home-cooked meal amid the current disruption of schedules.

Most of the conversation grew intense and passed above Jilly's six-year-old head. She nibbled idly at her food. After a time she got up and leaned against Evan, watching him chew and talk. It was not something that would have been normally allowed at mealtime, but since they could only spend these few precious moments together, Rick and Connie let her dawdle with him. He was deeply appreciative.

Jilly reached periodically toward his moving mouth, making gentle contact there. It was a test. Could she stop him in the middle of a sentence? Yes. Could she turn his head anytime she wanted? Yes. And would he look at her and smile? Yes. She snuggled against him and felt warm all over. He was still her Daddy Number One.

"I didn't notice anything unusual happening at the mansion this morning," Connie said. "Of course, I can get busy around here and not notice. What do the guards say?"

"Nothing happened according to them," Evan replied between bites of steamed broccoli. "But we've got the police questioning everybody."

"I'm just afraid that the police will attract the press," Pauline worried.

"They will," he promised, kissing Jilly's fingers as she placed them across his mouth. "I gave the police a one point five million dollar market value on the icon. I still don't think the forty mil is a legit figure. Something else is being paid for there. Or paid off, as the case may be." He gave his daughter another gentle squeeze.

"Something is really bothering me," Pauline said. "In everything else that's going on, I still haven't found Neva. According to Danna—uh, excuse me—" She glanced at Connie.

"You can use the D word around here," Rick quipped with a mischievous grin.

Pauline waited for a cue from Connie. It was *her* feeling about Evan's "other woman" that mattered. Awkwardness seemed perfectly natural. She couldn't quite adjust to the fact that Evan, Rick and Connie seemed so easy with each other anyway. She waited until Connie returned a smile and a nod. Only then did she continue. "Danna says Dad called Neva about the icon. According to her, he put Neva in charge of getting it shipped."

"We should *both* have a talk with Neva Sylvan when we're done here," Evan suggested.

Pauline took up her napkin and rose from the table. "Something's not right with that woman. She's never available for me. Never. I'm going to call and see if I can corner her right now."

"Why would Neva have anything to do with the icon?" Rick asked. "She's med director."

Evan shrugged. "Dad's missing, she's missing, the icon's missing. Maybe we'll find them all in the same place."

Rick looked up. "Now there's an idea."

"I'll say one thing about all of this," Connie commented. "In my years of being around Grace Ministries, it's never been like this before. This thing feels . . . completely *weird*."

"Nothing surprises me anymore," Rick said, looking up from a forkful of baked chicken.

Jilly had heard none of this—and *enough* of it at the same time. She pulled herself squarely into Evan's lap.

"Jilly, where are your manners?" Connie chided.

"No, I'm through. Really," Evan insisted. In fact, he could think of nothing more important for the moment. Putting his fork down, he snuggled his baby close. Softened by her innocence. It was a temptation to become totally lost in it.

"Why don't you stay here tonight, Daddy?" she asked, tilting her head at him coyly. "I want you to."

"That's very generous of you, sweetheart," Evan said, winking at Rick.

"No, really, Evan," Connie added. "We're fine. Why don't you stay the night? You and Rick leave for Dallas early anyway. It will make things easier."

As nearly as Evan could tell, they were both sincere. He felt a rush of gratitude. "You two are really something," he said. "I'd love to stay." He tickled Jilly. "See there? You really had to twist my arm, didn't you?"

She giggled with pure joy.

51

GRACE HOSPITAL OFFICE
6:01 P.M.

It had been a long and trying day for Danna Lavalle. Her hair had been pulled to the back of her head and tied with a ribbon. Her tongue explored her upper lip as she patiently listened to Pauline's voice on the other end of the telephone.

"We need to see Neva tonight," Pauline insisted. "No excuses."

Danna stared sternly at Neva who sat across the desk from her. "You won't believe this, but she says she had a family emergency," Danna replied. "I'm not sure that Neva is dealing straight-up with any of us, Pauline. Anyway, she's gone and left us with no contact for tonight."

"Danna, there is too much going on for her to do this to me. It is completely irresponsible. I've got to clear things up with her. The icon was stolen today."

Danna's eyes registered surprise at this news.

Pauline continued, "I'm going to have no choice but to make Neva a suspect. I'm reporting her to the police."

Danna's mind whirred like a computer. "I understand. I would do the same," she replied smoothly.

This was no real help to Pauline. She had been hoping to pressure more information from Danna by this threat. Apparently the secretary was telling all that she knew. "What about the board meeting tomorrow? Is she skipping out on that too?"

"She left an absentee vote with me. I believe it's in favor of your interim presidency."

"Truly?" Pauline was puzzled at this, but pleased. It meant that she now had five, instead of the needed four, votes.

Meanwhile in the office Neva glowered at Danna as if she wanted to physically attack. But her arms were securely pinned between two commandos in camouflage fatigues. They had been among those at the raid on the shack near Matamoros that morning.

"I'll call you if I come up with any clues," Danna said.

Pauline's voice betrayed weariness. "I'll be at home. Call me anytime."

"I'm sorry things are such a mess, honey. I've got a feeling they'll get better soon. OK?"

Danna hung up and her blue eyes dropped their "secretary" veil. She watched her boss now with open contempt. "The icon is missing, Neva. I think you should tell us about that too."

Neva glared. "You little spy."

Danna signaled one of the men guarding the door. He opened it and allowed another man to enter with a black satchel. One of the men guarding Neva began forcibly rolling up her sleeve.

"I'm warning you. All of this is coming down on your heads, whoever you are," Neva seethed.

"You still don't seem to understand," Danna replied in a deceptively reasonable tone of voice. "You're going to tell us everything, whether you want to or not. You might as well cooperate."

The man who had entered the office held up a syringe.

Seeing it, Neva choked. "You have no idea what you're dealing with! Please, please, Danna, don't do this. Don't!" Seeing that her words made no difference whatsoever, she added, "This will kill Dr. Grace. Do you understand? *Kill* him. Not to mention everything he's worked for."

Danna shook her head slowly. "I swear, Neva, if I didn't know what you were, I'd almost be convinced."

52

GRACE FAMILY COMPOUND
Rick Gresham's Residence
8:03 P.M.

Rick and Connie stood in the kitchen archway having completed the dishes. They watched Jilly playing with Evan on the floor of the living room. She had him pinned down with doll furniture, like Gulliver and the Lilliputians. The six-year-old had perched a Paddington Bear on his belly and now marched Barbie up his arm. Evan relaxed quietly, absorbing every minute of it.

Rick shifted uncomfortably. "Are you sure you did the right thing divorcing Mr. Wonderful there? He's a pretty irresistible guy."

"According to whom?" Connie turned and slipped her arms around her husband. "You know better than that."

She kissed him lightly. Looking back at Evan and Jilly, she grew thoughtful. "I divorced him alright. He didn't want it to end. Most people think I left him because he played around with Danna. The truth is, I could have forgiven him for that." She looked up and pinched Rick's cheek. "But don't *you* get any ideas, fella."

"Hey, I'm getting ideas alright," he said, sliding his hands teasingly downward.

"Stop that now." She wanted to finish her thought. "I left him because he didn't love me. Do you understand that? It's important that you understand. Completely."

"I understand that if he didn't love you he was some kind of idiot," Rick growled.

"You're just in love," she kidded. "But do you understand the difference it made to me? He was a kid when we married. A very religious kid trying to please God. I worshiped the ground he walked on. I loved him, but . . ."

"So what were you? The bad girl who ruined his life?"

"No. The other way around. To him, I was a good Christian girl. The perfect wife. Just what God wanted for the heir to the throne of 'Grace.' That's why he married me. A logical choice. His heart was never in it." She paused. "I loved him, so I tried to live up to that standard and be all the things he needed, and it about killed me. We both grew, and we would have made it if he had ever been in love with me. But he wasn't." She smiled past the painful memory. "I have no trouble with Danna anymore. She just showed me what Evan really wanted. He had always been good to me. It is just that finally I came to believe that I deserved to have someone whom I could tie around my little finger the way Jilly does out there. Look at them. He can't help himself. It's magic. I wanted that too, that's all. I ended it when he and Danna gave me the chance." She snuggled closer to Rick. "And you've made me glad that I did."

Rick smiled and kissed the top of her head. "You know something? You're a pretty tough customer, babe."

"You better believe it. That's why you can use the D word around here."

"Excuse me," Rick replied, "but it seems to me Evan still doesn't know what he wants. He doesn't have you or Danna—neither one."

Jilly giggled loudly from the other room, and they both turned to watch her bounce her Paddington Bear up and down on Evan's face. "Now what's this?" he protested happily.

Rick mused. "I think right now, he only knows what he lost. And believe me," he turned, kissing Connie's forehead, "it was a lot."

She smiled. "You're such an animal."

He picked her up easily and carried her backwards into the kitchen, kissing her neck softly. "Tell you what. Since we've got a free baby-sitter, I've got some very *unreligious* ideas banging around in my head. What do you say, bad girl?"

She giggled softly. "I'm *your* bad girl."

"That's right. Private stock."

53
PAULINE'S BEDROOM
9:43 P.M.

Pauline paused in the middle of pulling her nightgown over her head. Something strange beset her. She could hear the magnified sound of the satin brushing past her ears. It echoed, like the sound of stone dragging over stone at the end of an ancient hallway. It was an impression. Shaking it off, she let the gown drop to her shoulders and torso. She plucked at the static cling, arranging the buttons and bows on her chest. Her fingers seemed to belong to another person. She had to instruct them twice before they obeyed orders from her brain.

This strange sensation had first begun in Jerusalem as she had gazed at the burning wreckage of the pale blue Renault. Since then, from time to time, she had found herself in a protective shock zone. Insulated from reality. It happened more often now. She went through the motions of dealing with the issues at hand, but from time to time would hear voices as if the people around her were speaking through a tube.

As she prepared for bed it seemed as if the real Pauline had retreated into an inner chamber of the soul. She had felt like a total stranger at dinner with Rick, Connie and Evan. Everything she heard or touched or felt or tasted had been processed by an outer person who was not quite real. This outer Pauline acted as a mask, a surrogate, carrying on the work of everyday reality. The outer Pauline could be hurt, shocked, tormented. The *real* Pauline experienced everything secondhand. Even the sounds of a nightgown brushing past her ear was unreal, or surreal.

She sat down on the bed, dreading the ordeal of trying to sleep. Sleep itself seemed secondhand.

The shock zone had become a lonely, frightening place. She longed to share the torment, speak of it with someone who cared. She needed more than a friend—she needed her father. No. More than that. She needed a true love. Someone who would curl up beside her and whisper words that would not feel secondhand.

Words that would not echo. Words that would touch the real Pauline.

She began to weave as she sat on the bed, eyes growing suddenly heavy, crossing from an irresistible urge that sprang from terror more than fatigue. She shook herself awake, pondering the insight that this drowsiness must have been like that which overtook the disciples in the Garden of Gethsemane when Christ had found them sleeping. Time after time He had asked for their company. Time after time He had found them asleep. Who could resist that sleep? She reflected that they must have been so uncertain, so terrified on the night of His betrayal that they, like her, could only escape through the drug of sleep. But such sleep promised no rest. Not to them. Not to her. Only fitful tossing and turning, nightmares and rude awakenings.

The telephone jangled and she leaped toward it, yanking it from its cradle to her ear. "Hello?" Her own voice echoed back to her. Had she really answered the phone? Had she? She couldn't be sure until she heard a reply.

Someone was sobbing.

"Hello?"

"Sorry to disturb you, Pauline. This is Verlin."

"Verlin, yes. What is it?"

"I just wanted to let you know . . . uh, uh . . . that my boy walked in here off the street tonight . . . just an hour ago. Whoever took him . . . uh, uh . . . has let him go."

A comforting breeze blew across her brow with this news. Only a breeze. She needed so much more. "That's wonderful news, Verlin. Wonderful."

"It is wonderful. I'm not sure how wonderful. We can't tell for sure what he's been through. He's not making much sense."

He paused for a long time, and Pauline felt the shock zone building around her again.

"I . . . we think maybe he's confused. He's telling wild stories about what happened over there. Anyway, I won't be going to the meeting in the morning, if you don't mind. I want to get him looked at."

"No . . . of course." His words slowly penetrated the inner Pauline, who finally responded again. "Of course. Sure. I understand."

"Don't worry. I will make my motion and vote *in absentia*. I'll send Myra. You'll get what you want from me, no problem."

Suddenly she didn't want anything from him. She had one too many votes already. "Oh, no, Verlin. It's alright. Well, thanks—uh, thanks for calling. I'm just glad Jesse's back. I'll pray that everything goes well for you tomorrow, and . . . and when you get back let us know, will you?"

There was no reply. Apparently he had hung up.

54

GRESHAM RESIDENCE
11:59 P.M.

Evan lay flat on his back, filling and emptying his lungs with long satisfied draughts of sleep. Pauline had called him after hearing from Stiles. He'd received the news of Jesse's safe return as a perfect nightcap, after spending several hours in play with Jilly.

The playing had been therapy for him. In a certain important sense, it defined him. How often he forgot who he was. But for now he had no doubt. He was first and foremost Jilly's Daddy Number One. No other agendas, ambitions, or unfinished business. No beer and venison sausage required. This sleep was a natural thing, like laying down to die after a good, full life.

But in the darkness a tiny hand poised above his lips, fingers wriggling ever so slightly, feeling the wind of his sleeping breath. Then the hand descended like a falling leaf to rest lightly against his lips.

His eyes blinked, then opened fully, uncomprehendingly for a moment. He was quickly sobered to realized what had happened. A little girl at midnight, unable to sleep, had crawled silently from her bed to lay beside her other daddy. What did she feel? What did she know? Why had she placed her hand there so softly?

He turned to see her. The pale light passing through the sheers revealed that her eyes were wide open. Solemn, eloquent beyond words. With one arm she clutched her Paddington Bear, the other extended to his face. This was Jilly, mirroring a sadness a six-year-old child should never know. And he instantly knew that he was guilty. Why should a little girl have two daddies? Why should her heart be so divided? Had this moment been foreseen years ago there would have been no "first time" with Danna Lavalle. No confession. No divorce—maybe. Beyond that, whatever the reasons he and Connie had found for going their separate ways, neither of them had fully considered their daughter.

He reached over, wrapping Jilly's cold little fingers in his own. His palm was warm around hers.

"I love you, Daddy," she whispered steadily.

His face broke into a helpless smile, even as his eyes spilled tears to the pillow. He let them flow. There was nothing to hide from his little girl. She already knew. Maybe nothing had ever really gone "over her head" in all of her years. Conversations, negotiations, and those actions that spoke louder than words—she had heard everything with her heart.

After a moment he swallowed and whispered back, "I love you too, Jilly. I do."

He had wanted to say, "I love you more" and carry on the familiar banter he had developed with her. But he was no longer sure that he *did* love her more. There was nothing left in his heart as pure as what he saw in her innocent face just now.

And so he simply watched, and ached, and watched, until her eyes grew heavy and she drifted to sleep. And then he watched and ached some more. Allowing his tears to ebb and flow at will. He felt privileged to own the pain. He had learned at least one thing through the awful tearing of divorce: pain was no killer. Somehow the ache in his heart was the right thing to feel. He knew that like he knew God.

After a time—he wasn't sure if he had slept or not—Connie's form whispered through the room. He could smell the nighttime residue of her perfume, though he could no longer name it. The fragrance was unmistakably hers, full of gentle strength and womanliness. She bent over Jilly and lifted her from the bed, holding her close. For a while she stood silently watching her ex-husband. He watched her. Something priceless remained between them. They had shared eleven years. Years of trying hard, of growing, of being friends, of helping each other. They had wrestled the errors of their youth together, struggled to overcome family curses. And there was something more between them, something both of them understood; for all that had been missing in their marriage, there had been an amazing grace at work to produce this sweet child.

"Time for you and Rick to get going," Connie whispered, carrying Jilly out of the darkened room.

VII

DUNAMIS

Lift up your heads, O gates,
And be lifted up, O ancient doors.

(PSALMS 24:7, NASB)

55
EASTERN TURKEY
Nimrut Dag
6 P.M.

The setting sun intensified the green and ocher hues of the limestone hills below, stretching for fifty miles around. A warm glow bathed the unshaven faces of Simon Grace, Max and Vardan as they walked across the ceremonial mountaintop. A gentle breeze rustled dry apples of Sodom scattered among the wilted lupin and bull thistle at their feet. Around them stood or lay broken statues, once thirty and forty feet tall. Two-ton carved stone heads stared randomly from the ground where they had fallen. Fifty feet above them, separating the eastern and western altar terraces, loomed an artificial mountain peak, a pyramidal tumulus of hand-carried rocks.

The visages of the idols seemed impervious to the weather, war and neglect that had reduced their sanctuary to a boneyard. Disembodied spirits lurked in the cold blue shadows of their eyes as the sun passed from the sky. Beneath conical Urartian war helmets, the giants glared to the four winds as if promising vengeance for their lost glory. A stone eagle's head with a proud, bold beak and alert gaze had fallen from its thirty-foot perch, rolling miraculously to the mountain's crest. It now gazed southward, as if summoning the Prince of Persia from the ruins of Babylon. A lion's head peeked over a foundational row of stones watching the strategic fords of the Euphrates. Its impassive eyes had no doubt witnessed the ancient Urartian wars, the Armenian ascendancy, Alexander's plundering armies, the Seleucid skirmishes, the invading legions of Rome, Paul's missionary journeys, the scimitar-wielding Seljuks, the crusaders of medieval Europe—and in the twentieth century, the frenzied slaughter of Armenian Christians. The seesaw of history had bloodied the waters of the Euphrates at the feet of these old gods. Across the pantheon's silent altars now dismembered stone arms, legs and torsos lay—as if the gods had sacrificed one another in concert with the march of history.

One Seleucid giant seemed unique among the gods of Nimrut

Dag. Crowned with a richly carved garland of oak and grapevine, it appeared more Greek, more civilized than the war-helmeted Urartian idols. "Fortune of Commagene, the last to fall," Max said, proudly resting a hand on the garlanded head. His namesake sculpture, the same head that had been photographed and displayed in the Dunamis boardroom in Mannheim, Germany. "A bolt of lightning threw him down here in 1963. Did you know that?"

"That should tell you something about who is in charge around here," Grace quipped.

"Ah, ah," the German chided with a twinkle in his eye, "no East or West here. Fortune reflects the Greek and the Oriental in one new image. That is why I am so proud of him. Some say 'Fortuna.' Actually, the idol embodies both male and female attributes, as do all the gods. But you saw him in '57, doc. Remember? Still standing above the others, nearly as tall as the tumulus itself? Magnificent."

"He's always been a puzzle to me." Grace took a seat on the lion's-head and continued thoughtfully. "You say that you see Greek and oriental influence in the image. I see something else. I can't forget that Antiochus put him up here."

"There were four named 'Antiochus' in the Dynasty, doc. Which one?"

"You know which one," Dr. Grace quipped, preparing to restate a familiar argument between the two of them. "Antiochus means 'opposer.' That name is no accident. In prophecy Antiochus became the ultimate abominator. The forerunner of Antichrist himself."

Max winced and placed his finger to his lips, signaling Grace to watch his words for the benefit of Vardan Kassabian. The Armenian psychiatrist, moved by private emotions, continued to explore the huge base stones that had once enthroned the giants. "Antiochus knew nothing," he declared with his back to them, having obviously heard every word. "Nor did any of the Seleucid *usurpers*."

Max and Dr. Grace noticed that he spat the words with the force of a wounded believer.

"The secrets of Nimrut Dag, The Tree, the invocations, 'The Songs of Jubal,'" Vardan continued, gazing about with glistening eyes at the gods of his pre-Christian ancestors, "they all belonged to the original Urartians. And of course the Armenian keepers after them. The Seleucids were usurpers."

"That's right, Vardan." Max sent Grace a look that seemed to say, *let's humor him*. Maximilian's connection to the more recent Seleucid Dynasty gave him a somewhat lesser claim to the mountain's secrets, though privately the German felt that his more civilized ancestors were far superior in every way to the original Urartians. Or to the Armenian pagans, for that matter. A fact reflected in the superior Greek stonework in "Fortune of Commagene."

Grace intended to prove them both wrong. For the moment he watched the interplay between the two men and assumed, *Max wants to soothe Vardan's zeal because he is using him*. As a religious leader Dr. Grace understood the rebellious nature of zeal. A wise leader nurtured it, but then provided guidance for its unpredictable force. It could topple a king if he failed to gauge its direction and power.

"We owe the Urartians," Max added expansively.

He means to placate the man, the preacher concluded. He had hoped otherwise, wanting to divide and convert their non-Christian minds.

"Without 'The Songs of Jubal,'" Max went on, "we wouldn't be standing here, now would we?" He turned to Grace with a wink and changed the subject. "I'm in awe of the ancients, doc. Aren't you? They make me feel small."

"The leaders of the ancient world wanted it that way," Grace replied. "That's why they invoked the giants, the champions." Reading Vardan's darkening mood from the corner of his eye, he added, "The idols were always intended to intimidate the simpleminded. The kings of the Urartians, later the Seleucids, Romans, Greeks, Syrians, Canaanites—Mayans and Aztecs for that matter—they all worshiped the Sons of the Watchers, the giants, trying to elevate themselves to a godlike power. The kings sculpted their own faces on these stones. In some form it still happens today. Channeling, 'spirit guides,' gurus and ascended masters and such. Solomon said, 'there is nothing new under the sun.'"

The preacher crossed a leg easily, reaching down to pluck a stalk of bull thistle. He examined its needle-like thorns. "Antiochus I was the first Commagene, wasn't he, Max?"

"According to Grandpa 'Wolfie.' The first Seleucid Prince of Commagene. Ruled this tumulus 265 years before Christ. Of course Vardan will point out that he built it on the ancient Urartian High Place. History has rather forgotten that."

"Antiochus borrowed shamelessly from Urartian mythology," the psychiatrist returned. "These are Urartian foundation stones. Much older than the Seleucid Dynasty. They plastered their Greek influence over the top of them. The tumulus is Urartian. Each stone hand-carried from Ararat. No Seleucid king ever wrung that kind of devotion from my people."

"You get no argument from me. The tumulus was the forerunner of the pyramids," Commagene acknowledged. "But Fortune was the unique god of Antiochus." Once again Max patted the head of the idol proudly.

"Antiochus borrowed from us. Like all of the others."

"We don't know his true name," Grace interjected. "Maybe he's the one I'm after. The sun god."

Max looked away. His eyes glowered with a secret fire. Yet he turned again and nodded for Grace's benefit. "Perhaps Jubal saw him before the Flood, huh? Perhaps he is Rimmon?"

Grace tossed the bull thistle aside. "I doubt it. But there's something about him . . ." He stood and began to walk around the head of Fortune of Commagene, examining it as he continued, "There's something about this whole place that even you haven't discovered, my friend." He stuffed both hands in his hip pockets and stretched up and down. "The Jewish prophets saw an evil empire here in the north. Isaiah, Jeremiah, Ezekiel, Daniel, Zechariah—all of them saw it in dreams and visions. 'Out of the north an evil shall come'—'Wail, O gate, cry, O city, for smoke comes from the north'—'Lift up a standard toward Zion! Seek refuge, do not stand still, for I am bringing evil from the north, and great destruction.' The prophets saw this place in the Spirit. Or perhaps some saw it with their own eyes. Who knows how far they might have wandered?"

He turned and braced a foot against the stone head of the lion, delivering his thoughts with the practiced eloquence of a preacher. "Through fifteen hundred years of history Jerusalem was raped from the north. According to prophecy, it's not over. The present age will end when the northern kingdoms come down 'to take a spoil, to take a prey.' Armageddon, the valley of Megiddo, is the northern pathway to Zion in which it will all end. Many armies have taken that route. The Turks met defeat there in World War I— thanks to the British. That ended the deportation of Armenians from Ararat too, I might add for Vardan's benefit."

He paused thoughtfully. "The north. I find it interesting that the lust of the heart of Satan was to possess the power of the Great

North: '. . . you said in your heart,' Isaiah wrote, 'I will ascend to heaven; I will raise my throne above the stars of God, and I will sit on the mount of assembly in the Sides of the North.' Well, here we are. The Sides of the North, if you will. In Heaven the Sides of the North was the seat of power, control. I think Nimrut Dag marks its earthly counterpart. These are the thrones of the princes of the north who are not idols, but rather the demon spirits of the Nephilim."

He pushed back from the lion and walked again. "Here was Eden, before the Flood. Six hundred miles *north* of Jerusalem. Here the Urartians conjured the spirits of the Nephilim to worship the images of the giants after the Flood. Vardan, you are right. Antiochus borrowed Fortune of Commagene from your ancestors. He's an idol of one of the Sons of the Watchers."

The psychiatrist stood resolutely, with his back to the preacher, hiding his petulant response.

"What happened to their great civilizations?" Grace asked. "Their armies, cities? Why did they vanish overnight like the Mayans of Mexico, leaving these ruins?"

Still no response from Vardan. Commagene had crossed his arms and uncomfortably drummed his fingers across his pursed lips as he listened.

Simon Grace relentlessly pressed his dissertation. "They lost their battle in history, my friends. As Isaiah prophesied, a child was born, a Son was given. The government came to rest on His shoulders. The princes of the Great North arose from their thrones to inspire Herod to kill the child. The innocents of Bethlehem died, but the Messiah escaped with the aid of angels, Watchers. They warned his parents to hide in Egypt, in the land of the necromancers, where Satan would never expect to find him. Ha! But thirty years later the Devil finally got the job done—except he inadvertently fulfilled prophecy. Golgotha was surrounded by clouds of invisible Watchers the day of the Crucifixion. Watchers from both kingdoms. Darkness and light."

Dr. Grace paced and gestured, making the stone idol his pulpit. "On the cross, the twenty-second Psalm of Passion tells us, the Lord was surrounded by the strong bulls of Bashan. Slavering, roaring in his ears, claiming the bloodbaths of the Urartians had been enough, the only sacrifice mankind deserved. They mocked the blood of the Son of God. They dared Him to call a legion from the clouds to wreak vengeance. They offered Him the world for it. The

Watchers of the Heavens were there. They would have gladly unleashed their swords for him, but—" Grace paused dramatically, feeling every word. "—He forgave His executioners, and in that one profound act He trapped His enemies. By giving up His life He took the keys to Hell and the grave and for three days invaded the invisible realm of the dead."

"The Good Doctor Grace" walked to the head of the largest god on the mountain and kicked it derisively. "Remember that day, Zeus? I think you do. You haven't been the same since." Grace turned to look at both of his traveling fellows. "Since the day the God-Man wrenched the keys of Hell from him! He could not touch Him then, and I am here to say the Sides of the North are His today!" He laughed with the joy of his own faith, feeling it well up in his chest.

Commagene was not amused. He lost his smooth composure. "I had no idea you were going to do this, doc . . . be like this." He pointed to Vardan, whose posture had become rigid like the stones before him. "Go easy here."

"You are scientists," Grace scolded in reply. "This is a history lesson. You should becomfortable with it." He smiled to himself mischievously. "Two thousand years ago the Lord, the Lamb slain from the foundation of the world, spoiled the grip of His enemies on the underworld. He also spoiled this High Place. He will continue until the end of the age when He comes openly to show His authority over all. They will cower before the Lion of Judah then. Every knee will bow. He will ruin them and will parade their ruin before the eyes of every soul who has ever lived or been deceived by their schemes. They are defeated, Max. But their humiliation has just begun." He walked slowly toward the German philanthropist.

> "'Time will run back and fetch the age of gold,
>   And speckl'd vanity will sicken soon and die,
> And leprous sin will melt from earthly mold,
>   And Hell itself will pass away, And leave
> Her dolorous mansions to the peering light of day.'

"John Milton. Written in the year 1629. He was a Renaissance man. Schooled in every science and religion. He said, and I say, Antiochus and all of the Seleucids made a mistake here. They chose the Urartian gods. A dead-end in history."

Vardan turned to face him. "Antiochus was just another conquering egomaniac. He wouldn't have known the truth if it struck him in the face. And look there, it has." He pointed to the bust of Zeus in the likeness of Antiochus IV, his nose broken by the fall from his throne. "There he is, presuming to sit with the gods," he snorted. "The pompous impostor believed in his army. He was a desecrator. Never important. It is the Urartian secrets that live on. As they have from the beginning."

Grace's eyes sparkled with the challenge in Vardan's logic. "The secrets have become nonsense. You are wrong about Antiochus. Antiochus IV took the occult knowledge of the Urartians to heart. He became so good at the secrets he claimed to 'channel' Zeus himself. He would become Zeus before his entire court, guiding the affairs of state with the wisdom of a god. He took it very seriously, finally declaring himself god. An epiphany. There are still coins of the realm bearing the inscription, 'God Manifest, Antiochus IV, Epiphanes.'"

"And how little you really know," Vardan muttered to himself, his face grown livid.

"Now enough of this," Max chided, looking between the two of them with dismay. "Our discussions should remain respectful at least."

Vardan glared from one to the other, then wheeled and stalked back toward the foundation stones.

Max grimaced. "I'm afraid you've struck a nerve."

"I would expect to."

"But there is no need. I see no threat in what you've said personally. There are other explanations. For example, I think Antiochus had more to do with politics than religion. Politics and power. That's the great sweep of history." He nodded toward the bust of Zeus. "He was pragmatic. He knew the Greeks were bringing the power of a new civilization into the world. He simply wanted to take the political high ground, so he made himself god. That's politics. Epiphanes didn't care about the secrets. He became 'Epiphanes' to win votes and influence Urartians, so to speak."

Grace remained steadfast. "I'm afraid it was much more than that. It is the delusion of politicians to believe they *have* power when they are really pawns on a cosmic chess board. Conquerors included. Nimrod, Pharaoh, Nebuchadnezzar, Darius, Alexander, Caesar, Pompey, Charlemagne, Napoleon, Stalin, Hitler, Idi Amin, Qaddafi, Saddam Hussein. Politics is a mask worn by the 'principalities and powers, the rulers of the darkness.' All of them subject to the one true God. Antiochus Epiphanes lusted to be a god. Beyond politics. He wanted to ascend to a seat in the Sides of the North. To prove himself worthy, he obeyed their voices, violating the Temple in Jerusalem. Only a serious devotee would attempt such a thing. He butchered the Jews who dared to worship the Lord High God there. Those who had gone apostate, he bought with bribes and paraded through Antioch. 'My Antiochian' Jews,' he called them. 'Whores,' Judas Maccabees called them."

Max watched Grace closely now. "We've never discussed this before. I can see that it troubles you."

"I'm trying not to be troubled," Grace said, pacing more slowly now. He felt as though he was doing a "war dance of faith," working himself up to be strong for what lay ahead. Reassuring himself of the reasons he had come here. "Antiochus IV, the ultimate 'opposer,' erected an idol to himself in the Jerusalem Temple. Only he gave it the name of the Roman god Jupiter, who was also called Zeus by the Greeks. The very god he had supposedly incarnated. Also called Jove, by the way. God only knows his real name. Talk about serious! Antiochus Epiphanes set his image on the altar in the sanctuary of the Lord God Jehovah. He committed the first 'abomination of desolation.' The next will trigger the final chapter of the Great Tribulation."

Grace tilted his head to curiously regard the head of Zeus in the likeness of Antiochus before resuming, "He instituted a pagan festival to celebrate the rebirth of the sun in his honor. You know, I recall the image referred to as 'the winged solar disk of Zeus.'" Dr. Grace mused aloud, "'Upon the wing of abominations shall come one who makes desolate . . .' The desolating sacrilege . . . a winged solar disk." Grace roused himself again and spoke to his companions. "I suspect we are dealing with Zeus in this foul disease of cancer. Jupiter, Jove, Hadad-Rimmon, Baal—all names for the same Nephil. Antiochus called his festival in Jerusalem 'a festival of light.' The source of the light was the sun. They slaughtered pigs in place of lambs on the altar of the Lord. Human beings as well, on the twenty-fifth of every month."

Max Commagene listened intently, watching the last of the sun's fire sink slowly beneath the horizon. "So the battle isn't over," he mused. He seemed invigorated by the approach of night. "And there's nothing new under the sun?" An implied meaning shaded his voice—There *is* something new when the sun goes down. But Grace missed it, lost in his own thoughts.

"Daniel's eleventh chapter predicted the whole march of Seleucid history," Grace went on, "three hundred and fifty years before it happened." He was obviously not finished with his sermon. "Just three years after Antiochus set up his abomination in the sanctuary, he died. Stark raving mad. His inner circle called him no longer 'Epiphanes.' They snickered behind their hands and called him 'Epimanes.' Did you know that, Vardan? 'Epimanes'—'the poor madman.' That is the end of the Urartian secrets—insanity. The Watchers were madmen to rebel with Satan. The Sons of the Watchers, the giants, were purely twisted beyond reason. And any man who has ever followed them has been, to some degree, mad. Sorry, Max, I find no middle ground here."

By some unknown transformation, Max seemed suddenly curious. Objectively so. "This was written by the prophets?"

"It was. And how did the prophets know? Because they listened to the One True God. The original war started in Heaven. Some say in the Sides of the North. A mutiny on the part of the chief musician before the foundation of the world. Or maybe when the earth became without form and void. God knows. Anyway, a third of the angels followed Satan. It's not a new war—we've just found a new battlefield."

"You're awfully sure of yourself," Max chuckled. "Shouldn't you qualify all of that with an, 'I believe' statement? At least for the benefit of Vardan there? He has *sensitivities*. I'd hate to spoil his better judgment when so much is at stake."

Grace's eyes held no fear for himself and no sympathy for the doctor. "My life is going on that slab down there. Vardan needs to get behind *me* whether he agrees with me or not. So do the others."

Max thought a moment, then nodded seriously. "You are right. This has got to be done your way."

"When are you going to join the winning side, Max? Every renegade power will be put under the Lord."

The German philanthropist shook his head and smiled with what seemed to be real affection. "If anyone can make a believer of me, doc, it will be you."

The Armenian psychiatrist listened with none of the good nature Max displayed. He had retreated into the shadows, clutching his leatherbound volume as if protecting it.

"So who is Fortune of Commagene, really?" Grace asked. "This pantheon is nothing but a pack of lies. You're beginning to see that, aren't you?" He didn't wait for an answer. "These idols are romantic visions of some very ugly realities."

"Maybe so," Max returned, "but think of the doorway. That's where we stand. Five hundred feet beneath our feet is the Tree where the Urartians conjured the antediluvian gods. And now for the first time in history, science will let us cross that barrier in the opposite direction. To conjure ourselves into their world. The Sides of the North, Hades, the Third Heaven or whatever it is. We have the opportunity to take back some of that evil ground. The domain of Cancer. If you're right in what you believe, we'll all know it soon enough."

"Not necessarily." Grace grew serious and confessional. "It's uncharted territory over there, except maybe to John the Revelator. Or to the writer of the 'Book of the Watchers.' Or maybe to the man Paul said was 'caught up into the third heaven.'" He walked thoughtfully toward the edge of the terrace. The evening star had risen over the eastern horizon. His eyes wandered up to it, then down to where the cargo helicopter from the Van airstrip sat hidden beneath a canopy of desert camouflage below the terrace. The sounds of diesel generators filtered faintly up the slope from a cavern entrance there.

He contemplated the coming ordeal in the bowels of the mountain and murmured Scripture into the night, as if reciting a private liturgy: "'I consider the sufferings of this present time . . . not worthy to be compared with the glory that is to be revealed . . . For the anxious longing of the creation waits eagerly for the revealing of the sons of God. For the creation was subjected to futility, not of its own will, but because of Him who subjected it, in hope that the creation itself—'" He paused. "'—the creation itself *also* will be set free from its slavery to corruption . . . into the freedom of the glory of the children of God.'"

He turned to Vardan and Max, who stared at him curiously. "Paul said the creation can be set free from its slavery to corruption, sicknesses, disease, decay. And how? '. . . into the freedom of the glory of the children of God.' If I'm one of His sons, then perhaps I can set at least part of that creation free."

They stood silently for a moment.

"We have to honor your faith," Max agreed. "We may not understand it, but we will honor it." He checked Vardan as he added, "scientifically speaking, of course."

Grace looked back toward the evening star and prayed silently,

Forgive me, Father, if I step beyond Your will. He wandered a few more steps more to his left, looking toward the whispering fords of the Euphrates. "You know, it's funny—I keep remembering the three Hebrew children facing the fire temple of Babylon for not bowing to the king's image. Remember that story? They said, '*If*— If it be so, our God whom we serve is able to deliver us . . . ' 'If' is a big two-letter word. They didn't *know* anything for sure. They hadn't seen a miracle in apostate Israel for centuries when Daniel lived. Those Hebrews walked into the furnace not knowing if God would save them or not. It was faith all the way." He stuffed his hands deep into the khaki pockets of his fishing vest and began to stroll toward the sound of the generators. "I think I know how they felt."

With a sigh of relief, Max signaled Vardan to follow. The two of them stepped over the foundation of the pantheon after the preacher. But Grace had suddenly stopped. Max grabbed Vardan by the arm and held him back. They stood waiting, wondering what would happen next.

The faith-healer faced south, toward Jerusalem, six hundred miles distant. Suddenly he cupped his hands to his mouth and shouted, "'Lift up your heads, O you gates!'"

Max's fingers dug into the flesh of Vardan's upper arm. Both men felt the hair rising on the backs of their necks. Grace's voice echoed from the peak, clear, powerful and resonant. It was a summons, a challenge, perhaps a battle cry that had first echoed from the Sides of the North—trumpeted now from this orator's chest. "'Be lifted up, you ancient doors!'"

56
DALLAS, TEXAS
D/FW Airport
10:34 A.M.

Dallas/Ft. Worth Airport seemed the ideal location for an emergency board meeting, equidistant from both coasts, closer to the sun than Chicago or Denver. Board members could attend on short notice with a minimum of inconvenience from weather or schedule.

Evan held a copy of *World Today* in front of him as "Spirit I" held on the D/FW taxiway behind an American DC-10. The "heavy jet" pulled from its berth into their path and rolled toward the active runway. The newspaper headline read, "SIMON GRACE MISSING." Seeing the paper as they had departed that morning, brother and sister had been emotionally broadsided. Who had leaked the story? They had been wrangling that answer all the way from Brownsville. Jann Parker bent busily over a pile of papers in the extreme rear of the cabin, distancing herself discreetly from the fiery conversation.

"Dad leaked the story," Evan concluded. "It fits. Or else someone on the board leaked, and in that case they are planning to scuttle us in this meeting today."

"You cannot rule out someone *else* doing it," Pauline insisted.

"Right. The Devil did it," Evan suggested with mock inspiration. "One thing's for sure—someone is pulling the strings. You and I still haven't done anything worth spit. If this vote doesn't give us some real power, I'm going back to the news business."

Pauline barely registered his threat. "I don't think Stiles did it," she mused aloud, remembering the vice president's call last night. She didn't think he would make up the story about Jesse's return for any reason.

Evan broke the silence. "If it was any of the board members they will probably nominate Stiles *in absentia* and make him interim president. You and I will be history in a heartbeat."

"Stiles is not involved. He assured me of his vote last night."

"Do you think he'd tip his hand on something like this? The story about Jesse could be the perfect cover for a takeover. You've got to ask yourself, what *wouldn't* these guys do to get off the hook? By the way, did you see Jesse yourself? Has anyone seen him?"

The relentless questions suddenly became too much for her to deal with. Under the strain, Pauline felt herself retreating into the shock zone again. Her own voice began to sound far away. "How can we go through with this? What will I tell them? I won't be able to produce Daddy if they demand to see him. I see everything falling apart today."

Evan looked at her with concern. "Buck up, sister. You've got no choice but to play your hand. Go in there and see how this thing shakes out. Tell them Dad is on a prayer mission. That he left you in charge. Now that's the truth. You can tell the truth, can't you?"

"The truth?" She sighed helplessly. "Are you kidding?"

He grew disgusted. "Well, believe some version of it for the next two hours, OK?" He muttered half to himself, "I knew you would have trouble with this, so I brought along the 'Tree of Life' letter. The one Dad sent through Dallas WordSmith. If we have to play hardball, it will prove that he's still in charge of the ministry. He's not missing. So get that out of your head."

Pauline did not believe her dad had sent the letter. She stretched her perception of the truth, trying to make herself accept Evan's scenario. It held a certain logic. But she would have to believe it enough to be convincing before the board. That seemed unlikely. Until now, she had been ready for this meeting, knowing the "dirt files" had secured the vote. But the newspaper headline had destroyed her confidence. Maybe a power play was in motion after all. "Do you think the files have lost their effect?" she asked.

"Dirt is dirt. But think of it as backup. Don't say a word unless you're forced to. If you don't get the vote, I'll have to assure the gentlemen that I'm the kind to publish their dirty laundry. That's our last resort, understand? Last resort. I'll do that myself. I'm the 'bad guy.' You just sit there and look . . . *righteous.*"

In the meantime, Rick had taxied the Falcon to its remote berth. He came aft from the cockpit and released the door, letting down the air-stair. A terminal shuttle waited below. Jann Parker came forward from where she had been at work in the rear of the cabin. She and Pauline gathered their things and descended. On a sudden urge, Evan dialed his boss at *Texas People*, using the skyphone. He had held Putnam back from the story of his father's disappearance. Now it had become headlines with the wire services and Putnam was left with nothing.

A secretary answered. "Charles Putnam's office."

"This is Evan, calling for Charles, please."

In less than three seconds he heard a loud curse, followed by, "What's this headline?"

Evan could hear his boss's throat working like a bellows on the other end of the line. The *World Today* headline had to be the ultimate burn for the publisher. Losing credit for breaking an international story like this was a major blow. A make-or-break event for a newsman.

"I just called to say I'm sorry, Charles. What else can I say?"

"You can say you're on my payroll and you haven't earned your keep or even bothered to check in. Where's that fax connection? Where have you been since San Diego? You can say you have used me, that's what you can say. You owe me. You can say . . . you can say you ought to be strung up by the nether parts of your anatomy. You could say a lot of things, boy. Just fill in the blanks!"

Evan was silent. "Yeah." He saw a thicker stew than he had anticipated. He knew he had compromised his professionalism. "It's suddenly hitting me, Charles, that I've got a serious conflict of interest here. I've either got to compromise my family or my relationship with you. Listen, I've got to run to a meeting."

"What do you mean 'run'? What about our story?"

By now Pauline and Jann had entered the shuttle and were waiting for him.

"I resign, Charles," he said suddenly.

Putnam laughed with disbelief. "Yeah, right."

"I resign. I'll give it to you in a letter." He hung up and hurried down the stairs to the shuttle, thinking, *I probably just lost a book contract in that little move.*

Putnam did not want to lose his investment in Evan. "Alright," he said, not realizing Evan had hung up. "Maybe I came on a bit strong. I'm hurt. I'm disappointed. Can you blame me? Look, use your own discretion on the conflict. I'll make you a paid source or something like that. We'll work it out. Evan?" He heard the dial tone engage and realized he had been talking to dead air for some time.

The gray-suited publisher hurled an epithet, along with the telephone receiver, across the office. The phone hit the limit of its coiled tether, shattering a decorative vase on the coffee table. It rebounded across the floor, banging loudly against the side of the desk.

The door opened and Putnam's wide-eyed secretary peeked in. "Is everything alright?"

"It doesn't pay to be a nice guy in this business," he exploded, retrieving the phone.

57

HYATT HOTEL LOBBY
11:04 A.M.

On the ride to the hotel Pauline stopped her endless, circular thinking processes and prayed. *Help me, God. Please help me. I need some kind of wisdom. Show me what to do.*

As soon as the prayer found voice, a nearly silent influence in her mind replied, *Why don't you pray what you really mean? You don't want God's will. You want your own plans to succeed.* The present ordeal forced Pauline to look at herself much more closely than she wanted to. Prayer seemed not a matter of real faith anymore, but a last resort. A way of twisting God's arm in a tight spot. She prayed for a way out of a self-created mess. The web of deception she had begun to spin with the "dirt files" became more tangled with each passing moment. It had driven her to prayer. *How hypocritical! Oh, please forgive me, Father. I don't know what else to do. Look at me. I don't even trust You anymore. I'm a terrible believer. Oh well, forget it.* And she really meant it. The little voice had spoken the truth. A significant part of her didn't really want God's will after all.

Evan spent the same quiet shuttle ride shuffling and reshuffling details of the upcoming meeting like a hand of cards. The weakest card seemed to be Pauline. She would have to make a convincing presentation. The board would need to be reassured that Dr. Grace had left her in charge. A call to Verlin Stiles might become necessary to confirm that, he noted, unless Stiles had joined a conspiracy. The threat of the "dirt files" had already been made clear to him. If he and the other board members needed a reminder of the kind of damage they could do, they probably no longer cared about the threat of scandal to their reputations anyway. That would be impossible to overcome. Still, the power play of threatening to reveal the files seemed an unlikely scenario to Evan. That's the way he preferred it.

The shuttle deposited the two of them at the entrance to the Hyatt lobby. They walked down the steps, pushing through the glass doors and on toward the elevators.

241

"Feeling better?" Evan asked.

"Feeling sick."

"Think of Dad. That's what this is all about."

In that moment Pauline made up her mind. He was right. She would put her objections to rest and follow the course of action they had begun without looking back. With that determination, her shoulders straightened and her pace quickened.

As they entered the elevator, she noticed an attractive-figured young woman in a large sun hat and dark glasses entering the car with them. Once inside, the woman quickly removed the hat and glasses—a disguise. *It was Danna Lavalle!* She stared boldly at Evan. Pauline burned with disgust. The woman showed no discretion in coming anywhere near her brother!

Meanwhile Evan stared back, hiding his own surprise and the sudden thunder of his heartbeat. Not that she hadn't crossed his mind in the past few days. She had—knowing that she worked at his father's hospital. It was just that he had not expected to see her here and now. *Her eyes are bluer, deeper,* he thought, *her lips . . . delicious, full . . .*

"Hello, Danna," he brought himself to say.

"Someone blew up dad's yacht."

Evan hid a flash of fear, still not knowing who had died in the explosion.

"Oh no," Pauline breathed. Her face had gone ashen. "Why wasn't I told?"

Evan looked at her helplessly, realizing that he had not wanted to tell her until forced to, feeling guilty for instigating the mess. "I've been waiting for Stiles to confirm the details, Pauline. Yesterday it was still hearsay, and I didn't want to alarm you under the circumstances."

"Dorothy and Bud are dead," Danna added. "That's not hearsay. The bodyguards too."

Evan heard, but his thoughts wanted to retreat stupidly into the rich highlights of Danna's auburn hair. How could he think of such a thing at a time like this? "How about your dad?" he forced himself to ask.

"He's here."

Evan felt a wave of relief.

"He wants to see both of you right now."

"He survived." Evan said woodenly. He was relieved but also secretly angered. If anyone had to die in that skirmish, why not

Alan instead of Bud or Dorothy? They were merely the foot soldiers. *The scales of Justice are never completely balanced this side of death,* he reminded himself, using words he recalled from one of his father's frequent sermons.

Danna continued, "Dad asked to see you before the board meeting. I think it will have some bearing on what happens there."

Evan nodded again. Strangely, for the first time he saw a trace of Alan in Danna's eyes. A dark curtain dropped behind those arresting blues, smothering their natural sparkle. He'd never seen it before, and it made him uncomfortable now. She was the same, yet not the same as he had known her. Older, wiser, craftier for sure.

The door of the elevator opened to the fifth floor and Danna led them silently out, turning to her right. As they followed her through several turns of the hallway, Evan began to steel himself, knowing that Alan might blame him for the death of Dorothy and Bud. *I won't take it from him,* he determined. *The scamming bum brought it on himself!*

"You should have told me," Pauline whispered hoarsely as they neared the door to room 531. "We're dealing with *murder.* That gives new weight to the Sudan story."

Danna rapped lightly, and Alan answered from inside. She identified herself, and he undid the locks, letting them in.

"Do they know?" he asked Danna as they entered.

She nodded, moving past him into the room.

Alan wore a Band-Aid on his upper lip. Evan recognized the work of his own fist, while Pauline assumed it had been a wound suffered in the explosion. The mail-order preacher bore no other visible damage. The bedcovers lay strewn about the room. Food trays and newspapers had collected. Evidently he mistrusted even maid service after what he'd been through.

Alan bolted and chained the door behind them, then entered the room and paced, hands stuffed deep in his trouser pockets.

"Could you tell me where the icon is?" he began.

"Stolen," Evan replied with irritation.

Alan nodded as if he'd expected as much. "We're all in this over our heads, kids. These people are big. Really big."

Evan felt a wave of disgust rising against the man. "Nice of you to come forward now that your payday has been blown. Where were you when the forty million deal was still happening? You're not our friend, Alan, so don't pretend."

"No, wait, "Alan protested. "At first I had no reason to suspect. They told me Dr. Grace was behind this deal."

"Dad has never made a deal this big. It's even out of *your* league, Alan. You didn't warn Stiles, or Pauline, or the police. Don't play games here."

"Because I didn't suspect anything until it was too late." He stopped pacing. "You know me. It was a *big money* deal!" His eyes earnestly pled, as if he had made a point in his favor.

The reprobate! Evan thought. He almost laughed aloud. Money had become his second nature. His excuse for a lapse in behavior. He saw no contradiction in it whatsoever.

Alan went on, "I was asked to handle the deal by some people representing your dad. No red flags went up. It seemed possible that your dad could pull something off like this in the international marketplace. Forty million is spare change to some of the players out there. I was just happy for him, that's all, and glad to help. But the murders, man! Bud and Dorothy! In case you didn't know it, that's just not your dad's style!"

Evan saw straight through his scummy explanation. He wasn't sure Pauline did. "Who asked you?"

"What do you mean?"

"Don't play dumb. Who asked you to handle the deal?"

Alan hesitated, and Evan could see the same curtain drop behind his eyes that he'd just seen in Danna's.

"A professional service," Alan answered.

"Uh huh. A professional service. Like Federal Express? Like UPS? Wells Fargo? Something like that?" Evan was growing hotter by the minute.

"No."

"So who? Tell them!" Evan already knew full well.

Cornered, the mail wizard realized that the truth was the only thing that could serve his purposes for now. "The people who killed Dorothy and Bud," he admitted.

"Some professional service," Evan scoffed. "We're talking organized crime here, girls. In case you missed it." He turned back to Alan. "And you saw no red flags with this deal? You sleaze. That's what you've always been. You scumbag!"

"Evan!" Pauline chided.

He was ranting now. "You didn't see the Mafia as long as the money was right. But this isn't 'laundry' anymore, is it, Alan?" He recalled how close he'd come to exposing that very corruption when Alan had leaked his file, prompting the board to defrock him. The memory of it drove this attack. He wanted no more hypocrisy from the self-appointed apostle.

"I'm not here to take your abuse," Alan said, his voice shaking. "I'm telling you these people can buy and sell the Mafia. And I can tell you've never looked down the barrel of a gun."

Evan laughed aloud. "The barrel of a gun? No. It was your stinking *commission* you were looking at. Let's see, at fifteen percent that's around six million."

Alan turned to Pauline and shrugged helplessly. "Your brother just wants his pound of flesh. In the meantime your father's *life* is in real danger."

Pauline quickly crossed to Evan and whispered, "Stop insulting. Maybe he can help us."

"Help us?" He laughed derisively. Seeing that his attitude offended her, he sobered. It panicked him to think that Pauline would become Alan's ally. She could have no pride if she did that. Turning back to the mail mogul he asked, "Did you find out who was behind the Swiss account?"

Alan shrugged dolefully. "I made that promise to keep a crazy person from dropping me in the Pacific. The CIA can't even get behind a Swiss banker. The icon was our best lead, and now you've lost—" He suddenly stopped himself, seeing an imminent explosion rising in Evan. "Look, let's bury the hatchet and find your Dad, OK? What do you say? I need you, and whether you know it or not, you really do need me. Whoever is behind this scheme is trying to bankrupt this ministry and buy it for a song. I can turn that around for you."

"That's what Evan says," Pauline said with sudden recognition. "He says the 'Reverse the Curse' letter was designed to fail."

"He's right. It is."

"Well, Dad wouldn't do that," Pauline said. "Would he?"

"I was told your father was the author of it, but now I believe that's a lie. Why would he want to drive his own ministry into hopeless debt?"

"Because he wants to control it," Evan interjected. "Let's say he lets the ministry fall until the board screams uncle. In the meantime, Dad's sitting on a forty million dollar salvation package from the icon sale."

Alan's eyes flashed. "That's perversely brilliant, Evan, but that's just not your dad."

"That's what I've been telling him," Pauline added, happy to have some backup at last. "But he acts like he knows everything."

"Remember who we're talking to here, Pauline," Evan warned, not believing the way she could betray confidential information so easily. "This is a man who sold out his own daughter's reputation—"

"Leave me out of this!" Danna replied sharply.

"Fine." He felt undercut. "You're going to defend him?"

"I just said, 'leave me out of it.' That's all I said."

He returned to Pauline. "Just remember who you're talking to, and who he's talking about."

Alan seemed encouraged that he had at least driven a wedge between brother and sister. It might allow him to hang in with Evan. "Here's my theory," he offered. "I think whoever is behind the icon deal is behind your dad's disappearance. They're trying to dry up the income this month to keep you from using the economic muscle of the ministry to find him." He grabbed up two local papers and waved the headlines. "That's what this story is all about. Don't you see? It was timed to kill your income this month. Reverse publicity."

"Evan predicted the other way around," Pauline said, looking at her brother triumphantly. "He thought it was for a big payday or something." She began to emerge from the depths of the shock zone. "Now this fits *my* theory. The board didn't leak the story. Dad didn't leak it. The people who are holding Dad leaked it."

"That's right," Alan enthused, coming nearer to look into her face. "But you can beat them at their own game, Pauline. You've got to. You can't let these killers have their way with your finances or your father. That's what I came here to tell you. I can put the income back into this letter. Listen to me! Listen!" He had a wide-eyed sincerity that made him seem absolutely trustworthy. "What they meant for harm can become a landslide of income for the ministry. Do you hear me?"

"How?" She waited, thinking, *If he's right, for the first time we'll have the real muscle to search for Daddy.*

Where's that reprobate going with this? Evan thought. His mind raced to get ahead of his old nemesis.

Alan pulled a rumpled letter from his pants pocket. "When I saw the headlines this morning I knew that you had the attention of the whole world focused on Grace Ministries. The problem is, it's exactly the wrong kind of attention. Nobody on earth will send money to a missing preacher. Are you with me?"

Pauline nodded, fascinated.

Evan listened. He hadn't heard anything new yet.

"But here's what you do. Call a press conference to categorically deny that your father is missing. Then let your own father answer for his whereabouts."

"How?"

"Read his letter." Alan held it up again. "The 'Reverse the Curse' letter is your father's own explanation for where he is. It explains why he cannot be contacted by the press. You'll have the attention of the whole world when you make the announcement. Not to mention your donor mailing list. You'll focus all publicity back on this letter where it belongs. Tomorrow's paper will print the letter in quotes." He cackled. "See? You'll sting whoever has taken your father. They'll know someone wears their head on straight around here besides old Simon. It will produce a fifteen million dollar month. I guarantee it. Minimum. Or my name isn't Alan Lavalle." With a smile he unfolded and read the letter:

"'Just as Jesus needed to separate Himself from His disciples and go alone into the wilderness to pray, so have I gone to a secret place. I have gone to pray for your sicknesses, your pains, and your diseases, your curses : . .'"

He handed the letter back to Pauline. "Everything is sitting here waiting for you. And it's just that simple. We can kick their tails with a brick. We can turn all the publicity back to your father's ministry, and the income will follow. Naturally."

"It's too neat," Evan said. He recognized Alan's genius, as well as his father's. This seemed to be the exact manipulation he had warned Pauline to beware of at Addison Airport. "It's brilliant, but that's what bothers me. It's too brilliant. How can we be sure you and Dad haven't cooked this very maneuver up from the beginning?"

Alan seemed insulted. He grew red around the collar and looked away. "Will you give me a break? Someone wants the ministry on the rocks. The same people who killed Dorothy!" His voice had grown shrill. "I may have made a lot of compromises—" He nearly screamed now, nearly ready to fight Evan. "—but I wouldn't compromise with whoever killed her! Not even if it was your father!"

Evan withheld further words. The con man seemed truly offended, but Evan still couldn't bring himself to trust him. Yes, he believed Alan would use the death of a loved one for gain. The reprobate needed to believe in *something* to salve his conscience, after exchanging everything precious in his faith for one kind of income or another. So the sleaze drew a moral line at murder. Big deal! He was the same man who had sold out Danna and Evan to save his corrupt skin. Evan couldn't afford to forget that. He *wouldn't* forget it.

He took Pauline by the arm and steered her toward the door. "We're late. If my sister wins her vote in this board meeting I may listen to more from you. Not before."

In the hallway once again, Danna spoke as they approached the elevator. "There's more going on here than either you or Dad knows, Evan."

The bell sounded, and the doors slid open.

"Want to explain that?"

He saw Danna's curtain drop again.

"Just a feeling," she said, dismissing it lightly.

58

EXECUTIVE MEETING ROOM
12:34 P.M.

The emergency board meeting adjourned with one casualty, Chester Sharpey. The Oregon cattle rancher had been incensed at the suggestion that Pauline would oversee the ministry instead of Verlin Stiles. "No insult intended, honey, but you're just not the man for the job." His ruddy jowls and stern, moral pout underscored his feelings on the matter. When the other votes sounded—Harris, Avanzini, Dewey, Danna voting for Dr. Sylvan, and Myra voting for Verlin Stiles *in absentia*—all voting, "aye"— old Chester promptly announced his resignation.

"Now, allow me to sound a warning on my way out the door,"

he said, standing at the table, trembling with contained anger. "No one loves Dr. Grace more than I do, but he's become a maverick ever since we let the foreign hospitals leave the fold. Most of you have disagreed with me about that, but I'm saying it again for the record. Grace has removed himself from accountability. In this old rancher's experience, any man who does that, no matter how good his heart, is headed for a fall. You can all look forward to a manure load of real trouble around here. And I pray to God you can handle a pitchfork. Good-bye." With that he left the room.

59

HYATT LOBBY
1:45 P.M.

A bank of microphones, television cameras and newspapermen waited for the new interim president of Grace Ministries in the hotel lobby after the meeting. Pauline emerged nervously and sat down to make her first statement to the national press. Each of the remaining members of the board stood behind her. She took small comfort in their presence, knowing they were the corrupted ones. Feeling sullied, she prayed, *Dear God, help me. Oh forget it, here goes . . .*

"I categorically deny the truth of the *World Today* headline," she announced. "They have published an unfounded rumor. I have proof that my father is in touch with those of us in authority, and he, uh—" She fumbled for the letter, holding it up. "—he furthermore explains his absence in this month's letter to his partners. His being out of touch is no surprise to those of us who read his letters, and it has been part of the public record for any reporter competent enough to look beneath a rumor." She cleared her throat, surprised at the acid eloquence that fell so easily from her tongue. She heard her own voice as if through an echo chamber, reading the section of the letter suggested by Alan.

Ignoring the flood of questions that immediately followed her statement, she arose and retreated into a back room.

60
EVAN'S APARTMENT
3:15 P.M.

Hastily packing a suitcase for his return to Brownsville, Evan heard a knock at the door. He paused curiously for a moment beneath the patient nose of his stuffed bull moose, then hurried down the hallway, crossing the living room to answer it. Jennifer Bridgeport waited there, dressed in a green suit of crisp linen with a figure-complimenting waistline. Beyond her normal "journalistically frumpy" *chic*, the girl had obviously dressed to impress someone. One arm held a bundle of loose papers, and she glared at him as if he had offended her.

"Come in," he greeted. "You alright?"

She walked through the living room and into the kitchen without a word, dumping her load of papers on the floor as she passed.

"Fax confirmations," she announced over her shoulder. "I pulled them from the mail-room wastebasket at WordSmith."

It took Evan a minute to realize that she'd pulled off a first-rate investigative *coup*. Somewhere in the pile might be the date, time and place of origin of the fax from his father to WordSmith. The one that ordered the "Tree of Life" letter. "Oh, hey! Thanks," he said enthusiastically. Never mind that she had dumped them on the floor. That fit her style. He began retrieving the papers, carefully placing them in a pile.

"Mind if I have a beer?" she called from the kitchen.

"Help yourself."

She had already twisted the top from a longneck and tilted it for a drink as she returned to the living room. Hiking one leg carelessly onto the back of the sofa she watched him chase papers across the floor. He had grown to accept her boldness as part of the *you-can-have-it-all* mentality she had swallowed wholesale from a magazine rack. Actually, he found it amusing. It had become an accepted part of their camaraderie as co-writers.

From her sullenness he assumed she had heard about his resignation. After a minute of silence he said, "I take it you've heard."

She ignored his "toss-up" question. "Do you know what I had to go through to get that stuff?"

He went back to collecting the fax reports. "You were crazy like a fox as usual."

"Nah. The account exec at WordSmith was drooling over my body like a buck rabbit. I think he would have walked in front of a car for me." She grew suddenly irritated. "Why is that? Why is it only the *creeps* go for me, huh? He was married!" She tilted her bottle for another sip. "Where are the good guys anymore, Evan? The Prince Charmings and stuff like that, huh?" She followed this with a loud belch.

He cracked a smile. Repulsiveness was her way of showing anger. Still, he saw an element of sly truth in the remark. "Maybe all the Prince Charmings are scared of you, Jennifer."

"Scared?" She belted the word like a rocker. "Are they afraid to mess around?"

He laughed at her outrageously. "Yeah, maybe they are scared of that too. Now would you simmer down?" He went back to gathering papers, thinking, *She scares off the men she needs in her life, attracting the other kind.* It seemed unfortunate because, to his way of thinking, she had it in her to be as strong as ten acres of garlic behind the right man. But it would certainly have to be the uniquely "right" man.

"What about you, Evan?"

It took a moment for him to process the question. He looked up more slowly this time, noticing a flush on the exposed skin of her neck. She watched him boldly, nostrils flaring. A smile tugged suggestively at the corners of her mouth. Most of the time he was amused by her "out-front" bluster, but he didn't appreciate this.

"Well?"

Stooping down, he gathered the last of the papers and stood again. "What about me? You mean, am I scared of you?"

"Are you scared to mess around?"

It hit him like a double-edged challenge. One edge confronted his manhood and the other the limits of his affection for her.

"Scared is the wrong word," he clarified.

"So, where have you been?"

His earthy co-worker had let herself become quite unprofessional in his eyes. She had never done that before. He cleared his throat. "Where I have been has nothing to do with playing around." He had felt secretly tempted by Jennifer many times. Not quite like this, however.

"Have you been daffy?" she teased. "Deaf, dumb, blind?"

"You're out of line," he said as kindly as he knew how. He really did feel affection for Jennifer, but his foolish years of making more of affection than friendship were over. For her sake, and for the sake of their working relationship, he would not go to bed with her. Not now. Not ever. And he needed more time for this discussion than he could possibly afford at the moment. "Jen, you need to excuse me—"

She lurched forward and set the beer bottle on the coffee table without the benefit of a coaster. It hit the surface with a hollow *clank*, causing Evan to wince. Beer foamed over the bottletop, staining the walnut finish.

"I understand," she said as she passed him.

"I don't think you do."

"Spare me!" Her heels assailed the hardwood. At the door she paused. "So everything was just going to be cut off in mid-sentence. Was that it? You quit? No good-bye, no nothin'?" So she had heard about his resignation. He sensed pain beneath her anger.

"Of course not. There was no time."

"Where was my warning then, partner? Where was my courtesy call?"

"I had a serious conflict of interest, Jennifer. I had no time to talk about it to anyone. But that shouldn't prevent us from working together again, if we don't spoil everything now."

"Spoil *what?*" She took a couple steps back toward him. "What was I spoiling? Wait a minute—what do you think I was talking about, buster? Well, you arrogant—! You thought I was coming on to you?" She whirled toward the door. "You are so arrogant!"

He grew irritated with her, knowing the ploy well. She was diverting attention from her own lack of discretion by attacking him. He shrugged. "I'm not playing games."

Without a reply she went out, slamming the door behind her.

"Fine. Good riddance," he muttered. He had far too many things pressing his mind to let this rift bother him for long. In the meantime, he had the incredible fax reports to search. *She can be a blessing in spite of herself*, he thought.

In the bedroom again he quickly went to his word processor and pulled up a report labeled "Icon." He sent the file to an attached printer. It began to zip out a hard copy of the file. In the meantime he returned to his closet, fishing for more clothes to pack.

Another knock sounded at the front door. A bold one. He hurried out and opened it. Jennifer stood there again. This time she couldn't look him in the eye as she spoke.

"I forgot to tell you," she huffed, "the buck rabbit at WordSmith let it slip that the letter is being paid through advance money transfers from a Swiss account." She sighed impatiently. "He also said it's the largest mailing they've ever handled." She turned and stalked away again.

So, he thought, *the icon and the "Tree of Life" letter were both paid by Swiss bank account.* "Jen, thanks. Really," he called. She retreated toward her idling Japanese sports car throwing only a scowl over her shoulder in reply.

61

D/FW AIRPORT
Grace Falcon Jet
7:10 P.M.

As "Spirit I" taxied into position at the end of the runway, a deep sense of abandonment settled over Pauline Grace, newly elected interim president of her father's worldwide ministry. She checked the security of her seat belt and cinched it even tighter around her waist. In the rear of the cabin Evan huddled with Alan, Jann and Danna around a table, examining the fax confirmations from WordSmith's wastebasket. Alan, eager to prove himself a part of the Grace brother and sister team, happily did the legwork for Evan, listing each location and telephone number meticulously on a legal pad.

Pauline could not bring her mind to bear on the task. She had retreated to the front of the cabin to be alone. Now that the "dirt files" had placed real power in her hands, she wasn't sure she wanted that power. She kept recalling a phrase in King James English from the story of Samson: "he wist not that the Lord had departed from him." Perhaps God had also abandoned her in the thick of things. The feeling fit her perception of the Great Tribulation, that apocalyptic age of the future when the Spirit of God is said to abandon the entire planet. All restraints on evil would then be loosed and God's "vials of wrath" poured upon the earth. What cup of wrath might await her now? *Will the Falcon fall from the sky because of my sin? Will I lose it all, including Daddy? Dear God, save me.*

Looking around the marvelously furnished cabin, it seemed even the convenience of "Spirit I" had lost its sweetness. Every accoutrement of ministry privilege held a taste of perversity for her now. She had entered her own private tribulation. The inner storm over the use of the files remained so strong that her deeper guilt for manipulating the press conference that afternoon didn't even enter her mind.

Rick spooled the turbo-fan engines to 3,700 pounds of thrust for a takeoff to the south. The tail-mounted Garretts screamed, glowing red in the night as the craft rocketed forward between the runway lights. Pauline's knuckles turned white on the armrests. As they approached rotation, that critical moment of no-return, a band of tight fear enclosed her chest. *Will we fly? Or will God strike us down?* She held her breath.

The French-built Falcon *Mystere* eased smoothly into the air, a triumph of human ingenuity. The ground flashed past her window. Then she saw the receding runway's edge, lights of houses and apartments appearing below, then the Irving water tower, the streaming headlights of Highway 183, Cowboy Stadium, finally downtown Dallas in the distance. She let her breath go in a long sigh of relief, forcing herself to breathe normally again as the jet continued to rise. Turning her mind to other business, she shoved her superstitious fears into a dark corner of her mind.

Something in Chester Sharpey's good-bye speech had bothered her all day. Now it returned to mind. Perhaps her father's secretary could explain. "Jann, would you come up here for a minute, please?"

Jann obediently unbuckled her belt and came forward to take the bulkhead seat next to Pauline.

"What did Sharpey mean about Daddy being a maverick?"

"Ooooh," Jann said, letting her mind pick up the relevant facts. "Well, back in '83 Dr. Grace felt that the missionary hospitals should no longer depend on donations."

"I don't understand. Why should they be any different than the rest of the ministry?"

"Because donations go up and down each month. It's unpredictable, you know? The same is true for any TV ministry. With no set income, budgeting is almost impossible. But in the Third World, when hospital budgets fluctuate, people die. Your father didn't like that."

"Of course he wouldn't like it."

Evan overheard this and came forward to listen.

"So," Pauline continued, "Daddy came up with a way to fix that?"

"Yes. He got the hospital budgets underwritten by the Dunamis Foundation. It is a German firm. They sort of became a financial 'safety net' for us. They are chartered as a benevolent medical research group. Very reputable."

This was news to Evan. "Ever hear of them?" he asked his sister.

She had not.

Jann continued, "So now when ministry funds fall off, like they have since all the recent ministry scandals, Dunamis guarantees that the hospitals will operate on an even keel."

"I don't see anything wrong with that," Pauline declared. "Why does that make Daddy a maverick?"

Evan interjected, "Because he's not letting the right hand know what the left hand is doing." He had become fascinated by the scenario, seeing how his father had created great freedom for himself in this maneuver.

Meanwhile, Jann continued, "Sharpey started complaining when Dunamis took the hospitals away from the ministry board. They restructured, placing them under a medical board at the Foundation. It's a much better arrangement, really. Perfectly legal."

"Legal is not necessarily ethical," Evan countered.

"We're talking about keeping people alive," Pauline countered.

"Dunamis is keeping them alive," he answered. "Essentially the hospitals belong to whoever controls the money. If donations are no longer the basis of our hospitals, then the hospitals belong to the Foundation, not the ministry. No wonder Sharpey had a cow over it."

"But they are still Grace hospitals," Jann countered. "Your father *is* the ministry as far as Dunamis is concerned."

"And back here Dad is Dunamis as far as the ministry is concerned," Evan said. "See? No accountability. I'm with Sharpey. It smells bad. You have to see that it was a move that put a lot of power into one man's hands—Dad's."

"Well, it's in the hands of the right man if you're asking me," the secretary blustered. "Your father wanted to do what was right for the sick people without a lot of nonsense."

"Right, right," Evan said. "He also had other motives."

"Well, aren't you uppity?" Jann asserted herself with uncharacteristic rigor. "He pioneered those hospitals. His name is still on them. I think it's Sharpey's problem. He didn't like having Dr. Grace under two separate boards in the same ministry. I think he's just a bit of an 'old fogy' myself." She sent a look of support toward Pauline.

Evan also looked at Pauline. "This is hot, sis. As soon as West Germany wakes up . . ." He checked his watch. ". . . let's see, it's 1 or 2 in the morning out there now . . . Anyway, let's get a call through to Dunamis and see who we're dealing with."

"I called yesterday," Jann said.

"You did?"

"I spoke to the chairman's secretary—Freida Heidl."

"How about the chairman?"

"He's out of the country."

Evan glanced at Pauline. "Who is he?"

"One of the wealthiest men in the European Community. His name is Maximilian Commagene."

Evan's mind connected several possible Swiss bank accounts to this name. The phrase "major player" came to mind. Forty mil might just be spare change. "How much is he worth? Any idea?"

Jann shook her head innocently. "I don't know. I've always assumed that he was pretty substantial."

"There's substantial and then there's *substantial*. What do you say we find out? Maybe Forbes has him on a list." He looked at Pauline significantly. "Maybe he paid a forty million dollar tithe this month."

Pauline's mind was rapidly filling with new possibilities.

"If one of those fax confirmations originates from Germany, I'd say we'd better get over there for a look around. I'm going to see what we've got." With that, Evan returned to the rear table.

In her own mind, Pauline began to assemble clues out of a medical file: Her father had left Jerusalem on a chartered 727. Could it have belonged to Dunamis? Then the icon sale. Could it have been Dunamis's money? But why the icon? What purpose did it serve? And why the explosives? Alan's yacht? The car bomb in Jerusalem? Suddenly she chilled, remembering Jesse Stiles's story that the hospital in Sudan had been blown up. Explosions. A hospital too? Dunamis should have known all about the situation in Sudan, and yet there had been no word. No telegram, no call. Why had they not informed the ministry? Did they have something to hide? *Are they hiding Daddy, perhaps?*

"Jann, does Dunamis have a liaison at Grace?"

"Yes, Dr. Sylvan. Oh, I almost forgot. She also serves on the Dunamis hospital board with your father."

Neva's on the medical side of the ministry! Pauline thought. *The Dunamis side. She's missing too. Daddy supposedly told her to handle the icon deal. But how does the icon fit in? It's a museum piece, not medical. Why would he coordinate through the medical director? Unless it is Dunamis doing the coordinating. They have separated the hospitals from the ministry through Daddy—*At this point her intuition filled in a few blanks.

"Evan, you're wrong," she declared, loud enough for him to hear at the other end of the cabin.

He turned around from the table. She sounded suddenly alive, suddenly sure of herself.

"We're not dealing with a ministry problem," she said. "Whatever it is, it's on the medical side."

Pieces of a mystery began to take shape like the polished *tesserae* of *The Seven Sleepers* mosaic. The image remained too obscure to reveal the guilty party, but at least she no longer chased a phantom. She had an enemy in sight named Dunamis. Lydia's supernatural nightmares aside, Pauline intended to confront some very earthly realities at dawn.

62

BROWNSVILLE
Grace Family Compound
10:13 P.M.

The Grace guest house seemed more than ample, even for the tastes of Alan Lavalle. It contained a comfortable sitting area with a rock-lined fireplace and large-screened TV. From a common area, a kitchen served four guest bedrooms, each with a separate bath. Beyond a billiards table and a row of sliding glass doors, the aqua waters of a pool waited invitingly in the South Texas night. A hot tub vented steam beside a terraced rose garden.

Security cameras scanned each entryway. Electronic motion detectors flickered on either side of the room, signaling Alan's presence to the office of Grace Security Central. He placed his suitcase on a tiled breakfast counter, loosened his tie and used the remote control to turn on a television. Then he removed a pitcher of orange juice from the kitchen refrigerator as the late-night newscast filled the screen. Suddenly he whirled around.

A female anchorperson introduced the story: "A *World Today* headline, announcing that Dr. Simon Grace is missing, was emphatically denied by his daughter Pauline at a news conference at the Dallas-Ft. Worth airport this afternoon. The heir apparent to the multimillion-dollar religious empire near Brownsville took on the prestigious newspaper, delivering a lecture to the assembled reporters in the process."

"They have published an unfounded rumor," Pauline was seen to say as she held up the newspaper. "His being out of touch is no surprise to those of us who read his letters, and has been part of the public record for any reporter competent enough to look beneath a rumor."

"Yes!" Alan whooped enthusiastically, spilling orange juice on his shirtsleeve. "Yes!"

The next video edit showed Pauline reading the letter:

"'Just as Jesus needed to separate Himself from His disciples and go alone into the wilderness to pray, so have I gone to a secret place. I have gone to pray for your sicknesses, your pains, and your diseases, your curses . . .'"

"We couldn't ask for more," Alan exulted, setting the drink down and hurrying to the telephone to dial Pauline's number.

Meanwhile, the anchorwoman concluded, "Miss Grace refused to answer questions following her statement, leading some to speculate about what else she may be hiding."

"Hey! Give her a break," Alan shouted, muting the TV with the remote switch. He listened to the telephone ringing.

"Hello?"

"Pauline, you're fantastic, kid! Fantastic! You're a credit to your father."

She seemed lost. "What do you mean?"

"Are you watching the news?"

"No."

"I don't believe this. You make national news and you don't watch yourself?" He paused, pondering this incredulously. "Well, then let me tell you something. You are a natural, girl. You couldn't have said it better. That part about the letter being 'part of the public record' was genius. 'For those of you who bother to read my father's partnership letters.' Girl, that's driving it all the way to the bank!" He nearly burst with glee. "That one statement must have opened a hundred thousand envelopes out there. I mean it. I see people going to their trash cans to dig that letter out if they threw it away. You gave yourself another million bucks, OK? Conservatively speaking."

She remained skeptical, having trouble believing that it might be that easy. "Are you sure?"

"Look, you're tired. Just hear this. That's how we do it in this business, honey. You can't learn that sort of thing. You have to be born with it, and you were obviously born with the instincts of your father. I'm telling you, you've got it, Pauline. You—have—got—it— *girl!*"

VIII

"THE SONGS OF JUBAL"

Such notes, as warbled to the string
Drew Iron tears down Pluto's cheek,
And made Hell grant what Love did seek.

(JOHN MILTON, *IL PENSEROSO*)

63

BROWNSVILLE
Dr. Grace's Mansion
5:30 A.M.

After only a few hours sleep, still in housecoat and slippers, Evan and Pauline sat at the long meeting table in the studio. They sipped coffee and planned strategy for the coming day. Evan rechecked his list of fax locations for clues. To his disappointment he found nothing from Germany.

In the meantime Pauline used the speakerphone to initiate an overseas call to Dunamis. The secretary, Freida Heidl, answered. In a heavy accent she explained that Mr. Maximilian Commagene had taken a "confidential leave of absence," not informing the Foundation of his whereabouts. She added that this was not an uncommon practice for him, since his family wealth meant that he had to take extra measures to enjoy any privacy at all.

Pauline plunged ahead, perhaps naively, asking if Dunamis had initiated the process of purchasing *The Seven Sleepers of Antioch* from Dr. Grace.

"I don't, uh . . . have heard of such thing," the woman replied.

Pauline sensed a cover-up behind her broken English. "Can you tell me the status of the hospital in Sudan?"

"Oh, that is bad. We hear of problems—"

"Problems? We hear that people have been killed!"

The woman paused. "Yes. But no one knows, except that is in report to Dr. Sylvan. The civil war there, the peace has, uh . . . det—deteriorated."

"Freida, if there are any more emergencies at our hospitals, if anything else 'deteriorates,' will you notify Dr. Grace's office immediately?"

"That is done through Dr. Sylvan."

"You don't understand. I want the information first. Before Neva Sylvan hears of it."

The silence became stony. "I think this is a procedural question, ma'am. It will have to be taken up between Maximilian and Dr. Grace."

"I am speaking for Dr. Grace now. As interim president of Grace Ministries I am changing the rules. Do you understand? I want first access to this information."

The lady tittered arrogantly. "I am sorry, but I am afraid I cannot be sure that you are who you say you are. I am not sure Dr. Grace even has a daughter, let alone an interim president daughter. I will have to check—"

"What?!"

"If you will excuse me, whoever you are, I have important work to do." With that, Freida promptly hung up.

Pauline looked at Evan. "She's stonewalling. Did you notice how clear her English became at the end? We're definitely onto something."

Evan nodded. "Let's send Stiles."

"No." Pauline's reaction was immediate and firm. "He needs to stay with Jesse. He's been through enough."

"Then one of *us* needs to go."

"How about Alan?"

"Are you nuts?" Evan snorted with disdain. "We can't trust Alan to act in our best interest. He needs to be under our thumb. Anyway, I've got an assignment for him right now." He reached over and dialed the guest house using the speakerphone.

"So who goes to Germany, you or me?"

"I don't know. Hello, Alan? Are you awake?"

The speaker rattled with his hoarse reply. "Barely."

"Listen, I want you to do some detective work today. Come by the house and pick up this agate cross. You know the one I mean? The charm in the 'Tree of Life' package? I want you to look up a mineralogist—Texas is full of them—and see if he can locate the place of origin. There may be some kind of geologic fingerprint on it. Something we can trace."

Alan yawned. "Sure. How soon?"

"See you over here in an hour?"

"An hour!"

"This is no picnic, Alan. Get over here." He hung up feeling pleasure at ordering his old enemy around. But when he glanced at Pauline, her face had turned nearly white.

"Look," she said, staring toward the darkened loft.

He felt a shiver between his shoulder blades and whipped around. A burglar in a black ski mask watched them steadily. The man quietly leaned on the rail, a pistol with a silencer in one hand. The other hand held a black canvas satchel.

"I'm so sorry to do this," said the burglar in a ringing baritone. Instantly a bell of recognition sounded in Pauline's mind.

Evan tried to pinpoint the foreign accent, but couldn't figure it.

Pauline knew that voice. *Who? Where? Not so long ago.* But she didn't have long to wonder. The man peeled off his mask. "Colonel Canaan!" she gasped.

Evan quickly rose to his feet. The panic in his chest began to subside. He had imagined that he was meeting the mad bomber of Alan's yacht, or the icon thief. Adrenal turbulence still raced in his blood.

"Evan," Pauline introduced incredulously, "this is Colonel Gershon Canaan, our military escort in Jerusalem. Colonel, why have you come here like this?"

Evan added wryly, "You might have called ahead. Something normal."

"As I said, I am sorry," the colonel replied, stepping down from the loft into the meeting room. He put down his satchel and extended a hand to Evan with a wan, tired smile. The weariness around his eyes suggested that he had recently passed through an ordeal.

Evan glanced curiously at Pauline.

She shrugged, with a nervous laugh. "It's fine."

He took the colonel's firm grasp and shook it. "So what were you tying to steal, colonel?"

"The icon."

Evan chuckled expectantly, feeling that he would soon learn a great deal. The burglar Jann Garrett had seen in his father's office had not been after the files at all, but after the icon. Evan knew this man was probably a deadly member of Israel's secret Mossad organization. Yet someone else had beaten this expert to the icon. Was that probable? "How do I know you didn't steal the icon?" he challenged.

"Danna told me about it being stolen last night. That's the first I had heard of it, although I should have known. I came to see for myself, not that I mistrust my sources—I just check."

"Danna works for you?" Evan asked, recalling her mysterious intuition in the D/FW elevator yesterday.

"She has been valuable. If I know anything, the icon has merely been delivered to the buyer—not stolen." Canaan stopped and lifted his eyebrows at Evan with partial admiration. "You really stirred things up when you switched the shipping cases on Danna's father."

Evan nodded, still stricken with feelings of guilt for the deaths of Bud and Dorothy. "I'm afraid I'm in way over my head."

Canaan holstered his gun. "We are all in over our heads." He sighed wearily. "They're staying ahead of us."

"Who are *they*?"

Canaan turned his intense brown eyes on Pauline. "May I have some coffee please?"

"Of course. Sit down." She took a thermal carafe from the counter and poured him a cup, recalling the impression he had made on her in Jerusalem. A noble warrior, confident. She had sensed then that he could be her ally. But was he?

"We had a long talk with Neva Sylvan last night," he said.

"OK, now who are *we*?" Evan insisted. "You're confusing me."

"I'm sorry. We are the Uriel Mission, a unit of Israeli Intelligence. You are absolutely right about who purchased the icon. I overheard your telephone conversation. It is Dunamis. But Dunamis is no answer. What Dunamis is depends entirely on which way you look at it. It is a medical research foundation. It is also the house of Commagene's family wealth. And it is other things too."

"I'll bet those 'other things' are quite interesting if they have *your* attention," Evan said. He still remained skeptical of this colonel. "So why would Dunamis bother to buy something for forty million if they could so easily turn around and steal it?"

"Again I say, they didn't steal it." Canaan gazed ominously over the steam rising from his coffee cup. "Your father will have to give you the full answer."

Evan wondered what he meant. Perhaps he meant that Dr. Grace was pulling the strings of Dunamis—something Evan had suspected but couldn't quite bring himself to believe. "You can spell things out here, colonel. I have my suspicions about my father. What do you know about him?"

"Let us just say that we are very concerned about his role."

Evan and Pauline each pondered the fearful significance of this statement as Canaan sipped more coffee.

"We learned a great deal last night from Neva Sylvan. None of which will stand up in an American court of law, I am afraid.

According to some, we violated her civil rights in the process of interrogation."

"What do you mean?" Pauline asked, not liking the militaristic arrogance of his statement.

"We put her under sodium amytal. Her testimony was involuntary."

"Truth serum," Evan explained in an aside to Pauline. "So who *is* Neva?"

"'*What* is she?' is more like it. She is Pandora's box. I don't know how this woman came to be your medical director. There are several people living inside of her body and not one of them is a legitimate doctor. Anyway, among other interesting things we learned that the tablets we have been looking for have been sealed in the icon shipping case for forty years."

"What tablets?" Evan asked. "You mean pills?"

Canaan laughed. "Not pills. Cuneiform tablets, the oldest known form of writing. But I am getting ahead of myself. As part of the Uriel Mission I was watching your father in Jerusalem because of his involvement with the Dunamis Foundation. Dunamis happens to be the sole proprietor of a series of cuneiform tablets which we have been after since World War II. By the way, I could not help overhearing your conversation this morning, and I do not recommend travel to Mannheim. We have not been able to crack the front door of Dunamis. You will not do any better."

Pauline grew suddenly impatient with all this explanation. "Colonel, please, won't you just help us find Daddy? Will you do that?"

"I am afraid there is much more at stake here," Canaan said. He looked at Evan, then back to her with troubled eyes. "Are you sure you want to find your father?" He asked as if he would be appalled to hear her say yes.

At this, Pauline felt a new stab of fear. She grew specifically afraid that her father might not be who she thought he was at all. She began to imagine him as a hideous monster. She continued to fight that image as she spoke. Her voice quivered. "Colonel, I'm not saying my father is perfect . . . or innocent . . . or anything like that." She swallowed hard, watching him sip more coffee. She didn't like the way he averted his gaze from her. "In fact, I believe he is 'bound' or somehow trapped into something beyond his control." Lydia's spiritual explanation seemed suddenly attractive to Pauline again, now that the alternative was her father's own treachery.

Canaan regarded her calculatingly. "When you last saw your father in Jerusalem, was he carrying anything? A document? A briefcase?"

Her mind retraced the scene on the Derekh Ha-Shiloah. Already it seemed like a distant dream. Images blurred: the Valley of Hinnom, Joel Lassiter, the limo ride, her father's strange mood, the envelope, his wild reaction to the news of Lydia's heart attack, his words about Evan, his Bible— "He was carrying his Bible," she said. "I remember it quite clearly."

"Can you swear it was his Bible? Could it have disguised another book?" He unzipped his black satchel and withdrew a loose-leaf binder, which he dropped on the table in front of her.

Both she and Evan leaned quickly forward. Pauline opened it and saw reassembled fragments of torn paper forming several pages of a photocopied manuscript. The printing was in a foreign language, and it contained handwritten comments in the margins.

"It's in German," Evan whispered.

"Your father met two terrorists in Jerusalem after he left you, Pauline," Canaan said. "They drove a pale blue Renault. You remember the one."

She saw it all again—the car receding in the alleyway. Later, the twisted wreckage, the awful carnage, the flickering tires.

Canaan continued, "What I didn't tell you then was that the terrorists blew themselves up when we caught them in that road-block. At first we thought they had your father with them in the car, but when we ruled that out, we found these fragments. It was then we suspected they had blown up the car to keep us from finding this document."

"What is it?" Pauline asked.

"A Gnostic text, or some kind of pseudepigraphical writing," Evan said, examining the Scriptural notation accompanying the lines. "Am I right?"

Canaan nodded. "Your father flew to Germany with Max Commagene, leaving this document with the terrorists. Our Nazi hunters have been trying to crack Dunamis for decades to find the original clay tablets of this codex. This is what we call the Mannheim translation of 'The Songs of Jubal.' The original is not in German, but in a Urartian dialect, written in cuneiform. That is a style of writing where the scribe would use a stylus on wet clay tablets. The tablets were then baked to preserve the record. This is the oldest form of writing, before the invention of papyrus."

The document was called "The Songs of Jubal." The name "Jubal" raced suddenly through Pauline's mind. *Lydia had said in her dream she had seen someone named Jubal! A musician.* A cold new level of fear accompanied this recognition. "The Mannheim translation was in the car with those terrorists after their meeting with your father. It is a photocopy of a text Hitler used to direct secret medical experiments in the Nazi death camps. We believe Dunamis fronts a secret society whose past initiates served as medical advisors at Dachau and Neuengamme, among others. The reason this has become a hot property with terrorists is because it contains Hitler's personal notations about conjuring epiphanies through butchery. I don't know what you know about religious history, but human sacrifice was used to invoke the gods of mystery religions down through the ages."

"What do you mean by 'invoke'?" Pauline asked.

"I mean, to make them appear. It was a ritual of bloodshed in which spiritual entities were caused to appear—if only in shadowy visions—on earth."

A palpable wave of fear flowed over Pauline's brain. It seared like something physical. Her scalp crawled with it. *Medical advisors? Something on the medical side of the ministry? Dunamis? Is Daddy mixed up in this? What part does he play?* "I can guarantee you my father doesn't know about any of this," she bluffed. "He wouldn't associate with people like that."

Canaan cleared his throat and spoke carefully. "Then what was he doing with the Mannheim translation of 'The Songs of Jubal'?" He pointed to the binder in Evan's hands.

"Daddy didn't have that thing. I told you he had his own Bible. I remember."

"Are you sure?"

"I'm positive," she said even though she couldn't be positive. She chose to believe this version of the truth for the sake of her sanity.

Canaan took the binder back from Evan. "I would like to believe you. But now I find out from Neva that your father has also hidden the original Urartian tablets here in this room since 1957. Inside the icon case. Who would have thought to look here? Because of your father, Dunamis has kept the icon and 'The Songs of Jubal' out of our grasp. Do you think all of that is a coincidence? Or do you think he knew what he was doing?"

"He could have been duped," Pauline defended, "not knowing

the tablets were in there. And what about the forty million dollars? Are you saying Dunamis paid Dad forty million just to keep their stuff for thirty-odd years?"

Canaan shrugged. "Where's the money? Anybody seen this forty million dollars?"

Evan and Pauline exchanged glances.

"Another theory," Canaan continued. "Maybe your father is one of the Society members."

"So would he be paying himself?"

"It is a theory."

"No," Pauline said, shaking her head violently. "You don't know him or you wouldn't even say that."

Evan's mind whirled through his own encyclopedia of knowledge about the icon. "Let me take a wild guess, colonel. The medical advisors to Hitler from Dunamis . . . would they happen to be known as the Society of Apostates?"

Canaan's face showed surprise. He smiled and leaned suddenly forward. "Very few people know them by that name. How did you learn it?"

"Snooping around about the icon. It's a hobby."

"Very good." Canaan smiled. "Did you know that the legend behind *The Seven Sleepers* is recorded in 'The Songs of Jubal'?"

"I've never even heard of 'The Songs of Jubal,' and I'm pretty well read in the *Apocrypha* and the *Nag Hammadi* texts."

"What are these songs?" Pauline asked.

"'The Songs of Jubal,'" Canaan began. "Jubal lived before the Genesis Flood. He is supposed to have written songs about the antediluvian giants, also known as Nephilim."

"Those are half-men, half-angels," Evan interjected for Pauline's benefit.

She frowned, having heard little of such creatures. Although Lydia mentioned something . . .

"Angels married women, and their children became giants," Evan continued. "They were supposed to have filled the earth with violence. The Flood wiped out the Nephilim."

"I don't understand," Pauline replied.

"Genesis 4 through 6. It's not exactly Sunday School 1-A," Evan said. Turning to Canaan he continued, "So the Nephilim songs were supposedly passed through the Flood, written down in cuneiform tablets, and put into this Mannheim translation by a secret society? The authorship of the songs, of course, was ascribed to Jubal, the first musician. A typical Gnostic or cabalist trick—ascribing authorship to a legitimate Biblical figure. How am I doing?"

Canaan nodded and smiled. "Quite well."

"I do some reading."

"No one has actually seen these tablets apart from the Society initiates, which leads us to suspect they are fakes. There are seven initiates in this Society of Apostates, just as there are seven saints pictured in the icon."

"*The Seven Sleepers of Antioch*. Of course," Evan nodded, "mystics are big on numbers."

Canaan paused to sip more coffee. "Sorry. Didn't get much sleep. I learned only last night that *The Seven Sleepers* were inspired from "The Songs of Jubal.' Neva Sylvan turned out to be the biggest information break we've had in forty years. Among other things, she confessed to being one of the seven current Apostates. I have her under guard in Matamoros because we expect her to commit suicide at the first opportunity. The secret oath directs an Apostate to do that if his or her identity is ever discovered."

Evan leaped to his feet and began pacing the room. These bizarre facts began to make sense of recent events. "Dad hired Neva. There's no question he's involved himself with these Apostates at some level."

"He doesn't know who they are," Pauline defended, despising her brother for his disrespectful conclusion. She turned to Canaan. "What about the icon? What did Jubal's book have to do with it?"

"The prelude to 'The Songs of Jubal' begins: 'Summon the old gods, Summon the Champions from their thrones invisible.' The translation is more than songs. It is all about invocations, orgies, blood sacrifices and other nonsense, supposedly with the power to conjure gods back from the antediluvian world. Or the underworld. The book also tells about seven underworld priests who were killed in a Christian persecution in the third century A.D. The seven unrepentant pagans were walled into a cave by their Christian tormentors, but a centrury later they walked out miraculously alive and well. Under a deal with the Christian King Tiridates, the pagan religious order was ordained wholesale into the Armenian Church. To the king it was merely good politics. But a legend grew up about the seven saints who had survived the ordeal in the cave. A century later *The Seven Sleepers of Antioch* icon was commissioned and canonized by the church."

"And the Society of Apostates became Christian."

"Right." Canaan played down the significance of this treachery to Pauline, whose eyes had grown wide and fearful. "'The Songs of Jubal' and the icon are harmless, of course. But when someone takes them seriously, as the Apostates obviously do, bad things can happen."

"It's all pretty much mumbo-jumbo," Evan agreed.

Secretly, Pauline was taking it all *very* seriously. Her brain reeled with the conviction that Lydia had seen the truth in her dream after all! Jubal, Naamah, Tubal-cain, Mithrael and the Nephil. Evan would only ridicule her if she tried to explain the intercessor's dream now. Or the antediluvian rituals the old woman had seen during her heart attacks. Canaan would reject them too. Pauline had earned an undergraduate degree in Administration from a liberal arts college, but at the moment she wished she had applied herself to Biblical and religious studies as well—to have an edge with these two. "Are you saying there are still mystery religions functioning in the modern world?" she finally asked.

"Absolutely," Evan confirmed. "The attraction of mystery religion is the sense of superiority. People are attracted to secret knowledge, midnight rituals. The Society of Apostates has been hidden in the power structure of the church for all these centuries. Only the initiates know the real secrets. They feel superior. They laugh up their sleeve at the authority of a church that would canonize their fake icon."

"What is more," Canaan added, "the Society actively works for the day when the old gods will return. They are serious. They look for a messiah, just as the Jews and Christians do. It is this idea that makes them a security risk for Israel. We know, for example, that copies of the Mannheim translation circulate through an anti-Semitic network. The document had a powerful influence on Hitler. The Apostates hope they will inspire even greater atrocities with it in the future."

"God is dead," Evan interjected, "Jesus is in decline, and Satan is in the ascendancy. That is the basic creed of all Antichrist religion."

Canaan shrugged at this idea, but looked inquiringly at Pauline. "So your father is a doorway into Dunamis for us. You begin to see why I am chasing him at least?"

"I . . . Yes. I think you are wrong about a lot of things," she defended, "but I understand."

"You know what gets me?" Evan said, walking over and straightening the small picture of himself and his father on the wall. "Dad has sheltered this icon since '57."

"Surely Dad didn't know about the Apostates when he took it in?"

Evan let his silence speak for him.

She looked to Canaan for support, but he only stared.

"Why did he hire an Apostate as a medical director?" Evan asked rhetorically.

"He didn't know," Pauline insisted. "You've got to believe that. Lydia says he hired Neva because she believed in prayer."

"Dad needs to show up and explain himself here. Why has he positioned himself between the ministry and Dunamis, where no one can oversee his actions?"

"That is correct," Canaan added. "He answers to no one."

Evan nodded. "Remember what old Chester Sharpey said? 'Anyone who removes himself from accountability is headed for a fall.'"

She did remember. Still, she couldn't believe her father would hide this kind of evil. Against all the evidence, there had to be an explanation that would vindicate him. She would find it.

Canaan got up and poured himself more coffee. "If we could prove that the original cuneiform tablets are fake, we could discredit Dunamis. Not to mention the Society of Apostates and Hitler's notes in the Mannheim translation. This is the Uriel mission—to strike a great blow to anti-Semitism worldwide. We could smoke the Society into the open. Expose them to the light of day, and we think they would simply wither and die of the exposure." He patted the loose-leaf binder.

"What if the tablets are not fakes?" Pauline asked.

Canaan stared at her as if surprised she would even consider such a thing.

"I mean, what if?" she elaborated. "Have you thought of that?"

He answered sharply, "My job is to capture them. The scholars can work the rest of it out." He stood to his feet, packing the loose-leaf binder into the black satchel. "Hitler's marginal notes contain descriptions of the epiphanies that supposedly appeared at Dachau. All tyrants eventually retreat into this kind of insanity. Hitler claimed that the 'final solution' would open the ancient doors to the invisible world, and the antediluvian gods would arise and save the super race. Men would become as gods and gods as men. They would again cohabit, as in the days just after Eden. That was Hitler's secret fantasy." Canaan paused to laugh, unable to conceal his disdain. "We have got to put an end to this kind of mental disease." He paused again, looking at Pauline in a moment of uncertainty. "You know, it is interesting though—the doctors at Dachau claimed that Moloch manifested at the surgeries, justifying the slaughter of the Jews because they had sacrificed their own children to his image in Hinnom."

Pauline's mind raced back to the Valley of Hinnom, remembering her father's words about the Jews bowing their knee to Moloch. She remembered Colonel Canaan's rapt gaze at him as he spoke. She got up and walked uneasily to the opposite side of the room, recalling the weirdness she had sensed that day. *Surely Daddy doesn't believe that the Jews deserved the Holocaust? Could that have been his intent in bringing up Jeremiah's "valley of slaughter"? Never.* She rested her head against a picture on the wall, fighting a wave of nausea. "My father is not against the Jews," she said. She could say no more, no less.

"I agree," Evan added. "If I know my dad, it's the forty million dollars he's after. That is what got him into this mess."

Pauline ran through all of the new pieces of the puzzle in her mind. Just when it began to make sense, everything was a square peg in a round hole again. Nothing fit with a convincing sense of reality. An image would seem to form, then vanish beneath a host of new revelations. Her brain grew tired, battered. Then an image returned to her. She saw her father's hands in the limousine again, extended before him, trembling. Why did she see this now? What did it mean? Then she recalled the moment; he had been trying to tell her something. What had he said? "Of all the people I ever laid these hands on, why did *she* have to die?" *That's it!* she realized.

She whirled around. "Evan, Mother died of cancer. Dad has never gotten over it. He started the lab in Matamoros to find a cure. That's what he's still after." She felt suddenly right inside. This seemed to be the missing piece that explained her father's motives. He was not a simple money-grubbing evangelist. He was not a monster. "Don't you see, Evan?" she pled.

In these simple words Pauline had finally put together a scenario that made sense to Evan. It didn't reflect his own view, but it made sense in its own right. He respectfully allowed the suggestion to filter through his own views, but after doing so, it still came up short. He recalled a statement his father had made to him when he was seventeen or eighteen, when he had openly challenged him about loading sermons with emotional statements designed to reap larger offerings. "No man has pure motives," Grace had responded. "In fact, success is satisfying more than one motive in a single stroke." Evan knew that his father was the artist of the master-stroke. His motive of finding a cure for cancer would not be pure. It also had a healthy payday included with it. Evan was sure of it. The more he thought about it, the more he saw that finding a cure for cancer by combining science and religion was an insanely utopian idea. And yet in that, it was pure genius. An impossible, noble quest. Something that would create the perfect cover for a master fund-raiser. Beneath its fabulous promises, he could disguise a host of secret ambitions.

"I think you're right," he conceded. "He's after the cure. But that's not necessarily good news. Just how far will he go to get one? How many compromises will he make? How many unholy alliances will he enter? That's the part that scares me." He paused, then wagged his finger like a lecturer. "And you can't tell me the answer to that, little sister. Even *you* don't know him that well."

In the pained silence that followed Canaan regarded Pauline steadily, trying to read the flexibility and strength of her character. "Do you want to find your father now?" he asked. "Even if he turns out to be more guilty than you imagined?"

She thought only for a moment. "Of course I do." Her voice was intense with dread and hope. "He's my father."

64

GRACE HOSPITAL
7:22 A.M.

Danna Lavalle hadn't slept. Upon returning from the board meeting, her Israeli operative, Colonel Canaan, had given her the order to close out her part of the Grace/Dunamis investigation. That morning she had only taken enough time to change into a cotton jumpsuit before printing out the latest medical research files from Neva's computer terminal. Two of Canaan's commandos worked beside her, binding printouts into booklets and storing them in cardboard files for shipment to Israel.

They finished the last bundle when Evan, Pauline and Canaan walked into the office dressed for an active day. Canaan had changed from his "burglar blacks" into civilian slacks and shirt. Pauline wore a pant and blouse combination, Evan wore green canvas denims and tennis shoes.

"You knew about this all along, honey," Pauline said to Danna. "Why didn't you tell me?"

"I only know part of it," she replied tiredly. "I tried to steer you in the right direction at least."

"When? What do you mean, 'steer me'?" Pauline couldn't help feeling betrayed. She automatically demanded loyalty from an employee. It was an instinct she had picked up from her father.

"Well, whenever you called about the icon, or Sudan, I tried to keep your suspicions moving in the right direction," Danna said, then shrugged. "For seven years now I've had to keep secrets. Night before last, when you finally got suspicious of Neva, we were just beginning our interrogation and didn't know what we would learn. I couldn't say anything then."

"I wish you had."

"I think you're going to see that things happened for the best. But you know, when you mentioned the missing icon on the phone, it turned out to be very helpful. I hadn't made that connection before. Neither had the colonel. It turned out to be important in his interrogation."

Evan spoke up. "So this is what you meant yesterday in Dallas when you said there was more going on than I knew about."

She smiled slightly and nodded, enjoying the new respect she heard in his voice. Picking up a bundle of papers, she said, "There is a friendship between your dad and Max Commagene. Both of them are looking for a cancer cure."

Score one for Pauline, Evan thought, sending her an acknowledging look.

"Both men believe diseases are supernaturally caused, but that's where things get strange—" Danna looked worriedly at both of them. "—as you will see. Are we ready?"

They followed her through the door and into an elevator. She narrated as they waited for six floors to pass. "Commagene and Dr. Grace met in a London museum in the 50s. Sometime after that,

Commagene gave your father the icon. I don't know if Dr. Grace knew the tablets were included or not. Do you?"

"We don't know," Evan replied. "They were news to me."

The doors of the elevator opened in the hospital lobby and the four of them headed for the main exit. Colonel Canaan separated from the group, moving toward two of his commandos stationed in the lobby. Danna continued, "It started out that your father was intrigued by the demon-possession cases he saw in Africa and India. They were common over there. He also had his greatest healing miracles in demon-dominated societies and he wondered why."

"Dad always said healing in America is like dragging a calf to a stall," Pauline commented. She had always accepted the idea that more healings occurred overseas because faith remained simple and pure in backward societies. In Western civilization medicine had revealed that exorcism was simply not the answer to every sickness. It had never occurred to her that her father might think otherwise.

Evan pushed through the revolving glass door of the hospital's main entrance. Danna and Pauline followed him. Beneath the canopy Manuel, Pauline's driver, held the door of the limousine for them.

Danna continued as they walked toward him, "Your dad invited Dunamis to begin experiments in our foreign hospitals to see if there was a link between sickness and the spiritual world. One area of research led to another. The Matamoros cancer lab was just one of many. Only Neva knows all that went on, but she may not be much help. She's hardly coherent."

The three of them took seats in the passenger compartment of the limo.

"In '83, just after I started my part of the investigation," Danna went on, "Dunamis took over the foreign hospitals. I was just out of nursing school at the time, but your dad asked me to help Neva with the new load of administration and communications with Dunamis. That put me in a position to get access to the computer. Over the years I have been able to send a lot of information to the Uriel Mission. A lot of it I didn't understand."

Colonel Canaan and one of his men in battle fatigues crossed the entryway toward the car. Pauline and Evan continued to listen to Danna as he approached.

"When I heard Canaan was coming in from Jerusalem, I knew

things were coming to a head. Then when I got Jesse's call telling me the doctors in the Sudan had murdered all of the patients and had blown the place up, I knew we had to intervene. Not to mention the explosion on dad's yacht."

The commando entered a car in front of the limo with several other men who had arranged to fly across the border via helicopter. Canaan came back and entered the passenger compartment beside Evan. Pauline signaled Manuel, and the limousine eased from the entry drive.

The Steeple stood boldly across the fourth fairway, gleaming in the morning sun as they passed it, going south.

65

MEXICAN BORDER CROSSING
Grace Limousine
8:15 A.M.

Less than an hour later they reached the toll bridge spanning the Rio Grande. Manuel maneuvered into an express lane, pausing briefly as the station agent waved them through. Decades of daily hospital operations across the border had streamlined customs arrangements for Grace personnel.

"I don't think you know it yet," Danna was saying, "but Neva kidnapped Jesse in Houston."

"That's why he didn't show up in Brownsville?" Evan asked.

She nodded. "Colonel Canaan ordered his men to rescue him. They released him in front of his house. Poor kid. He's not really sure who the good guys and bad guys are anymore. He's going to need some professional help."

"It was not one of our objectives to rescue Jesse," Canaan explained, "but Neva had arranged to have him killed by a Santeria priest down here. Apparently they've been doing human sacrifice rituals for some time."

Hearing this, Pauline's scalp crawled with renewed anxiety. She couldn't imagine such a beastly crime in the name of religion. "How can that sort of thing go on so close to our border?"

"You will have to answer that one yourself. At any rate, Danna wouldn't let us stop short of bringing Jesse home. We were hoping Neva would lead us to Commagene before we blew our cover with her organization, but there is not much chance of that now. Under the influence of truth serum she betrayed her Apostate identity and will attempt suicide to keep us from learning anything more."

As they neared the Matamoros side of the bridge, Pauline became filled with curiosity about Dr. Sylvan. The more she thought about her, the more troubled she became that her father had placed any trust in the woman at all. "Lydia told me Neva began as a research assistant in the Matamoros cancer lab. Later she became a doctor. Is there any truth to that?"

"Yes and no," Canaan replied. "After leaving the lab she lived at a Hindu Temple on the Tamil Nadu coast. It is a well-known shrine for the insane—or the demon-possessed, depending on your point of view. After that she volunteered her services in Jonestown, Guyana. How's that for a resumé?"

Pauline's stomach knotted, and she again felt that palpable wave of fear creep across her skull. *Dear Lord Jesus, please, when will this nightmare end?* She regarded Jonestown as the epitome of religious insanity. Something she had never understood and did not want to understand. Far removed from her own reality.

Canaan went on, "Our operatives placed Neva at several Dunamis medical board meetings during her People's Temple and Jonestown period. Her experiences must have elevated her esteem within the Society of Apostates. Afterward she emerged as a 'rebirthing' practitioner, showing up in Santa Cruz, California."

"What in heaven's name is a 'rebirthing practitioner'?" Pauline demanded, feeling disgust and anger rising above her fear now.

"'Rebirthing' is a new kind of religious career."

"New Age," Evan interjected. "It's a very old idea, actually."

Canaan nodded. "It is Eastern. People need to be 'birthed' from one level of consciousness to another. It follows the 'born again' idea of Christianity."

"No, it doesn't," Pauline quickly insisted. "I can guarantee you that the two do not even relate."

"Perhaps not. Neva helped people 'rebirth' from their old levels of consciousness into higher levels."

"Well, I don't appreciate your mixing of Christian terminology with anything that woman does," Pauline snapped. "How many 'rebirthings' had to happen before four hundred people would commit suicide for Jim Jones? There was absolutely nothing Christian about that maniac."

"Exactly." Canaan remained quiet, watching her for a moment. "Suicide is sort of the ultimate 'rebirth,' I suppose. You just need help getting used to the idea, right? That's why they need 'rebirthers.' It is not natural." He nodded at this idea, as if sorting it out in his own mind. After all, his work demanded not so much moral judgment as mental competence. To him, Pauline seemed obsessed about the morality of everything. He continued, "All I know is that Neva found a large clientele in California. Mostly self-proclaimed Christians. Yuppies. I guess they were looking for something less sensational than suicide in her practice. Material gain probably. Self help. Harmless stuff."

"Well, I don't like Neva, and I don't understand how she ever got into our ministry."

"We live in a post-Christian world," Evan interjected wanly. "Americans have forgotten their heritage. It's Judeo-Christian, not Hare Krishna. Any trendy idea that comes along nowadays can get a following. 'The Force be with you' and all that stuff. It *sells*."

"Who sold whom?" Canaan asked, eying him steadily. "Your father made Neva Sylvan medical director here."

Evan carefully sorted it. "I don't think my father understood the implications of what he did."

"He didn't know," Pauline declared positively.

"But we have to admit that he was embarrassingly stupid, at the very least," Evan added.

Pauline saw that he was right. For a moment she allowed herself to feel the humiliation she would certainly have to face if and when the revelations about Neva Sylvan became public. Not to mention the medical experimentation she seemed to be involved in with Grace Ministries. And what might it reveal about the murderous excesses in Sudan? The press would run riot. Someone would have to face the cameras. No doubt many of the pictures of her standing with her father in Third-World crusades would be splashed across newspapers nationwide. She would be dragged to center stage, like it or not. *No! I've dragged myself to center stage*, she suddenly remembered. She had attacked and manipulated the press in the D/FW press conference. She had it coming from the press. And they would love their revenge, as usual.

Danna seemed to read Pauline's troubled thoughts and reached over to touch her arm sympathetically. "Neva didn't advertise her background around here. As far as I can see, your father may not have known about her."

Pauline sighed and paused before answering. "Even if he didn't know, he's still responsible."

66

MATAMOROS
Grace Missionary Hospital
9:01 A.M.

The Grace Medical facility in Matamoros took up half a city block. Housed in a white two-story *hacienda* of sunbaked brick with a shaded courtyard, it offered free walk-in health services to the poor.

As Evan and the others crossed the courtyard, rows of Mexican peasants waited on benches for the kind of care they could not afford elsewhere in the Gulf State of Tamaulipas. Broken bones, cuts, flu, emphysema, skin rashes, poison ivy, pregnancies, diseases of malnutrition and filth. This had always been the part of his father's ministry Evan had wanted to serve as a young man. The "good Samaritan" binding of wounds had seemed more charitable than the hit-and-miss prayers for the sick. In the long healing lines, so many went away as they had come. Sick. Except, perhaps, carrying more disappointment and disillusionment than before, wondering why God had passed them by. But it had been a long time since Evan had felt these things. Ten years since he had lost his place of power with the ministry and the hospitals.

He reminded himself as they moved toward the rear of the courtyard, even the hospital did not run with a pure motive. The city fathers and *barrio* dwellers alike considered Dr. Grace a living saint for providing the free clinic bearing his name. Thus, his needs for electrical power, sewer, cheap labor and favorable zoning laws were liberally supplied.

The Matamoros clinic included much more than met the eye. Passing through an archway at the rear of the *hacienda* the group came to a locked iron gate. Danna produced a key and let them into a second, larger compound surrounded by a twelve-foot-chain-link fence with tangles of razor-sharp barbed wire nested along the top. A hundred yards away, a helicopter pad occupied the center of a cement paved square, now crowded with Grace's bullet-riddled CareFlight chopper, flanked by two unmarked commando craft.

Around the square sat an assortment of buildings. On either side two large warehouses of corrugated metal dominated the other structures. Neither building had windows. Several air-conditioning units hummed along the rooftops. Six emergency diesel generators were parked there, three beside each building. Large transformers and surge control units sat next to the generators, busily filtering Mexico's "dirty" power. These units supplied the main hospital building where most of the serious care was provided. They also powered the old cancer research lab, supposedly abandoned for many years now.

Danna led them straight through the maze of helicopters and generators toward an older stucco building at the very back of the lot. Across a gravel yard, standing two stories tall, it looked like a gymnasium structure from an early-sixties schoolyard. Three of Canaan's men stood guard at the door with automatic weapons.

"This is the original cancer research center," Danna explained as they neared.

One of the men knocked on the door. It opened, and another commando led the group inside. Evan, Pauline, Canaan and Danna proceeded down a short hallway past several offices. Turning left, they entered a larger office.

Inside, the two commandos who had been helping Danna at the main hospital now watched over Neva. They had flown ahead from the Texas side, using one of the helicopters.

Pauline immediately noticed that Neva's hair was unkempt. She remained handcuffed. A sleepy half-moon bagged beneath each eye. A bruise disturbingly pocked her left cheek. The now responsible interim president of Grace Ministries quaked a bit, feeling some responsibility for the confrontational feel in the room. It seemed like a violent atmosphere to her. Satanic. She recalled Canaan's offhanded mention of "violating Neva's civil rights."

"How did she receive this bruise?" Pauline demanded, looking directly at Canaan.

"She did that to herself," he replied steadily. "Threw herself into the arm of a chair."

She didn't believe him. Watching his eyes, she was convinced he held something back. *He always does,* she thought. *What kind of man is he really?*

Danna broke the silence. "OK, Benji," she said, moving to the door. "It's time for us to see the lab."

The commando named Benji unlocked and removed the medical director's handcuffs.

Pauline wanted to say something to Neva. Something normal, something sympathetic. But she didn't know what to say, having recently learned details of Neva's vile spiritual odyssey. Still, she seemed human and should be treated with respect.

"Who are these men?" Evan asked, indicating two other civilians handcuffed in the room.

"Neva's pilot," Canaan explained. "The other one there is a lab assistant. We'll be letting them go later, but you will want to press charges of some kind when you learn what they were up to."

"You have no idea what you're doing," Neva suddenly growled. Her voice sounded hoarse and unnatural.

Ignoring her, Danna led the way out of the office. Neva followed sullenly, Benji firmly holding her arm. The rest of the group strung along behind.

They proceeded down a wide hallway to a metal door. Danna's keys rattled the lock. The door swung open and they entered a large, well-lit room that could once have been a gymnasium. Around the walls were counters, sinks, petri dishes, metallic canisters, rows of test tubes, thousands of minutely labeled substances, electronic devices, examination tables and a glass-enclosed vivisection area.

Pauline recalled Lydia's mention of a prayer loft her father had built in the early 1960s. She glanced around and located it. A balcony on one wall above the main floor. It had an open stairway leading to each side. Above it on the wall hung an old canvas banner, drooping at one end, trailing a train of cobwebs. It still displayed a quote of Matthew 16:19, in faded blue brush strokes. Pauline imagined the banner, shiny and bold, in those early days, when the idea of medicine and prayer had been exciting and new—and her mother, Ruth, had still been alive.

In the meantime Evan had spotted the banner and read it aloud rhetorically;

"'Whatsoever thou shalt bind on earth shall be bound in Heaven: and whatsoever thou shalt loose on earth shall be loosed in Heaven.'"

"That loft is where Lydia prayed for a cure," Pauline explained. "You remember that, don't you, Neva? You were here then."

"Hm?" Neva looked bewildered, as if she had forgotten the old banner. She found it, then chortled, "Primitive. The results were very disappointing." The derision in her voice filled the chamber.

Danna cleared her throat and began to narrate her tour of the facility. "This research lab has been sealed off from the clinic and hospital staff. This has been 'Neva's baby' out here." She walked toward the lab tables against the far wall and pointed to a series of stainless steel canisters. "These are malignancy and viral 'motivation' experiments which have continued under Neva's supervision in recent years. Remember, the key to this research has been to scientifically measure spiritual influences on physical disease."

"Like the banner says," Evan interjected, "'bind' a disease on earth and so 'bind' it in Heaven."

"Primitive," Neva said again. "We're well beyond that now."

Danna resumed her talk. "Dunamis called the research in this lab 'motivational.' What did that mean? There are as many labs as there are Grace hospitals in Third-World countries. Each hospital conducted part of the overall plan. Here they were interested specifically in psychic atmospheres' that would turn a disease on and off, so to speak. Also atmospheres that would speed up or slow down the normal processes of viral activity, or motivation. Much of their research could be very dangerous as biochemical weaponry. In an attempt to measure the influence of various 'spiritual' environments on malignant and viral cultures, some of these specimens have been exposed to concentrated prayer, meditation, laughter, horror, satanic worship, psychedelic drug ceremonies, orgies, and animal and human sacrifice."

"You can't be serious," Pauline groaned, feeling a taste of gall rising from her stomach.

"I wish I wasn't."

"Witch doctors," Evan spat.

"Don't misunderstand," Neva blurted at him, "we didn't do these things ourselves. We found where these things were already going on, and we introduced our scientific research there. Plagues have been unleashed by these extreme cultures, but who has had the courage to look for a scientific cure in the same environment? It takes a *real* scientist who puts aside moral judgment to do that."

"The bloody little shack in the cornfield?" Canaan asked. "Was that one of your extreme cultures?" He turned to Pauline and

Evan. "Jesse was about to meet his end there as a ritual sacrifice. She is more than a scientist. She is a murderer."

"Canaan, you could achieve so much," Neva purred, showing an insane admiration for her tormentor. "Yes, 'the bloody little shack.' You've spilled enough blood yourself, Jew. You should understand sacrifice! Who are you sacrificing on the West Bank? On the Temple Mount? In Gaza and the occupied territories? I know you . . . Christ killer!"

Suddenly the air in the lab seemed to grow stifling. Benji increased his grip on Neva's arm and shook it roughly.

"You'll only speak when asked from now on," Danna warned. "Is that clear?"

"At least she's beginning to show her true colors," Canaan commented dryly.

Neva glared.

"According to the computer files," Danna continued, "certain atmospheres have shown dramatic results. Especially in the negative direction, meaning that they have been able to 'motivate' worse malignancies through these experiments, but they have not come close to a cure."

Danna went on to explain that one of the more encouraging experiments took place in Haiti, involving AIDS and herpes patients. They had been able to establish that anger and anxiety levels were linked to the outbreak of symptoms, while positive emotions worked to keep them in remission. It was an interesting example of New Age medicine. Nothing criminal.

"Still primitive," Neva snorted.

Ignoring her, Danna went on, "The shining star of Dunamis research is what they call Near Death Experimentation, or NDE." She explained that the most recent work had taken place in Sudan, where a team of doctors began simulating the NDE through a combination of drugs and life-support equipment.

Pauline grew numb, hearing this about the Sudan hospital. That meant that Jesse Stiles's wild reports of killings probably had nothing to do with the civil war there. She glanced at Evan. He appeared grim, beyond anger.

Danna continued, "For years people have described going through a tunnel and experiencing vivid things on the other side of death, including supernatural beings. Dunamis has conducted aggressive research in this area, hoping to pinpoint the supernatural beings as motivating factors in cancer malignancies. They evidently feel they are close to a breakthrough. Perhaps a cure."

Neva breathed, "Your father is a visionary."

Pauline felt a surge of anger burning at her face, stinging her eyes.

Neva went on, "The cure is what this is all about, and *you* want to bring it all down. You know not what you do! Everything Dr. Grace dreamed of, all of the sacrifices that have brought us to this day . . . You want to destroy it because your minds are fearful and superstitious and unscientific. Provincial. Too small to contain it." She suddenly declared with conviction, "Dr. Grace is no less than a Christopher Columbus, sailing to a new world."

"Un-be-lievable!" Pauline screamed, unable to contain herself any longer. All of her frustrations, the insinuation about her father, and her simmering fears united in a rush of pure hatred for this woman. Neva had brought about all these things. She was the demon behind the evil in Grace Ministries. Pauline lurched at her across the floor, grabbing the doctor by the lapels. A surprised Benji stepped back as she shook the stout little woman with all her strength. "What have you done to us? Where is Daddy? You filthy witch—" She clawed at her face.

Evan leaped forward to intervene, but as he did Neva writhed free. Before Benji could stop her she raced to a nearby table and snatched up a beaker of "motivated" virus. Popping the lid free she sloshed a greenish gruel onto the tabletop. Whirling around with an evil laugh she gulped half of it in a display of suicidal glee.

"It's virus," she panted, the green stuff clinging to her teeth and oozing from the corners of her mouth. "Highly motivated."

The others fell back as she advanced insanely, poised to throw the beaker.

"Let her go," Canaan barked. He and Benji leveled their guns. "She is dead. Everybody get out."

Pauline started to run, but then froze hearing Neva's scream. "You all must die for your ignorance!"

The mad medical director spun and hurled the culture at Pauline. By instinct she fell flat to the floor. Evan grabbed her shoulders and half lifted, half dragged her backwards toward the door.

"Out!" Canaan shouted. "Don't shoot," he hissed to Benji. "She's dead already. That stuff will do it."

Neva grabbed a second beaker and pursued him as he backed away. She leered. "Why did you have to mess with me, Jew dog? I was there, you know." The green slime spit hideously from her teeth as she laughed. "I mixed the Kool-Aid! Ah-ha! You should have been there—then you would have known. Listen to Jim Jones's tape sometime. Why do you think he recorded it? For a joke? Are you kidding? You can hear the epiphanies in the distance . . . on the perimeter of Jonestown. As . . . as the people died, in one moment they burst the veil to the invisible realm. We could see them, Jew dog. The epiphanies. We *know* they are rising to take their rightful thrones. Listen to them. On the tapes, above the screams. Everybody saw them. Those were screams of ecstasy, you know? Do you know?"

Canaan continued to back toward the door, silently motioning the others to run for it.

"You should know this, Jew. In the gas chambers, the death-camp operating rooms . . . ecstasy. Because the gods had come to help us. We sent a fresh message to the world from Jonestown, that's all it was. A fresh message because the world was forgetting. The old gods will rise again! They will return! Listen to the tape. You can hear them. Rising. Ha, ha, ha, ha!" She sobered and snarled with the voice of a slavering panther, clicking her teeth between words. "We'll come against you, Jew dog. Oh, I will be there when my lord comes to take back his throne. The one *you* and the filthy Christ you begat have stolen! I will see you in *Megiddo*, dog. In the valley where your God dies."

Evan, Pauline and Danna huddled outside the laboratory door now, watching with transfixed horror.

The evil doctor suddenly lunged toward Canaan, throwing her beaker of "motivated" virus like a weapon. Canaan hit the floor, but the virus caught Benji on the side of the face. He grabbed his head and began instantly retching and vomiting, throwing himself backwards toward the door. Canaan loosed a burst of gunfire at Neva, but she dodged behind a table like an agile cat. He then dragged Benji the rest of the way through the doorway and slammed the metal door behind them.

A stainless steel canister slammed immediately against it. Neva screamed from inside, "I was in the bunker, Jew dog! Ha, ha, ha, ha!"

"Now she thinks she's Eva Braun," Canaan panted, his back braced against the door. "She's insane."

"She's gotta die soon with the amount of culture she downed,"

Evan said. "Did anybody get a good look at what it was? I mean, we're going to need an antidote for Benji."

They could hear him in the bathroom, gagging and flushing his skin with water. Danna had gone to assist him.

"I think he'll be alright if the culture didn't enter a break in the skin," Canaan said. "Neva is going to be alright. The plan is to let her escape. She will try to warn the others."

Evan looked at the clever intelligence officer, amazed.

Beyond the laboratory door all grew quiet.

Canaan's radio suddenly crackled, relaying a message in Hebrew. He leaped to his feet and opened the lab door. "She went out the back way," he said smiling with admiration. "She's crazy like a fox. I'll bet you that culture was benign." He laughed heartily, and with a measure of relief. "I have a man out there to follow her."

67

BORDER CROSSING
11:47 A.M.

The Grace limousine crossed the border bridge on its return to Brownsville, its four passengers deep in thought. Neva had managed to lose the tail Canaan had sent following her escape from the lab. The myriad alleyways and hovels of the Matamoros back streets had provided her a quick hiding place. In the meantime Benji had been flown to Sinai Hospital in Houston to have his viral exposure checked. The question that remained was, where might Dunamis and Dr. Grace have gone to conduct their fantastical cancer experiments? Neva's revelations at the lab had fired all their worst fears.

Canaan asserted that they could eliminate Sudan, Jerusalem, Mannheim, Matamoros, and Brownsville as possible locations for the current experiments. Pauline relayed that Jann Parker's telephone survey of Grace hospitals and of Dr. Grace's personal contacts had failed to produce a clue. She added that perhaps the Haiti hospital should now be checked again. Canaan agreed.

"You won't learn anything by talking to the ministry staff,"

Danna suggested. "They've been kept out of what's going on. And the Dunamis people are going to outright lie."

In the meantime, Evan had become intrigued by the idea of the NDE experiments and their use in the search for a "supernatural" cause and cure to cancer. As his mind flitted between details of the bizarre events of recent days, he became suddenly struck with an unexpected new possibility. "The desert that sin made," he mused aloud, envisioning the picture of Nimrut Dag on the wall of his father's studio.

Pauline overheard, remembering their discussion of the picture.

"That picture," he murmured again, looking at her. "Why does Dad keep it around? It doesn't fit the others in the gallery. I thought maybe he kept it because it was the only picture of me, but that doesn't make sense. He has piles of pictures of me. Why that one?"

She nodded, trying to imagine where the picture had been taken. A desert.

"Nimrut Dag," he explained. "That's the name on the photo. When we made that picture he called it 'the desert that sin made.' Maybe that's where they are."

"Why?"

"Because to find the cure for cancer, you first have to find the cause."

"Right . . ."

"Sin."

She paused. "Sin caused disease? Well, maybe original sin."

Evan felt something click into place in his mind. Was the connection original sin?

Canaan's brow wrinkled with interest at this new line of thinking. "Any idea where this 'Nimrut Dag' is?"

"The Middle East or North Africa," Evan replied. "You tell me. I was just eight years old when we went there. It's a mountain with some kind of ruins near the top. It shouldn't be hard to look up in an atlas once we get home."

Pauline shrugged. "So why would they go there?"

Evan searched his gut-reaction for an answer, trying to put words to feelings, to intuition. "Because it's Eden," he replied with sudden conviction. He had not been sure until this very moment. "You said it yourself, Pauline . . . original sin. They've gone to the place of original sin where sickness and every form of evil first entered the world. With this Dunamis bunch, that makes sense."

Pauline felt a chill. Once again she remembered Lydia's dream and knew that Eden had perished with the Flood. "That seems too fantastical, Evan."

"Not for Dunamis. They're doing nothing halfway. Are they?" He looked at her and laughed with amazement. "Dad thinks he's found the Garden."

"From the name, I would guess it is in Iraq or Syria," Canaan offered, still puzzling the location question. "They have mountains up there called 'dags.' Nimrut Dag is no doubt a mountain. Probably an ancient High Place."

"What is a High Place?" Pauline asked.

"Idol worship in the Middle East was always done on the highest point of land. It dates back to the Tower of Babel, I suppose. A way of getting closer to God."

"Wherever it is," Evan said, "you can see the ruins of a pantheon in the picture. I was there in '57. Dad called it the 'desert that sin made.' That means he believed it was Eden that far back. It was a big deal to him. He kept saying that to me for years. Every time he referred to the picture, like there was some lesson in it for me."

"'57?" Canaan mused. "That was near the time Commagene gave him the icon." The intelligence officer's interest in the theory suddenly grew stronger. He now connected Dunamis to this mysterious Nimrut Dag. "I want to see that picture."

"You bet," Evan replied. "You know, Dad and Commagene have been after the original Garden all along. They're after a supernatural cure to cancer. *Supernatural* is the key." He looked around the car with new excitement. "Do you realize they are totally nuts?"

"But of course," Canaan replied. "Eden is purely mythical. It was not a literal place."

"Perhaps," Evan replied, "but if you *believed* it was a literal place, how extreme might you become? See my point?"

The colonel nodded solemnly.

Pauline had been both surprised and disappointed in this exchange. She had assumed that Jews believed in a literal Eden. Once again she had been naive. Romantically so. This forced her to pause and adjust her thinking. Evidently she was the only person on the trail of her father who believed in the Bible word for word. Why? *How can they pick and choose from the Word of God?* she wondered, feeling even more isolated and alone.

"Pauline, what is the name of the grand slam letter Dad just sent to Dallas WordSmith?" Evan asked. "What did he call it?"

The question was a setup and she knew it. She resented it, but the answer came to mind with a sickening confirmation. "'Tree of Life,'" she said.

"And where do we find the 'Tree of Life'?"

She refused to nod. The answer was obvious.

"Now I know we're tracking right. There's more. What is the response device in the 'Tree of Life' letter? The piece I sent Alan to check out today?"

She remembered the small charm cross, but failed to see its significance. "It's just a cross."

"That's the New Testament 'Tree of Life,'" he exclaimed. "A charm cross made of agate, right?" He shook his head. "Wrong. I just realized what it is made of, sis. Another form of agate. Silica-based. Pauline, it's petrified wood!" He shouted it. Calming himself, he laughed as he continued, "If you were to find the Garden of Eden today, what form would it be in?" His mind began making even more connections. "The mosaic pieces of the icon are petrified wood." He yelled, "When we're hot, we're hot!"

Pauline remembered well. The stunning faces of *The Seven Sleepers of Antioch* which used to make her dizzy when she stared at them as a girl. The Apostate Saints in their leaf-gold halos. Up close, she had found that the patterns of wood grain in the individual *tesserae* gave the artwork its visual power. She also chillingly recalled that Lydia's dream of the Nephil had included a description of a fallen forest.

Evan shrugged with his palms outward, resting his case. "Again, how important would Nimrut Dag be to Dunamis? To Dad? To the cure for cancer? If they knew, or even if they only *believed*, that it was the original site of the Garden?"

Without waiting for a reply he reached for the car telephone and dialed Rick Gresham's telephone number. He ordered him to prepare "Spirit I" for flight to the Middle East, possibly to Syria or Iraq. He then asked him to meet them at the mansion studio for travel orientation at 5:15 P.M. As he hung up, it hit him that he had upstaged his sister's authority. "Was that OK with you, sis?"

"Of course," she quipped, looking out the window broodingly. Her tone of voice indicated that it was OK only because she had no other choice.

68

BROWNSVILLE
Dr. Grace's Mansion
5:30 P.M.

Preparation for travel began in earnest as soon as the group returned to the family compound. Nimrut Dag had been positively identified as a mountaintop pantheon in Eastern Turkey. Atlases, notebooks, encyclopedias and reference books had been pulled from Dr. Grace's private collection and spread on the table to assist in planning.

Alan Lavalle had joined the group. Upon hearing about the Turkish location he grew very excited, remembering that one of the fax confirmations had originated from a place called Antakaya, Turkey. They quickly looked it up, only to discover that Antakaya was the modern site of Antioch on the Orontes River. The same Antioch for which *The Seven Sleepers* icon was named. The city named for the infamous Antiochus Epiphanes. Alan added that it was the city where the followers of Jesus were first called "Christians," and where Paul had made his missionary home.

In Evan's mind, this news solidified the probability that Dr. Grace had been the author of the "Tree of Life" letter after all. He (or someone) had evidently carried the concept from the remote location of Nimrut Dag to Antioch, the nearest location with the modern convenience of a telephone. Knowing this, Evan was even more convinced that his father had been orchestrating the media all along. Pauline's fears grew that her brother had been right about that too.

Alan Lavalle made himself a part of the teamwork, typing and retyping an itinerary from the changing flight plan supplied by Rick. First they had planned to fly to Antakaya. Then upon a more thorough investigation, they discovered that an airstrip to the north, near Lake Van, would place them closer to Nimrut Dag by auto and helicopter.

Danna spent the next two hours on the telephone getting clearances for "Spirit I" to fly to the Lake Van airport. She succeeded only after persuading the Ministry of Health in Istanbul that Grace

Ministries International would be scouting a possible hospital site in the remote Eastern provinces. Which was not true, but a seemingly necessary lie to get into the country. Passing that hurdle, she was able to secure a Turkish helicopter service to ferry them from Van to Nimrut Dag. She was emphatically told, however, that the mountain pantheon had been strictly closed to tourism for the past six months. Orders of the Turkish Ministry of Archaeology and Antiquities. She concluded that something strange was going on there, no doubt the work of Dunamis.

To one side of this action Canaan used the private line in Dr. Grace's bedroom to lay plans for a commando raid on the site. Evan coordinated details with him. It would be a nighttime desert operation similar to the Iran rescue attempt ordered by President Carter, infamous for its failure. "Only we won't fail," Canaan promised.

Three new *Aerospatiale* stealth helicopters would fly low over the Mediterranean between Cyprus and Syria. The Israeli commandos would enter Turkish airspace at the landfall of the Gulf of Iskenderun. Turning eastward, they would proceed to the upper Euphrates Valley and follow it to their target. These Super Frelon aircraft had been specially designed and painted to reduce their signature to enemy radar. Carrying six to eight commandos each, they were further equipped to fly knap-of-the-earth at 184 miles per hour—*at night!* The pilots wore super-sophisticated night-vision goggles to allow them to navigate in this computer-controlled environment, and the Israeli pilots were very good at it.

The raid's single objective would be to capture the cuneiform tablets of "The Songs of Jubal"—if they were there—in order to bring them to Jerusalem for scientific study. Hopefully, the scholars would prove them a hoax and discredit the anti-Semite network that had circulated translations throughout the world.

Canaan had not been able to prove to his superiors that the original tablets were indeed at Nimrut Dag. At first the decision-makers had wanted to back out for lack of hard evidence. Through several heated telephone discussions they questioned the colonel's facts and found them lacking. Finally Canaan put his rank on the line. "The tablets will be there!" he bellowed. They had reluctantly agreed to risk the raid.

It seemed to Evan that Canaan went too far in this. He felt a suspicion that the colonel steered the decision in order to provide help for Pauline. It was not one of those things he could prove. It was just an impression that arose from watching the process.

With Canaan's assurances, however, the plan received secret approval by a special committee of the Knesset. This group had already weighed the risk of an international incident against the possible benefit of capturing the secret "Songs of Jubal." It was the same kind of approval given to the preemptive strike on Iraq's nuclear facility years before.

In the process of planning the Nimrut Dag raid, Canaan privately promised to supply Pauline and Evan information on the whereabouts and well-being of their father. After outlining the details of the raid, he learned that "Spirit I" had been given clearance to land at Lake Van. This surprised the colonel, knowing that Turkey was highly protective of the region. With that break, he suggested that he enter Turkey as Rick's copilot rather than accompany the commandos. That would give him the advantage of arriving ahead of the others. His own air-force credentials won Rick's approval of the idea, and it was agreed.

Returning to the studio they found that Pauline had produced Dr. Grace's personal scrapbook on the pantheon of Nimrut Dag. It had been tucked above her father's desk. As they entered she was spreading it on the meeting table. It was filled with stunning photographs, diagrams and survey elevations. Much of it had been taken from a book written in German, and from mapping done by the American School of Oriental Research. Extensive descriptions of the history and archaeology of the place abounded. Close-ups of the broken gods bore identifying labels.

Evan read the German spelling of their names aloud. "Zeus, Herakles, Oromasdes, Artagnes, Ares, Dexiosis, Mithras—one of the twelve high Aryan gods," he commented. "The neo-Nazis will love this place. Apollon or Apollyon, Abaddon or Apollo, depending upon whether you're Roman, Persian or Greek. Helios, Hermes, Antiochos, Kommagene— Hey, colonel," Evan called excitedly, "you won't believe this—Kommagene." A robust image with a garlanded head of oak and grape clusters bore a familiar name. "This place holds the secret to Mr. Dunamis himself."

"Maximilian Commagene. What is this page from?" the colonel asked. He flipped backwards to a frontispiece which read, *Die Kommagenischen Kultreformen Unter König Mithradates I. Kallinikos und Seinem Sohne Antiochos I.* "Roughly translated," he said aloud, "'The Commagene Culture under Kings Mithradates, Kallinikos and Antiochus.'"

"Max's family tree," Evan commented. "Where has this been

all my life?" He continued to pore through the pages. "Does it make more sense now? They're looking for the demigod behind cancer and other diseases. If this pagan worship site is Eden . . . Do you see what they're up to? Like the book of Hebrews says, 'They serve at a sanctuary that is a copy and shadow of what is in heaven.'"

"'Summon the old gods . . .'" Canaan rhetorically quoted the phrase from the preface to "The Songs of Jubal."

"Look at this." Evan had turned to a pencil-drawn sketch of a cave beneath the pantheon terrace. A hand-written note identified it as "The cave of the Seven Sleepers." "This was a high-level pagan holy place. Any doubts about whether or not this is where they are should be gone now," he said. "Do you realize the significance of this find? This may be the site where the seven original Apostates were walled into that cave, and if it is also the site of the Garden of Eden—that is why the Apostates walked out alive after two hundred years. The Tree of Life is in there. That's the legend behind the icon."

By now Alan, Danna and Rick had joined them.

Alan tossed the cross of petrified wood to the tabletop. "Alright. Danna told me about the Garden idea. Do you realize that this cross of petrified wood is the hottest response device ever invented? And I've heard of them all." The mail-order religionist began to dance a little jig around the table. "The genius of Simon Grace! He outdid the master—me, of course." He nudged Canaan with an elbow. "In case you forgot, the fruit of the forbidden tree was death and disease. Christ was hung on a tree, a cross. Out of the tree of death—" He held up the relic cross. "—we now have the 'Tree of Life.' The possibilities are endless. Simon bought a twelve million list? Are you kidding? He should buy another twelve million names. This is gonna bury you in money! It's the great whopper response device of them all!" He nearly choked with glee. He couldn't seem to help himself.

Canaan had been viewing Alan through this entire revealing speech with a darkly cynical eye. "I have heard it said that 'it pays to follow Jesus,'" he commented dryly.

Evan and Pauline simultaneously felt a slap of shame in this remark.

"I'm sorry you had to see this," Evan apologized, taking the charm from Alan. "When Christ cleansed the Jerusalem Temple, I think he drove out all the Alan Lavalles with a whip."

Canaan remained thoughtful a moment. "But is he right? Is this the greatest fund-raising device of its kind?"

Evan felt confused, trapped into discussion by Alan's naked greed. "We don't know. Alan is the expert in these things."

"Then aren't you just a bit hypocritical?"

Evan shook his head slightly. "What do you mean?"

"This mansion, the limousines, the private jet, this whole religious Disneyworld, not to mention the hospitals and the preaching . . . Was not everything in your life paid for with this kind of money?"

Evan looked at his sister helplessly. For the moment he felt proud to have been defrocked so long ago. He wanted to put great distance between himself and the money of ministry.

Alan began to chuckle, eyes sparkling at Canaan. "Spoken like a real Jew," he said. "I can always count on you people to respect the value of a dollar sooner or later."

Evan and Pauline turned angrily on him for this racial slur.

He threw up his hands in protest. "Nothing gets done without money! Why don't you people give me a break?"

69
THE STEEPLE
7:03 A.M.

Lydia knelt at her prayer station. Pauline quietly entered the apartment and stopped for several minutes in the dim glow of the stained-glass wall, listening to the murmur of the intercessor's prayer. She carried her father's scrapbook of Nimrut Dag, wanting to share it with the old woman before leaving the country.

Above the Bible on the lectern, the public relations image of Dr. Grace smiled reassuringly at her from across the room. It was pure illusion to Pauline now. She knew that her father was terribly compromised, corrupt, and perhaps mad. Pursuing a quest beyond the lawful bounds of medicine. He had invaded the realm of the demigods, perhaps the netherworld, in search of a cure for cancer. All of which was surely forbidden.

Yes, Lydia, he's bound, she thought. *He—is—bound!*

She crossed the bedroom and knelt at the lectern facing the intercessor.

Lydia felt the movement of the air and the heat of her body. Her eyes fluttered open and she reached across, placing two warm hands on the younger woman's forearms. "How do you want me to pray?" she asked.

Pauline thought about it. "I don't know. For 'journey mercies,' for wisdom, for safety. For Daddy. For me and Evan. We're leaving before daybreak. There's so much to tell. I can't even tell you all of it. But can I ask you to look at something?"

She nodded. Pauline opened the book, laying it atop the Bible on the lectern. She pointed out the pictures of the ruined pantheon at Nimrut Dag, the tumulus, the thrones, the dismembered statues, their fierce visages. She passed it all before the intercessor's gaze, page after page.

"This is where Daddy has gone. I wanted to know if you saw any of this in your dream."

She looked carefully and shook her head. "No. These are nice-looking statues compared to what I saw. The Nephil was hideous, deformed. It was a buck-skinned ape with dilapidated bat wings, a—a dog-like mouth, drooling, with huge canine fangs. And it talked. Isn't that strange? The creature talked around all those flashing teeth. It asked me its name like it was playing a game or something."

"Maybe that's it. Maybe that is the key to all of this, knowing the monster's name. It must be Cancer."

"Hmm . . ." Lydia felt within her mind for an answer. She remained unclear, puzzled. "Maybe so. I don't know."

"That's what Daddy is after, a cancer cure. We know that now. He has involved himself with some very evil people, Lydia. He has done things in the foreign hospitals that would be illegal here in the United States. He's joined an international organization that has performed atrocities. A lot of people have died. Do you understand? We'll never outlive this awful thing. Our whole lives will be lost in the shadow of it."

"Oh, honey . . ." Lydia lamented with sympathy for what this knowledge did to the young woman. "Are you saying your father actually planned these things?"

"I don't know. But, Lydia, he did open the door. He is responsible. I think he did it out of grief for Mother."

"That could be."

"It started in Matamoros when Mother was sick. But Neva has become a monster and has gone so far beyond what is right. It is sickening. She says she was in Jonestown, Lydia. Can you believe it?"

"My, my!" The old woman's mind puzzled through this new revelation. "I'd be careful of anything that woman says. If she is under the power of evil spirits, then all she can do is lie. Remember," she thumped the page of pictures, "all these gods are liars. They came from the father of lies. They deceive. They even take the truth and twist it so that it means something perverse, but the end is always death. That's how you can know them."

Pauline looked again at the idols in their corroded glory on Nimrut Dag. "Evan says Daddy believes this place was once the Garden of Eden. The place of original sin. He thinks Daddy is going to medically cross over to face the god of cancer. That's what I think you saw in the dream. They are using some kind of medical procedure to send him over there, you know? People who have died and been resuscitated have seen things. Like maybe where you went that night of your heart attack. Barry swears you died three times."

"Now I don't know about that. I died in the dream, but . . . well, I saw things. Oh! I saw things I can't describe, and yes, I believe I saw the Garden. It must have been after the Fall of it. All the trees had been knocked down except for two. The Tree of Life and the Tree of the Knowledge of Good and Evil. That Tree of Knowledge was old and ugly and gnarled-up."

"If the Garden was dead, then today it might be a petrified forest, mightn't it?"

"Oh, I don't know about such things. I suppose. I imagine the Garden was still there on earth until the Flood destroyed it all."

"One thing I believe, Lydia. I believe you saw the truth about what is happening with Daddy. It's a spiritual truth somehow, don't you think so? He's bound. But how do we set him free?"

"I don't know what to make of it all. The dream was so real. I felt like I was there, Pauline. I'm not so sure I wasn't. But your father was bound up in that arena. The Nephil was full-grown and he was tied to a pole. The angel Mithrael was there fighting with him. And Naamah was there too. It was a tragic place."

The old woman gripped her arm and whispered with sudden

wonder, "You know, he was beautiful, Pauline. More than I can say. I could see why women would want to . . . be attracted to one—an angel, I mean. At the beginning I was inside Naamah's body. Their love was so intense and romantic. But then I felt that terrible Nephil in her womb, and believe me, it was much better for the angels to keep their proper place and stay away from women. They must have had many wives, because no woman could survive the birth of one of those giants. Huge monsters. I do believe it is Naamah's Nephil that binds your father. It is a cursed thing, whatever it is."

"Cancer," Pauline whispered. "Dad needs to get out of that arena. Forget the cure for cancer. He needs to come home and straighten out this ministry. I believe that is my mission. To get him to see that. His priorities have been warped by this obsession." Pauline felt herself brighten with new purpose as she spoke. For the first time she seemed to have answers born in her own soul. Not just questions.

Lydia spoke. "Well, we know he's at this Nimrut place, and you are going after him, right?"

Pauline nodded, feeling dwarfed by the enormity of the whole idea.

"I wish I could go with you."

"Oh, so do I, but it is going to be dangerous."

"Well, that's no reason for me to stay home. I think I would just slow you down, that's all. Besides, I feel that I've already been there in the Spirit. I'll be in prayer until you return. The Lord will have to deliver you no matter who goes or stays."

Pauline grew quiet. She no longer felt like retreating into an inner sanctum, a shock zone. She no longer heard voices that echoed or felt things secondhand. She emerged from her inner self now. Afraid, terribly afraid, but no longer hiding. It was a much better feeling to face a real fear than to hide from an imagined one. Even though the real danger became more threatening with each passing moment.

She looked up at Lydia. "There's something bothering me that I want to share with you." She paused to collect her thoughts. "Among the other things, it looks like Daddy has involved himself with a group called the Society of Apostates."

"No way." Lydia shook her head vigorously. "Apostasy? Are you serious now? Your father might be caught in heresy, or even reprobate. Those sins can be forgiven. But to be an apostate is to be no child of God at all. Do you understand? That would mean he is under judgment with no hope."

"Oh, Lydia, I don't understand these things. I'm so afraid."

"Don't be," the intercessor replied with a stiff lip. "It just ain't so."

In her heart Pauline couldn't imagine her father as unforgivable. But he had surrounded himself with unforgivable people, for sure. "Neva claims to be one of the Society of Apostates," she said, "and Daddy has been close to her. Also, he has placed the foreign hospitals under the Secret Society through a company called Dunamis. A foundation."

"Did he do this knowingly?"

"I don't know. I have learned that this Society operated medical experiments under Hitler during World War II."

"Your dad is not involved with that," she replied sternly.

"I don't want to believe it either, but I've been wrong about so many things. How do you know?"

"I know your father and so do you. Don't let the Devil steal what is right in your heart. That's his way. He deceives you into thinking that because you were wrong on one point, you're wrong on the rest of them too. But he's a liar. He's the deceiver. The confuser. That's all the power he has left in this world, honey—lies, deceit and confusion. Get thee behind me, Satan!" The little woman was trembling with righteous anger.

Her words glowed like a candle in the dark for Pauline. But the candle illuminated only Lydia. Only *her* determined faith. "They are doing medical experiments, Lydia. People have been killed. An entire ward of patients was experimented with cruelly. Then they were exterminated."

"Your father wouldn't have anything to do with that, and you know it!"

Pauline heard rebuke in her voice. "Maybe it is the Apostates. These Apostates are over there with him now, supposedly looking for a cure. Maybe they have taken him hostage. Maybe that's what has him bound. What am I to believe? I just don't know."

"Nonsense. Nonsense. You know your father in your heart, Pauline." She clapped a hand to her own chest. "Simon Grace is a healer, not a killer."

Pauline had seen too much to be as sure as Lydia. She wanted to believe, but she had to keep her mind open or she might become a pawn for her father's manipulations again. Lydia couldn't understand that. She had not been through the pile of evidence, the files, the letters that Pauline had seen. "I don't know anymore," she said. "I wish I did, but I don't."

"Yes, you do." Lydia paused and sighed, waiting with her eyes closed. *What does she need, Father?* She felt an answer come into her mind as naturally as the breath filling her lungs. "Pauline, there are two kinds of evil that bind men in this world. There are evil minds that hatch evil plans. That is a high kind of evil. A controlling evil. And then there's the evil that traps a man because of his feeling heart. Maybe he feels things too deeply. Your father is like that; most men are not. Do you understand me? Whatever your father's involved with, whatever it is that has him bound, it's the second kind of evil, honey. Go find him. Do what you have to do, and I'll be here doing my part. I love you, sweetie."

Lydia had put into words the things that remained true in Pauline's heart. Regardless of the revelations about her father, no matter how much Evan and Canaan caused her to fear, she would not allow that light to go out again. Not in her heart of hearts. For her father's sake, and for a desperate piece of her own soul.

"Thank you, Lydia," she said, standing and collecting the picture album with new resolve.

"Let's pray together before you go," the intercessor said, taking her by the hands. The old woman closed her eyes without hesitation and tilted her head back.

"Father, Great God above all other gods, we come before You by the blood of the Lamb. We speak to You in His holy name. Nothing is hidden from Your eyes. If we ascend to the stars You are there; if we go down into the depths of Hell, You are there. You know each sparrow that falls, You hear each secret heart, You count the hairs of our head. Nothing is too hard for You. I give You Pauline now. I ask that You keep her and those who travel with her. I ask that You bring Simon Grace home and that You loose him from the terrible bonds of this demon. This is Your daughter Lydia, Lord, asking these things in Jesus' name, Amen."

70

RICK GRESHAM'S RESIDENCE
9:39 P.M.

"Will you say prayers with me, Daddy?"

Evan glanced over his shoulder at Connie and Rick. They stood in the doorway of Jilly's darkened bedroom, watching him tuck her in before leaving for the airstrip and the waiting Falcon. Rick signaled thumbs up to the bedtime prayer idea. He and Connie promptly bowed their heads, waiting for Daddy Number One to begin.

Evan turned back around. The six-year-old sweetness of his life lay on her ruffled pink pillow, smiling up at him in the dark. She folded her hands over the paws of her Paddington Bear, never doubting for a second that her daddy would do exactly as she had asked.

"Of course, honey, I'll . . . be glad to," he said, clearing his throat. He folded his own hands. "OK, here we go. Ready? Dear God . . ."

"Dear God . . ." she repeated.

It had been a long time since Evan had prayed a bedtime prayer, or a prayer of any kind for that matter. He fished his memory for the next phrase.

She opened one eye, peeking up at him, waiting.

"Now I lay me down to sleep . . ." he said at last.

Her tiny voice repeated slowly and deliberately, savoring each precious word, "Now I lay me down to sleep . . ."

"I pray the Lord my soul to keep . . ."

71

EASTERN TURKEY
Nimrut Dag Cavern
MIDNIGHT

Simon Grace eased his body onto a padded table in a huge cavern. Several stands of electrical lights poured brilliance around the experimental area of the room. Grace wore a green smock and string-tie pants. Inserted into the main vein of his right arm was a catheter attached to an intravenous saline bag hung above the bed. Electrodes attached to his head trailed their leads to a brain wave monitor. Other electrodes sprouted from the button vents on his chest, snaking off to an EKG. A respirator and defibrillator stood ready.

The table lay in the center of a huge underground room. Across the floor, the trees of a petrified forest lay embedded at regular intervals. The doctors of Dunamis stood around in sterile surgical garb—Sutphen, Osis, Lester, Kassabian and Santesteban. The German philanthropist Maximilian Commagene bent near his head.

"Start the drip," Grace ordered.

"Remember," Max said cheerily, "you'll be back in twenty minutes, so don't try to save the world."

Grace hesitated. "Are you nervous or something?"

Max nudged his shoulder playfully. "Yeah. You'd think it was *me.*"

"You told me these people were the best. Now, why should you be nervous?"

In a wider circle of light seven more tables and monitors could be seen. Other patients occupied them, already comatose, their monitors humming in the background. The icon of the golden-haloed *Seven Sleepers of Antioch* glowed against the earthen wall beyond the beds illuminated by a row of votive candles. The Seven Apostate Saints watched the proceedings through petrified eyes— fashioned of the crytallized bark of the Tree of Knowledge.

Kassabian stood before an easel which held a computer-generated chart. It revealed a parched plain stretching to a rim of dark mountains in the distance. It was not an artistic rendering, but representational, a computerized conception. In the foreground stood two trees, one alive, one dead. Kassabian continued, "It is our hope that the terminal cancer patients around you here will create an atmosphere to carry you into the same transcendental landscape with them. This is a composite of visions from all the experiments we've run at this site. We have no assurance that you will end up with them, but trying it first with the atmosphere is safer than using the malignancy you've requested."

Grace shook his head negatively and muttered. "Cancer's the only way to go. This trial run is a waste of time."

"We've lost one doctor already," Sutphen cautioned.

"Because he was one of yours," Grace asserted. "You get help from the wrong gods." He laughed at his own outrageousness. "Of course, I don't know if my God will deliver me."

Vardan sighed disagreeably, then used a pointer to indicate features on the easel as he spoke. "If you encounter any of these—the wasteland surrounded by the distant mountains or cliffs, or the two trees—then we'll know you have entered the same environment described by the other patients. We will conduct experiments the next time you go over."

"You'll have to use the tumor sample," Grace insisted with disdain.

Dr. Lester, the cancer specialist, stepped forward. "We do have your wife's frozen culture ready for you, Dr. Grace. We are prepared."

"Thank you."

Lester nodded assuredly. "We've had it shipped from the Matamoros lab."

"Then I guess I owe you this trial run in good faith. Sorry to be so crotchety. It's just that I'm doing this fool thing for *her* as much as for anything else. Do you understand?"

Dr. Sutphen signaled Dr. Osis to release the drip. "Any creatures you encounter will be considered a bonus," he said. "We'll go to amytal interview to get a complete description when you return. Then we'll plan some kind of strategy from that information."

"Wait a second," Grace responded, holding his hand up. "There's only one strategy, Mr. Sutphen. Get this straight, all of you. You boys can chant or mumble or cut yourselves up on an altar to Baal when it's your turn, but there's only one plan for me. Is that clear?"

"They understand," Max assured him quickly.

Grace seemed unsatisfied. "I won't go after this bugger until I know that my letter has arrived in the homes of my partners. When they have started praying for me I'll know it. I'll feel their prayers around me here. Then you can infect me with Ruth's culture like I told you. Not before." He settled back again. "This time, let's just say I'm going over to spy out the land. To see where the giants live."

"No problem." Max shook his head. "Don't misunderstand, doc. We're in total agreement. The doctor just misspoke himself, that's all. You're the man of faith."

Grace let out a weary laugh. "If I had the faith of a sand flea I wouldn't be here. I've pursued the healing power of the Lord all my life, son. I've made mistakes. Seen a few people healed too, and I'm talking miracles here. Things that few scientists have ever seen. All that's good, but—" He paused and swallowed with difficulty, "—but when it came to my Ruth, my faith failed. Now I'd like to *know* why. Wouldn't you want to know? If you were me? Wouldn't you want to know the big answer to that one?"

Max nodded. He'd heard this talk before.

"In the meantime, all I ask is to get my hands on the devil who took her. Is that so wrong? I got theologians out the wah-zoo telling me I'm nuts, I'm over the line. But what do they know? Hey, Jacob wrestled an angel to get something from God. And he got it too." He shifted his arms, looking at the electrodes streaming from his body. "Of course he walked with a limp for the rest of his life, but shoot, I don't have much life left. Anyway, this demon or fallen angel or Nephil—Rimmon-Hadad or whatever it is that's got cancer's name on it—I want to get ahold of him just once. I'd like to tread on that serpent for a while, that scorpion, put my foot on his neck if the Lord will let me." For a moment his aging eyes blazed with a faraway light, then focused once again on Max. "And if he's too big for me—well, fine! I want to spit in his eye. Let's go."

The doctors glanced at one another uneasily.

Max smiled smoothly. "You sound ready for this, my friend."

"You aren't going to find anyone more ready. Let's go."

Dr. Osis, the anesthesiologist, reached up to the saline bag hanging above Grace's bed and released the tested mixture that would send him to the nether world.

"Win or lose," he said, "don't build me a statue, Max. Promise?" He chuckled. "Don't put me up there with Fortune of Commagene and the rest."

"Promise," Max replied with a reassuring smile, crossing his heart.

"The Lord is . . . the only one worthy . . ." The preacher felt the first relaxing flush of Hypnos-3 enter his veins and his head fell to one side, eyes rolling back. Dr. Lester quickly reached forward to check his breathing with the back of his hand. "Stand by with respirator."

". . . old Jacob . . ." Grace whispered, ". . . wrestled him an angel . . ."

And in the next instant he was moving through a timeless tunnel at the speed of thought.

IX

LORDS OF DISEASE

The Nephilim were on the earth in those days . . .
(GENESIS 6:4, NASB)

72

EASTBOUND, SARGASSO SEA
41,000 Feet; 470 Knots
9:32 A.M.

Colonel Canaan sat opposite Rick in the cockpit, relaying orders in Hebrew to his operatives in Israel. In the meantime Evan, Pauline and Danna huddled over the table in the rear cabin, piecing together more information from an assortment of books found in Simon Grace's library.

Once again Pauline could not concentrate. She had second thoughts about the raid, worrying aloud about the danger Colonel Canaan and his commandos might bring to her father. Since the Dunamis people seemed highly educated, she reasoned, they might respond to a civilized appeal to release Dr. Grace without military arm twisting. Evan reminded her of the murderous explosion aboard Alan's yacht, and of the mass killings of the Sudanese cancer patients. These were examples, he said, of just how civilized the educated folk at Dunamis could be.

She could only agree. But her worried thoughts—like an ulcer-producing stomach acid, once flowing, not so easily shut off—turned to Canaan's motives. It seemed he only wanted to capture "The Songs of Jubal" and forget the well-being of Dr. Grace, she said.

Her brother disagreed. He related his impression that Canaan had actually risked the mission for her benefit. He told of how he had witnessed the tug-of-war between the colonel and his superior officers via telephone. How they had wanted hard evidence that the original "Songs of Jubal" were actually at Nimrut Dag before committing to the mission. Canaan could only offer the circumstantial evidence of Grace's disappearance, the stolen icon, the fax from Turkey, and Neva's amytal testimony. Finally, the High Command had agreed to risk the raid based on the colonel's personal assurances that the tablets would be found. From Evan's point of view, "He stuck his neck out to help you find Dad."

Pauline flushed unexpectedly. She had not even considered that the colonel could be more than professionally interested in her.

Besides, he had impressed her as the kind who would never let his personal feelings cloud his military judgment. This gave her something new to worry about. Suddenly she felt responsible for the lives of the commandos who would fly over hostile territory simply because of the colonel's care for her. In her mind she recalled pictures of the downed helicopters of President Carter's aborted mission to Iran. *Things can go wrong. Why hasn't Canaan been up-front with me about his feelings? If he really has them. Why does Evan have to be the one to tell me?*

"Excuse me," she said, leaving Evan and Danna and making her way to the forward passageway. Reaching the cockpit she pulled down the jumpseat and sat between Rick and Canaan as they guided "Spirit I" though an enchanted cloud canyon forty-one thousand feet above the fabled waters of the Bermuda Triangle.

"Hey there, babe," Rick said, smiling back at her through his ever-present sunglasses.

"Hi."

Canaan looked up from studying an air chart in his lap. "Hello," he grunted. His eyes softened as he watched her, his mind ready to shed some of its load of flight plans and mission details in favor of sweeter, softer things.

Her attitude remained all business. "Colonel, what happens to you if you don't find the cuneiform tablets?"

He paused thoughtfully before answering. "I suppose we will gain useful information in that case."

"But what about *you*? What if you send all those men in there and don't find the tablets? What happens to you?"

"That's not important."

"But it is."

He glanced at her, then quickly turned to look out the window at the passing clouds.

She detected hidden feelings in this uneasiness. "Turn them back, colonel. Call off the mission. We'll go in alone and bring Daddy out."

He turned quickly. "Your father is not my objective, Pauline. Getting him out will be your part."

"But we don't know that the tablets are really there. We can't even be sure Daddy is there. You're risking lives and maybe an international incident."

"I am doing my job," he said resolutely. He could see that she was not satisfied with this. He waited thoughtfully before speaking again. "Israel is in the business of protecting herself these days," he began, then cleared his throat determinedly. "You see, you and I were not around then, but they tell us the whole world heard Hitler's threats against the Jews in the 30s. But no one was willing to risk an international incident." He smiled grimly at her.

"So you are willing."

"Never again," he replied, voicing the aggressive self-defense posture of the Jews since World War II. "I suppose freedom of speech gave Hitler the right to make his threats against us, but we have not forgotten that it was the British prime minister Chamberlain who went over and negotiated a treaty with him, knowing the position he had taken against us. The world did not really believe until they saw pictures from Auschwitz, Bergen-Belsen, Dachau—and of course, by then, for six million Jews it was too late." He put on a softer air of cynicism. "So we are taking our own risks these days, thank you."

The weight of this truth was self evident. His reasons for going after "The Songs of Jubal" were intensely Jewish. She nodded slowly and turned forward, watching as Rick bent their flight path between two cotton-topped thunderheads.

"Zero niner seven," he said, dialing in a new heading.

Canaan continued, "So we have different reasons for what we are doing, yet we are on the same journey."

She felt a twinge of regret. The handsome soldier may not have been personally involved with her after all, but at least he sounded like the Colonel Canaan she had imagined—one of Yahweh's superior warriors. "We've both got our hands full," she acknowledged. With that, she folded the jumpseat to return to the main cabin.

"Wait a sec," Rick said, reaching beneath his seat. He pulled out a padded brown envelope. "I almost forgot. When I reached the hangar this morning a car followed me to the gate. A friend of Evan's—said her name was Jennifer—" He shrugged. "She laid this on me. Said it was extremely important."

"Jennifer? Who is that?" Pauline took the package, and a bolt of fear hit her. A package bomb! In her mind's eye she saw "Spirit I" disintegrating in midair. But with relief she noticed that the envelope had already been opened. "What is it, Rick?"

"Oh yeah," he said. "Looks like a letter."

The "Tree of Life" letter! Pauline thought, tearing open the envelope.

"I'm sorry," Rick apologized. "I was in such a scramble this morning I just forgot to give it to you before takeoff."

She noticed the Dallas WordSmith logo on the enclosed work order. "Evan! Come look at this!"

Emptying the contents into her hand, she quickly scanned it. Four faxed pages, hand-written, signed by Dr. Simon Grace! She figured the pages had been sent from Antioch, as the others had been. A photocopied picture of her father fell into her palm. "Daddy," she pled under her breath, feeling suddenly closer to him. She examined it closely. It showed him sitting in front of a huge carved stone face on Nimrut Dag, his Bible held open in front of him. Across the bottom of the picture he had written a caption: "Lord of Cancer. Let the sons of God spoil his land and live. Numbers 33:51-53."

"Colonel, look," she said leaning into the cockpit. She held the picture in front of Canaan. "I told you he didn't have the 'Jubal book' when he disappeared. He has his Bible. See it there?"

Canaan examined the picture closely. "True. If this picture is a recent one."

"It just arrived. You heard Rick."

"He has been visiting Nimrut Dag for years. This could have been taken on one of his other trips."

She looked for a clue that would tell her this wasn't so.

"We have to at least consider that," Colonel Canaan continued. "Or who knows, he might have posed in front of a poster of the mountain in a Dunamis studio. Didn't Robert Schuller do that once with the Wall of China?"

He sounds like Evan now, she thought, turning to go. As she entered the narrow hallway she ran smack into her brother.

"What's up?" he asked.

"It's Daddy's letter, and a picture. Rick got it early this morning."

He took the package eagerly and examined it. "'Lord of Cancer'?" he read. "No question we're on the right track. Where did this come from?" he asked, turning back to the main cabin.

"Someone named Jennifer delivered it this morning."

Surprised, he warmed to the thought that Jennifer had gone back to WordSmith on his behalf. Especially after the insults she'd dished out at his apartment. He couldn't know for sure if it had been professional pride or personal shame that had caused her to go this extra mile. Whatever it had been, once again his "earthy" writing assistant had produced a blessing in spite of herself.

As he approached his seat, Danna sat watching from the cabin table, where she had continued to examine her medical printout. "So who is this Jennifer?" she asked, her tongue posed mischievously against her upper lip.

"Nobody," he returned quickly. "I mean she's somebody, of course. Nobody you would know. What I mean is—she is—she *was* my research assistant at *Texas People*."

"Oooh, I see," Danna cooed smoothly. "It's just that I've never heard of her."

"Yes," he returned sarcastically, "there are so many." He laid the mail pieces on the table, ignoring the face Danna made in reply.

For a moment the three of them silently studied the photocopied picture of Dr. Grace in front of the idol.

"'Lord of Cancer'?" Danna asked, reading the note.

"Yeah, me too," Evan answered.

"I wonder which one of them it is?" Pauline asked.

Danna grabbed Dr. Grace's scrapbook and began flipping through the pages, looking for a match-up. In the meantime Evan scanned the letter. He looked up suddenly.

"Pauline, it's his handwriting. Did you see?"

She had already noticed that. She looked again. Closely this time. Even with the fax and copier distortions, the hand revealed itself to be unmistakably her father's. That meant the "Tree of Life" letter and the charm cross were also his inventions. He was not being controlled by hostile kidnappers. These facts had become inescapable.

He's so faulty, she thought, *so manipulative.*

"Here it is!" Danna said excitedly. She plopped the scrapbook on the tabletop next to the picture of Dr. Grace. Reading the German captions beneath the matching picture, she said, "Zeus-Oromasdes. Two names for one god."

"Those are the names given by different mystery religions," Evan explained. "Same demigod. Apparently Dad believes Zeus is the god of cancer."

Danna picked up a copy of the WordSmith work order, scanning it. "They plan to have this letter in the mail in a week."

"That soon? That makes it a mid-month letter," Evan said. "This has got to be a super-strong concept because payday is the first of the month for most people. Dad's sailing against the wind asking for donations at that time of month." He read aloud:

> "'My Dear Partner,
>   "'Greetings in the name of our Lord and Savior Jesus Christ.'

"A fine apostolic opening," he commented sarcastically.

> "'By now you have no doubt heard the reports of my disappearance in the news media. But I told my partners in my last letter where I was going—'"

Evan looked at Pauline. "What did I say? He's been pulling our strings all along, sis."

"No, *my* strings," she replied resignedly, realizing for the first time that her father had planned to use the publicity of his own disappearance after all. He had use her to cover it up until this letter could be mailed. "Keep this out of the press," he had written in the note he handed her in Jerusalem. "It wasn't 'we' who got used," she said to Evan quietly. "*I* was the one whose strings got pulled. I even went the extra mile for him, lecturing the press about his letter."

He appreciated the fact that she had made this difficult admission. He wanted to soften the blow just a bit. "Yeah, but I can't blame you for doing that. Alan is a very persuasive guy. I have to tell you, I'm still not sure he isn't in this with Dad." He glanced at Danna for what she might know about her father.

She shrugged. "He doesn't confide in me."

"He's probably not involved. How else do you explain Dorothy and Bud?" He read on:

> "'I have gone aside to a secret place in the desert to pray. What I have not told you, my dear partner, is why I have gone.
>   "'Neither have I told you that I need your prayers and support today more than ever before. My life is literally in the balance.'"

Evan drew a deep breath. He looked at Danna. "Your father wrote the textbook on this kind of letter. I know the formula. This statement is called an 'ask.' You have to get an 'ask' built into a good fund-raising letter up-front. Then you have to repeat it in several places in order to get the kind of money you're after at the end." He shook the four pages between his fingers. "But this is the ultimate ask: 'My life is literally in the balance'? Send money or I die?" He turned to Pauline. "If you were one of his ministry partners, how would you feel reading this? 'Poor Dr. Grace. He needs my Social Security check?' Right?"

"Our partners are middle- and upper-income," Pauline quickly replied. She had done some looking at statistics recently.

"Not on this list. Don't forget, they've included past donors and have purchased other lists for this letter. Twelve million new names." He rattled the pages again. "And notice, he doesn't simply say, 'I need your prayers'; that would kill the possibilities in the up-front 'ask,' see? In ministry mail it's always, 'I need your prayer and support.' One is tied to the other. The experts know it's easier to send money than to pray. That is what most people will do—send money instead of pray. The money is a kind of 'guilt money.' A substitute for not taking the time and effort to pray. Guilt is an effective motivator for giving, but it's downright un-Christian if you ask me." He grinned wanly. "That's why nobody asked me. Anyway, it is assumed that the ones who go to the trouble to pray for Dr. Grace will also go to the trouble to send money. So you always say, 'I need your prayer *and support.*' You get both groups that way. As brother Alan Lavalle always says, 'Don't leave holes in your net.'"

He dodged a quick look at Danna. She appeared unfazed.

"'Most of you know that my beloved wife Ruth died of cancer years ago.'

Evan felt sadness and shame reading this line. "Where's his decency? He'll use anyone—even his dead wife."
Pauline's insides hurt. How could she deny it?

"'This was a great loss to me. In my years of laying hands on the sick in accordance with the Great Commission of Jesus in Mark 19:18, I have known—'

"By the way," he interjected, "this is called a credibility statement. Quoting Scripture reminds the partners that their giving is of Biblical proportions.'"

Pauline had grown tired of his interjections. "We are impressed with your knowledge of fund-raising, Evan, but would you please just read the letter?"

"I am sorry. It's just something I've had to deal with over these years. I guess I want you to deal with it too."

"I will when I'm feeling better," she promised hastily.

He continued to read:

"'—I have known that it is God's will to heal. So I have asked myself, why did my dear Ruth have to die after so many prayers were prayed for her? Others were healed.'"

"Now that is real," Pauline pointed out. "These are the things he really feels and believes. He's not just *using* Mother's death. This is a personal quest for him. It was on his mind in Jerusalem."

Evan had learned to constantly be alert to how his sister's emotions would unbalance her better judgment. "Perhaps so," he replied. "It's just not *all* that he feels and believes. Remember that. He knows what he's doing in this letter and he's angling for the biggest offering of his life.'

"'In past centuries great pestilences wiped out precious populations on the earth. Plague struck Athens in 430 B.C. In pre-Christian Rome 5,000 died every day in the epidemic of 262 A.D. 150,000 died in Europe around the time of the Crusades. But the worst was India where more than 10 million succumbed to black death at the close of the past century.

"'From the beginning, the Creator has been at war with the Destroyer. In life, in love, and in medicine. Christian believers and unbelievers alike died horrible deaths in the plagues of history. Many of their dying prayers seemed to go unanswered.'"

Evan paused, turning the page:

"'Many who lost loved ones, as I lost my wife, have asked, "Where is God?" And many cursed God in their misery and pain. Others kept faith through the time of darkness. They continued to pray to God for deliverance and for mercy. Such a one are you, my dear partner.'

"Personalize, personalize. These letters are always personal to the max . . .

"'Paul the Apostle speaks of Christ when he writes in I Corinthians 15:25 & 26, "For He must reign until He has put all His enemies under His feet. The last enemy that will be abolished is death." So you see, this battle will not be over until Death itself is abolished.

"'But if death has not been defeated, we *have* seen many diseases controlled, have we not? Measles, smallpox, tuberculosis, black plague and many others. But there is still much more to do until every power is placed under the feet of our Lord.

"'I declare to you that in God's mercy, He has raised up science and medicine to put a stop to some of these medical evils. Medicine does not truly cure disease, but places it under arrest by a natural power. In some cases surgery is an answer, in others radiation and new drugs. For all of this we thank God. He is merciful to send us this temporary help. He is merciful while we wait for the ultimate defeat of death itself.

"'But as sons and daughters of the Most High, I say to you there is more we can do! We can carry this battle beyond the natural realm of medicine into the invisible realm of the spirit. For as we read in Ephesians 6:12, ". . . we wrestle not against flesh and blood, but against principalities, against powers, against the rulers of the darkness of this world, against spiritual wickedness in high places."

"'My dear partners and friends, as I write to you today I am sitting in the ancient High Place of Satan. I am in a foreign land. I need you to pledge your prayers and support for me today as never before. I have come seeking a cure for cancer. I am praying that God will allow me to take this high ground for Him. To take this land from the hand of His enemy in a great spiritual battle. Just as the Children of Israel took their Promised Land and drove out the giants and the enemies who lived there.

"'Hear the command of the Lord to the Israelites in Numbers 33:51, "When you cross over the Jordan into the land of Canaan, then you shall drive out all the inhabitants of the land from before you, and destroy all their figured stones, and destroy all their molten images and demolish all their High Places; and you shall take possession of the land and live in it, for I have given the land to you to possess it."

"'My partners, what was true in the natural realm for Israel is now true in the spiritual realm for those of us who are in Christ Jesus. Do you want to enter the spiritual promised land of health? Do you want to see cancer driven from the planet, as I do? Join me today.

"'Let me explain. The origin of all disease was the Garden of Eden. As I write, I am sitting on a High Place of evil in that lost Paradise. Around me are the stone gods that ruled the early civilizations. I believe I am among the petrified trees that once shaded the Garden of God—'

"Notice," Evan commented, "he said here, 'I believe I am among the trees of the Garden.' He knows there will be a storm of controversy over the location of the Garden of Eden, even if he has found his petrified forest. Most Jewish and Christian scholars will laugh. Eden was a metaphor at best."

"How can you know that for sure?" Pauline asked, looking toward Danna for support. "Do you believe the Garden was real?"

Danna looked up at the ceiling and back, searching for a diplomatic answer. "To tell you the truth, I never thought it mattered before. But this is the first time I have ever found myself actually, you know, headed for Eden. If there is one. Frankly, I hope there is. It sounds wonderfully romantic."

"*Romantic* is exactly the right word," Evan quipped.

Pauline ignored him as he began to read again:

"'—I'm near the very spot where Adam and Eve ate of the Tree of Knowledge and loosed death and disease upon the prehistoric world. As you know, God drove them from Eden for this. He placed a sword of fire to watch the Tree of Life and so keep men from gaining eternal life in their sinful state. But the Tree of Life has been given back to us in the form of the cross of Jesus Christ! That is why I have come boldly back to that Garden. I have come in the name of the Cross of Christ Jesus.

"'Paul tells us, "The first Adam became a living soul. The last Adam became a life-giving Spirit." My partners and friends, I am convinced that the cure for cancer is in the spiritual realm of the second Adam, not in the natural realm of the first Adam which includes medicine. I have come here because the real battle will be fought in the heavenlies. I will need your prayers.

"'I cannot reveal to you the name of this secret place because it is in a land where the authorities are not in favor of our cause. At the dawn of the twentieth century more than a million Christians were slaughtered here for their faith, in the shadows of the mountain on which I sit. I am in enemy territory. I sit among the stone idols of Baal and his cohorts, praying for the cure to cancer. Won't you help me? Satan has come against me here. Do not ask me to stand alone, my friends and partners. If I am not successful in the next two weeks, surely my secret mission will be discovered and I will be sent home. Or perhaps worse. Above all, pray for me.'"

Evan could read no further. He felt an involuntary thrill run the length of his body. He hated to be moved by such primitive eloquence. He had learned to resist it for most of his adult life, but his father had drawn upon deep symbolism in this letter. Symbols as deep as the Scriptures themselves. Deeper than history. "Pauline," he said, "there is a crazy kind of logic behind this, but it's just—"

"Yes?" She felt it too—not craziness, but conviction. Truth.

Her father's cause as expressed in the letter had become her cause as Evan had read it. "Yes?" she asked again. He didn't seem able to reply. She saw with more clarity now the vision that drove her father. Truly if he chose wrongly in this quest, it had been an error of the heart. *The heart!* Simon Grace was a passionate man, bold, brash, dancing, like David. A man after God's heart!

Evan shook his head to clear it, and attempted to read again without falling under the spell of the words.

"'Children of God, this is a spiritual battle. The broken idols around me here—'"

Pauline reached out and took hold of the pages of the letter. "I'll read it," she said firmly.

He let go of the letter, reminding himself that 86 percent of his father's donations came from women. It figured that Pauline would be swayed.

She read in a womanly, open and sympathetic voice:

"'Children of God, this is a spiritual battle. The broken idols around me here are the physical reality. They have fallen into ruin and become desolate, just as the prophets of Israel predicted. But the demon spirits that inspired them are still at large, working havoc in the earth. I have traced the idol Baal from the Old Testament Scriptures to this place. He is known by many other names—Zeus, Jupiter—but in the modern world I believe his name is Cancer. I may be wrong. But if I am, God save me. I am here praying that we can prevail against this evil spirit. Will you at least stand with me?

"'Will you pray that God will allow me to face the demon god of Cancer and in the name of Jesus command it to be bound and cast into the eternal pit! This cannot be done by medical science. It is not a natural matter like these idols of stone. It is a spiritual matter like the spirits they represent.

"'Paul explains in I Corinthians 15: "If there is a natural body, there is also a spiritual body." Pray that I can invade the enemy's spiritual High Place in my spiritual body and bring him into captivity.

"'As written in II Corinthians 10, "For though we walk in the flesh, we do not war according to the flesh, for the weapons of our warfare are not of the flesh, but divinely powerful for the destruction of fortresses. We are destroying speculations and every lofty thing raised up against the knowledge of God, and we are taking every thought captive to the obedience of Christ, and we are ready to punish all disobedience, whenever your obedience is complete—"'"

"Now there's a key," Evan interrupted. "Is his obedience complete? I think not. You have to remember, this is the same man who used the 'dirt files' to get what he wanted in the ministry. His 'obedience' is far from complete, Pauline, so how can he expect success?"

Pauline fought to filter the truth of Evan's words without receiving the poison in them. She swallowed and continued:

"'Cancer is a rebellious spirit, disobedient to God. As I said, medicine is a weapon of the flesh. A natural weapon. By God's mercy it can be used to arrest this enemy, but only a son of God can bind the strongman. I want to see this enemy judged, don't you? Did not Christ, who healed all the sick who came to Him, say in John chapter 14, ". . . he who believes in Me, the works that I do shall he do also; and greater works than these shall he do because I go to My Father"? This may be the day we will see one of those "greater works." Not just a healing of one person with cancer—but a spiritual cure! Will you pray with me? Will you support me in this great battle?'"

Evan sarcastically falsettoed the four-note signature from "The Twilight Zone": "Do-do-do-do, do-do-do-do."

Pauline remained steadfast. "He means every word, Evan."

"He means *money*. Go on, read some more."

She sighed disagreeably, remembering Lydia's words, "Simon Grace is a healer." She agreed. Much more than money moved her father. Why did Evan remain so obstinate?

"'A medical staff is with me here. They are conducting experiments, helping me enter the enemy's High Place. I will share more with you about that later.'"

"Well, he's talking about Dunamis," Evan pointed out. "The Society of Apostates. Is he telling the truth here?"

"All that he knows," Pauline defended. "To him Dunamis is simply a medical foundation.

"'I need special prayer-helpers in this fight. Those who will pray every day for the next two weeks, and those who will also send a gift of fifty dollars—'"

Money. She paused, realizing that with every line of this letter now, her father was proving Evan to be right. Her brother mercifully remained quiet. She steeled herself to read more.

"'—to help me pay the past due bills of this ministry. To symbolize our covenant together against cancer, I want to send you a cross made from the petrified wood of one of the ancient trees of the Garden of Eden, where I am praying today. It will remind you of our prayer-covenant together, as we seek to bind the strongman of Cancer.'

"'Just think of holding a piece of Eden in your hand in the form of the cross, the spiritual Tree of Life. Think of having it with you as a necklace or charm on a bracelet—'"

At this, Evan pulled the sample charm cross out of his shirt, where he had placed it on a necklace. "Here it is folks, millions of these. Only in America."

Pauline continued:

"'—When someone asks you about it, you can say "I covenanted for the cancer cure with Dr. Simon Grace, when he fasted and prayed on the mountain. This cross is made from one of the original trees of Eden." Next, I am asking for a special army of prayer-helpers who will give a thousand dollars each to help me during this fight. As you know Satan has attacked our finances lately—'

"Whoa! Now that's a lie," Evan declared angrily. "This is a financial crisis he engineered himself. *He* sent the bogus letter out this month. Right? At least Alan says so, for whatever that's worth. If he and Alan are in this together, then he's lying even more than we think. He crippled his own ministry. At the same time he made a forty million dollar icon deal on the side. Then he says to his dear partners, 'the Devil has attacked my finances'? Yeah right—if he's the Devil."

Again Pauline couldn't fight. She hoped against hope that somehow her father hadn't seen all the ramifications of his strategy. His obsession had blinded him. After all, he had gone to a remote location, remaining out of touch with his day-to-day operations. She recalled how he had ignored Stiles and his business decisions the day he had disappeared in Jerusalem. He had seemed so preoccupied. Any man might make the same error under these complications. She read more:

"'—and we are sixty to ninety days behind on some of our obligations. These thousand-dollar givers will help me be strong in this fight. They will keep me from being distracted by the pressing financial burdens of the daily ministry so that I can devote myself totally to fasting and prayer. To these special helpers, I will not only send the cross made from the trees of the Garden, but I will also prepare a confidential video message from the actual High Place where I am now in constant prayer. In this tape I will show you the various idols in this secret hideaway. Especially the one I believe to be the demon of Cancer. I will explain how he got his name and why I believe he is our enemy in this fight. The material on this tape will be sensitive and confidential. I can only afford to make it available to my thousand-dollar partners. So won't you pray about it today and ask God what you should do?'"

"Is the videotape here?" Danna asked.

"No, it's part of the fulfillment package," Evan replied. "That kind of thing is usually made as late in the game as possible."

Pauline continued:

"'Whatever you feel God telling you to give, let's join our prayers together. Together we will ask God for this mountain. Pray with me now.

> "'Your Servant,
> Dr. Simon Grace.

"'P.S.—'"

"There is always a postscript in a fund-raising letter," Evan explained. "It always contains the 'ask' in capsule form because marketing studies have shown that some people will only read the P.S. in the letter, and they need to know what he wants without having to read the whole letter. And most people read the P.S. first, so it's very important."

Aren't we impressed? Pauline thought sourly as she glanced down and saw that her brother was right, yet again—

"'P.S. Please pray about the thousand-dollar gift to defeat the god of Cancer. I have never needed it more than today. Above all, send the amount God speaks to your heart. Remember the widow's mite.'"

Pauline rubbed her eyes, feeling temporarily exhausted.

"Alan's right," Evan said. "Dad should buy another twelve million names. It's insane, but I can tell you, when you put the unprecedented publicity about his disappearance together with this letter, and the cross of petrified wood from the Garden of Eden, the income is likely to go higher than anything in history."

Pauline heard nothing. She had gone far away in her mind, growing even more sure that Lydia had seen her father bound in the very spiritual realm described in this letter. A holy spiritual force had caused Lydia to enter her prophetic dream. That same spiritual force now guided their mission to find her dad, making a path for them through a myriad of difficulties. A timeless war raged here. Pauline's new confidence grew from knowing that she had chosen the right side in the war, the opposite of Evan's natural point of view. "Danna, Evan," she said, "the one thing missing in the letter is a description of how he is getting into the supernatural. He played down the medical side when actually medicine is the only way he can cross over."

Evan acknowledged the point with a solemn nod.

Danna did too.

Evan quickly added, "Once again, I think he was dishonest."

"Dishonest? You would think that!" Pauline uncoiled, strongly incensed. "What did his letter say?" she challenged. "He said . . ." She shuffled the pages of the letter until she found the quote. "'A medical staff is with me here. They are conducting experiments and helping me enter the enemy's High Place. I will share more with you about that later.' There's nothing dishonest about that. Why should he tell everything?"

"Especially if he has something to hide."

"That's unfair, Evan. Hold some kind of court on your big, fat mouth before you let fly with every paranoia that just pops into your little mind, will you!"

"OK," he said, holding his hands up resignedly. He thought she had overreacted on a valid point. "I overstated myself. I'm sorry. I guess I'm trying to make you see things my way, and I can see that you are not going to do it. So why whip a dead horse?" A smile played at the corners of his mouth. "I don't mean to imply that *you*'re a dead horse." In spite of their differences, he genuinely liked the way she had stood up to him just now. Especially since she had been right about a fine point of difference. He had never seen that in her before, a willingness to fight for a fine point. Still, she worried him. He definitely saw her falling back under "Daddy's" spell.

Pauline had mentally moved on. She felt a strong urge come over her. "There's something I want to tell you guys," she said in an uncharacteristically confessional tone.

Evan and Danna checked each other's eyes as they moved to the sofas in the back of the cabin. Pauline seemed her old assertive self again. The three of them took opposite corners in the lounge area.

"Please hear me out before you jump in with comments, OK?" She wanted them both to take her seriously and thought now, after reading the letter, perhaps they would. "I got a call in Jerusalem just before Daddy disappeared," she began. "It was Barry Malone telling me that Lydia had died three times from a heart attack." She glanced at Danna. "You know who I mean? Lydia, the intercessor?"

Danna shrugged. "I've heard of her."

"Well, she lives in the Steeple and has prayed for Daddy for many years. She had been fasting and praying for ten days when all of a sudden she had a cardiac arrest. At least that's what Neva said. Lydia called it the effects of 'travailing prayer.'"

"Travailing prayer?" Danna asked.

"It's a kind of prayer where something is brought forth. Like a birth," Pauline explained. "She was dreaming about a birth when this thing happened, as a matter of fact. But I'll get to that in just a minute. Anyway, in that first call I got in Jerusalem Barry was at her bedside, and he told me she was trying to get a message to Daddy. She couldn't talk, so she relayed a Scripture reference, Luke 22:31, 32. I looked it up later. It said, 'Simon, Simon, behold Satan has demanded permission to sift you like wheat, but I have prayed for you, that your faith may not fail; and you, when once you have turned again—' I like this part, if it turns out to be about Daddy, because it is full of so much hope—it says, 'when once you have turned again, strengthen your brothers.' Well, within fifteen minutes of getting that message, Daddy disappeared. Do you think there might be a connection?"

Danna nodded sagely, as if she had previous knowledge of such things.

"Perhaps," Evan added. "I'd check it out at least."

"Well, I did check it out. But if there is a connection, the connection is spiritual, not natural. Lydia told me she had a dream, a supernatural dream in which she entered the body of a woman in another dimension. This woman died trying to give birth to a horrible giant. She thinks this giant was what they call a Nephilim."

"Nephil," Evan corrected "Nephilim is the plural form of Nephil. It's like cherubim is the plural of cherub. It's Hebrew."

"What, pray tell, is a Nephil?" Danna asked.

"May I?" Evan asked.

Pauline nodded, not knowing much about it herself.

"Genesis chapter 6 says giants roamed the earth before the Flood. It also says that these giants occurred when the 'sons of God' saw that the 'daughters of men' were beautiful—at least they had good taste, if bad morals. Anyway, they took wives. The implication here is that the 'sons of God' were angels. Perhaps the angels that guarded the Garden of Eden." He glanced between the two of them. "Where have we heard of Eden lately? Anyway, their offspring, the giants, became the gods of pagan mythologies. There is a Jewish tradition in the book of First Enoch that indicates the Nephilim died in the Flood and their spirits became the demon hordes. These views are disputed, of course, but I suppose it is OK to speculate—"

"But there is a Jewish tradition to that effect?" Pauline asked quickly. It would lend credibility to Lydia's dream.

"Oh yes. Christian too. Genesis called the race of giants 'Nephilim.' The book of First Enoch has a lot more to say about them, and about the angels who married women. In fact, I believe I saw a copy of the Pseudepigrapha in the books we brought from Dad's library. If he is 'going over,' as we say, then he has probably drawn his ideas about the netherworld from the book of First Enoch. That's why we found it with the books about Nimrut Dag. I never thought of that possibility until just now, but let's see—"

"The psuedepi—what?" Danna began to rummage through a box of books looking for it.

"Pseudepigrapha. I believe its official title is *The Old Testament Pseudepigrapha*." He spelled the word for her.

"Is it an apocryphal book?" Pauline asked dubiously. She put little confidence in anything quasi-biblical.

"Pseudepigraphical," Evan corrected with a smile. "Yes, that's about the same as apocryphal. It's not included in the New or Old Testament canon, if that's what you mean. It's part of the apocalyptic writings made in the period between the Old and New Testaments. Jesus said in Matthew that '. . . all the prophets and the law prophesied until John the Baptist.' So technically at least the Book of Enoch falls into that intertestamental category. The Old Testament Bible may have been closed, but divine communication didn't go out of business between the two Testaments. At least according to Jesus. Nevertheless, First Enoch was rejected from the Bible after about four centuries of Christianity."

"But this book can't be reliable then, if it's not in the Bible."

"Well, that depends."

"How can it depend? It's either Biblical or it's not."

"Well, it's both. It's not in the Bible, OK? Let's be clear about that. But it is quoted in the book of Jude. How can a canonized Scripture quote an unreliable source?"

Pauline's mind spun. To her the Bible had always been the absolute *Bible*. Flawless. Perfect. "Are you sure about this, Evan?"

"Please, I'm not trying to take away from the Bible," he continued. "I just understand how Dad might have found something on this subject in the Apocrypha. Especially First Enoch."

"Listen to this," Danna said, holding the fat volume of the Pseudepigrapha sideways. "These are marginal notes. 'First Enoch was accepted as Scripture in early Christian writings by Origen, Justin Martyr, Clement of Alexandria, Irenaeus and other Church Fathers.' Also . . ." She tilted the volume the other way. " . . Jude verses 14 and 15 quote from 'The Book of the Watchers.'"

"There you have it," Evan agreed, explaining, "'The Book of the Watchers' is a part of First Enoch. As I recall, it's the part about angels and women."

Pauline stood up in an instant and headed to the bulkhead seat. Reaching behind it she pulled out her Bible and returned quickly to her seat, flipping through, looking for the Jude reference. *It's near the end, near Revelation*, she reminded herself. *"First, Second and Third John, Jude and Revelation"*—the Sunday school rhyme of the Bible books sang in her head. Then she found it. Jude verse 14. She read aloud:

> "'And about these also Enoch, in the seventh generation from Adam, prophesied, saying, "Behold, the Lord came with many thousands of His holy ones, to execute judgment upon all, and to convict all the ungodly of all their ungodly deeds which they have done in an ungodly way, and of all the harsh things which ungodly sinners have spoken against Him."'"

"That's First Enoch, word for word," Evan replied. "So if you accept the Bible, you have to give First Enoch some kind of credit too, unless you throw out the book of Jude. You can't say it's *totally* uninspired. Especially 'The Book of the Watchers,' which is quoted there. It's the same part of First Enoch where you read about angels marrying women and having giant children."

"Right here," Danna said, looking up, her index finger pressed to a page of First Enoch. "It's in chapter 6:

> "'And it came to pass when the children of men had multiplied that in those days were born unto them beautiful and comely daughters.

And the angels, the children of the heaven, saw and lusted after them, and said to one another: "Come, let us choose us wives . . . and beget us children . . .""'"

"Good," Evan interjected. "Now, Pauline, find Genesis 6 verse 4. I think we are getting close to Dad's thinking on the subject."

She quickly flipped her Bible back to the beginning and read:

"'The Nephilim were on the earth in those days, and also afterward, when the sons of God came in to the daughters of men, and they bore children to them. Those were the mighty men who were of old, men of renown.'"

"See there?" Evan said. "You've got Genesis talking about the Nephilim, and you've got the book of First Enoch expanding that story, and you've got Jude in the New Testament quoting from First Enoch."

"Listen to this," Danna said eagerly. "Down further in chapter 7 it says:

"'. . . And they became pregnant, and they bare great giants . . . the giants turned against them and devoured mankind. And they began to sin against birds, and beasts, and reptiles, and fish, and to devour one another's flesh, and drink the blood—'"

She looked up, making a wretched face.

"That sounds like the Nephilim or the Nephil or whatever in Lydia's dream," Pauline added thoughtfully. "It was a horrid creature. So were the people who worshiped it." To herself, she thought, *So maybe Lydia's dream came right out of First Enoch. In the Spirit somehow she became linked to what Dad is doing out here on Nimrut Dag. She saw it in advance, and in the invisible realm. Like a prophecy.*

"OK," Evan interjected, sensing that the girls were running amok with his information, "remember, all we're trying to do here is understand what Dad is up to. I'm not saying that Lydia saw anything real, but these sorts of ideas have been in the 'collective unconsciousness' of our society. Dad has used this Enoch text to guide his research with Dunamis. I'm not sure that he necessarily believes it. He's just found it useful, like anything else. It's good for another multi-million dollar offering. Anyway, a case can be made that First Enoch is at least partially reliable, and if that is so, then the part about the angels marrying women could be considered reliable too. Dad wouldn't want to draw from a non-orthodox source, you understand. Although you'll run into theologians who scream heresy at the very mention of Enoch. It's a can of theological worms."

Pauline felt torn between two reactions. On the one hand she wanted to believe in the angels and women producing Nephilim as recorded in First Enoch. It verified Lydia's dream. It also gave clues as to what her father had in mind when he had become involved with Dunamis. On the other hand she felt fear that if the book of First Enoch contained any inspired passages, then the "rock" of Holy Scripture might not be as solid as she had always believed it to be. To her, the Bible had always been the Word, the entire Word, and the *only* Word of God. God had nothing more to say to the world until he showed up at the Second Coming. To think that God had in any sense inspired writings beyond the pages of The Book scared her. *Terror* more accurately described the feeling. *If the Bible is just another book, then nothing I believe is absolute,* she feared. But then, that was not the dilemma, was it? "Evan, I always thought the Bible was an open and shut case," she said.

He sensed her fear and sympathized on one level, despised it on another. "Well, maybe the Bible is an absolute record," he said. "I don't know." He said this, realizing how much she wanted absolutes in her life.

For himself, he believed God to be absolute. God had given a few Scriptural absolutes to men, but beyond that, had left an open field. He saw faith as a life of multiple choice in a broad relationship with God, full of adventure and discovery. Seldom predictable. The world held too many surprises for him to cling to extra absolutes. That is, any beyond those few that had been clearly given. He didn't want to miss any of God's good gifts in life, some of which might well lie beyond the boundaries of his own fear.

Intriguingly, in the course of this conversation Evan had begun to see a slight chance to win a place of fellowship for himself within Pauline's religious mind-set. Something he had lost in his fall with Danna so many years ago. In that regard, he wanted to push his sister beyond the safe limits she had set for herself. If she stepped outside of her own fears, even for a minute, she might come to see him as a believer, even though they believed many things differently. Still, in order to do that, he would have to find a bridge—some common ground between them.

"There will always be Christians who see the Scripture as

inerrant," he said. "You've got a lot of company in that. Then there have always been believers who see them as inspired, but not *equally* inspired in all passages. So how do you resolve that in your mind? Is one group in and the other group out of the Kingdom?"

"I don't know," she said honestly.

He definitely liked this answer, seldom hearing it from his absolute-minded sister.

She continued her personal debate aloud. "I don't see why I should have to close my eyes about First Enoch. Why should I? But I really feel like I'm betraying my faith to think that this book has some—*any* shred of truth in it."

"It does have some truth in it or it wouldn't be quoted in Jude. You can accept that absolutely if you want to. That doesn't take away from the Bible."

"Right. But what about the other parts of Enoch? You can't trust them. We can't really trust this stuff about the angels and the women and giants. It might be true, but it might not. I just hate that sort of thing!"

He smiled and agreed with a silent nod.

"I've always felt like the Bible was my rock," she lamented. "But I guess maybe Jesus didn't say that the Scripture was the rock, did He? What was the rock? You know, the rock upon which He would build His church and the gates of Hell would not prevail?"

Evan had been required to memorize the King James Version of this passage in a college course. He recited it by heart. "'But who say ye that I am? And Simon Peter answered and said, Thou art the Christ, the Son of the living God. And Jesus answered and said unto him, Blessed art thou, Simon Bar-Jonah: for flesh and blood hath not revealed it unto thee, but my Father who is in Heaven. And I also say unto thee, that thou art Peter, and upon this rock I will build my church; and the gates of Hades shall not prevail against it!' So anyway, there you have it. He said Peter was the rock upon which He would build His church."

She smiled, realizing that for millions of the world's Catholics this was the true interpretation of the passage. Their faith rested not on Scripture but the authority of the Church. The Popes claimed they had inherited the Church from Peter, the Rock. Apostolic Succession, or something like that. She also knew that Evan did not believe the Catholic interpretation. She knew him that well. But interestingly, for the first time she understood how the Protestant Reformation must have shaken the Catholic world so terribly. She had always taken her Protestantism for granted, not realizing how frightening it had been for the first Protestants, who had dared to defy sixteen centuries of Catholic authority. She empathized, now that her own rock of Protestant faith in the Bible seemed to move beneath her feet.

"The rock is revelation," she said aloud, quoting a sermon she'd heard her father preach many times.

"Revelation?" Evan asked rhetorically. "*Written* revelation?"

"No. 'The letter killeth.'" She recalled the words of Paul in Second Corinthians. "'. . . but the Spirit giveth life.' The revelation happened when Peter said, 'Thou art the Christ,' and Jesus told him 'flesh and blood' couldn't reveal that to him. Only the Spirit. Then the Lord said, 'Thou art Peter and on this rock I will build my Church and the gates of Hell shall not prevail against it.' The rock is the revelation that Jesus is the Christ, the Messiah, the Son of God." She thought about it for a moment. "But then, I can see how someone could easily take Jesus' words to mean that *Peter* was the rock. After all, his name meant 'stone.'" She suddenly demanded in the voice of a spoiled little girl, "Why didn't God make it more simple?"

"God doesn't give you absolutes on demand, does He? If you make an absolute of your own, you are playing god. That is idolatry." Evan smiled at her with what he hoped was sympathy, not gloating.

In this exchange he felt something he hadn't felt for many years. A feeling of home. A feeling of conviction. A feeling of faith. He believed in something. For one thing he believed God had designed revelation to frustrate the human lust for absolutes. *The desire for more absolutes than God has revealed is an evil desire.* That had become one of his few convictions. He stood on it. His personal search of history had revealed that the lust for absolutes was a trait shared by the worst dictators and tyrants of all time. *A murderer is someone who has to be absolutely right*, he mused, *even when he is absolutely wrong. Jim Jones had to be absolutely right to force his suicidal will on so many victims. Hitler as well.*

It seemed fitting to Evan that the conversation between Jesus and Peter could be taken both ways in Scripture; the rock *might* have been Peter, or the rock *might* have been Jesus Christ. Theologians could run in opposite directions, both claiming to be right. He saw a divine genius in this paradox. Perhaps it explained why Jesus had spoken in parables, leaving as many applications as he had hearers. The truth could only be known through revelation. To those with ears to hear, it was a spiritual experience, never a catechism.

He noticed that his sister had succumbed to staring out the window. "The rock is revelation, Pauline," he repeated.

She turned and looked at him blankly.

"On that point we agree," he insisted.

"Don't give me too much credit for agreeing," she sighed.

He could see that she did not enjoy looking beyond the familiar limits of her fears. "Faith, Pauline," he said. "Faith." He wanted to encourage her.

After a silence she asked, "Why have I never dealt with this before?"

He wanted to say, Because you have been hiding rather than growing! Because you demand easy answers where there are none! Because men like your father have told you what you wanted to hear for so long you don't know the truth when it hits you in the face! Because false religion sterilizes the good gifts God placed within you! He wanted to say all of that, but he held his tongue. He suddenly wondered what would remain if he destroyed all of her religious idols. He wasn't really ready for that responsibility. "Maybe it's not very important, sis," he replied. In a certain way he really meant this. "Truth is nothing without love."

"But for me truth is important," she replied surprisingly. "My father is involved with a Nephil, and I don't even know if that is possible."

Once again she was running the wrong direction. "That's not truth, that's knowledge. And don't take Enoch literally," he cautioned.

"Well, I do take it literally. I think Daddy is really in the spiritual realm, bound up by a Nephil like in Lydia's dream. What if we can learn something about it that will help us release him?"

"OK. Just for argument, let's say he is up there with the Nephil. What do we do? This is where you and I part ways. I'd say it is a spiritual reality that we can only deal with from here on earth. You don't think you're actually going to find Dad up in the clouds with the harps and the angels? Excuse me—unless he's dead!"

It was a frightening thought. "How about *near* dead?" she asked.

"I never put any stock in that near stuff myself," he replied. "You're either dead or you're not."

"Oh ho," Pauline replied, pointing an accusing finger. "So you lust for absolutes! I want them for Scripture, you want them for an absolute death. That's a very interesting difference between us." She laughed high and long. It felt good to catch Evan in hypocrisy.

His face turned red. "You're going to find Dad at Nimrut Dag," he went on defensively, "and whatever we can do for him will be done with both feet firmly planted on *terra firma*. The spiritual realm is real to the spirits. If Dad is not a spirit, then I don't see much we can do for him except bring the Old Man to his senses and yank him on home. OK? I think he's been led out onto a freaking limb like some freaking Shirley MacLaine. Only *he* got out there chasing money. Who knows, maybe she did too."

Pauline was confused. "Let me get this straight. To you, Lydia's dream and all of this Nephilim stuff doesn't have to be thrown out? I mean, you think it could be true? In a sense?"

"True . . .?" He paused carefully, wanting to cool her fervor about the "truth" part of it. "True is not quite the same as 'truth.' It is true only in a partial sense."

"But it isn't against the Bible for me to believe it literally. According to . . . to Jude and the early church fathers. Right?"

"Some say it is against the Bible, some say no. I'm sorry, but I can't give you an absolute there either."

"I want one," she said, laughing at herself. "Did you learn all this stuff in Bible college, Evan? Is that what I missed?"

He smiled sheepishly with the memory. "No. In fact, they didn't like me much in Bible college because I asked the wrong kind of questions. You know, the ones that led to more questions. I've just always been curious. I keep reading."

Pauline wondered how they had come from the same mother and father. For the first time in her life she began to appreciate Evan's mind. That in turn opened her own mind to possibilities she would never have considered alone. "Lydia says she died in the dream and then rose out of her body. Then she saw Tubal-cain take the Nephil from Naamah's womb by a postmortem cesarean. The woman in the dream had already died, mind you. Then some priests or the like chanted and worshiped the creature. Then she saw more scenes leading up to a scene where she saw Daddy tied up with chains in an arena with the grown-up Nephil."

"Yeah, well, are you sure the old woman was fasting?" Evan asked dryly. "Sounds like bad pizza to me."

Ignoring his remark, Danna, who had been listening quietly, asked, "Lydia's dream happened the day Dr. Grace disappeared?"

"Yes."

"That gives me goose bumps."

"Goose bumps are pretty worthless," Evan muttered.

Pauline ignored him, adding, "Lydia died three times. They had to resuscitate her with those electrical shocker things."

"Defibrillators," Danna prompted.

"Right. Lydia's view of it says she had supernatural dreams resulting from her prayer and fasting for my father. Now I'm beginning to wonder if there isn't a medical explanation too. She had a spiritual experience, a dream or a vision or whatever. Went out of her own body, she says. At the same time there was a medical explanation, which says she died of cardiac arrest. Maybe *both* happened. She describes a Near Death Experience as a spiritual experience. Maybe that's what it is. Lydia saw into the actual spiritual dimension. I am sure she saw what Daddy is writing about in this letter. And this letter hadn't even been written yet."

"Pauline, honey," Evan said, "crazy people think this kind of stuff is real, and they do terrible, antisocial things because of it."

Danna objected, "What Pauline is saying is making more sense than anything yet. The Near Death Experience is a place where . . . where medicine opens a door to the spirit realm. That's what your dad is after. If he's with Dunamis, then he's betting his life on it. What is the truth?" She groped for words. "Maybe it's just that medicine creates the doorway so a person can go through to the other side. And come back. Hopefully."

"Possibly," Pauline continued. She felt pleased that at least Danna respected her thoughts. "Maybe we're not *supposed* to cross over. Maybe Dad is trying to do God's will, but he's doing something wrong, something forbidden, and that's why he's bound over there." She shrugged.

"But then," Danna interjected, "that would be like forbidding resuscitation. I'm not a doctor, but I've always accepted that if it is medically possible, then we automatically know God allows it. Because He could put a stop to medicine if He wanted to. He's God, after all. So it's not strictly forbidden to use a medical doorway." She looked back and forth between the two of them for a response.

"You know, that's interesting," Pauline offered thoughtfully. "In Genesis you have the story of the people at Babel who came together to build a tower that would reach into heaven. Now I know that heaven probably meant the sky, but maybe it included the spiritual heavens too, I don't know. But I remember the part where God said if he didn't stop them, nothing would be impossible that they had decided to do. In other words, they would have ended up in heaven—whatever heaven they had imagined."

"See there?" Danna replied. "God put a stop to it at the Tower of Babel. He can put a stop to it at Nimrut Dag. I say, let's go find your dad and leave God's business up to Him."

Pauline smiled weakly. "Thanks, Danna. Somehow that isn't very comforting."

Evan stood up, stuffing his hands deeply into his pockets. "You're both getting too far out in the ether zone for me. The problem with Dad is money—not some freaking Nephil Lydia saw."

Pauline ignored him again. "In the final scene Lydia sees Dad wrapped up in chains in this old colosseum. Like the one in Rome. The angel is there. He is blind, and he is all scarred and bloodied-up from a fight. Naamah is there tending to his wounds. Dad wrote in the letter, 'if there is a physical body, there is a spiritual one.' Anyway, in the center of the ring Lydia sees this same Nephil, all grown-up. It is terribly ugly and . . . well, the thing is just a demon. She said it seemed that Mithrael and the Nephil fought over Daddy, and Daddy couldn't get away. She thought if the angel won, he could go free; but if the Nephil won, he would stay bound up in chains."

"What did she say we could do about it?" Danna asked.

"She said for me to find Daddy. She would pray."

"Pray," Evan declared. "I'm beginning to think that's exactly what we should have done."

Pauline ignored him again. "That's what his letter is all about. He's asking for prayer."

"Prayer and support," Evan reminded her.

Pauline turned back to Danna. "I think Lydia has been right all along. She has been tuned in spiritually. She prays for Dad. The rest of us just work for him, or live off of him, or—" She nodded toward Evan. "—some of us just criticize him. But at the risk of sounding corny, Dad is my father, right or wrong. If he is bound, I'm going to do everything in my power to get him back. I want to learn about these Nephilim because Lydia saw one in her dream. And I want to learn about this medical process, this NDE or whatever Dunamis has been studying because that is the method Daddy is using."

"Do you know what you're saying?"

"Why do I have to know what I'm saying?" she demanded irritably.

"Because it's pretty serious stuff."

"So is life. I didn't ask to be born, but I've got to deal with that. Ready or not. What's your point?"

"My point is, it seems to me you've educated yourself in a very thin slice of life. What you *don't* know can be the death of us all."

"There comes a point where I just don't care anymore," she said with as much self-realization as argument. "Can you understand that? I'm only human, and somehow I think that ought to be *enough* in this case!"

Evan wanted to end the conversation, but he could not. He cared too much for both of these women. "Your father's recklessness has put us here. Excuse me, but if you had read something besides your Bible and your Dad's fund-raising letters over the years, you'd know that only dangerous utopians, drug-crazed radicals, and Nazi lunatics believe in this kind of stuff." His voice had a cutting edge to it. "You girls are being sucked in."

"Who do you think you are?" Danna blustered. "And who do you think you are talking to?"

"OK." He threw up his hands and walked forward to the bulkhead.

"You're coming on like God Almighty," Danna continued. "Like you're the only one with any brains around here. And I'm getting tired of it. I've been around the block a few times, and I say it's important to hear what Pauline is saying."

"OK, hear it," he argued. "Then rule it out. Sorry about the attitude, but I really am concerned. Hear what I'm saying too." He came boldly back into the rear section. "Can I give you my scenario?"

Pauline and Danna looked at each other doe-eyed. They knew they were about to hear it anyway.

He gathered himself to make his point. "Lydia may have seen something. Maybe something real. But it's like Joseph's dream of his brothers' wheat stalks bowing down to his wheat stalk in the Bible. Remember that? It's symbolically true—not literally true."

"You've already said that," Pauline said.

"I'm summing up here, OK?" He sighed, regathering his thoughts. "What I believe is really happening—what has Dad bound—is a power struggle. And the whole thing is about money. Like Alan says, Dad is about to reap the greatest fund-raising letter of all time. Not to mention a forty million dollar personal pay-day from the sale of the icon—whether or not they find a cure for cancer. You keep forgetting the amounts of money involved here. Enough to mess up a man's better judgment, believe me."

They pondered this thoughtfully. Then Danna spoke up. "But I've seen Dunamis operate for years now. They are dead serious about the supernatural. Don't forget, Neva spent some time at Jonestown. According to Canaan their predecessors were at Dachau, learning what they could do in the spiritual realm of medicine before any of us were born. I think these people are more serious about the spiritual dimension than they are about money, if you ask me."

"OK, maybe," Evan conceded. "But for Dad, it's still about money. If they come up with a cure for cancer, they stand to reap billions. We can't let ourselves get into the crazy ozone with them. It's their territory, so to speak." He turned to Pauline pleadingly. "That's all I have to say."

She remained quiet. Questions of right or wrong seemed totally beside the point for her now. In setting out after her father, she had begun a course beyond her ability to comprehend. She was traveling to Eden not because of what she believed, but because of who she was. She was Simon Grace's daughter, and perhaps a good deal more than that. Everything she did now would reveal her true identity, beyond anything she had ever done before. And because she knew herself so little, she was truly flying into the unknown.

X

ARARAT

Then God said to Noah,
The end of all flesh has come before Me . . .

(GENESIS 6:13)

73

EASTERN TURKEY
12:02 P.M.

Rick and Canaan piloted "Spirit I" toward its initial descent over the north end of an inland sea. This maneuver provided a bird's-eye view of a snow-laden mountain poised on the Russian border between Muslim Turkey and Russian Armenia.

"Pauline, come here and see this magnificent mountain," Danna said with a tone of awe in her voice. She pressed her forehead against the glass of the pressurized window to take in its full expanse.

Pauline stood up, feeling more than ready for a break. Her mind had grown foggy from absorbing too many medical statistics. For the past several hours during the flight, as they left the last fuel stop in Casablanca, she and Danna had been pouring over pages of the Dunamis files, looking for clues to their methods of experimentation with Near Death patients.

"That's Ararat out there," Evan narrated as she crossed to the left side of the plane. Through the same quiet hours, he had been studying his father's scrapbook of the region and had found a wealth of information on the enticing land of Eastern Turkey—not to mention a volume of confirming information about the quest at Nimrut Dag.

As Pauline approached the porthole, she became struck by the unexpected size of the mountain. Huge glaciers crawled from its ragged peak toward the valleys on all sides. The surrounding landscape seemed in upheaval, breaking away, eroding, sliding beneath unknown geological pressures. In fact, Evan informed them, a huge chasm had once opened on a lower slope of Ararat, swallowing an entire village. This event had been documented, happening in the twentieth century. He showed them a news clipping in the scrapbook.

Inspired, he quickly flipped to another section. "Let me read you some of Dad's notes about the mountain. 'Ararat rises 14,500 feet from the floor of the Araxes River Valley, the greatest unbroken slope in the world. It can be seen from Iran, Iraq and Syria in the south. It dominates the Turkish highlands from Anatolia to the Caucasus of Russia, and north to the Black Sea. It is without a doubt the resting place of Noah's Ark—' Ah, well, that's his opinion. '—and from this mountain descended every living animal of our present world.'"

Evan paused. "Pardon me, but I have a hard time believing all of the duckbilled platypuses crawled off this here mountain and hiked down to Australia, you know?"

Perhaps the sight of Ararat had suddenly inspired her. Whatever it was, Pauline's brain rose to defend her "literalist" faith. And her father's. "The fact that those animals are mostly in one place today might suggest that they *came* from one place after the Flood, mightn't it?"

"What did they do, come off the Ark and go down there before supper? I mean, it took generations for them to make the trip. Assuming there was still a land bridge between the continents back then. Surely they dropped a few babies along the way? Laid a few eggs? Where are they now? Why don't we find populations of platypuses in Asia or Africa? We only find them in Australia. It's like they evolved there."

"Maybe God made them migrate. Like geese. How do the birds know to fly from the Arctic to the Tropics every year? Explain that scientifically. Are they navigators like Rick? With intelligence? No. So maybe God placed a homing instinct inside the marsupials when they came off the Ark. It caused them to go to Australia. He could have done that if He wanted to. He *is* God, after all."

One of the few things Evan believed about God was that He made good sense. He was neither arbitrary nor capricious. Pauline's argument made Him sound that way. He knew that the Bible stated that the Genesis Flood covered the whole earth and that it had destroyed all flesh, and that all life had originated from the Ark of Noah. But that seemed like a typically "flat earth" conception of the world to him. The story had been told in the language and understanding of the times. It seemed too absurd for a modern mind to take Noah's Flood literally, as a whole-earth upheaval. But he had no time to explain to Pauline about the possibility of a continental disaster of some sort that had flooded the Fertile Crescent, *seeming* like the whole world to the ancients of the region. It wouldn't matter anyway. She believed God had authored the Bible. It was word for word His point of view, not the points of view of the men who wrote under inspiration. "I guess we have to say there are still some things we just can't know," he replied, "and leave it at that."

"Unless you know by revelation," she returned.

He looked at his sister with amazement. It seemed she was experiencing a resurgence of gray matter before his very eyes. "Moving right along," he said with a sly smile, looking down to read again: "'Our interest is not with the mountain itself but with the people of Ararat. The forgotten Urartians who lived there when they called the region "Urartu." They became the keepers of the secrets of ancient Eden, and the conjurers at the Tree of the Gods.'"

"What Dad is saying about this place is the same stuff in Lydia's dream, Evan." Pauline continued to be inspired by the sight of the Genesis landmark as she spoke. The mountain seemed to add a dimension of frightening reality to Lydia's dream of Mithrael, Naamah and the Nephil. "She is just a simple woman. She lives in a small circle, yet she prays around the world, and then some."

"OK, her dream seems on target. But consider this—Dad may have let some of these things slip in conversations over the years. These notes were not made yesterday. He may have said things to her that she just forgot she heard. The same way he said, 'the desert that sin made' to me when I was a kid. He might have said some of these things and now it affects her subconscious mind even though she's forgotten it. Now it's coming out in her dreams, or something like that. Just consider it. Please."

She considered it. It was a reasonable doubt that would have provided a safe emotional distance from the present ordeal had she been back home in Texas. But somehow in the shadows of Ararat the comfort quickly vanished.

Evan resumed reading with reluctance, afraid that he might be adding fuel to Pauline's literalist fire. "'The wife of Noah's cursed son Ham descended from an ancient angel marriage, though she herself was not a giant. I propose that she carried a recessive gene of giantism in her DNA from the past inbreeding of angels, or perhaps even one of the giant Nephilim offspring of the angels. The Nephilim bred copiously between the various species, especially the dinosaurs, which led to their extinction. The text of "The Songs of Jubal" tells us that when Ham's wife conceived children after the Flood, she remembered the "Sacred Songs of the Giants." She sang them as lullabies to her son Canaan, and to her grandchildren. Later, out of Canaan's family came Nimrod, the first giant born after the Flood, according to Urartian legend.'"

Evan looked up with fascination. "Can you believe Dad has dug all this up?"

"I can now."

"'The Urartians descended from Nimrod. They built the Tower of Babel, and sought to perfect the artifices of Tubal-cain. They sang "The Songs of Jubal." Out of the Urartian line came the race of giants known as the "sons of Anak," who became the champions of the Canaanites. Also the giant Rephaites who bred the great sacrificial Bulls of Bashan in the land of Canaan. They are mentioned by the Promised-Land spies in Numbers 13:33. One of the giants was Goliath of Gath, later slain by the boy David.'"

He looked up again commenting, "I've always wondered about the giants after the Flood, how they differ from the original Nephilim, but I've never heard of this particular explanation. It's interesting."

The Falcon banked sharply away from Ararat and dipped toward the southern end of the great lake beneath them. Rick's voice crackled over the intercom. "Buckle up, pigeons. We're descending toward beautiful downtown Van. We'll be on the ground in less than ten minutes, so please check the security of your seat belts, and keep them fastened about you at all times—as we do here in the cockpit—when seated. And when awake." He yawned loudly. "Uh-hum. And thank you for flying Apocalyptic Airways. We'll see you in the Rapture."

Pauline could barely bring herself to snicker at Rick's insanity. She felt a knot in the pit of her stomach. Her father grew uncomfortably near in that strange land below. Yet she felt farther from him than ever in her life. Danna seemed to sense her tension and gave her a supportive hug as they returned from the windows to their seats.

Oblivious to them, Evan read on. "'The Urartian priesthood eventually preserved "The Songs of Jubal" in cuneiform tablets. They built fortresses throughout the region, like Toprak Kale and Van Kalesi, near the garden city of Van. They built High Places and pantheons to preserve the memory of the old gods. They created ceremonial caverns. As civilizations migrated from Ararat after the Flood, they unknowingly carried with them the legends and myths of the antediluvian gods. According to "The Book of the Watchers," when the Nephilim drowned in the Flood, evil spirits arose from their bodies and entered the invisible realm, animating idol worship thereafter.'"

Evan eagerly swiveled around to face the girls seated behind him. He locked the seat in place for the landing. Danna stowed books in the boxes they had brought with them.

Pauline stared from the portside window at an emerald crater nestled in a peak passing beneath the plane. She heard everything Evan said, but she remained preoccupied, storing the words away in her mind like meaningless, individual *tesserae*. By themselves the pieces revealed little: her father's notes, his disappearance, Neva Sylvan's odyssey, *The Seven Sleepers of Antioch*, the cancer cure, Dunamis, the Urartian priesthood, idols, Nephilim, "The Songs of Jubal," Commagene, Eden, Nimrut Dag, the "Tree of Life." The pieces could be put together to form many pictures, depending upon how they were arranged. They could be made to show her father as a monster. Another arrangement revealed a healer trapped by his own obsession. Another a victim of an evil conspiracy. At times the preacher's own fund-raising manipulation rearranged the picture altogether, making him worthy of censure. Maybe none of the arrangements revealed the truth. Maybe all of them did. Such was the nature of a mosaic. *God, why can't things be clear?*

Evan observed, "Dad has obviously done his homework on this place. Listen to this. 'I myself have seen the chamber of Van Kalesi and the stone channels in the floor for the slaughter of bulls used in the great Urartian bloodbaths, later associated with Mithraism.'"

"Oh really!" Danna protested. "Do we need to hear this?"

"We need to know what Dad was thinking when he came here," Evan replied before continuing. "'The Urartians built sacrificial caverns all over Urartu and Anatolia, until they succeeded in locating the Great Antediluvian Tree, and the remains of the Garden at Nimrut Dag. There, or so they claimed, a chorus of Nephilim announced the doorway to the Sides of the North. According to Urartian legend, the Sides of the North had existed on the great northern shoulder to the Mountain of Eden. But the Fountains of the Deep had broken it up, along with portions of the earth's crust during the Flood. The entire Garden Mountain vanished, as well as the Sides of the North. Only the Urartians remembered that the Sides of the North had once stood higher than Ararat above the land of Eden.'"

"Like an island in the sky," Pauline murmured. "Lydia mentioned such a place, above the clouds, in her dream."

He paused. "I am aware that this fits well with her dream, but I think it is more important to understand Dad's view of it right

now." He read again. "'Only the Urartian priesthood understood
that the Sides of the North had become a spiritual place after the
Flood, existing parallel to life on earth—' OK, Lydia's dream again.
'With the knowledge of these secrets, they began to build the great
High Places, which later appeared in Canaan and the rest of the
world. They developed rituals from "The Songs of Jubal." By the
blood of bulls and by the sacrifice of infants and slaves, the Urartian
priesthood conjured the epiphanies of the antediluvian gods from
the Sides of the North. In the sacrificial caves first appeared
Annamelech, Asherah, Ashtoreth, Ishtar, Baal, Baalzebub, Bel,
Chiun, Dagon, Moloch, Nergal, Rimmon, Satyr, Succuth, Tammuz
and Tartak of the Canaanite cults.' Man, he has done some homework. 'The Urartians originated the secrets used later by the witch
of Endor, as well as the spells and incantations of sorcerers, medi-
ums, warlocks and shamans throughout history. The Egyptian
priests took back with them the secrets of Anubis, Hathor, Isis,
Osiris, Re, Seth, Horus, Sphinx and Thoth. The antediluvian
demigods took other names and entered the rich Pantheon of
Greece: Aphrodite, Apollo, Aries, Atlas, Cronus, Dionysus,
Nemesis, Zeus and a host of others. Not to mention the Titans and
all the monsters and heroes of these celebrated mythologies. In turn,
they spawned Romulus and Remus, and fed the legends of Rome
with Jupiter, Aurora, Bacchus, Cupid, the Furies, Neptune, Mars,
Saturn, Somnus and Vulcan.'"

He paused to clear his head and catch his breath before plung-
ing in again. "'The Urartian High Places became duplicated centuries later by the Aztec and Mayan cultures in the Americas, and
by the Polynesians. Demon spirits passed through the Ancient
Doors to inspire and honor their ritual sacrifices around the world.
The rites of African witch doctors with their variety of fetishes
sprang from the antediluvian songs. In the British Isles, Celtic legend and the secrets of Stonehenge belonged first to the Urartian
priests of the Nephilim. The Teutonic myths of Balder and Loki—
the dark son of the giants who forced an apocalypse against the
white German gods and heroes—all of these arose from the bloody
rituals of Urartu.

"'Bastardized versions of the original gods formed the Indo-
Aryan pantheons. The Hindu Bhagavad Gita, Juggernaut, Manu,
Shiva, Thug, Vishnu and the Vedas all crawled first from the caves
of Ararat. But the Urartians themselves remained near the source,

in the land of the secrets. They became the keepers of the Ancient Doors to the Sides of the North.'"

He paused again. The intensity, the accumulated spiritual mass of the subject matter had become heavier than his own curiosity to know it. If not for the fact that they were presently chasing the author of these notes, his own father, he would have put the scrapbook aside as the ramblings of an undisciplined mind. And so, he continued . . .

"'By the time of Darius the Mede in 590 B.C., the Urartians became known as the Armenians. There remains a dispute among scholars, but my own research has convinced me that these people are one and the same. During the transition time, the Urartian priesthood kept the ancient secrets alive. While in the meantime the citizenry of Armenia provided all of the famous wine for Babylon the Great City, with its luxurious Hanging Gardens. Armenian wine pots, which Commagene uncovered here in the land of the Turks, were once floated the length of the Euphrates River in skin boats. The Armenians traced their proud wine-making skills directly to the drunken patriarch Noah. Their wines were the finest of the ancient world.

"'Alexander the Great conquered the region, then the Seleucid Dynasty. Still, the Armenian pagans held to their unique culture and religious identity. For this reason the Armenians martyred the Apostles Thaddeus and Bartholomew for preaching Christ in the first century A.D. But in 280 A.D. everything changed. King Tiridates of Armenia converted to Christianity under the preaching of a wandering charismatic named Gregory the Illuminator. Armed with the holy bones of John the Baptist, the Christians began to tear down the High Places of the Urartians. They built Christian churches on the ruins of the ancient fire temples. By kingly decree, the first Christian nation on earth sprang up around Ararat. This happened a half-century before the conversion of Constantine and the Holy Roman Empire. At this time the secret Urartian rites almost died, persecuted by the ambitious Christian king. A sworn Secret Society of Apostates was initiated to preserve the old ways. They negotiated a crafty deal with the king, and he secretly ordained their priesthood wholesale into the state church. Once in power, the Secret Society preserved "The Songs of Jubal" for later generations and canonized "The Seven Sleepers of Antioch" as Christian saints, later creating the Apostate icon from the petrified Trees of Eden.'"

Evan paused again. "Well, he knows more than I do on the subject. I'd like to pick his brain, but I still can't tell where he stands. What is he doing with these people? Is he into this stuff or against it?"

"Final approach," Rick called over the cabin page. "We've got a crosswind in beautiful downtown Van today. Might touch down a little hard, so everybody hang on."

Each of them obediently rechecked their seat belts.

As she watched the ground rush toward her through the window, Pauline did not have the usual feeling of descending from the sky in the jet. Rather, she felt as if this hostile, ancient land of Ararat was rising up to swallow her in a conflict older than the planet.

Glancing from the left side of the plane, Evan saw a crumbling fortress riding the crest of a ridge along the lake. "There's Van Kalesi," he said, pointing to it. "The Urartian fortress Dad mentioned. We're here." He slammed the notebook shut.

Pauline continued to look out the window at the wind-driven whitecaps lashing the briny waters of Lake Van on the opposite side of the plane.

The Falcon's wheels touched the uneven runway with a squeal and a small explosion of black smoke. The craft knifed along like a bird of prey in a flock of prop-driven transports. The dark eyes of the locals watched with wonder as the sleek jet taxied to a fuel depot.

No sooner had the engines cut than Colonel Canaan came aft and lowered the air-stair. Pauline, Evan, Danna and Rick were all more than anxious to stretch their legs after the six-hour flight from their last fuel stop in North Africa.

Stepping to the tarmac, Pauline filled her lungs with the high, thin atmosphere. It smelled of a mixture of salt from the lake and dry herbs from the arid hills. The September sun burned high above them, bright but not hot. The ground felt warm, the air cool.

"Better see if you can locate that helicopter right away," Pauline suggested to Rick.

"Right. Don't want to be caught with our pants down."

"See if they will let one of us pilot the thing," Canaan added. "If my men don't secure Nimrut Dag, we will still have the problem of getting past the authorities."

"Will do."

Canaan turned to the others with a look of sympathy. "I know that the hardest part for all of you will be waiting until my men arrive at Nimrut Dag. I am with you in that."

"If it wasn't for the business at hand, I'd love to explore this place," Evan said. "What do you say we check into the Bes Kardes?" He returned to the plane to pick up luggage.

Danna joked, "It looks like the Van chamber of commerce has sent out the local limo service."

A twenty-year-old International Harvester pickup slowly made its way toward them, backfiring repeatedly, laying down a carpet of multi-hued exhaust. The three-quarter-ton bed sported a canvas sunshade held up by four flexible two-by-twos, which swayed dangerously with each bump in the tarmac.

74

VAN
Bes Kardes Hotel
2:00 P.M.

Leaning over the second-story rail of a guest room in the hotel, Evan eyed a busy Turkish market below — called a *sook* by the locals. Piles of wares, stacks of pottery, woven wool and cotton sweaters, hand-knit Kurdish socks, hemp sacks of vegetables, fruits, tea, herbed goat's cheese, spices, hand-hammered copper pots, snowdrift ice, Black Sea salt, and sides of freshly butchered beef were displayed between the busy stalls along the street. Live goats, pigs and pigeons strained at the ends of tethers, or sat quietly, caged for sale. The street burst with the color, sights and smells of an exotic tourist location. Ignorant of the tourist potential, the *sook* was essential to the dwellers of the garden city of Van. The shops bustled with peasants from the countryside, bartering everything from garlic to grain to shoe leather.

Evan's mouth began to water at the exotic aroma of a yogurt-marinated lamb kebab, wafting its scent across the balcony. Leaning out, he could see the meal roasting in a *tandir* fire pot, nestled in the ground below.

Behind him, Pauline and Danna continued to pore over the computer data from Neva Sylvan's medical files. Colonel Canaan watched them closely, fingering the Uzi he managed to get past the local agent by engineering several sleight-of-hand returns to the plane after being checked through customs. He had smuggled it in pieces, reassembling it in the room.

Meanwhile, Pauline picked Danna's nursing brain about everything that might have happened to her father. They had discovered that Dr. Osis had developed a secret drug compound called Hypnos-3, administered by IV, which would induce a coma deep enough to produce a full Near Death Experience. Danna explained that the true NDE always included the three basic phases. The autoscopic—more commonly called, the "out-of-body" episode, followed by the traversing of the tunnel, followed by something called a "transcendental experience" beyond the tunnel. Another drug would awaken the patient from the NDE, although cutting off the supply of Hypnos-3 would also bring a patient out of the sleep in fifteen or twenty minutes without any assistance. Failing that, other standard resuscitation methods were available.

In the sheets of data, they had not been able to locate the secret drug formula. However they had found Dr. Osis's dosage instructions for Hypnos-3:

> NDE threshold is usually reached between 150 mg (3 cc) and 350 mg (7 cc), but can be as little as 75 mg (1.5 cc) in the elderly patient or the patient with organic illness. Begin the infusion until either sustained rapid lateral nystagmus is present or drowsiness is noted. Slight slurring of speech will occur just before the NDE threshold is reached. If speech slurring continues for longer than thirty seconds, increase the rate by 0.2 cc /5 minutes. To maintain the level of narcosis, infuse the formula at a rate of about 0.5-1.0 cc /5 minutes.

"Do you understand these instructions?" Pauline asked. They seemed completely over her own head.

"In theory. If you don't do something every day, you know, it's like—well, like baking a cake. You can do it, but you just have to follow the directions to the letter."

Pauline nodded. "Could you follow this if you had to?"

Danna looked at her, sensing the quiet determination that was growing in her mind. She nodded.

"I'm going for some fresh air," Evan said, not hearing them. He passed through the room on his way to the front door, signaling Canaan to follow. The colonel set his weapon down, and the two of them went out.

In the meantime, something new had taken Pauline's attention.

She became puzzled over nearly twenty pages of data of nothing but combinations of the numbers 0 and 1. "What are these?" she asked.

"As I understand it, that is the mapping information they fed into the computer. They made a grid out of all the interviews of people they sent over to the third stage of NDE, the transcendental plane. All of this information has been turned into binary numbers. The computer puts the numbers through a formula and generates a three-dimensional line drawing of what they have seen."

"A composite?"

"Right. The more information they add to it, the more accurate the picture becomes. That is, if you believe in probabilities. They are trying to see what's on the other side through that method. A Dunamis research doctor named Santesteban developed the grid idea for use with Dr. Kassabian's sodium amytal interview . Kassabian is another Dunamis doctor. A Russian psychiatrist from Armenia. All of them are probably Apostates. So anyway, somewhere in all these numbers they think they have found the 'transcendental landscape' of cancer."

"And that is where Daddy is going."

"I think so," Danna agreed.

"Then that is where Lydia saw him in chains."

"I don't know if your dad knows it or not—" Danna stopped herself.

"What is it, Danna? Tell me."

"Oh, Pauline, you already know this is dangerous."

"I need to know more. What is it?"

"The last patients they sent over became the most successful and the most tragic at the same time. At least from what I have been able to make of the report."

"How so?"

"They saw the same thing. The report called it 'similarities,' with only two 'anomalies,' which means only two of the patients *didn't* see what they predicted they would see on the other side. However, the report ended with the note that the patients returned to a state of what they called 'complete dysfunction.'"

Pauline envisioned her father as a vegetable. Perhaps that explained the meaning of his chains. Would he die that way?

"The patients went insane, honey. I believe those are the very ones they took back to the hospital in the Sudan and—"

"Killed them?"

She nodded.

Once again Pauline's mind retreated from this knowledge. She thought instead of Lydia. "Lydia's dream gives me hope. She must have seen behind all of this. You know, she went through all three of the NDE stages. She came out of her body, then she went through the tunnel—several times, and then she saw several different places with people, the angels and the Nephil. It's like she entered a transcendental landscape alright. I think it was the world before the Flood somehow."

"We hear these stories from a lot of patients now that we can bring them back by defibrillator and heart massage, you know."

"Maybe Lydia saw the Sides of the North."

Danna pondered this. "That's funny. From what Evan read to us on the plane, the Urartians concentrated on getting the gods to come down from the Sides of the North. Can it work the other way around?"

Pauline felt fervor steal through her. Something akin to what her father must have felt writing that letter from Nimrut Dag. "Why not? Didn't Christ come to spoil principalities and spiritual wickedness? Didn't God send the Israelites into the giants' land to possess it? We are spiritual Israel. We should do even greater things than Joshua or Caleb if we believe what we preach."

75

VAN BAZAAR
2:21 P.M.

"I had to get out," Evan said, wiping perspiration from his forehead. He and the colonel strolled through the Turkish *sook*. "I was going a little nuts in there."

They walked a half-block, milling through a throng of men in threadbare suits and cloth caps, old women carrying huge bundles of groceries and firewood, groups of young girls passing in colorful cotton costumes, sharing whispered secrets behind their hands.

"You won't find many Jews around town," Canaan commented wryly. "Eighteen thousand families were deported to Persia in the fourth century."

"The Christians fared worse."

Canaan nodded sagely. "They had their own holocaust at the turn of the century. The sources I trust say two million vanished."

With these words Evan felt a hostile presence invade the street. It blanketed the sunlit scene like a shadowless cloud. An evil history lurked beneath the smiles of the Turkish merchants. They were not the enemy, but an enemy had found refuge among them. A spiritual enemy.

"Not many people realize how many German officers were here during World War I," Canaan murmured, "to advise and observe the slaughter. From the experience with the Armenians, Hitler learned that the civilized world would forgive a successful genocide. The Turks showed him that it had to be a complete job. No halfway measure. He was serving in the German army at the time. The 'final solution' to the Armenian problem inspired him as to how to handle the kinds of ethnic problems dividing Europe. In 1939 he said, 'I have ordered my death units to exterminate without mercy or pity, men, women, and children belonging to the Polish-speaking race. . . . After all, who remembers today the extermination of the Armenians?'" He raised his eyebrows and looked steadily at Evan. "The Holocaust began here."

"Commagene is German," Evan said with new understanding. He could taste death in the name. "Was he a Nazi?"

"Not Max. He was too young. But his uncle Otto Commagene was. He served here in Turkey during World War I. He saw the Armenian deportations and advised Hitler in the second war."

"Otto?"

"He masterminded the medical atrocities committed in the death camps. The Uriel Mission remembers him well. Otto was organized. He had a purpose. Today he is either dead or running from Simon Weisenthal in the hills of Argentina—we are not sure. He assembled the Society of Apostates during the Armenian slaughter, bringing the secret order to Mannheim, Germany. He created Dunamis during the Second War, orchestrating the Apostates to conduct the radical research at the death camps. He was sure it would be their Golden Age. If you can imagine it, he wanted to bring medical advances out of the Jewish genocide."

Evan felt a tightness in his chest. "You knew all of this before we came here?"

Canaan nodded soberly. "I know too much."

"Too much?"

"It was Otto who gave your dad the icon. Not Max. He was probably around when that picture of you was taken at Nimrut."

Evan's memory raced back to his eighth year. "The desert that sin made," his father had said. Suddenly that phrase seemed to mean more than he had ever imagined. But still, he recalled no image of a German on the mountain. Just shadowy figures of many people who had come and gone in the course of a healing crusade spanning three continents. He had only been a boy.

His mind raced forward through all of his years with his father. Corruption? Manipulation? Yes, he'd seen it. But he could not find the evidence for this kind of maniacal evil in Dr. Grace. He feared it, but he could not see it.

His insides began to quiver the way they had as a boy when he had no choice but to face a schoolyard bully. He detested violence, but had resigned himself to the fact that for the sake of what was innocent, good or right, the world required it now and then. He and Canaan had come to Turkey to spoil his father's multi-million-dollar scheme. They were likely to face the wrath of Dunamis in the process. He still didn't know how much control his father exerted over the Apostates, or vice versa. Or if it would even matter when push came to shove.

Surely Dr. Grace had not become so blinded by his own devices that he would turn against his flesh and blood? But then, he had wrecked Evan's career once, defrocking him for adultery when he had threatened to expose Alan Lavalle. Another msterstroke, killing two birds with one stone. Furthermore, Simon Grace had used his children, and even the death of his own wife in a fund-raising letter. Where would he stop?

As for Dunamis, they had demonstrated their willingness to shed blood with the bombing of Alan's yacht. Neva Sylvan had shown her true murderous colors in the Matamoros lab. He put nothing past her. The more he considered it, the more he appreciated Canaan's armed Israeli unit. "When do your men arrive?" he asked.

"Early morning. They leave the north Israel staging area at sundown, make Turkish landfall at 8:46, fly up the Euphrates. If all goes well they'll drop on Nimrut Dag and secure the caverns by 1 A.M. or so. I don't think our coming will be a complete surprise. Surely Neva Sylvan has alerted them since she escaped the Matamoros lab. At any rate, my radio will pick up within a three hundred mile radius. My men will signal when they have secured the area, and we can take the helicopter out to meet them. If Turkish troop movement is detected, however, they will have to leave immediately. I don't expect them to stay longer than four hours."

"So you'll be going back with them?"

Canaan remained silent for a moment. "That will be up to High Command. If they think there is a danger of my being caught here in Turkey after the raid, the answer will have to be yes."

Evan smelled a mixture of frankincense and hashish. During their discussion they had wandered aimlessly to a cutlery booth in the *sook*. A toothless Kurdish proprietor sat cross-legged on a pillow watching them. Canaan reached down and picked up an antler-handled dagger, turning it in his palm, admiring the hand-forged steel and craftsmanship. The Kurd's shrewd eyes glinted as he silently puffed a long-stemmed pipe.

Evan watched the old man, who seemed an enigma beneath his sun-leathered wrinkles. He wondered if his eyes had witnessed the atrocities upon the Armenians seventy-five years past. Recalling a note he had read in his father's scrapbook, he wondered if the old man had seen the pile of children's hands hacked off in the city square? He tried to imagine the religious-nationalist zeal that would release such blood lust in men. How could anyone who committed such atrocities go on living a normal existence? How could they ever nurture children of their own? What sort of curses must they inadvertently pass on to the next generation?

Canaan replaced the knife, nodding appreciatively to the shopkeeper before moving on. They strolled the busy *sook* in silence for a time.

"The intercom in the Falcon goes two ways," the colonel mentioned suddenly.

The comment seemed out of character. Evidently the copilot had overheard something through the intercom. Perhaps part of their in-flight discussion, Evan surmised. "Yes?"

"I heard something about the Book of Enoch."

"Yes, you did."

"I found it interesting. In fact, it brought something to mind. You may recall, I told you I am a member of the Uriel Mission. Do you know that name?"

Evan thought a moment. "It rings a bell, but no."

The colonel walked to the middle of the cobblestoned street, turning in a circle, scanning the people as he continued, "According to *Midrash Rabbah*, Uriel is one of the four angels of the Presence of God: Michael, Gabriel, Raphael and Uriel. In 'The Book of the Watchers,' I believe it is First Enoch 9, Uriel addressed a prayer to God, asking for an end to the violence and bloodshed the Nephilim had brought to the earth."

Evan stopped abruptly in the street. "I remember. And God sent the Flood in response to Uriel's prayer?"

"Exactly."

"That's why your organization is called the Uriel Mission. That's spooky, colonel."

Canaan continued to look about, a smile prying at the corners of his mouth as they walked. "There is more than meets the eye to our mission here." He paused again. "I don't know what it means, but I could get *religious* over something like this."

Canaan's words about Uriel had opened unexpected doors in Evan's mind. Doors to the supernatural which he preferred to leave shut. But in the context of their discussion, supernatural explanations had begun to make sense. How less than supernatural was the order to commit genocide—Turkish or German? But then, Evan was suddenly reminded, the God of Israel had ordered the first genocide—the Great Genesis Flood. Near-complete extermination of a world filled with violence. Even more disturbingly, in the Promised Land a thousand years before Christ, the God of Israel had ordered genocide at the hands of His own people. Evan recalled well the unflinching Deuteronomic command, ". . . thou shalt save alive nothing that breatheth: But thou shalt utterly destroy them; namely the Hittites, and the Amorites, the Canaanites, and the Perizzites, the Hivites, and the Jebusites; as the Lord thy God hath commanded thee: that they teach you not to do after all their abominations, which they have done unto their gods." He imagined suddenly, not Canaanite soldiers falling in battle, but Canaanite women and children screaming for mercy beneath the God-ordained swords of the Children of Israel. How could such a thing have ever been God's will?

It troubled Evan greatly to deal with these Old Testament Scriptures in light of his own faith. He wanted genocide to only belong to the gods of evil. Not to Jehovah. Not to the Father of Jesus, the Savior, the Christ. But apparently in the war between light and darkness battles in the supernatural were very much more real than he wanted to imagine. Serious enough to command incomprehensible losses to mankind. Either all religion was an illness, he reasoned, or there was some hellish kind of *truth* to this supernatural war. Something which remained too great for any human mind to squarely face. Armageddon became suddenly thinkable in the light of the supernatural.

With a shudder, putting three thousand years of enlightenment between himself and Jehovah—modern genocide still seemed decidedly different to Evan. It seemed purely evil. Satanically evil. Whether the vengeful Crusades against the "Christ killing" Jews and "infidel" Muslims, the Turkish "deportation" of Christian Armenia, Hitler's celebrated atrocities, the "Killing Fields" of Cambodia under the Khmer Rouge, the Stalinist purges, the Gulag Archipelago, the Russian *pogroms*, the Maoist Red Guards, or even the suicidal horror of Jonestown. Who, in the age of the forgiving Christ, could order a "final solution" on men, women and children? "Without pity or mercy," as Hitler said. How less than demonic were the men who decided such a thing should be done? How fiendish the soldiers who saluted and followed their orders? In that twisted sense, Neva Sylvan had been right—these modern slaughterers *were* "epiphanies"—gods manifest in the flesh—the *old* gods, indwelling the flesh of men. Perhaps they were the very antediluvian Nephilim who had once filled the earth with so much violence that even the angels had prayed for an end to it.

He suddenly had no more stomach for walking this Turkish road. Tilting his head toward the hotel, he said, "What do you say we go back?"

"Not yet," Canaan returned furtively. "A woman has been following us. Come with me." He walked to a nearby shop and feigned interest in a Persian rug. "She's right back there. Looks like a tourist. See her at the corner? Over there."

Evan moved to the other side of Canaan's stooped figure, his eyes flitting back and forth across the crowd.

"I thought I saw her earlier when I was on my way back from the airstrip."

Suddenly Evan saw the woman. She peered back at him from beneath a head scarf. She was half-concealed near the corner of an alley two blocks away. She wore sunglasses which she had dipped below her eyes to get a better look at the two of them. At that distance, the shape of her head beneath the tied scarf resembled a sculpted skull with skin stretched over it. *Am I getting crazy? For heaven's sake, she has flesh on the bone!* he thought. But the eyes seemed larger than human and glared across the bustling bazaar with dark, penetrating hostility. They were the eyes of a damned soul. One who no longer hoped or appreciated anything of value, or knew remorse.

"It's Neva," he said automatically.

Canaan straightened. "Are you sure?"

He felt fear melting like ice cubes into his bloodstream. "Pretty sure. What do you think?"

Canaan grew puzzled. "Where is she?"

Evan's eyes returned to the spot. "She's gone! She was right there at the corner of that alley."

Canaan sprinted toward the place. Evan followed, growing quickly winded in the mile-high air.

Entering the alleyway, they saw that it wound between several buildings of clay-brick, littered with overflowing garbage containers and burning refuse drums. A foul-smelling black smoke eddied in the alley as they ran. Rounding a curve, they came suddenly into a side street fronting a series of multi-level stone buildings. There was no sign of the woman.

Canaan stopped and turned completely around, his eyes fully alert to danger now. Across the street an old woman beat dust from a rug hung over a balcony rail. To their left, the street held a flock of feeding chickens. No sign of Neva, if in truth it had been her. Immediately to their right, a group of three men cleaned a rifle with an ornately twisted Damascus barrel as they sat on the porch of a residence watching the two strangers—though pretending not to notice. From a distant minaret the shrill voice of a *muezzin* called the Sunni faithful to their afternoon prayers. Without a word, Evan and Canaan hurried back in the direction of the Bes Kardes Hotel.

XI

THE SIDES OF THE NORTH

Then Uriel said to me,
"Here shall stand . . . the spirits of the angels
which have united themselves with women
. . . this place is the end of heaven and earth:
it is the prison house for the stars."

(I Enoch 19:1; 18:14, The Book of the Watchers)

76

VAN
Bes Kardes Hotel
1:49 A.M.

Colonel Canaan had been right. Waiting became the hardest part, each member of the party suffering some stage of jet lag. After their foray into the streets, Evan and the colonel persuaded Rick and the women to stay inside the hotel until word came from the commandos. The two made no mention of seeing Neva Sylvan since neither Evan nor Canaan could be certain it had been she trailing them in the Turkish *sook*. That had been almost twelve hours ago, as long as they had been in the air from Texas, minus the fuel stops. The minutes and hours of waiting had wound each of them like the mainspring of a watch.

During the wait, Pauline had continued to probe Danna's medical data until she could no longer concentrate. Her mind would simply go blank without warning and she'd find herself staring at walls.

At ten o'clock Canaan insisted that she get some sleep in preparation for the coming ordeal. If not sleep, then quiet rest at least. Pauline had reluctantly agreed to do that, *if* they would all please join her in a prayer.

Rick, Canaan, Danna, Evan and Pauline had joined hands in a circle in the middle of her room, bowing their heads. Her prayer had been halting, inarticulate, but heartfelt. She prayed a simple plea for the mercy of God, and for help in what lay ahead. Evan felt honesty in the prayer and actually said "Amen" at the end. Something he hadn't done for years.

After separating to their rooms—Rick and Canaan shared one, Danna had the room next to Pauline's, and Evan's room lay at the far perimeter of the group—Pauline lay down and, surprisingly, fell into an exhausted sleep. She had not expected to sleep at all. As it turned out, her dreams engulfed her immediately, full of fits and starts.

She dreamed of computer data sheets that suddenly made sense. Jerking awake she would stare into the darkness, unable to recall the significance of the insight. Still, the sensation remained real, pulsating through her body with the conviction that even as she lay in this strange bed, she lay near a doorway of awful discovery. She had glimpsed new realities while unconscious. She knew that her father was near. Nearly in the room with her. She could feel his desperation—bound and gagged on the brink of Hell somewhere.

"O Jesus," she prayed, tears rolling to her pillow, "don't let him go . . . be there with him."

She fell asleep again, lost in another abstract sequence that only made sense in dreams. Another door opened in her mind, revealing another world, brilliant, stark and vivid. Blue, blue sky. Parched land. Another reality parallel to her own. This time there were visions, juxtaposed at the speed of thought, with no regard for time or space. Armies of warrior-angels, men of incredible physique and radiant beauty, fighting creatures of a thousand disfigured varieties on a vast wasteland plain. Some of the angels wrestled directly, hand to hand, with reptilian demons. Angels of a particular rank seemed to use weapons directed by commands in an angelic tongue. Fire, hail, lightning, stones obeyed them, hurling themselves against the cursed demons at the angels' bidding. Still others were armed with brightly flashing swords.

Out of this battlefield an angel stumbled, bowing to his knees, wounded. Looking up, he gazed wearily into Pauline's eyes, releasing a storm of emotion in her breast, making it hard for her to breathe. A familiar feeling she had known at other odd times in her life. Yes, the feeling in the Valley of Hinnom! She instantly understood that she had been given a part to play in a spiritual battle. For one thing, prayer penetrated the veil between the worlds. She knew it now. *Binding on earth what is bound in Heaven, loosing on earth what is loosed there. That is why the Spirit prays through us with "groanings which cannot be uttered,"* she realized with wonder! *We cannot see the battle, so how can we know what to pray? Nor can we know the full will of the Father in anything.*

Suddenly she saw her "daddy," bound with chains in an ancient arena. But then the arena disappeared. It became a medical laboratory, as only happens in dreams. Then the lab transformed into a church sanctuary with pews filled with mounds of envelopes and stacks of checks and cash. Evan and Pauline sat in the pews among the piled millions. And suddenly Ruth, their mother, sat with them! Television cameras, the only other viewers in the hall, aimed their electronic eyes mutely at the pulpit. As they all watched, the pulpit became a sacrificial altar, and her father suddenly lay upon it, bound again with chains. A giant door opened into blackness behind the dais. Something horrible was coming! A creature—

Everything changed to a hospital scene. Dr. Grace now reached forward to lay his hand on the head of his dying wife as she lay comatose on a hospital bed, cancer consuming her vibrant beauty. His hands began to tremble violently and paused short of her forehead, unable to move. "She's gone," he whispered as if in shock. And then, not his wife—his hand descended upon the head of an emaciated villager, held erect before the preacher in a sea of black, upturned faces. A scene Pauline had witnessed hundreds of times in dozens of Third-World nations with her father. As he prepared to pray, a demonized witch doctor hissed and writhed on the ground beneath the crude wooden platform, his eyes blazing up at the preacher with carnivorous fury, daring him to pray the prayer of faith. Meanwhile, the sick man's empty eye sockets festered and spilled pus down his cheeks, as if screaming out to a modern medical mind—"We are impossible! Impossible! Legion! Legion! Legion!"—as the preacher's trembling hand came to rest on the man's head—could he believe for his sight?

The people had come in simple faith. Dr. Grace had no choice but to pray, even as his own faith melted. Pauline understood that behind her father's closed eyelids now, he saw the lifeless face of his own wife, her sparkling laughter forever silenced by the power of an evil malignancy. It mocked him. His prayer for the blind man choked to silence as between his tightly closed lids hot tears spilled the length of his face.

"Daddyyyy!" The cry ripped from Pauline's throat, and she awoke to find herself on her hands and knees beside the strange bed in the hotel—no longer addressing "Daddy" in her heart, but "Father" from her spirit. Out of her belly sobs arose and poured uninhibited from her mouth. "Abba! Abba! Abba!" She rolled to her back on the floor literally beside herself. She could not stop anymore than she could have wished to be born. Her body arched upward, not with pain but with a powerful contraction. She knew that she was giving birth to something in the Spirit. Something beyond her comprehension.

This is what Lydia felt, she realized. No fear invaded the experience. In her mind she knew only peace, light, and a sense of being connected to God Most High by an infinitely wise and Holy Spirit.

She became almost an observer of the event, watching the Spirit move her body at His will. Her mind filled with the perfect confidence that *nothing is impossible* to the Lord of the Universe. Healing, resurrection, virgin birth. She had recited the creeds all of her life, but had conceived God far too small in her mind! She had believed, but in this moment she knew beyond human knowledge. It became illuminated as a truth revealed. *He is omnipotent! He answers to no one! He is the Lawgiver! The Judge! On earth He is not willing that any should perish! But in the face of His great enemy he must sometimes endure the tragedies of time in order to purchase the victories of eternity. Grace, mercy, majesty belong to Him!* Her mind worshiped with complete abandon. The Hosts of Heaven sang along with her. She could hear them in her spirit, music more splendorous than any note sounded on earth!

As she held her stomach and rolled from side to side, unintelligible moans of prayer continued to flow from the center of her being, like a river.

Sudden reality! Danna's concerned face bent above her in the dim light. She had heard the sounds of anguish from her room and had run to Pauline's aid.

"It's alright, Danna. I'm alright, honey. Don't be afraid." She thought, *How crazy I must look, moaning here on the floor. She thinks I'm sick.*

She reached up and took the nurse's hand, wanting to laugh. How could she tell her that this was not agony she saw? That she was perfectly alright? Not in pain, not insane. For the first time in her life she knew that nothing could be wrong because God ruled the universe from His crystal throne. Alpha, Omega.

With Danna's help, she managed to pull her trembling limbs back onto the bed, but the contractions continued to pour through her body, exhilarating her with their power. Looking upward, she sensed a host of witnesses like a cloud above the bed. She couldn't see them, but she knew their presence was as real as the walls and ceiling of the room. They were *there!* Watching. With her somehow. She could feel countless sets of loving eyes beholding her strange labor with enthusiasm and perfect understanding from beyond the veil of life. Like a cheering section. Some of them had waited for centuries for this time of revelation. *They have purchased this moment*, she thought. *Yes, they perfectly understand. But wait! What does that mean, Lord? They purchased? Who are they?*

The answer came clearly . . . devastatingly . . .

They are more than two million: from Ephesus, Smyrna, Pergamum, Thyatira, Sardis, Philadelphia, Laodicea, Antioch, Tarsus, Lystra, Iconium, Colosse, Hierapolis, Derbe— Then came names Pauline had only recently heard, or read on maps of Eastern Turkey. —*Kars, Ani, Erzurum, Ercis, Van, Silvan, Bitlis, Siirt, Mus . . .*

"This is a land of martyrs," she sobbed with sudden understanding. She clung to the nurse as another contraction arched her body. "Aaaah! I couldn't know these things. Do you understand? They are coming to me. This knowledge is not natural." Her voice thinned with weeping. "Not one dying martyr's cry went unheard, Danna. How do I know? How? I know *Him*. I *know* Him. Every martyr died for a purpose. Every defeat has become a victory on the other side. One day the whole earth will see it . . ." She began to sob uncontrollably again, gasping for air, not with sadness but with a high form of grief, something pleasing to the cloud of witnesses above. "The trees will clap their hands, the hills will sing—" she gasped. "Every knee will bow. They will all bow. No more faith then, no more faith. They will *know* Him! The Lamb slain from the foundation of the world."

Pauline squeezed Danna's hand so tightly, the nurse's fingers grew white at the tips. "Oh, if you could only feel what I feel," she sobbed. "Can you feel the cloud? Watching me?"

Danna nodded vigorously, tears streaming freely down her face as well. She felt something invisible and real in the room. No explanation necessary. What she saw in Pauline witnessed to her own heart. It had the ring of a greater reality. In spite of the powerful emotions, the Spirit dominated the room with peace, far beyond the ability of words to describe. She had felt a similar reality once at the beside of a dying old man who had told of seeing angels. He had died with a glow on his face in contrast to the cursing last words of so many bitter souls she had seen at life's end. Cursing even beneath their heavy blanket of sedatives.

Until this moment Pauline had *never* considered herself to possess the stuff of martyrs. She had shuddered at the description of John Hus raising his arms in the fire, crying, "He is faithful! He is faithful!" She had paled to read the last words of Stephen, "Lord, do not hold this sin against them!" as the cruel stones had struck him down. She had run desperately to save her own life just two weeks ago in Jerusalem, with no charity in her heart for the Palestinian youths and their rocks and slings. Now she understood.

The martyrs were not heroes. Like the account of Stephen in the Book of Acts—"being full of the Holy Spirit, he gazed intently into Heaven and saw the glory of God . . ." Now she understood seeing "the glory of God." Taken by the revelation of the Holy Spirit, the same Spirit that John the Baptist had seen descending upon Jesus without measure —with the Spirit's river of "living water" flowing from her belly, she too could sing in the fire, or as the lions tore her limb from limb. Sing! Not by might, not by power, but by *the Spirit she could sing!*

"I know how the martyrs died," she cried. "They were people just like us, Danna. There was no pain. They saw too much glory for pain. We could do it if He called us to. You and I. We could do it."

Danna looked stricken. She nodded in spite of herself, barely grasping the significance of these words, hardly conceiving the magnitude of the bloodbaths of history.

"It's OK. I'm OK, you know?" Pauline felt urged to reassure Danna.

The nurse nodded, wiping her eyes again and smiling.

Suddenly Pauline convulsed in the grip of a very old reality that only now became true for her. A passage of Scripture poured rapid-fire from her mouth—so rapidly she couldn't recall its source, nor could she remember memorizing it. She had only heard it. Her father had read it from a pulpit sometime in her past, yet now the words came forth verbatim, accompanied by sobs of pure emotion: "'Women received their dead raised to life again: and others were tortured, not accepting deliverance; that they might obtain a better resurrection: And others had trials of cruel mockings and scourgings, yea, moreover of bonds and imprisonment: They were stoned . . . they were sawn asunder . . . were tempted, were slain with the sword: they wandered about in sheepskins and goatskins; being destitute, afflicted, tormented; of whom the world was not worthy!'"

Pauline gripped her stomach, rolling from side to side as if mourning the passing of each priceless martyr. Yet on the other side of the veil of life, she became aware that each moan of grief became a shout of triumph to the God of Heaven and earth! How could she ever have guessed as much? "Eye hath not seen, ear hath not heard . . ."

Danna had taken a grip on Pauline's body to keep it from thrashing from the bed. Sob after sob continued to pour from her, unstoppable, unimaginable—short of the unction of the Spirit. "'They wandered . . .'" Pauline continued, catching visions of the nameless heroes of Heaven, "'in deserts . . . and in mountains . . . and in dens and caves of the earth . . .'" The bed shook beneath the quaking of her body. "'And these all, having obtained a good report through faith, received not the promise: God having provided some better thing for us, that they without us should not be made perfect.'" She panted from the exertion of this utterance.

"Danna," she said, pleading with her to understand, "our Lord has always been among the poor. Can you see Him? With His cross? A man of sorrows. Never the hero of nations or religions. All rituals have missed Him. He is the God of the heartbroken. He is the Lamb. In history His victories have seldom been recorded, considered unworthy of mention. That's why there is a new heaven and earth, a place to celebrate His victories. No earthly council ever served Him. His Kingdom has never been with the mighty. He remains among the nameless of earth and when He puts an end to time . . . the last shall be first!"

Looking toward the ceiling again she could feel the warmth of more than two million smiles beaming back at her. She smiled up through her tears at the nameless martyrs of Urartu now gathered in their glorified cloud. Her mind heard the music of their praises, understood the power of their witness which had humiliated entire armies of Hell in centuries past.

"Praise to God Most High," she whispered.

She continued in a subdued, happy and husky voice, coming to the end of her revelation. "'Wherefore seeing we also are compassed about with so great a cloud of witnesses, let us lay aside every weight, and the sin which doth so easily beset us, and let us run with patience the race that is set before us, looking unto Jesus the author and finisher of our faith; who for the joy that was set before him . . .'" Her eyes crossed involuntarily, and she had to rouse herself before she could continue. "'. . . endure—endured the cross . . . despising the shame'—my sweet Lord," she whispered. "He—'is set down . . .'" Her words began to slur. "'. . . at the right hand of the throne . . .'"

With that, the last contraction released Pauline's body, and she descended into a deep and quiet sleep. Danna remained, wiping her eyes, sniffling, holding Pauline's limp hand and crying softly in the dark for another hour. She would never be the same.

✤

Unaware of his sister's revelation, an hour later Evan lay awake, staring at diagonal streaks of moonlight crossing the floor and wall of his room. The cold influence of the moon painted the spartan interior of the hotel through vented window louvers above the bed. The window looked across a second-story breezeway at the wood and straw rooftops of shops and stone houses. Farther across the lake, the northern mountains were silhouetted against the stars.

The piled cotton bed sheets smelled of perfumed alkaline soap and the silky saline waters of Lake Van. The scent blended in a pleasant, exotic way, adding to the other foreign sensations in this mile-high city.

In the distance the sound of a dog fight erupted in the stillness. Shouted Turkish curses ended the match with one dog yelping in pain, no doubt pegged with a rock by a disturbed sleeper. As quiet returned to the streets, Evan became aware of just how primitive that silence was. It reigned supreme in this outpost of civilization. Neither the sound of an electric fan, nor air conditioner, television, radio, nor the drone of a plane in the sky, nor the prowling of an automobile disturbed the wee hours. Though he lay on the bed fully clothed, he felt as if he had become naked, stripped of his modern comfort zone as he waited for the signal of soldiers from Nimrut Dag.

A crossing shadow interrupted the pattern of light on the wall, and shortly thereafter a soft rap sounded at his door. He knew Canaan would knock boldly. Puzzled, he got up and moved silently to the door. "Who is there?"

"Danna."

He felt an old thrill at the sound of her voice. He opened the door and she stood there, her robe tightly wound around her body, her thick auburn hair wet from a shower. She wore no makeup.

"May I come in?" Her voice sounded husky from crying.

How often he had heard those very words from her during his Logos Mail years. How his ego had soared to be desired by this voluptuous and willful woman. But time had changed both of them. They had grown to understand that passion can never purchase what true love desires: true intimacy, self-giving, commitment. Their past lay between them like a deep and rocky gorge across which a small, swaying board now waited. They would have to help each other across. Very carefully.

"Come in," he said, stepping back.

He had read trouble in the sound of her voice. Yet, in their lust-filled past, any kind of trouble had been excuse enough to bring them together in the night. It had been part of the game. Part of the cruel deception of an affair. Substituting brief intensity for the complicated work of caring for real needs. Never leaving them more than empty.

"Have a seat?" He pulled a wooden chair near the window.

She shook her head no and leaned shakily against the wall.

He couldn't help but notice the prize she had become. Even more than when she had thrown herself at him at the age of twenty-two. He tore his mind away from an erotic memory.

"Can't sleep?" he asked.

"Pauline is sleeping like a baby, Evan."

This surprised him. "I didn't think anything could make her unwind."

"You just wouldn't believe what I've been through with her. I can't even begin to describe it." She sighed helplessly and walked to the window, staring out.

Evan watched as the light of the moon caressed her full lips and fell lightly across her shoulders.

"Your sister is special, Evan. Be careful with her."

He waited for a moment, wondering what she meant. "How should I be careful?"

"Listen to her."

"OK."

"No!" Danna suddenly spun around, and he saw a splash of tears fly from her face like diamonds in the moonlight. "I mean *listen* to her. Listen when you disagree. Do you hear me? *Especially* when you disagree."

He felt lost. "What are you saying?"

She made no reply. Her shoulders shook, and she cried silently into her hands.

Evan moved toward her in sympathy, not understanding what he saw. He reached out to touch the points of her shoulders, then moved his hands carefully forward until his arms enfolded her in a gentle embrace. She held her stance. He understood why she remained reluctant to receive his affection. The past could not be erased. Still he held her. After a moment, as she continued to cry softly, she took one hand from her face and placed it around his waist. Then the other. The two of them swayed together, holding each other on that shaky plank above passion's chasm. Their balance would have to be perfect.

Evan read the touch of her hands. They were full of appreciation. Full of relief, knowing that for once his arms around her were meant only for comfort. Nothing more.

After several minutes her crying subsided. She wiped her face against the terry cloth of her robe.

"Let me find a towel," he offered and hurried to the bathroom. Returning with the thin cotton cloth supplied by the Bes Kardes, he handed it to her. "Go ahead. I won't be needing it."

"Thank you, Evan," she said.

He knew that her thanks extended to much more than the towel.

She moved to the door and turned the knob.

Suddenly Evan felt the desire to say more. Much more. But in very few words.

She paused.

"Let me walk you to your room."

They proceeded from the door to the second-floor breezeway and walked side by side. He wanted, every step of the way, to place his arm around her shoulder. Or her waist. Was it presumption? No. More than that.

At the door to her room he turned in front of her, reaching a hand to her chin. He caressed it lightly, allowing his fingers to explore upward to the damp softness of her hair. He stroked the drying tresses backwards from her temple. *A prize, a priceless treasures*. His fingers said it all. In that moment he realized that he had never really known this wonderful woman. He bent forward and found her lips waiting. Full and tender. His kiss fell as soft as the moonlight, and in its gentleness he said everything that had been in his heart to say.

He turned for his room with a new kind of satisfaction. One that he would continue to crave. He had changed. Never again would he want anything from Danna that was not his to take.

As he passed Canaan's door he stopped, hearing a small electronic beep, followed by a few baritone words of Hebrew. Almost immediately the colonel's door opened.

"It is time," he said.

77

THE CASTLE OF HOSHAP
6:13 A.M.

I t had taken less than an hour to get into the air. Twenty minutes of that hour had been consumed by the *walk* to the airstrip. No predawn taxi service had been available in Van.

Rick and Canaan had obtained the keys to the helicopter the night before by paying the craft's owner, a Turk who ran a local sight-seeing service, two million *lira*. That amount equalled a month's profit for the happy man. With a deposited bond for the full price of the vehicle, he had further agreed to let Rick's party use the chopper for the next two days, saying nothing about a night-time takeoff.

Upon receiving word from the Israeli commando unit at Nimrut Dag, Canaan had suggested Rick stay in Van with the jet in case something went wrong on the trip. The colonel would try to obtain permission from High Command to return to Van with Pauline and Evan. Failing that, he would radio Rick to bring a four-wheel drive to take them out of the wilderness. Of course, if everything turned out to be friendly with Dunamis after the Uriel commandos had secured the cuneiform tablets, which seemed unlikely, they would be free to return with their father. Or whatever they wished.

Canaan piloted the helicopter, lifting off in the dark with Danna, Pauline and Evan. Holding a road map between his legs, he proceeded south through the rugged Hakkari Uplands, following the only known overland route to the pantheon.

The knot of anticipation had left Pauline's stomach. She felt absolutely refreshed and vigorous. No fear. Only an incredulous wonder at the magnitude of the journey she made. The others were making the same trip, but not with the same understanding. For the first time in her life her mind was free from self concern. After the illumination of her spirit that night, she had changed. Her concern for the life of her father had nothing to do with her own happiness anymore. She longed to see the will of the Father done. Whatever it turned out to be, like Job she would trust Him.

369

❖

An hour later, dawn broke as they ascended into the highest *vilayet* in Turkey, a mountain pass guarded by a huge medieval castle. The valley resembled a moonscape. The castle had been surrounded by an earthen stockade enclosing a thousand-acre compound. Its walls were serrated with cones, shaped like the mosque domes of the region. Each dome sat atop the wall, ten feet apart. The contrast between the *minaret* wall and the square-shouldered bulk of the European castle seemed purposeful. As if the Seljuk Turks had built the wall to remind the world that the Latin States of the Crusaders had indeed fallen to the "infidels."

The helicopter prattled along the old road at one hundred and twenty miles per hour, roaring over the heads of two loaded donkeys and a startled drover. Racing past the domes of the Turkish wall like pickets on a roadside fence, Canaan shouted over his shoulder above the noisy rotors, "Crusaders built the castle! It was the northernmost lookout for Christian Antioch and Edessa!"

As they swung to the west, following the Hoshap River toward its confluence with the Tigris, Canaan began receiving more data through the radio bug in his ear. He cupped his hand over the earpiece and listened intently. After a while he signaled Evan and Pauline to come nearer.

"Your father is in the cavern. He is comatose. Maintained on life support. You are going to have to find a way to get him free and take him out of there using the vehicles they left behind. I have been ordered to return with my unit."

"Why is he on life support?" Danna shouted.

Canaan shrugged. "They don't know."

Pauline had not understood this possibility from her study of the medical data. She huddled with Danna. "Why is he on life support?"

Danna shook her head, watching the passing countryside. "I don't know. If the drug has run its course he should be awake. I would be afraid to disconnect him without the guidance of a doctor."

Pauline noticed Canaan signaling Evan to come nearer for a confidential message.

"No secrets!" she shouted above the roar of the engine, and scrambled close to hear. "No secrets," she repeated, looking Canaan in the eye. "You can tell me everything."

Canaan pretended to check his instruments for a while, then cleared his throat before speaking. "There are five dead doctors in that cave. Apparently Neva got word to them that their secret was out, and they committed suicide. Six of the seven Apostates are now accounted for, including Neva. Who is the seventh one—the Patriarch?" He hesitated. "Your father is the only one still alive in the cave." He watched her face for reaction, then went on, "Commagene has cleared out. Probably on his way to Mannheim. Maybe he's the Patriarch. The icon has been removed." With a grimace he added, "So have 'The Songs of Jubal' tablets. The Nephilim are staying ahead of Uriel."

"So Neva warned them," Evan mused. "Which way did Commagene go to get out of here?"

Canaan shrugged. "Like his uncle Otto, he is one slippery devil."

78

NIMRUT DAG
Pantheon
7:21 A.M.

The ground-hugging helicopter climbed out of the breaks of the Euphrates River from the south and followed a scant four-wheel drive trail toward the 7,000-foot summit of Nimrut Dag. Its pyramidal cone came suddenly into view.

"The pictures didn't do it justice," Evan declared with awe.

The peak of the tumulus sat at the top of a high valley, dominating the landscape for fifty miles around. For the first time they could see the massive duplicated thrones of the gods on both the east and west terraces of the High Place. From this vantage point, Ararat's snows glowed like a cloud on the northern horizon.

"If you were a prophet of Israel and you had come on this sight in the sixth or seventh century B.C., what would you call it?" Evan shouted above the noise of the rotors.

Canaan now hovered the aircraft, studying a topographical

map of the mountain in his lap. He looked up at the mountain again.

"The Sides of the North?" Evan prompted.

Canaan nodded and smiled accommodatingly, more immediate navigational thoughts on his mind. "Look there." He pointed to a limestone spur that descended exactly between the eastern and western terraces. "The cavern must be in there. What does the map say?"

Evan bent forward to read the finely printed notation. "'Ice caves.'"

Canaan accelerated. "Let's go above it for a look. We'll have to land on one of the terraces."

The helicopter's engines began to complain in the thin atmosphere as it shuddered and began its climb, slowly gaining elevation like a rusty elevator.

"There . . . look!" Evan pointed to a desert camouflage canopy concealing several diesel generators near a rocky prominence. "Electrical power units."

Canaan nodded and continued to climb. Now they drew even to the great High Altars of the western terrace. Among the heads of the giant demigods sat three assault helicopters, painted the camouflage colors of the desert.

"Israeli?" Evan inquired.

Again Canaan nodded. "See the Matra pods?"

"Under the sides there?"

"Yes. Those are Matra Mistral air-to-air rockets." He smiled proudly. "They came prepared to knock interference out of the sky if necessary."

He continued to climb the sight-seeing craft above the mountaintop, then maneuvered it forward to hover over the military helicopters, looking for a landing-place.

As he did, Evan examined a topographical diagram from his father's scrapbook. "Pauline, Danna, look at this," he said as he placed the map before them in line with the scene below. "The terrace held the High Altars, see? Can you imagine the sacrifices that took place up here?"

Pauline could imagine. A great battle still raged over this ground. The Urartians had spilled the blood of bulls and virgins, seeking to purchase the Sides of the North, but they could never have it. The blood of the martyrs cried out from the surrounding valleys, *Never!* She felt a singular urge to extract her father from this place and flee.

Pointing to each of the giant thrones, first on the map, then on the ground, Evan began to name the pantheon of Nimrut Dag as they descended upon it. "On the right flank, a guardian eagle and a lion. Next to them, Herakles-Artagnes-Ares. Then the throne of Antiochus I. Next to him, his great-grandson Antiochus IV—the largest statue on the mountain is his, Zeus-Oromasdes the awe-some-Jupiter. Epiphany. Better known as Baal."

"Cancer," Pauline finished.

"That's the one. The sun god of several religions. Then the odd god there, Fortune of Commagene, placed by Antiochus I after taking over the High Place from the Urartians. Commagene's idol. Then comes Apollon-Mithras-Helios-Hermes. And on the far end you have another eagle and lion and several *stellae* with religious and historical inscriptions."

The helicopter settled to the ground, scattering dust over the site. Canaan immediately cut the engines. Two armed commandos peeked from behind the ruined thrones of Jupiter and Commagene respectively, guarding the Israeli craft, each leveling an Uzi, steadying his aim against the ancient stone rests. Behind them the hand-carried pyramid of the tumulus climbed into a clean blue sky.

The four passengers climbed from the craft and hurried across the terrace, weaving between the heads of the giants. The nearly deafening noise of the idling twin turboshaft engines on each of the assault Israeli helicopters made the journey through the idols seemed even more frightening. The gods stared fiercely at them as they passed through the wind-whipped dust.

A third commando appeared from below the crest of the hill and hurried toward the group. He stopped, motioning them to join him. He also waved off the guards on the thrones above. They retracted their weapons and commenced scanning the surrounding horizon with binoculars.

As the group passed the unique head of Fortune of Commagene, Evan shouted, "Notice the garland. Greek influence, more civilized. That's Commagene. All the others wear those crude Urartian war helmets." Next they passed the largest head. A fierce, bearded specimen. "Zeus. Antiochus IV," Evan shouted as they passed.

Then he shut up, having grown quickly winded in the altitude. They all panted to keep up with Canaan and his companion. The women, wearing trail boots and walking shorts, struggled to stay close to Evan, watching how he negotiated his way through the unstable rocks around the tumulus. They tried to step in his steps as he followed Canaan.

Pauline's mind raced. How would her father appear? Would he be the same? She hadn't laid eyes on him since he had walked away from her in that awful Palestinian neighborhood. It seemed so long ago. Even then the gods of Nimrut Dag had been waging war, sending that stone-throwing mob to kill her in the Derekh Ha-Shiloah. They would have succeeded except for Canaan. Except for God. She felt a bit like the hound that had finally hunted down its quarry only to find it had cornered a bear too big to handle. *The battle is the Lord's*, she quoted to her mounting fear, and kept moving ahead.

They followed a faint trail toward the diesel generators below the terrace, which could be heard humming ahead of them. In five minutes they were near enough to see the mouth of a mine shaft beneath the canopy. Two land rovers sat near the entrance, their noses pointed down the four-wheel drive trail toward the distant river.

Approaching the cave, Colonel Canaan came back to escort Pauline. "It is a big operation in there," he said. "They have enlarged the original ice cave to haul in equipment. Very sophisticated."

As they passed the land rovers the colonel opened the driver's side door to the nearest vehicle. Reaching inside he pulled up two loose wires hanging beneath the dash. "This is how you will leave," he said. "Twist these together and then jump-start the vehicle by letting it roll down the hill in second gear. Pop the clutch. Know how it is done?"

"Got it," Evan said, looking at Pauline and Danna.

"No problem," Danna replied.

"How about you?" he asked, looking at Pauline.

"Maybe."

"Let Danna drive," he suggested as they turned into the cave.

Canaan moved quickly through the entrance of the shaft, stepping over an assembly of large cables which snaked from the generators into its darkened depths. "I do not believe Commagene had government clearance for all of this or he would have stayed around and used the Turkish army to keep us away. He probably had worked out an under-the-table trade agreement to keep their heads turned."

They moved past the parked land rovers and followed a string of electrical lights down a long sloping corridor that had been blasted from the mountainside to enlarge the original entrance. The sounds of the generators grew dim behind them. Limestone formations showed the marks of jackhammers and explosives. Temporary braces reinforced the ceiling in recently exposed sections of the cave.

"They probably told them this was an archaeological dig or something," Evan said, making small talk. Anything to hear the sounds of sanity. Each of them knew they were about to enter the inner sanctum of the original Urartians. The natives of Ararat, , the children of Nimrod, builders of Babel, keepers of the Ancient Doors, and now—the modern version of Dunamis. Evan knew from Dr. Grace's notebook that this cave had begun in baths of blood, the ancient conjuring rituals, spawning the hybrid mystery religions of the world. Disguising itself in the Christian age through the Society of Apostates, it had seduced the power structure of the church itself, perpetuating lying signs and wonders through *The Seven Sleepers of Antioch* and countless other deceptions. It had blossomed into vivid fruition from the darkened minds of perverted Popes and tyrants, finding perhaps its most fertile soil in the medical experimentation of Nazi Germany. And now, Grace Ministries too?

Canaan stopped suddenly, leaning toward the wall. The barrel of his Uzi pointed to a veritable logjam of petrified trees embedded in a deposit of sandstone. They looked at one another in wonder.

Evan quipped, "Say hello to the antediluvian world."

They moved deeper, sensing a slight breeze on their faces. The air felt surprisingly comfortable, nearly 70 degrees or so. Rounding a final corner they came suddenly upon a huge room. Budding stalagmites had been cleared from a large central area of the floor. It had been swept and polished until it bore the sheen of marble. Embedded at regular intervals in the floor were the remains of petrified trees. Each trunk had fallen in an expanding outward radius from an invisible point of origin behind the back wall of the cave. A darkly stained channel had been cut in the floor from the wall to a deep recess beyond the reach of the electrical lights.

Between the tree trunks, near the rear wall of the cave, seven medical tables were arranged, each bed surrounded by a full complement of heart and brain wave monitors, lung and heart machines. Five of the seven stations were occupied by sheet-covered bodies attached to IV lines. Their monitors remained attached as well, registering flat signals. These evidently were the suicidal doctors of Dunamis. Society initiates. Nearer to the group, a single table held Dr. Grace's body. His were the only monitors showing the activity of life, the only body employing the medically heroic breathing apparatus.

Seeing the form of her father, Pauline broke from the group and ran forward. Suddenly her heart raced again. In spite of the night before, fear returned in force. She no longer knew anything for sure. *Why does revelation forsake me now?* she screamed inside. Once again she groped for hope and faith.

Evan and Danna quickly followed her. Arriving at the table, they found Pauline mutely stroking her father's unshaven face. He looked more gaunt than when she had seen him last. An IV had been attached to his right arm and the tube of a lung machine inserted into his mouth. This had been sealed with scotch tape across his nose. The pumping interval of the breathing machine continued with inhuman regularity. To all appearances her father had become a vegetable, except for the activity of his heart and brain wave monitor, which Pauline could not properly interpret.

"It's OK, Daddy," Pauline said into his ear. "We're here with you now. We're with you, Daddy."

Canaan nudged Evan's shoulder and signaled him forward. He accompanied the colonel to the other beds. The second commando who had led them inside pulled down the first sheet covering the nearest corpse. "Dr. Karl Lester," Canaan said. Replacing the sheet he moved toward the next body.

"He was known to the Uriel Mission," Canaan explained to Evan. "A cancer specialist. One of the Society initiates."

The commando pulled down the next sheet. "Kassabian. No surprise. He's a Russian Armenian psychiatrist," Canaan commented, "a KGB operative, Society initiate. We thought he might be the Patriarch because he was Armenian, but now we know better. The Patriarch must stay alive to initiate seven more Apostates."

The next table held a woman's body. He peered at her waxen face. "Osis. Anesthesiologist. She brewed up the Hypnos-3 formula."

Next. "Sutphen. South African surgeon. Mastermind of the

NDE simulator using advance life support and resuscitation methods."

They came to the final bed. "Santesteban. Viral disease specialist." Canaan turned to Evan. "What we have here are five of the seven. All dead by suicide." Canaan looked at his watch and pointed to his earpiece. "I don't have much time, so listen carefully. Neva told us under sodium amytal that the Apostates would commit suicide when they were discovered. All of them except one."

Evan's mind raced. *Five dead, plus Neva makes six. Who is number seven? Who is still alive?* He turned to look at his father. He saw Pauline kneeling beside the old man, stroking his face. Danna knelt beside her. *Could it be him?* The very thought of it seemed to threaten every happiness he might ever know. His own father the Patriarch of Apostates?

"The one who must stay alive," Canaan continued.

Evan looked back at him grimly.

Canaan returned the gaze. "Since joining Uriel seven years ago, we have assumed your father was an initiate. That is why I was assigned to provide his guard in Israel."

"And now? Do you think he's the Patriarch?"

"And now . . ." Canaan swallowed with difficulty. "I think the Patriarch is Maximilian Commagene. Or perhaps Otto, if he is still alive somewhere." He bent suddenly, listening to his earpiece, nodding at instructions from the command helicopters on the terrace above, which were unintelligible to Evan. Looking at Pauline again, Canaan added, "Maybe I do not see as clearly as I once did. I pray that the Patriarch is not her daddy."

The colonel looked at his fellow commando and nodded toward the door. He walked quickly to where Pauline knelt. Shifting his gun, he knelt beside her.

She only had a vague awareness of him. She continued to quote Scripture steadily into Dr. Grace's ear. "'. . . yea, though I walk through the valley of the shadow of death I will fear no evil, for thou art with me . . . thou preparest a table before me . . . in the presence of mine enemies—'" As she continued, her eyes roamed to the other seven tables and the doctors of Dunamis lying there. "'. . . I will fear no evil . . .'"

Canaan spoke gently, with great care. "Pauline."

She didn't seem to hear.

"Pauline, I *have* to go. Rick will have to bring a doctor to help you get your father out. Do you understand? I have done all I can do for now. I—"

She seemed lost to him, quoting again, "'. . . though I walk through the valley of the shadow of death . . . I will fear no evil . . .' Daddy? Daddy?" She patiently tried to reach him with her words, even as she tried to reassure her own heart. "Can you hear me, Daddy? 'Fear no evil.'"

Canaan stood abruptly, torn between his military duty and his desire to help this captivating woman who loved her father as no one he had ever seen. He turned and ran toward the entrance of the cave. His companion had already disappeared up the sloping entryway.

Evan caught Danna's eye. "I'd better see that Rick orders a doctor for us here. I'll be right back."

He ran to catch up with Canaan.

79

PANTHEON
7:38 A.M.

As Evan emerged from the mouth of the cave he could hear the Super Frelon helicopters roaring from the terrace one hundred yards above the cave. Dust billowed from the site. Canaan had already made it halfway there and continued running along the old processional trail.

Evan still felt surprise that the colonel had not reassured him that he would inform Rick Gresham of their situation. He feared that the commando leader had been put off by Pauline's state of mind and had forgotten it in his own emotional turmoil. Evan remained sure that the competent colonel would remember to call Rick once in the air, but he couldn't afford to make that assumption with so much at stake. So he ran hard to catch him.

Several other commandos emerged from hiding around the pantheon as Canaan neared it ahead of Evan. They fell in with the colonel, running toward the waiting assault helicopters on the terrace.

Canaan paused at the rim, looking back, seeing Evan struggling up the rocky slope behind him. He motioned his companions into the churning machines and waited.

When he arrived, Evan had to shout between gasps for air. "Don't forget—to tell Rick—we need a doctor here!"

Canaan smiled, surprised at his own oversight. "Of course." He slapped a hand to Evan's shoulder and spoke with sudden depth of feeling. "Evan, you are *oher Yihsrael*. A true friend of the Jewish people." Then he sobered. "Take good care of your sister, will you?"

Evan saluted and smiled. He felt a bond between them. He felt that perhaps they were brothers of the faith of Abraham, whether their religions acknowledged it or not.

Canaan turned and sprinted for the open door of the nearest helicopter. The craft already held in a low hover, and he dove headfirst, four feet above ground, landing neatly inside. The three churning machines slipped easily off the mountain terrace, skimming the contour of the slope to reduce their radar profile. Their twin turboshaft engines spewed fire as they hurled themselves suddenly downward with the pull of gravity to a near maximum speed of 200 miles per hour.

Alone in the settling dust, Evan felt a hollow vulnerability without the soldiers. What if the Dunamis crew returned? His eyes wandered over the silent idols, half-expecting one of them to come to life, like a Hollywood special effect, and chase him from the mountain. Looking into the valley again, he was amazed to notice how quickly the engine noise of the helicopters faded in the desert air. Their rotor blades caught his eye, flashing like the wings of giant dragonflies, winging to the distant Euphrates.

Beneath a growing anxiety at the back of his neck, he felt compelled to pull his father's charm cross from inside his shirt. He held the necklace curiously in his palm, regarding it with new appreciation. It was his father's response device, yes, but it was much more than that. He belonged to the God of that cross. *He belonged!* None of the stone idols of Nimrut Dag laid a single legitimate claim to his life. He had been called to this site, unprepared and unworthy in himself to carry out a mission of spiritual importance. In that, he realized that his life was not his own. Had never been. Just as Lydia had told him.

80

CAVERN
7:41 A.M.

As Evan burst into the main room of the cavern, his mind did not fully register what he saw. His brain had been busy sorting the cards in his hand. What if Rick didn't show up with a doctor? Could he take Dr. Grace out of here himself? He had checked the fuel level on the land rovers at the entrance to the cave and had found one three-quarters full and the other half full. *Enough to return to Van? Or to the nearest hospital? Or fuel source? Which is nearer in this primitive land?* He had no idea.

He saw Pauline sitting on the sixth of the seven tables behind Dr. Grace. Denim jacket half removed, right arm exposed. Danna stood beside her, focusing her eyes intently, inserting a catheter into her vein. Unbelievably his sister was preparing to enter the Near Death zone in pursuit of her father.

Still halfway across the room he exploded, "No! What is this?"

Danna whirled around to face him. "This is what she wants," she insisted.

"This is just what I was afraid of!" Evan shouted, running to the bedside, frustrated and overwrought at her ignorant desires. Evidently Pauline had pulled Danna into her plan. "Haven't you seen that this whole thing is crazy?"

"I'm not afraid, Evan," Pauline said. "I want to go after him."

"It's not for you to do! I told you to keep your wits about you here. We don't need this. We need a doctor."

"Call a doctor. That's for *you* to do," she returned steadily. "This is for me to do."

Her decision had been coming to this from the beginning. She realized it now. The search for her father had also become a search for her Heavenly Father. What would He allow? What would He forbid? Had her own father committed a deed worthy of death by entering the netherworld, or whatever it turned out to be? So had King David, she reminded herself. He had committed murder and adultery, both worthy of death. She would throw herself on the

380

mercy of God as David had done. She would do it on behalf of her father.

Her own will had become locked on this unconscious goal like a heat-seeking missile. It had pushed her forward against all other thoughts. Now that goal emerged into her conscious mind, and she agreed openly with it. Willfully. She wanted to know that if she threw herself from the mountain, if she fell into Hell itself, would He be there for her? *Who is God? What kind of Father is He?* This had become her private quest.

Looking at Evan again, she explained herself in words she thought he might understand. "If this is the last chance I ever have to see Daddy, and if I can help him, I don't want to live with the regrets of not going." She nodded to Danna to start the drip.

"I won't let you do this!" Evan leaped for the IV bag and yanked it from its elevated stand.

The catheter had already been attached to Pauline's arm, and Danna grabbed it protectively. "You can rip out her vein!" she screamed, watching his eyes. "Evan, listen to your sister."

"This is where my listening ends," he said determinedly. "Someone should have stopped Dad before he went this far, and if it has to be me, then it will be me!"

Danna's eyes filled with disappointment. She desperately wanted Evan to learn to let go of those things he couldn't understand. Not only with his sister, but with any woman he might come to know.

A cackle erupted from a darkened recess of the cave. Beyond the blood channel in the floor, a damp, contemptuous voice draped itself across their ears. "Stop Christopher Columbus? Haa, ha, ha, ha, haaa! You would!"

"Neva," Evan whispered with instant recognition. His mind nearly froze with fear. "We're in deep trouble here. Deep trouble."

Pauline sensed death a breath away for them all. She was ready. She resigned herself to it immediately. *OK then. It is time.* "Do it," she whispered between clenched teeth to Danna. "Do it now!"

Danna tried to quietly retrieve the IV bag from Evan's grip, but he held to it firmly and would not let go. He had heard Pauline's whispered insanity.

In the meantime Neva stepped from the shadows holding a pistol leveled at Evan. "I think it's a good idea, scientifically speaking," she said. "Let Pauline go see her daddy."

"You're all completely mad," Evan breathed.

Neva's eyes bulged, and her mouth twisted downward. "Maybe you misunderstood me!" She raised the pistol, a 9 mm Luger, aiming it between his eyes. "I said I think it's a good idea."

Evan felt faint. Powerless. "Pauline, I'll stop her. She can't shoot us all."

"Oh, but I can." Neva cocked the hammer.

Danna tugged the IV bag from his reluctant grasp. "Buy time, *stall* her," she whispered.

"Raise your hands," Neva ordered, looking at Evan. She walked forward to the last vacant bed, checking its apparatus in preparation for her own suicide. "Oh, I am looking forward to this," she said, patting the padded mattress. She pointed the gun at Evan suddenly again, with a swift change of personality. "Back off! Over there by your father. Now go!"

Evan raised his hands and backed up until he could feel his father's bed against his backside.

"Do it! Turn on the drip," Neva hissed at Danna. "You little spy. Turn it on, that's right. You know how it's done. Oh, I get to kill you too." She chuckled derisively. "That's too sweet. Ha, haaaa."

"Lay down, honey," Danna warned Pauline as she hung the bag on the rack. "This is going to hit you fast."

"It's OK," Pauline said smiling at her. "I'm supposed to go this way." With that she lay down, feeling the same peace she had felt as she went to sleep in the Bes Kardes the night before.

Neva began to chuckle as she watched Danna release the Hypnos-3 into the solution. "We're all going to be together soon," the medical director purred. "Very soon." She wagged the gun at Danna. "Now get over there with him!"

Pauline watched Danna walk over to Evan. With her eyes she loved them both. More dear to her in that moment than they had ever been in her life. Death and the presence of evil only magnified the beauty and love in her heart. It couldn't touch her. "Evan, Danna," she said, and her words began to slur, "I love . . . you . . . I . . ." Her physical eyes stared at nothing. Nevertheless, she continued to watch them lovingly as she began to rise . . .

. . . *rise* . . .

. . . *from her body toward the ceiling of the cave.*

"What kind of body or being is this?" She couldn't tell. Her gaze turned upward, and the ceiling of the cave became exceedingly clear. Every crevice, each texture of limestone, crystallized silica and rock

grew vivid. Her mind read their geologic histories in a moment of revelation. She instantly knew that the earth was young. How so? It was part of a universe that had suffered more God-ordained catastrophe than any scientific method could register or comprehend. The epochs had been spoken words from the imagination of the Creator. And His imagination was vivid! Beyond her wildest dreams!

Turning in midair she found herself gazing down upon her own body, lying very still on the table. Beyond it, she saw Neva Sylvan bending at the corner of her father's bed, feverishly binding Evan's arms behind him with industrial tape. The tape became a chain. It became magnified in her vision until she saw each microscopic fiber of reinforcement within its adhesive design, and knew that her brother was being bound for death. Neva had become a doctor in a death camp. Working as others had worked—Otto Commagene, Dr. Mengele, Hitler and his cohorts. Neva had placed Evan with his back to one of the table legs, his own legs extended straight out before him on the floor. Danna waited for death similarly against the opposite side of the table.

"Save them, Father," Pauline prayed. Not a wishful prayer. Nor uncertain. From this side of the veil of life, the prayer was answered even as she thought it. "They are saved because I asked. Nothing is ever lost to my Father. Nothing!"

Had she used the human brain she had left on the table below, she would have marveled at her own faith in this prayer. However, in this state of being she had naturally prayed "believing," as she had never believed on earth. "When you pray, believe," Christ had said, "and you shall have what you ask." This faith had been the object of her father's lifelong healing ministry. Here it sprang naturally from her mind. "I ask, He does it," she thought. "It's just that simple."

In another second she would have used her newfound faith to cast the evil High Place of Nimrut Dag into the sea. But not having charge of her own being, she heard instead the cloud of witnesses in song. Just as she had heard them in her room in the hotel. Beautiful! Beyond her ability to resist. She felt as if she belonged to the sound of it. Her face radiated rapture.

And then suddenly a Tree stood where the back wall of the cavern had been. Gnarled and ugly, standing in petrified defiance, reaching toward the sky above the cavern. A hole yawned in the center of the Tree, and she followed the music through its doorway into an infinitely long tunnel. Instantly she found herself moving impossibly fast . . .

81

THE SIDES OF THE NORTH

. . . she emerged from the hollow of the tree onto a parched, surrealistic plain surrounded by distant cliffs. She flew above the prone trunks of a petrified forest, lying parallel like the trees in the cave below. "How can this be? I am flying, yet I have a body as light as mist." She recalled her father's words: "There is a physical body . . . there is a spiritual body." The feeling of the spiritual body exhilarated her. So alive, so free!

And yet not free, because, beyond her own control, her body flew toward a dark blotch on the horizon. As she drew near she saw that it was a castle-like structure. She recognized it as a ruined stadium, like the one in Lydia's dream. Except this one existed within the parched landscape, not in the beautiful place Lydia had described. She wanted to stop and inspect the dead vines which clung to the ancient walls, but no. By the mysterious force that propelled her, she flew straight through its walls, just as Lydia had flown.

Inside she was deposited, not in midair above the pole, but on her own two feet. Swish! She could move herself on feet as light as a feather. "What a feeling of freedom!"

But a blast of agitated air instantly assaulted her wisplike body. In unthinking terror, closing her eyes, she whirled and threw herself against the wall like a gust of wind. She plunged again and again against its cold unyielding stone, unable to pass through. "Solid?" How then had she passed through it to come inside? And why now did she suddenly find herself in a quasi-corporeal form? Half-human, confined to this prison—yet half-spirit, able to move so lightly within it. Oh, to have no body at all, but only spirit! She would fly away from this awful, suffocating place.

The agitated air in the arena threatened her ability to concentrate. It disintegrated each thought into a thousand fragments, none of which she could stop to examine. Racing, racing thoughts flew from her. The air pressed against her skin incessantly, crawling, irritating, stifling. Lydia had not mentioned this. It vibrated before her face like a thick cloud of mosquitos. She brushed and slapped at her cheeks, but her face was not the problem. The air in the arena itself

384

actually hummed, as if charged for an approaching bolt of lightning. The sound of the humming, or whispering, seemed to emanate from a pulsating caldron. Like the drone of a million lamentations, the endless festinations of the damned, the mindless babble of The Pit. Never satisfied. It persisted like the compulsive sexuality of an automaton, grinding on and on without the slightest possibility of pleasure. It was the sound of weeping, of wailing, of gnashing teeth. Yet this misery lusted for company. It reached out to engulf her in an embrace of eternal death. By intuition she understood that it lusted to consume anything that had once been called "good" in creation. Like the waters of a flood, it ran mindlessly to any low place in the cause of evil. Its thoughts were only evil. Continuously. "You are mine, you are mine, you are mine, you are mine, you are mine," it rasped in her ear. "Liar!" she thought. "Liar!" Accuser was its name. Opposing its purpose. It had come against her here, which should have assured her that she belonged to the side of right in the conflict, but she lacked that perception. The atmosphere crushed, overwhelmed, pressed her mercilessly. It was the "anti"—the very "Anti-" of Antiochus—Anti-Christ! And suddenly she remembered why she had come here—her father was in this place.

She turned back to face the arena, fighting the suffocating air. Immediately she quailed. A huge looming Nephil panted his horrid breath deliberately over her body. His breath had produced the pulsating atmosphere. His canine mouth twisted now in the permanent grimace of laughter. His eyes were bright and purposeful, dancing with glee as he watched her terror. He had been watching all along, about twenty paces distant, tethered to the pole in the center of the arena. Just as Lydia had described!

"What's my name?" he asked, hissing hotly afterward, "Ha, ha, ha, ha, ha, haaa!"

Now that he had her full attention, he flexed his ten- or twelve-foot bulk upward, crowing like a proud rooster. His huge clawed hands, feet and fangs were his prized attributes, and he knew it. He roared and displayed them with a flourish, rattling them through the air like Saracen blades. The vestiges of his bat-like wings beat the air vigorously, ridiculously, uselessly. The Nephil's pleasure would never be the ecstasy of flight, but ripping, tearing, any manner of devouring. He sported a buck-skinned coat with stiff, pig-like bristles which ran between his pointed ears, down his backside to the broomed end of his tail.

He stopped crowing abruptly, and his bold gaze traveled up and down the length of her body with vile admiration. He appeared aroused, like a lecherous executioner, knowing he had time to torture his kill. Shrugging powerful shoulders, he leered at her, rubbing one clawed hand over the other with anticipation.

Lydia's descriptions had not prepared Pauline for the terrible visage of this demon. The faith she had felt as she rose from her body in the cavern melted away. Only desperation remained. Desperation that grew and grew until suddenly it burst from her lungs in an explosion. "Daddy!" she screamed insistently. "Where are you, Daaaaddyyyy?"

The Nephil yodeled with her, "Daddy! Daddyyyyy"—drowning the sound of her cries, filling the arena with the echoes of his own distorted mockery.

Horrified, she knew that no one had heard her cry. No one who cared. Not even the few strangers she now noticed scattered among the stone bleachers. They were doctors, dressed in lab clothes and surgical "scrubs." Strange. "The dead doctors from the cave below?" she wondered. "Of course!"

The Nephil began to jump up and down like an oversized child, shaking the chains of his tether against the pole. The weight of his pounding feet shook the colosseum, dislodging several loose stones from the highest balconies. They bounded downward through the stands, causing the doctors to scramble for cover. Still, the Nephil kept its attention on Pauline, drooling copiously at the chaos he had been able to generate in her heart.

Despair came down on her like a blanket, and with it came the knowledge that she had transgressed God's order. She had gone too far, following her father to this place between Heaven and Hell where no human spirit rightly belonged. No revelation existed here, no comfort, no reassurance from the Holy Spirit. No conviction, no invitation to repent. Even the faith she had known wilted and died. All was relentlessly controlled, and she seemed only a pawn, no longer human. Certainly not divine.

But even as this curtain of hopelessness enfolded her, a huge hand came to rest on her shoulder. She screamed and whirled, unable to imagine the next horror she must face. A warrior-angel stood by her with a sheathed broadsword, and she felt instantly as if her whole being were a tiny feather about to be consumed in a holy, purifying fire. There would be nothing left of Pauline. Her life had been called from the void of nothing, and to nothing she would *return in this fire. God is a consuming fire, she knew in that instant, more to be feared than any other.*

"Do not be afraid," the angel said.

"At least there is mercy here," she thought as her panic began to subside. "God has shown me mercy."

The angel's voice thundered like a waterfall. Not loudly, but musically. The utterance sounded multilayered, as if he spoke in several languages at once. Or more precisely, to several realities at once. His kind but wearied eyes told her that he had come from afar, and that he had come as a friend.

"Do not be afraid," he repeated.

She recognized this greeting from Scripture and took comfort in its familiarity. It had always been the words of angels to the prophets of Israel who fell prostrate before their heavenly messengers. "Fear not." Forgetting fear for the moment, she thrilled to the majesty of the messenger. "His are the largest, most beautiful eyes I have ever seen," she thought.

"I have been opposed as have you," the angel explained simply, then looked away, squinting carefully in the direction of the Nephil.

No longer afraid, she felt over-awed. She wanted to laugh out loud with relief. "Now here is help," she thought. "He is magnificent. Seven or eight feet tall, I'd guess. Marvelously muscled." A crown of fine gold chain mail draped his brow beneath thick black hair. The locks were highlighted with rich auburn streaks and held in place with a knot of blood-red fabric at the back of his neck. He wore a tunic of fine linen. Exotic threads of silver held the seams together, and an armored plate of gold, like a brilliant sunburst, adorned his chest.

"I am Uriel," he said, still watching the Nephil. "I am sent from the Lord by the prayers of one who is well-known in the Presence." He turned and smiled as if she knew who he meant.

"That would be Lydia," she thought. Her heart pounded with renewed hope. This man was handsome beyond compare. She remained speechless. Her spiritual body felt much too human to remain steady under his gaze. "No wonder God keeps them invisible," she thought. He was the living reality behind every Prince Charming of every fairy tale ever told! She understood now—fairy tales had not sprung from empty imaginations, but from the memory of a time when these god-men walked the earth. "They would

have no trouble finding wives today," she marveled. *"Not now, not ever."*

"I am to take you across the arena," the angel said.

"Don't go. Please." Pauline found her voice. It sounded strangely muffled in this environment.

The angel pointed to a place beyond the Nephil. Her eyes followed the length of his massive arm to the tip of the finger. There on the opposite side of the arena, the figure of a man lay chained on an elevated slab of stone. Pauline could barely make out a shock of white hair and a clerical collar, but that was enough. *"Daddy,"* she breathed.

"I am to take you to him," the angel said. He unsheathed his blade and grasped it in both hands with surety. She could see that he needed no practice using it. The blade sang with the slightest movement through the heavy air in the arena. The shining metal sang with the strength of a million voices, instantly plucking a chord of recognition in Pauline's heart. She knew that sound! The song of the blade cut through the atmosphere laden with the Nephil's foul breath and stilled it instantly, perfectly.

She laughed suddenly like a delighted schoolgirl, clapping hands to her cheeks. Not only because of the power of the sword to bring instant peace, but even more, because the song of Uriel's sword was the song of the cloud of witnesses she had heard the night before. One and the same! She laughed again, wanting to cry at the beauty of this idea—the songs of martyrs empowered the weapons of angels! Only God could be so creative! *"He is an artist,"* she blurted. *"He does everything so well!"*

The angel's eyes sparkled at her knowingly, losing their tiredness for a moment. He threw his head back and laughed along with her. The sound he made seemed like a thunderclap of multilayered joy. It fluttered across the arena, causing the Nephil to cower, almost to shrink before their eyes. Uriel watched Pauline and, for the sport of it, flailed the air with his sword, releasing the song of the martyrs again and again like a symphony of glory. Pauline became nearly hysterical, falling against the wall with elation, tears of joy streaming from her eyes. It was a moment that would never have entered her human heart. A moment beyond imagining. Laughing with an angel! In praise to God Most High!

Modestly Uriel nodded and stilled his sword. Weariness crept again into his expression. *"It is not yet the time for this,"* he said soberly.

Pauline contained her laughter and nodded in quick agreement. She didn't want to do anything but obey. Still, it had been such a moment to share. They would relive it again after her death, she thought. She would find Uriel and remind him of it. So she believed. Surely she would see him again.

"You must cross now," he said. "I will give the Nephil more than he can handle. I will drive him that way." Uriel motioned toward her left. "You will run straight to your father."

"Yes," she replied. "That is what I will do." She felt an instant sadness at the thought of running away, increasing any distance at all between herself and the angel. If there were any other way—

"Wait." He held up his hand. Backing several steps into the arena, he turned around with a flourish. Cupping a hand to his mouth he shouted, "Mithrael! Son of God!"

"Mithrael! Mithrael!" the Nephil mocked in his chaotic, shrieking voice.

"Silence!" Uriel commanded, leveling the point of his sword between the creature's eyes. "Your disobedience will allow me to go beyond my orders."

The Nephil seemed to know what this meant. He scowled like a thwarted schoolboy and pouted at the pole, drooling sullenly into the dust.

Pauline observed, "Chaos is the only game the Nephil knows. Order binds him, limits him."

In the meantime a battered angel had raised himself from the dust at the far edge of the contest arena. Pauline had not seen him before. She noticed him now with astonishment. He appeared to be of the same species or rank as Uriel, but blond, and oh, how forlorn. Stripped of his honorable tunic, he wore tattered sackcloth. A bright metallic band gagged his mouth. He appeared wounded and blind, humiliated, like a shorn Samson. A beautiful woman stood beside him, helping him to his feet. "That is Naamah," Pauline thought, recalling Lydia's description.

Behind them, a stone paddock held a host of other women. All of them as beautiful in their own way as Naamah.

Pauline didn't think, she just found the question blurting from her mouth: "Who are the women?" They continued to watch every move Mithrael made, whispering among themselves obsessively.

"He lived long on the earth," Uriel said sadly, turning to look at her. "He took many wives."

"Did he have many children?"

Uriel didn't respond to this. He either didn't hear the question or chose to ignore it. "Mithrael," he called, "I have been sent here from the Presence!"

Mithrael threw himself immediately to his knees, using his bandaged fingers to sign feverishly into the palm of Naamah's hand.

"My husband asks, 'Who are you?'" Naamah called back to him.

"I am Uriel."

Once again Mithrael communicated to his wife by signs.

"'How long?'" she said. "My husband asks, 'How long will He afflict me?'"

"It is not for you to know the times nor the seasons of the Lord," Uriel replied.

"Then why have you come?"

"To give passage to one who has become lost here."

Mithrael paused. He tilted his head as if pondering something hidden in this message. A possibility. A gesture. His wife bent her lips to his ear and whispered.

Mithrael began to sign to her again.

She replied, "My husband asks, 'Allow me your privilege, as in the days of vengeance to come. For I am counted among those who go down to The Pit; I am set apart with the dead who are cut off from His care. Why does the Lord reject me? Will He hide his face forever? I have suffered His terrors. They surround me like the waters of the Flood—'"

"Silence!" Uriel commanded, pointing his sword at Naamah.

With a pained expression, the woman grasped her husband's head protectively to her breast. Mithrael remained on his knees, swaying in her arms.

Pauline looked hard at Uriel. The angel's face had flushed unexpectedly. A husky emotion had torn at the layers of his voice as he commanded this silence. Too harshly, it seemed.

"Hear the Word of the Lord to you, O Mithrael, Watcher of the Heavens!" This utterance became a clarion call, trumpeted by Uriel as if God Himself were speaking. "Your star once burned brightly in the Firmament of Heaven, yet you have forsaken your place. You have taken the daughters of men. Before mankind, you sinned the sin of Esau, forsook your birthright, and now your cursed sons vex the righteous of the earth in their age. Therefore, the Holy One declares: 'Your glory is removed from among the stars of God! I am the Lord, who was, and is, and is to come and

---

I have spoken it. By My name you shall never return to your place.'"

Pauline noticed that the proclamation of this judgment had caused the doctors to huddle together in conference at a far entrance of the arena. Within herself she felt the awful tragedy of this pronouncement, and for the first time in her life the true guilt of sin. It was something that could only be accounted before God Himself. Not even angels understood it. Sin confronted God. Not created beings. It flew in His divine face, and He alone would judge it.

The angel's sword continued to extend toward Mithrael. "Yet you shall live, Mithrael, declares the Holy One!"

"He is holy!" Naamah called at the insistence of her mute husband, who signed furiously into her hand. "He is holy, righteous and true!"

Uriel's voice softened, no longer trumpeting. "He has not forgotten your former service. He has not forgotten how you warred against the Opposer in the Sides of the North. He remembers that you threw down lightning at His command upon the rebellious Watchers. Your own brothers. You resisted the proud and seducing words of the Evil One. The heart of the Lord is toward you, O Mithrael, Watcher of the Heavens—"

Uriel's voice seemed to falter. Pauline noticed with wonder that his face now glistened with tears.

"—Be strong. Endure your time. Endure to the end, my brother. For you are a son of God."

Slowly, deliberately, the fallen angel gathered his remaining strength and stood to his feet. He extended his left hand toward the angel of the Presence, clenching it into a tight fist. It slammed solidly against his chest. Pauline heard the impact shortly after seeing it. He then extended an open palm in what must have been an angel's salute. Uriel returned the gesture silently.

Then the guilty father of Naamah's Nephil shook himself free of his wife's comforting grasp. Against the pain of his wounds, he began to jump, bobbing and weaving his head like a boxer awaiting the sound of a bell, another round in a bloody contest.

Seeing this, Uriel smiled. "He asked for the privilege," he whispered with pride and wonder.

Stepping near to Pauline, he looked into her eyes as his tears continued to fall. At first he remained speechless, as if trying to figure out how to explain a high mystery to a child. "He has asked

*for the privilege of giving you passage," he said finally. "It can only
be given once."*

He looked back over his shoulder to where Mithrael now
jogged back and forth, beyond the tether of the monster. His movements were growing limber, yet it was obvious that he was in great
pain. The Nephil stalked him on all fours, walking stiffly like an
insulted cur, its hackles fully erect, its pace synchronous, beat for
beat, with the angel, as if daring him to come within reach.

"You must run for your father when he engages the beast,"
Uriel said. "I will be here if he should fail. You will be safe. Now
prepare."

"Yes," Pauline said. She had drawn courage from Mithrael's
display, as well as Uriel's presence. She would not disappoint either
of them. If necessary, she would leap the entire stadium. "I am
ready," she declared.

Without warning Mithrael rushed the Nephil.

"Now!" Uriel shouted.

Pauline fixed her eyes on her father and ran like the wind. In
her ears she heard the Nephil's challenge as it closed with the angel
behind her. In the stands the doctors hooted and cat-called, watching the contest like rowdy fans.

Pauline had never known such fleetness of foot. She accelerated
so rapidly that the wind in her ears drowned the sounds of combat.
She felt a shadow at her shoulder. Turning once, she saw Uriel lop-
ing easily beside her. He watched the fight carefully as he ran. She
heard Naamah's screams of agony and glimpsed the hunched back
of the Nephil in the distance, bending over what must have been
Mithrael's prone body. The monster flailed viciously with its clawed
hands and feet.

In the next split second she arrived at the stone platform where
her father lay bound by a large rusty chain and padlock. He shook
his head vigorously as she grew near, and closed his eyes as if to
deny that she had come to this place. But opening them again, he
saw the apple of his eye still kneeling above him.

Pauline had expected to feel a rush of sympathetic emotion
upon arriving at his side. But she did not. The sight did not seem
tragic. His chains looked surprisingly proper. Of course he would
be bound in this place. He had bound himself on earth through
manipulation and schemes. Through unconsoled grief and disappointment he had entwined the healing power of God with the evil
of Dunamis to seek a cure for cancer. "Perhaps his earthly body is

dying," she thought. "Perhaps Cancer has exploited an inner weakness to snare him." At any rate, the chains she now saw binding him were simply the heavenly manifestation of his earthly state. She accepted it.

In the cave below, his body remained unconscious. So did hers. Here, by the mercy of God, they were face to face, as she had wished it. He was alert, but unable to speak. She looked into his eyes with a new kind of love. No longer hero-worshiping a man of God. No longer seeking to draw strength from him. She had come on the prayers of Lydia to help him. And he so obviously and desperately needed it.

"Daddy, I'm here," she said, her voice steady. "I found you, Daddy. I love you."

He struggled to reply but could not. His mouth was tightly gagged behind a metal strap identical to the one Mithráel wore. Somehow she knew she had to remove the gag before anything else could be done to release him. But the apparatus had been honed of a finely milled space-age metal. There was no clasp to it, front or back. At least, none that she could see.

"Uriel!" she cried as she worked her fingers around the strange contraption. "Uriel, how can I undo this?"

There was no answer. All she could hear were the snarls of the contest in the arena behind her.

She whirled around. Uriel had gone. Instinctively she looked through the sky above the arena, but saw no trace of the kind and handsome warrior. "How could he leave me?" she lamented, and immediately the answer came—"He goes nowhere of his own accord."

Her distress had somehow aroused the Nephil from his violent frenzy. He stood up now, eyes glazed, and turned slowly toward her. Blood dripped from the long scimitar claws of his right hand. The angel crawled frantically in the dust toward the perimeter of the monster's leash, his back and sides freshly lacerated. Naamah watched, sobbing at the new wounds on her handsome treasure. The other wives wailed in chorus behind her.

"Here!" Pauline shouted, standing up and waving her arms to distract the beast. "Come here, you foul thing!"

The Nephil's attention locked onto her immediately. Forgetting the angel, it leaped across the ground toward her, bucking like a colt, expelling a continuous braying wheeze through its nostrils.

*The demon loomed larger and larger until Pauline lost her nerve
and fell backwards, clutching her father protectively.*

*With a sound like a thunderclap, the Nephil hit the end of its
tether. The pole swayed and moaned from the shock of the colli-
sion, but the tether held firm, keeping the creature from reaching
her. She began to understand that its limits had been established by
a power much greater than itself. Now if she could just convince
her pounding heart to believe that.*

*A faint tinkling sound reached her ears, and for the first time
she noticed a set of keys vibrating at the very top of the Nephil's
pole. They were on a large ring hung on a peg there.*

*She returned to her father's side. "Are they the keys to free
you?" she asked, picking up what must have been a fifteen-pound
padlock. The lock secured the chains around her father's body, and
she felt sure the keys would fit the lock. They were the prize in this
arena. If only Mithrael could reach them. From the mismatch she
had just witnessed, there seemed little chance of that.*

*"Guess my name, woman," the Nephil purred, watching her
intently.*

*She turned to glance at it, and the Nephil smiled. The monster
exuded charm like a cobra. Frightening. Intelligent. It had grown
perfectly tranquil after hitting the end of its leash. It sat now on its
haunches, head tilted to one side in the manner of a sweet puppy.*

"Play the game. What's my name?" it rhymed.

*It occurred to her that perhaps the name was another kind of
key. A riddle that might deliver the real keys into her hand. The reason Mithrael and her father were gagged was to keep them from
revealing the true identity of the Nephil. His true name. Of course!
"I know who you are," she seethed. "Baal-Zeus-Jupiter. Whatever
you may call yourself—you are Cancer!"*

*The face of the Nephil grew exaggeratedly round with surprise.
"She plays!" it falsettoed, brusquely leaping from its haunches and
dancing in a circle. "Wrong!"*

*"You are Cancer!" shouted one of the doctors in the stands
above.*

*Surprised at the sound of support, Pauline stood up to see who
had spoken. Five doctors had come together from various sections
of the stands. They all looked at her now and nodded in unison.
"Cancer," they agreed.*

She turned to see what effect this might have on the creature.

It had clapped a clawed hand over its mouth, suppressing a spasm of mirth.

Suddenly its countenance grew fierce. It began to pace. "Come on, play! Am I Thor? Thunder?" Now it minced effeminately in a circle. "Am I Adonis?"

"I said you are Cancer," Pauline replied firmly. "I know who you are, you filth. You're nothing but the rot of cancer! You are the very malignancy, the curse of it. You killed my mother." Aiming her finger like the point of Uriel's sword she suddenly screamed, "I command you in the name of Jesus and the Most High God, go into The Pit!"

The giant's eyes grew suddenly wide. It fell to the ground in a violent convulsion, gagging, choking, clutching at its throat. Through ever-weakening spasms of twitching, it finally grew very still.

Pauline watched awestruck, ready to shout for joy, but the creature bounded with full vigor to its feet, like a powerful jack-in-the-box. "Just fooling," it chimed. Roaring with laughter at its own joke. The creature milked approval from the doctors in the stands with broad, begging gestures. Chaos reigned in the arena. The doctors responded insanely, begrudging the Nephil a sparse round of applause for his victory.

It took a deep bow. "Command me again," it mocked, looking sideways at Pauline. "Please? Command me."

She had no intention of casting more pearls before this mocking swine. Apparently the name of Jesus was not hers to use in the arena. She would not repeat the error. Noticing a motion behind the creature, she saw that in spite of his many wounds the angel now limped toward the pole. She assumed that his purpose would be to reach the set of keys at the top while the Nephil remained distracted. "Could this be the answer to my and Lydia's prayers?" Pauline wondered. She could see that the move promised failure if she didn't hold the demon's attention longer.

"You're Apollo," she said, grasping the first name that occurred to her from the long list Evan had read in the plane.

"No."

"Fortune of Commagene."

"Uh, uh." It shook its head, crossing its gruesome feet as if embarrassed, like a child.

"What a wretched parody," she thought. She could hardly endure the Satanic charade, but what could she do to change it?

A surgeon called from the stands like a rowdy fan, "You are a rebel from the pantheon of justice!"

The other doctors applauded with shouts of, "Yeah, yeah. Take your place again. Serve your father."

The Nephil snickered at them.

Pauline tried not to look at the angel, who now began to pull himself up the pole in the center of the arena. The muscles of his ample back glistened with fresh blood as he climbed.

"You are a viral motivator!" another doctor called out. "A malignant cell."

The Nephil fell to one side in a fit of mirth, pounding the ground with its fist. It rolled onto its back, kicking with glee. Then the beast suddenly arrested itself—

To Pauline's distress, it had spotted the angel climbing the pole. "You are Isis! Osiris! Thoth! Nemesis!" she screamed, throwing names at him from her memory, to no avail. As the Curse lunged toward the pole, she raced into the arena after it. "Here! Here! Get back here, you filth, you half-breed!"

The creature continued on heedlessly. It seemed completely obsessed with the attack. Gathering the slack of its tether as it ran, suddenly it whipped the thong in a wide arc through the air, creating loops which fell around Mithrael's body, lashing him to the pole. The Nephil leaped viciously backwards, cinching the loops tightly around the angel, pinning him helplessly, just out of reach of the ring of keys.

"No!" Mithrael moaned, his hands straining upward.

"Eeeulff! Euulff! Euulff!" The Nephil brayed like a randy jack-ass.

In the stands Pauline noticed the weird doctors nudging one another, applauding the demon's skillful maneuver as if attending a Roman circus. Naamah and the other wives filled the arena with another chorus of vocal distress.

Pauline plugged her ears to the hellish cacophony and shrank helplessly toward her father. What could she do for the angel?

"Be strong"—she remembered Uriel's words—"Endure your time."

Was the arena a place of judgment for a fallen son of God? she wondered. Or a cruelly poetic punishment of some sort? Or perhaps an angelic purgatory? These questions remained unanswered.

She had to turn away as with uninhibited glee the Nephil began to flog its father, using the heavy chained section of the tether

*attached to its own collar. Again and again as she hurried from the
arena, Pauline heard the angel's cry and the splattering thud of the
heavy links of chain against his lacerated back.*

"*Eeeeeeulff! Eeuulf! Eeuulf!*" *squealed the Nephil.*

82

CAVERN
8:15 A.M.

Neva eased herself onto the last vacant table in the cavern.
Immediately beside her, Pauline's unconscious form lay, with
none of the heart or brain wave monitors attached, which meant
her vital signs could not be verified. That mattered little to Neva.
She knew that all of them would soon be dead. Immediately in front
of the evil medical director, Evan and Danna were securely strapped
to the legs of Dr. Grace's bed.

Methodically the mad doctor inserted a catheter into her own
vein. Then she ran her fingers up and down the surgical tubing leading to the IV bag on the stainless steel hanger attached above her.
Her lap held a loaded syringe and a pistol. She had already shaved
patches of her scalp and had attached brain wave leads to an elec-
troencephalograph. For reasons of her own she had foregone
attaching the heart monitor.

At last she seemed to have everything ready, to her own satisfaction. Smiling wearily at Evan she picked up the Luger and aimed
it between his eyes. "You're dead." Then she aimed the gun at
Danna and chuckled. "Oh, what an unexpected gift from the gods
you are, my dear. Vengeance is just too sweet."

She placed the gun back down and picked up the syringe,
squeezing the air from the needle, along with a cc of fluid. "It's
going to be terrifying for you," she said as she removed the reservoir bag from the IV stand. Stabbing it with the needle, she began
measuring the unknown fluid into the saline solution.

"You see, when the others heard that our time had come they
designed a beautiful exit." Gesturing toward the dead doctors on
the other tables, she added sadly, "Such a loss to the scientific

world. It will take years to rebuild the team. But then they'll be back." She smiled wickedly. "They always are. In the meantime, sacrifices have always been necessary with the gods. Many, many more sacrifices than you can imagine." She sighed, glancing around the cavern. "Everything is wired to my brain, you see? Isn't that brilliant?" She looked at Danna. "Of course you're not legally dead until you're brain-dead, right? When my alpha waves stop, you little ones will die under several tons of this mountain. Of course the dust will choke you before the end comes. Who knows? It might strangle you and get the job done early." She placed her own hands around her throat and mimicked a choking sound. "I, of course, will be on the other side with the gods. But it pleases me to know the kind of death you will suffer. The gods grant us, their true children, even these small pleasures."

Evan's mind raced. *Buy time, buy time.* His wrists were tightly bound with the tape, but he continued to wrench his hands against their reinforced strength anyway. Anything for another chance at life. "Neva, what about your research? Don't you care about losing that?"

"We're passing it on. Nothing is permanently lost here. We've been experimenting for centuries like this. Didn't you know that? We've gone to the ends of the earth to learn how to use the Ancient Doors. Anyway, I can go over now. My part here is finished."

"What about the Patriarch?"

She smiled cagily at him and chuckled as she reached up to turn on her drip. She answered as she lay herself comfortably down. "He's protected by the gods. Perfectly safe."

Evan struggled against his bonds, tying to think of a way to keep her brain waves active for another minute, another second. "Neva! As long as we're all going to die, talk to me! Were you close to a cure? Were you?"

"Yes . . ." she murmured sleepily, "we were so close . . . I tried to tell you, but you wouldn't . . ."

As she replied, he worked feverishly against his taped wrists.

Suddenly she stiffened on the table. Her voice seemed to rasp through a constricted throat, sounding like a man's voice. "You should've been there, then you would know. The epiphanies were everywhere. Listen to the tapes . . . they were there, 'rising from their thrones' . . . ha, haaa . . ." The voice trailed off into nothingness.

"Dear Jesus," Danna whispered, her eyes closed, leaning back against the leg of the table. She felt only one glimmer of hope remaining. Something she had not told Evan about Pauline's dosage of Hypnos-3. She had cut it by half. If everything worked correctly Pauline would be coming back early. *Please, God, make it work.*

Evan worked violently against his tape, straining to put his feet under him. Pushing back against the weight of his father and the equipment holding the medical table behind him, adrenaline flooded his bloodstream. As far as he could see, only one chance remained for all of them—no spiritual answer could be found to this life-threatening dilemma. He must free himself to live. With a mighty heave of his legs, the table lifted into the air behind him. His father lifted with it.

"Wait, Evan," Danna whispered, "it's OK—"

He wouldn't listen. Time for talk had gone. He continued to strain, tilting the entire table higher. Suddenly Dr. Grace's body slipped sideways to the floor of the cave, toppling the table and dumping his body beyond the limit of the IV line. The catheter needle ripped from his vein. Electrodes popped from the leads on his scalp and chest. He dangled for a moment, held only by the respirator tube inserted into his bronchial tubes. It supported his weight briefly, then ripped free, dropping the preacher to the floor. His head impacted with a dull crack, and blood streamed the length of his forearm, dripping into the ancient channel in the floor.

Evan felt the table lift him high into the air, suddenly relieved of its burden. *We're going to die anyway,* he thought. Shoving once more with all his might, the bed rolled sideways. Still tightly bound to the leg of the table, his arms bent violently at an impossible angle. As the table rolled, he tumbled over the top of Danna, forcing her into an upside-down position too. The muffled crack of Evan's breaking arm immediately preceded his cry of excruciating pain.

83

THE SIDES OF THE NORTH

Mithrael cried out as the Nephil slammed the heavy chain once more against his backbone.

"*Lord of Cancer!*" The voice of a woman sounded from above.

Pauline looked toward an archway at the top of the arena.
Neva Sylvan appeared suddenly there, silhouetted against the azure
sky. Short, solidly built, salt-and-pepper hair. As Pauline watched
helplessly, the medical director ran lightly down the steps to join the
other doctors in the arena. Now there were six of them. Seeing
Neva, Pauline received the inner confirmation that indeed the spectators in the arena were the Doctors of Dunamis. Six of seven of
the Society of Apostates. Where was the seventh?

With a knot of revulsion growing in her stomach, she had simply seen enough. Turning back to her father, she feverishly began
prying at the gag on his mouth from every possible direction. As she
worked over him, he wrenched his head violently from her grasp.
She noticed that his eyes seemed desperate to tell her something. She
paused. He paused. As her fingers reached again for the gag, he
nodded encouragingly. But as she explored behind the plate for the
constricting band that held it in place, he shook his head vigorously
no. She repeated the attempt with the same result and realized that
he attempted to guide her.

"Oh, Daddy, what is it? Tell me."

She stopped to examine the gag plate itself. Very deliberately
he nodded his head. She felt hope rise in her heart. An answer. She
bent near and squinted at the smooth plate. Disguised in its mirrored surface she detected a hairline seam. It traveled from one side
of the plate to the other. At one end, the seam took a right-angled
turn, enclosing a larger square of metal. "This is an inlaid mechanism of some sort," she thought. Her fingers explored the nearly
perfect seam directly over the mouth. Her father shook his head
encouragingly.

"It has a latch," she said. She used her fingernail to seek a catch
in the seam. But she couldn't find a hold that would allow her to
lift it from its flush position in the mouthpiece. She continued to pry
at it until her father again shook his head no.

"What is it, Daddy? How does it work?" She tried again and
again with the same frustrating result. She could find simply no way
to pull the mechanism. "Pull—that's it!" she thought. "I'll try to
push." Placing a finger on the large end of the seam, she pressed.
The small end lifted ever so slightly from its resting place on the
opposite side, exposing a nail's width of plate.

"That's it! I've got it!" she said. At last, by pushing one end and
using her fingernail to lift the other at the same time, the entire

assembly fell miraculously free into her hand. She stared at it in shock and disbelief.

Looking up, for the next millisecond her father's lips began to form a word. A desperate word which she with all her concentrated willpower attempted to emulate as it came from his mouth. Lips moving in what seemed to be slow-motion dream time, his mouth formed the word—

"Mmmaaaaa—"

84
CAVERN
8:26 A.M.

"—Mmmaaaaamaaa!" she screamed, sitting up abruptly on the medical slab.

"There is a God," Danna laughed with relief from her upside-down position beside the toppled bed. "I only gave her a half-dose, Evan. She's back."

"Pauline! Help us, honey!" Evan called, his voice edged with pain from the broken arm. "We've got to get out of here. The cave is going to explode! Come on, get us free!"

"She can't really understand yet," Danna cautioned.

Pauline sat there, still attached to the drip. She felt confused, as if she'd just awakened from a deep sleep in a stranger's house. Not remembering who she was, nor how she had gotten there. There remained the feeling that a powerful volume of air had recently ripped from her lungs, along with a word. A word she did not hear or understand. But she had spoken it as he had formed it—her father. She had just been with her father in an arena.

Who is yelling at me? She tried to focus her eyes, but they wanted to wander all over the place at their own bidding. She saw Neva beside her. *Neva is here and she is up there*, she thought woodenly. The other doctors were under their sheets. *Them too! All of them are up there with Daddy—Oh, no! He's hurt!* Her drug-dulled mind tried to process all that she saw. Her father's bed upside-down. His form sprawled awkwardly on the floor. The stream of bright-red blood.

"I 'ave to 'elp Daddy," she slurred, scooting to the edge of the bed and sliding off the edge to her feet.

"Take down the IV bag first—" Danna's words of caution came too late.

Pauline hit the end of the line and felt the sharp sting of the needle in her vein, followed by a deep and bruising pain in the soft crook of her arm. She reeled backward against the table.

"You've got to take down the bag first, honey," Danna said. "Bring it all over to me and I'll help you."

Pauline turned around and for the first time saw Danna and Evan lying upside-down. She tilted her head crazily, feeling suddenly upside-down herself. "Wha's a matter?"

"Leave the needle in," Danna instructed patiently. "Just take the bag from the hanger and bring it to me. Can you do that?"

Pauline hurt all over. Especially her head. It felt like something sour and sick had entered the bones of her skull. Her legs buckled beneath her, and she sagged against the table. After a moment she replayed Danna's instructions. *Just take the bag from the hanger and bring it to me.* Steadying herself with her arms, she walked around the bed to the IV apparatus.

"That's it," Danna coached. "Reach up and take it down."

After three attempts she managed to get her fingers to obey and take hold of the bag. After four more attempts she managed to pull it along the hanger arm by an eyelet, freeing it from its perch.

"OK, now bring it here," urged Danna.

It soaked slowly into Pauline's drugged brain that she needed to help Evan and Danna first, before she could help her father. Carrying her IV bag, she wandered to a place on the floor where she had seen Neva put down her scissors. Every detail had been observed with superior clarity as she had hovered above the room. Returning to the table she knelt down and used the scissors to chew at the tape binding Danna's wrists to the table leg.

As soon as she had severed most of it, Danna wrenched her sore wrists from the remaining tape, righted herself, and immediately grabbed the scissors.

"Hurry," Evan pled.

But she leaped first toward Neva's table, cutting her IV line. "That should buy us some more time," she said. "I hope."

Checking Neva's brain wave monitor, the alpha waves burst

erratically in response to the cut-off of the drug. They flashed upward, then plunged dangerously low again.

"Please hurry!" Evan pled.

She ran to his side. Kneeling, she cut through the bands of tape around his wrists. He rolled to one side with a moan, tears of pain flowing from his eyes. Not only had the left arm been savagely broken, circulation had been cut off for the past ten minutes. It hung unnaturally twisted as he stood shakily to his feet, moaning again.

"At least it's my left," he said. "Let's get Dad."

Pauline knelt groggily at her father's side.

"Get away, Pauline!" Evan demanded, having no time for courtesy. "It's got to be you and me, Danna—she's useless," he said. "Come on."

"Wait. Be quiet," Danna demanded, picking up Dr. Grace's wrist between her thumb and forefingers. At the same time she placed her cheek near his mouth. After ten seconds she raised up. "He's ticking."

"Then let's go." Evan knelt, placing his right arm under his father's armpits. Danna used both of her hands to lift him from the other side. Her strength was simply not enough to hold him, nor was Evan's one-armed grip. Dr. Grace slipped limply back to the floor.

Without a word Evan leaped back to the overturned table and found the roll of reinforced tape Neva had used. "Help me make a sling with this stuff," he instructed handing it to Danna.

She understood immediately. Stripping loose enough tape to cross his chest, she passed it under each of Dr. Grace's arms, forming a loop behind his head. Several such loops, layered one on top of the other, would provide a handle that would allow them to drag him backwards out of the cave. Evan could use his strength with one arm that way, and the women could assist as best they could.

As she doubled and tripled the wrap, Evan bent close to his father's face. Placing the back of his hand beneath his nose, he felt a slight tickle there. "You're right. He is breathing."

"I don't know why," Danna said. "He was on that machine until a few minutes ago."

Evan stood up, glancing about the cave, wondering where the Dunamis operatives had stashed the explosives. They had very little time. Three wraps of the tape were enough. Grabbing the makeshift handle, he heaved with a grunt and began dragging his father across the polished floor toward the shaft. The strain on the one side of his body sent pulses of hot pain shooting against the torn tissue of his opposite arm.

Danna quickly placed an arm around Pauline and helped her toward the door. Pauline's knees buckled, and she fell to the floor.

"Hold that thing over your head!" Danna demanded, handing her the IV bag she had dropped. She had to shout to penetrate the fuzz on Pauline's brain. Getting her to focus on something, even a simple task like holding the bag, would help.

Pauline struggled to her feet with Danna's help again, this time holding the bag over her head. Evan had already neared the entrance to the sloping shaft.

Behind them, Neva's brain wave monitor began to show signs of agitation with the interrupted flow of narcotic. Suddenly she cried out of her sleep in a piercingly clear voice, "Sacrifices were necessary!"

Evan knew the fear of a fleeing prey, as if Hell itself stretched out to entrap him in Neva's voice. Something in his own mind fought to drag him backwards, to allow the mountain to come down on him. Enough is enough. Giving up would end the hard work of living, the torment.

He prayed. Something stronger than his own willpower must fight for his escape. "Dachau, Jonestown," he bellowed suddenly over his shoulder. His voice was full of angry mockery. "You should get the Nobel prize for that, Neva!"

A chorus of voices answered from the doctor's mouth, screaming in furious unison, "Do not touch our work! There is Hell to pay!"

"Come on, Danna!" Evan yelled, waiting for her to catch up.

"Go on!" she replied, struggling to hold Pauline upright. "We're alright. Get him out of here!"

"I'll be back for you," Evan promised, throwing all of his strength into the harness, dragging his father almost at a run up the ramp. Rounding the final corner, he seemed to gain strength with every step as he struggled toward the light of day.

At the entrance Evan hurried to the nearest land rover, depositing his father unceremoniously on the ground beside it. Then he stumbled painfully back to the cave.

Pauline continued to sag repeatedly against the wall of the shaft as Evan rounded the corner from above. The two had not made fifty feet of progress since he had left them behind. The pain in his left arm screamed at his brain, but he used the pain to clear his thoughts and push himself forward. He placed his right arm under Pauline's left side, supporting her. Together he and Danna hustled her toward the entrance.

"Let's put her—in this first car—" he gasped. "Then help me with Dad."

Reaching the first vehicle, they pushed Pauline into the passenger seat. She sat weaving back and forth unsteadily, holding her IV bag obediently above her head.

"Hold on now," Evan urged. "We're almost done. Dad is OK. He's alive." He shut the door of the vehicle firmly after her.

He and Danna ran to where Dr. Grace lay beside the other vehicle. Evan used the sling to drag him to the rear door. Opening the doors to both sides, he stood inside the floorboard and lifted the homemade harness with all his might. Danna pushed Grace's limp one hundred and seventy pounds from below. Evan's rising blood pressure throbbed in every broken splinter of the left arm as they deposited him across the differential well.

"Remember now," Evan reminded her. "Twist the wires on your vehicle together. Second gear . . . let it roll down the mountain . . . pop the clutch."

"Got it."

Evan scrambled around the vehicle to the driver's side. He knew it would be a circus to try to shift the vehicle and steer at the same time, but he had no time to quibble. He twisted the wires together beneath the dashboard, shifted to second gear, and released the brake.

Danna's vehicle moved forward quickly, responding well to the tug of gravity. After rolling forward about twenty feet she popped her clutch. The land rover lurched, and Pauline's face smashed into the windshield.

"Oh, honey, I'm sorry!" Danna cried helplessly.

Pauline, still in a stupor, pulled herself back onto her seat, blood running profusely from her nose. Meanwhile, the engine of the land rover had sputtered to life. Danna gritted her teeth to consider first things first. Getting down the mountain before it exploded remained definitely *first*. Pauline's injuries could be helped later.

"Hang on!" she screamed, gunning the engine and bounding down the trail.

Behind them, Evan's vehicle had rolled to a stop. He took the land rover out of gear, got out frantically, and pushed with all his might to get it in motion again. As it began to roll, he leaped for the door but was dragged, nearly losing his grip with his good arm. Throwing himself desperately forward he rolled onto the seat, over his broken arm, sobbing with blinding pain. Pulling himself upright in the now careening vehicle he was thrown cruelly against the steering wheel. He screamed with agony before he could use his legs to right himself again. He depressed the clutch and selected a higher gear to lessen the engine drag when he let it out. He had observed Danna's mishap with Pauline and didn't want his father's body to receive similar damage.

The engine ignited and began to purr smoothly as he dropped around a limestone outcropping onto the trail. Braking hard, the wheels spit in the gravel and turned onto the slice of roadway. Feeling an explosion building like a volcano beneath the mountain, he pushed the accelerator to the floor and chased Danna toward the breaks of the river below.

In ninety seconds the sound of their engines had faded from the mountaintop. All that could be heard for the next two minutes was the metallic complaint of their vehicle frames as they bounded over rock and gully. Ten minutes later twin trails of dust streaked silently across the dusty Cilo/Sat plain beneath the pantheon of Nimrut Dag.

❖

Halfway down the mountain Evan caught the flashing blades of a helicopter rising out of the breaks of the Euphrates, across the plain. *A Turkish patrol?* he wondered. It hugged the contour of the ground as it flew. *Israeli?* As they neared the base of the mountain he realized that the low-flying craft was hurrying directly toward them. "Frying pan into the fire," he muttered. "It must be Turkish." What could be done?

Once on the plain Danna signaled Evan to stop. He pulled up beside her, rolling down the passenger-side window.

"Are we far enough away to stop?" Danna asked. "Pauline's got a nose bleed."

"Sure." Evan got out of the vehicle and hurried to Pauline's side of the vehicle. He glanced at the approaching helicopter. "If this is the Dunamis people coming," he warned, "we are going to have to run for it. If it's the Turkish army, we're in trouble, but they might help us get Dad to a hospital at least. Then they will arrest us. We can handle that, I suppose."

He saw that Pauline bled profusely from her nose. Instantly he felt pity and admiration for his sister. He told himself that he would never underestimate her courage or her love again. Taking his handkerchief, he held it to her nose to stop the flow. She looked up at him groggily.

"We're a fine bunch of wounded ducks, aren't we?" he commented.

Across the vehicle, Danna shook her head and smiled, her eyes bright from a pounding pulse. "But we're alive."

"And we've got you and Dad back," Evan said patting Pauline's cheek. "Did you see anything over there?"

"I saw Dad," she said in a thin squeak. "Where is he?"

"He's in my car. He's still in a coma, but he doesn't seem to need life support. We'll worry about that when we get out of here."

The helicopter engine could be heard rapidly approaching now. "I'd better see who this is," he said, ducking his head back out of the doorway.

To his surprise he recognized the chopper as one of the Super Frelon craft. The pilot put it into a steep bank overhead, its exhaust jets screaming. Hovering quickly in front of them, the craft landed directly in their path amid a cloud of swirling dust.

Colonel Canaan leaped from the pilot's seat and ran toward them. Evan met him halfway.

"One of my men told me he had found the place wired up there," Canaan explained. "I nearly shot him out of the sky. I offloaded the whole group in a canyon. I have four hours to get you out of here. So who have we got?"

"Everybody. Me with a broken arm, Pauline with a broken nose, and Dad's comatose—"

The colonel looked at him quickly.

"She went over."

"I should have known," Canaan muttered, more as a reprimand to himself.

"Me too," Evan added. "She's groggy. Her face hit the windshield on the way down the mountain."

Canaan looked angrily at him for a moment, then softened. "I should have stayed. I was worried about getting her father out alive. I thought you would need a doctor for that."

Evan allowed himself to feel some relief. He glanced back up at the altar terraces now several thousand feet above them. "We'd better get out of here before things blow."

Canaan ran to the passenger side of Danna's vehicle and looked in at Pauline. He inspected her bloody nose and the IV. "Are you alright?"

She tried to answer, but her head hurt too much. Following the ingestion of Hypnos-3, her body refused to respond properly. She managed only to hold the IV bag aloft and keep the bloody rag to her nose.

"I can't leave you alone for five minutes," the colonel scolded with a twinkle of admiration in his eye. He reached beneath Pauline, lifting her easily from the seat. His strength brought a "little girl" feeling to life inside her. It was something she needed to feel. She had lost it in Jerusalem two weeks ago. As he carried her toward the roaring helicopter, she laid her head against his chest, and when he set her gently inside, a damp stain remained on his shirt where her face had been.

He took a few precious seconds to brush the tears from beneath her eyes. "Someday I want you to tell me what you saw over there, angel." His voice brimmed with respect. "Will you do that for me? For a friend?"

Looking into his eyes she felt something respond in her heart. She saw a depth in him she would not have recognized had she never seen Uriel in the Sides of the North. Whether by heritage, education, or experience, the blessings and curses of the Jewish Covenant marked this man. He would understand what she had experienced, if anyone would.

"I promise," she replied.

He hurried toward the other land rover, where Evan and Danna now struggled with Dr. Grace. The colonel took the doctor's limp body from them and carried him into the waiting aircraft.

"Let us go now," the colonel urged.

"You don't have to say that twice," Evan said as he helped Danna inside. The colonel shut the landing door. Soon the churning rotors began to vibrate through the craft as it lifted from the ground. Seeing his sister staring out the portside window, Evan moved nearer to her. He took the IV bag from her weary fingers and hooked it to a luggage rack over her head. Then he sat down beside her.

"You OK?" he asked again.

She didn't reply. Following her fixed gaze he saw that she stared toward the western altar of Nimrut Dag.

85

CAVERN

Neva Sylvan's alpha waves flickered and went out like an expiring candle. Instantly the entire mountaintop erupted. Six Apostate doctors arose simultaneously from beneath their sheets in the cave, howling with surprise and madness. No longer arena spectators in the Sides of the North, they had mysteriously been restored to flesh and bone. Brain wave monitors, which had remained deceptively dead for more than twelve hours, returned now to full animation. It had all happened in the twinkling of an eye—in the flash of a single blasting cap, wired to the medical director's brain.

A chain reaction of plastic explosives ripped through every supporting structure of the Urartian cave. The wall behind the medical beds fell first in a curtain of dust, revealing a petrified tree standing as if by the power of magic. Its defiant branches twisted from the bowels of the cave like the scaly hand of a dragon.

The doctors clamored and clawed at one another, tangling their monitor leads in terror and confusion as a gaping hole opened in the ceiling above them. Against the brilliant sky, the throne of Fortune of Commagene loomed for a final moment of reluctance, then slowly responded to the pull of gravity, toppling forward, followed by its two-ton head, which came rolling out of nowhere as if on cue. Both tumbled end over end into the entrails of the cave, falling in a shower of dismembered idols, and the twisted wreckage of the tourist helicopter. Close behind, twenty thousand tons of displaced mountain rushed downward to fill the void. Each of the tumulus stones forming the pyramidal peak of the mountain— stones which had been hand-carried millennia ago by the Urartian faithful from every corner of Ararat—now rushed eagerly downward to seal the Apostates in a common grave.

And for one brief eternity, the electronic memory of their brain wave monitors remained etched mockingly on the blanket of darkness. A moment to be witnessed and remembered by the wide-eyed Doctors of Dunamis forever.

XII

KEYS TO THE KINGDOM

And sullen Moloch, fled,
Hath left in shadows dread
His burning Idol all of blackest hue . . .
He feels from Judah's Land
The dreaded Infant's hand . . .

(JOHN MILTON, "ON THE MORNING OF CHRIST'S NATIVITY")

86

BROWNSVILLE, TEXAS
Dr. Grace's Mansion
Studio

His broken arm encased in plaster and cradled in a sling, Evan stood at the head of the long meeting table and raised his right hand to elevate the charm cross of petrified wood. The one on his own necklace. Those seated at the table could see it clearly. He stood near the windows in his father's studio, searching his vocabulary for the words to help him phrase the proposal. "Do I hear a motion, then, to employ the revised letter from Logos Mail, using this response device for the month of September?"

An atmosphere of awkwardness descended on the heels of this question. It suddenly permeated the room. Each of the board members seemed sensitive to it, in one form or another, corrupted though they were (with the exception of Chester Sharpey). Pauline had pled with him over the telephone to attend this emergency board meeting as an advisor, even though his resignation letter still stood. She had made it clear that she didn't want to accept it, and that imminent changes in the ministry would likely cause him to change his mind anyway. So, at her insistence, he had agreed to attend.

Following Evan's question, Harlan Harris slouched uncomfortably at the far end of the table. He scanned the picture gallery rather than make eye contact with any of his fellow board members. Peter Avanzini looked hesitantly from Jann Parker to Myra and back to Jann. "I'd like to hear what Verlin says about it," he grunted.

"Verlin recommends the letter and the device," Myra replied quickly.

Verlin Stiles had not come to the meeting. He continued to work from his house since receiving his son Jesse back. The boy's mental and emotional confusion continued to require mild doses of thorazine every four hours, plus daily psychiatric interviews. For that reason Myra, Verlin's secretary, represented him in the meeting.

Avanzini had seemed put off by Myra's quick response. He

413

drummed his fingers twice before rapping the table nervously with his knuckles.

More silence followed.

"I . . . I don't know . . ." Avanzini said with a shrug. He began fiddling with the Bible he always carried.

The hypocrite, Evan thought, recalling the financial skulduggery recorded in his "dirt file." *What possible objection would he raise to any Lavalle scheme?* "Let me remind you that you have a cash flow surplus for the first time in more than a year," Evan prodded. "The 'Reverse the Curse' letter has been a big winner. Alan is primarily responsible for that. Of course Pauline did her part, as Alan will tell you." Evan reiterated this fact for the third time in the past half-hour. The decision to go ahead with the new letter seemed as if it should be cut-and-dried to him. He wanted the board to hurry up, give approval, and move on to a round of golf before dark. "The fact remains, however, that we—or *you*, I should say— still have a long way to go to clear up the past-due debts. Far be it from me to judge the rightness or wrongness of the proposal, but are you arguing with success?"

None of them would look at him.

"I don't understand. What's the hang-up?"

"Something is wrong here, son." Chester Sharpey solemnly voiced his considered opinion. "Something is definitely wrong."

Evan sat promptly down, feeling suddenly dizzy, a bit dazed and agitated. With Sharpey's words, the uncomfortable effect had intensified, coiling like a suffocating constrictor in the room. *What is wrong here?* he wondered. He had only recently begun to discern the supernatural, since stumbling through the revelations of Nimrut Dag with Pauline. *Chaos* best described the feeling in the room, yet that word had been used to describe atmospheres of less disorder. He could almost taste it. A foul, odorous sludge at the back of his throat. It made him want to spit. Yet it was more than a taste to be expelled. A foul *presence* had invaded the room; a personality with chaos in its wake. And somehow it had come riding on the words of his own mouth as he had innocently proposed the Logos Mail package. Humbling himself, banishing as many judgmental thoughts of these corruptible men as he could, he waited. Deliberately, quietly.

His mind flashed over a confidential report given to him by the Uriel Mission earlier that morning. Canaan had kept in constant touch with him since their return from Turkey, regarding Uriel's pursuit of Dunamis and Max Commagene and their involvement with Grace Ministries. Today's report had outlined the goings-on of the Santeria cult operating near Matamoros. The same one that the late Neva Sylvan had contracted for experimental purposes, and for the near-extermination of Jesse Stiles. According to the testimony Canaan had extracted from Neva under sodium amytal, a Cuban-American named Jesús had allegedly committed more than a dozen human sacrifices just over the U.S.-Mexican border. He remained at large, funded liberally as the spiritual "guru" of a marijuana smuggling ring. The Uriel report recommended that a police investigation be launched at once. Evan had turned the information over to Mexican police that same morning, only to have them respond with incredulity. No matter how he had urged them to look into the allegations, they had refused to treat them as more than hearsay. "The kind of thing that circulates among the peasants down here who can't afford TV," the Tamaulipas detective had sarcastically replied. Evan had felt a threatening cloud move over him with those words, similar to the feeling he'd experienced in the *sook* in Van, Turkey. He was sure the Matamoros evil would break out again, engulfing more innocent victims.

Now he couldn't help but wonder if a demonic power hadn't followed him from the Matamoros police station. Perhaps Evan himself had led it into the room. He had never considered such possibilities before. They seemed superstitious to him, and he would rather dismiss them as such. He waited.

After fifty or sixty seconds, Pastor Cecil Dewey began to weep. Quietly at first, then suddenly convulsing. He bowed forward, tears falling on the polished oaken table.

What is this remarkable thing? Evan wondered. *If it is remorse, then let the tears come. They are fitting in this room.* After all, the board had just heard Evan's report of the goings-on between Grace Hospitals and Dunamis, Dr. Grace's continuing coma, the possible murders in the Sudan cancer clinic, and Neva Sylvan's hideous revelation at the Matamoros cancer lab. They no doubt were feeling a weight of real guilt about now, knowing that it had been their own corruptibility as a board which had allowed Dr. Grace the improper powers to create this tragic mess.

Jann produced a kleenex for the weeping preacher, stuffing it between his clenched fingers. Peter Avanzini stood to his feet and moved closer behind him, placing a comforting hand on his shoulder.

Again Evan could not help but wonder if this was a display of true compassion by this man of documented greed. Co-conspirator for years with the likes of Alan Lavalle. What, besides money, truly moved him?

Harlan Harris, the auto dealer, cleared his throat and abruptly rose from his slouch at the end of the table. He walked to the far corner of the room. Placing his forehead against the loft, he stood in a stance suggesting that he carried the weight of some kind of overriding sorrow.

In all of this, Evan felt that each of the men's reactions was being directed somehow against the invading atmosphere he sensed in the room. Still his mind played against that possibility. Perhaps they had become disturbed with a hidden political aspect of using Alan Lavalle's revised letter. Something Evan had stumbled ignorantly across in his wording of the question. Perhaps, or maybe they disliked Evan's handling it at all. No. The atmosphere better explained their uneasiness. Evan began to think that if this room full of reprobates, with the exception of Sharpey, was actually responding to a spiritual enemy, perhaps God didn't need a holy people to do a holy work. That was something to consider. He knew God so little. He watched Oregon rancher Chester Sharpey, bowed sagely over his hands of honest toil.

Pauline's voice crackled suddenly over the speakerphone, breaking the spell. The speakerphone, for the purpose of this meeting, had been placed at the head of the table. Pauline had followed the meeting's agenda from her bed. "Evan, what is happening out there?"

"Uh . . . I'm not sure," he replied. "Will you . . . uh, ask Lydia about it? We're up against something here."

Upon returning from Turkey, her father's master bedroom had been redone at Pauline's request. She had arranged it so that she could recover near his comatose body. She still suffered dizziness and blackout spells from the Hypnos-3 she had taken. Bedridden for the past week, she remained where she could oversee a rotating shift of nurses who watched her father around the clock. All of the medical personnel had been screened for this work by Danna Lavalle upon returning from Nimrut Dag.

Dr. Grace had remained in an unexplained coma. The family doctor visited each day. He had told Evan and Pauline that sometimes people do not wish to wake up from sedation. This was a phenomenon sometimes observed when surgery patients have awakened in the middle of an operation, experiencing the horror of the pain and the blood. Often the trauma keeps them unconscious long after the effects of the sedation have been eliminated from their bloodstream.

Evan agreed with the doctor, but to Pauline and Lydia the explanation remained supernatural, not physical. Dr. Grace remained comatose because he was still bound in the invisible realm of the spirit.

Under the direction of Danna Lavalle, the nursing staff had installed a hydro-therapy unit in the den to work Dr. Grace's limbs twice a day in order to keep his muscles from atrophying. They also took blood samples daily, trying to determine a medical cause for his continuing unconsciousness. None had been found.

At Pauline's request, Lydia had brought her prayer vigil from the Steeple to this bedroom. Her prayer station had been placed beside Dr. Grace's bed. At Lydia's suggestion a constant atmosphere of recorded worship music played through a headset placed over his ears when she was not immediately present. For much of the rest of the time, Lydia and Pauline took turns reading Scripture to him. Pauline felt urged to read constantly from the book of Psalms.

The only real business Pauline felt well enough to handle was conducted through the use of a speakerphone at her bedside. Still, she found herself growing quickly exhausted from even the most minor demands of administration. She had begged Evan to stay on and help her. He had agreed, which explained the role he now played in this emergency board meeting, carrying the ball in her stead.

Over the speakerphone, she had sensed this awkward moment in the meeting and now turned to look inquiringly at Lydia, who sat near her father's bed.

The old woman's concentration burned with intensity. "You've got a decision to make, Pauline," she said. "This is up to you."

She had not expected to hear this. Furthermore, she had not wanted to hear it. "But I'm so tired, Lydia."

"The time has come," the old woman replied firmly.

"What do you mean?"

"I mean it is time for you to quit waiting for someone to rescue you, young lady. It is time to act, and act decisively."

Her voice carried the tone of a rebuke, and it pained Pauline to hear it. It caused a clutching pain in her chest, as she thought of dealing with another fund-raising letter, and all of the moral and ethical implications involved. A wave of slumber rolled against her battered mind. She wanted to hide her head under the pillow, escape in sleep. "Please, no more responsibilities," she pled. "I can't take one thing more."

"Be strong, Pauline," Lydia said, her eyes bright and alert. "Endure this time."

Pauline suddenly flushed with renewed vigor. The words seemed to come not from Lydia but from Heaven itself, bypassing her senses, ringing bells in her spirit. These had been the words of Uriel to Mithrael in the arena. Lydia had not been there. Did she know? Of course not. Her choice of words had been prompted from a higher source! They called to a deep reservoir of strength in Pauline's soul. A river, tapped by the spirit, stronger than emotional, physical or mental fatigue. In response to the call, the river began to flow through her limbs like an adrenaline pump. *It is time!* Pauline had become wide awake now. *Act. Act. Do something. Do it.*

"Evan, come in here, please," she called into the speaker.

"Be right there," he replied from the meeting room.

Lydia nodded. She folded her arms and began to rock back and forth, her lips moving in silent prayer.

In the meeting room Chester Sharpey heard, raised his head and nodded at Evan, acknowledging his leave of them.

He stood quietly and slipped past the table, secretly relieved to be leaving the room with its weird atmosphere. Climbing the stairs into the loft and crossing to the far corner, he passed the empty place on the floor where *The Seven Sleepers of Antioch* had been encased for so many years. The hair tickled up and down the length of his spine as he walked, introducing a host of butterflies into his stomach.

Moving into the bedroom with Pauline and Lydia, the atmosphere did not diminish. The chaotic sense in the board room had invaded this room as well.

Lydia looked up.

Evan looked at Pauline, and she stared back at him befuddled. Around her bed were a half-dozen floral arrangements. A new one had been added today, he noted. Colonel Canaan had sent flowers and potted plants nearly every day since her return. He had called her every day too. Something more than friendship was blooming between the two of them.

Looking down, he realized that he still held the charm cross he had held up at the meeting table. He held it up again for Pauline and Lydia. "In there I asked them, 'Do we use the revised letter with this response device?' And then everything got kind of strange. Is there something wrong with this cross?"

"No," Lydia said, dismissing the thought with a wave. "The charm is nothing. It is what is behind it that we are dealing with. Trinkets come and go."

"What do I need to do?" Pauline asked, feeling more within herself for direction.

"You don't need to do anything," Evan offered, putting the cross in his pocket. "It seems to me the board needs to make a simple decision out there, that's all. We have stopped the Dallas WordSmith contract. That was the right thing to do since Dunamis was paying them anyway. And we've had Alan write this new letter using Dad's response device. That way you don't have the expense of creating a new one. Good fiscally responsible decisions if you ask me. All we need is their approval now. It seems simple. But somehow it's not."

"Well, maybe . . ." Pauline fished for her thought. "Maybe we're supposed to do something instead of Alan's letter."

Evan turned to Lydia. "What do you think?"

She drew a thoughtful breath. "I have prayed about everything I know how to pray for."

"So do we wait?" Evan wanted to know.

"No. You make the decision. Something in this decision strikes at the very heart of this ministry, the right and wrong of it. How do you feel, Pauline?" she suddenly asked. "What does your gut say you should do?"

Pauline found the words slipping from her mouth without thinking. "Stop the letter." She felt right as the words emerged from her mouth, but as soon as her ears heard them and processed their meaning, a host of doubts arose.

"And why?" Lydia asked.

"Because it is wrong." Again the words seemed to come of their own accord.

"Good reason." Lydia looked at Evan. "Do you feel that way too?"

He had felt confirmation as Pauline spoke, but remained naturally cautious. "My feelings are seldom reliable for important decisions," he said. "I like information, you know? The more the better when it comes to a decision like this."

Lydia nodded, then waited. She closed her eyes.

Evan had to confess he didn't know exactly how to make this decision. What more information could he gather? He had grown less sure of his mental processes through the recent ordeal. He had learned that a kind of wisdom existed—not from superior reasoning, but from *listening*. Danna had said it best: "Listen to your sister. Especially when you disagree." He was determined to listen now, and not to judge Pauline too quickly. Finally he spoke up again. "If Pauline and I both agree that this *feels* wrong, why don't we just go ahead and make the decision based on our feelings this time? I can do that. Maybe it's the right thing to do. I mean, nothing else makes sense."

"Why not?" Pauline agreed. "We will destroy the letter. We will not use it." She glanced at her father's comatose body once again, thrilling to the notion that he had heard her.

"Did you feel that, Evan?" Lydia asked. "When she said that, did you feel your spirit say yes the way mine did?"

Evan had felt right about it. "Yes, I did," he agreed.

Gazing hard at her father's prone form now, Pauline received a new insight. She saw him trapped in this coma, but now suddenly she saw *herself* trapped with him. She had fallen to the same manipulative tactics of fund-raising that he had. The sudden guilt of it came back to her; she had used the files against Verlin Stiles. *Oh, with good reason, but that is how it always begins—good reasons used to justify manipulation. Where does it end? That is the question. It can end anywhere, she told herself, in places no one dreamed of! Oh, Lord, she prayed internally, my heart is not pure enough to always do right. Neither is Daddy's. That is why we must never manipulate to accomplish Your work. No flesh will glory in Your presence.* She knew further that with her tacit approval Evan had used the files to guarantee the votes she needed in the D/FW board meeting. For another good cause, of course. Then she had gone on to accept Alan's scenario for the letter, manipulating the press after the meeting, reaping millions in the mail as a result. What had Alan said to her in Brownsville that night?—"You can't learn that sort of thing. You have to be born with it, and you were obviously born with the instincts of your father." She looked at Dr. Grace now, and knew that she must break this family curse. That was the action she must take—break the curse. She could not break it by prayer, nor by "guilt giving," nor by good deeds rendered out of her ill-gotten gain. She could only do it by *doing it!* Reversing the curse herself. In that moment Pauline decided to do much more than either Evan or Lydia suspected.

"Bring the speakerphone to me," she suddenly ordered. "I have decided."

Evan crossed the room quickly to help her. He placed the machine on her lap. If he had learned one thing in recent days, it was that Pauline could surprise him. He felt excitement, as if on an adventure of discovery.

"Put this conversation on the speaker for the board members, will you?" she asked.

"Of course." He flipped a switch and spoke into the speaker himself. "We have reached a decision in here. All those in the meeting room, please listen up."

Jann Parker and Myra arose shakily from their knees where they had been in prayer since he had left the room. Dewey and Avanzini did the same from the other side of the table. Harris remained with his head in the corner, but the entire room had grown calm and quiet.

"Dial Alan Lavalle first," Pauline said.

Evan felt his face smiling uncontrollably as he punched the now-familiar button. So much of what he had first urged on Pauline now came from her own heart. He could see that. Now that he had given up changing her, she acted with understanding. Through the course of their ordeal, he had grown weary of fighting her anyway. He enjoyed just letting her be herself.

A secretary answered the line. Apparently Dorothy's replacement. "Logos Mail Incorporated."

"May I speak with Alan Lavalle please?" Evan said. "This is Evan Grace calling from the Grace Ministries board meeting. It is urgent."

The board members listened to this, solemnly seated around the table in the studio.

After about fifteen seconds Alan's voice responded, "Evan, what do you think of that package? It's not your father's letter, but it's a strong compromise, don't you agree? Should help you get back on your feet, at least."

"Yes, Alan. Thank you. Listen, we're looking at that package right now as a matter of fact. The board is present. I have you on the speakerphone here, so you might want to watch your language."

He chuckled. "You're a funny guy."

"The boss wants to talk to you."

"Hello, Alan," Pauline greeted.

"Pauline. How you feeling, honey?"

"Much better, thanks. I want you to listen to me, and listen carefully because I can't raise my voice quite the way I would like to."

"That's alright, honey, just do your best."

"You're fired."

Quiet reigned in the library. Each member of the board remained frozen. Not breathing. Listening.

In the bedroom Lydia's lips moved in silent prayer.

Pauline continued, "I don't want to say it again. We can be friends, of course, but your professional relationship with Grace Ministries is over. Is that clear?"

After a long pause Alan replied, "You make yourself mighty clear, Pauline. No need to raise your voice on that one."

"Thank you, Alan. There will be a time when I can tell you what is behind all of this, but for now, good-bye."

Evan nodded solemnly and hung up. What a bombshell! His sister had come of age.

"We're not quite through," she said. "Would you dial Verlin now, please?"

Evan dialed, watching her with ever-deepening respect. He felt a new kind of joy between them. Here was real power, the power to set things right. He could get used to this! How seldom one recognized that they had such power, or used it rightly. But wow! Pauline could write the book on it. What a feeling!

Lydia remained in quiet prayer, eyes closed, palms open and extended before her.

The telephone rang and was answered. "Hello?"

Evan responded. "Hello, Verlin. This is Evan. How's Jesse tonight?"

Verlin's voice was a dead thing. It contained not a spark of life. "He's getting some rest."

"We hope you are too. Sorry to disturb you."

"Thank you."

"I hate to bother you at home like this but, as you know, we're in the board meeting and we've reached a number of important decisions. Pauline needs to speak with you."

"Fine."

Evan signaled her to begin.

"Hello, Verlin. I have you on the speakerphone with the other board members present. First of all, can you tell me what deposits we have made so far from the letter that went out last month? I'm talking about the one just before my news conference at D/FW? 'Reverse the Curse'?"

"Right. More than fifteen million. It's still coming in."

"Is that fifteen deposited?"

"Yes."

In the library the board members swallowed hard and looked at each other nervously, sensing another unprecedented action.

"Does our computer have a record of each individual gift?"

He hesitated, anticipating the frustration and costliness of a massive personalized accounting process. "Yes."

"Individually?"

"Yes."

"Good. I'm going to write a new letter this month, Verlin. And we're going to send back all fifteen million dollars, plus any more that comes in. I will ask our partners to give it back to us again, of course, but this time it's going to be for the right reasons. Do you understand? They may choose to keep it, but this is how they will give to our ministry from now on—with their eyes open. We'll tell them the truth, and they'll respond to the truth, or they can keep their money and we'll go off the air. That's my commitment."

He grew silent. Then he lost control of an involuntary wheezing laugh. "We'll be bankrupt."

"Nonsense, Verlin. We can scale back. Sell the plane, the limousine, the property, whatever it takes. We'll reduce our television time. Make a priority list and do it. That's all. We will not run a ministry for money for one day more. Do you see my point?"

He was slow to respond. "Uh . . . Yes! But it takes—it takes some getting used to, that's all."

"What if you do go bankrupt?" Evan challenged, watching her eyes.

She didn't waver. "Then so be it. But I don't think we will. The original vision Dad had for the hospitals is too good. There is too much need in the world out there, and people want to be a part of meeting real needs. That's what I believe. We'll give them that opportunity." She spoke to the speakerphone again. "Even if it means we go under, Verlin, I need a pledge from you right now, in the presence of the board, that you will follow these orders to the letter. Without variance. Will you see that it is done for me?"

He considered it thoughtfully. It occurred to him that so much of the game of religious politics would go down the drain with this new policy. It was a game he had always lost anyway. He was reminded of how often he had found himself blindsided by someone's ambition masquerading as a "mission from God" or a "can't miss" fund-raising letter concept. "Consider it done, Pauline. Really. It *is* done."

"Thank you, Verlin. And by the way, since I have you on the phone—I had a little file of yours. You know the one?"

He was taken off guard. He cleared his throat dourly, recalling her humiliating use of the file from his past. "I think so."

She had not planned to say this. It hadn't occurred to her before this moment of inspiration, but the words came easily from her mouth. "Well, I'm sorry, Verlin. I burned some trash in the fireplace tonight and I must have—I must have dropped it in there by mistake. I'm just not myself these days." She paused, feeling the last vestige of a recent darkness leave her soul. "Can you forgive me for that, Verlin? I've destroyed your file." Her eyes stung with hope as she posed the question. Her throat tightened.

A choking sound came from the other end of the line as Verlin realized the Sword of Damocles had been removed from his life in this gesture. He finally brought himself to reply quietly, "Absolutely." It was all he could say, but his voice was full of feeling once again.

Pauline's heart sang a sweet song of absolution. "Thank you, Verlin. I *am* so sorry. I love you. Let me know if there is anything more we can do to help with Jesse, will you?"

"I sure will." He paused. "Thank you, Pauline. Again . . . I . . . I don't know what to say."

"Say good night then."

"OK," he chuckled. "Good night."

In the stunned silence that followed, each board member—with the exception of Chester Sharpey who had nothing to hide—reflected on the contents of their own secret file.

Two hours later Evan saw the last of the board member out of the front door. They left Dr. Grace's mansion with expressions of renewed personal commitment. Following the decision to fire Alan Lavalle and write a new letter, Pauline had moved the agenda forward with a special viewing of the one hour TV special "Grace in the Holy Land." Joel Lassiter arrived with his proud "baby," having only finished post-production of the program earlier that day. The hour was highly polished, fascinating, state-of-the-art TV. And it was moving. Dr. Grace seemed at his very best delivering the message from Jerusalem locations. Lassiter received their words of praise with his usual aplomb, actually soaking up every compliment like an insatiable sponge. He had worked hard and deserved the generous praise.

Keeping her word to her father, Pauline cleared the delivery of the program to a syndicated network for national prime time airing. On schedule.

Following that, there had been a bonfire in the fireplace in Pauline's bedroom. Privately, one by one, the board members had been invited in, where they watched Evan drop the contents of their files into the flames. Tears, prayers, and at least a show of repentance had been made by each of them. Only God could read their hearts.

Then Pauline had firmly asked for each board member's resignation. In the powerfully cleansed and charged atmosphere, they had humbly submitted.

Finally Chester Sharpey had been called in. Evan and Pauline explained that a new board would be selected, requesting that he submit names for consideration. They expressed a determination that Dr. Grace—should he recover—would remain subject to this new board and its governing influence. No more "maverick" maneuvers. Not that the board would be perfect, but then, neither had been their father. In light of that reality, checks and balances seemed the best policy. Since dealing with the "dirt files," Pauline had gained a whole new appreciation for the concept of submission and how essential it must be for accomplishing the work of the Kingdom.

✣

The last guest had been dismissed from the main entrance. With a strong sense of readiness for the many trials ahead, Evan returned to his father's bedroom to say good night to Pauline and Lydia. As he neared the room, Jilly ran into his arms, joyfully surprising him. Evidently Rick and Connie had walked up the hill for a visit, entering by a side door. He lifted his daughter, kissed her sweetly, and carried her into the bedroom. To his further surprise, Danna had also slipped into the house unnoticed. His heartbeat quickened at the sight of her. She seemed to grow more lovely each time he looked at her. The recent ordeal had awakened new feelings between the two of them. They had yet to sort them out.

"Hello there," he said.

"Hi yourself," she replied, as she adjusted Dr. Grace's bedcovers.

He nodded to the rest of them, standing around Pauline's bed. "Some day, huh?"

"Daddy, how long are you going to have a broken arm?" Jilly asked, reaching up and turning his head away from looking at Danna.

"A few months, honey."

"I'm sorry you got hurt," she pouted sympathetically. "How long will Grandpa be sick?"

At that unexpected moment Dr. Grace cleared his throat and stirred on his bed as if responding to Jilly's voice. They turned to watch, transfixed. He yawned widely. His hand moved across his face and vigorously rubbed his eyes. When he removed his hand, his eyes fluttered open. In that moment Dr. Simon Grace found himself face to face with his astonished son Evan and Jilly. The preacher's brow wrinkled with curiosity, and he shook his head slightly, as if to ask, "What on earth are you doing here?" His eyes roved over Jilly and down to Evan's broken arm.

"Dad," Evan said hoarsely, "do you know me?"

Grace swallowed painfully and nodded with a mischievous twinkle. "Of course . . . you're Jimmy Hogan's boy," he rasped.

They all laughed. It was his trademark humor to tease like that. The old man was still intact after so long asleep.

Clearing his throat, he tried to say something next to Jilly, but gave up and merely nodded, smiling at her gamely. He seemed to be in considerable pain. It was small wonder, with all the life support attachments he had endured. Especially the breathing tube that had ripped from his throat in the cave. Not to mention the bang he'd received on the head when the table had overturned.

"Let me help you," Evan offered, setting Jilly down and hurrying to his side.

Dr. Grace waved him off, determined to rise on his own. But after several tries he could not get up. He looked up apologetically.

Evan took his hand. "Here, you rusty old prophet."

The others tittered nervously.

Grace smiled, hearing their voices. Evan sat on the bed and placed his right arm under his dad's shoulder. Danna assisted him on the other side, helping him into a sitting position. She quickly stuffed pillows behind his back. The preacher looked around shyly, taking inventory of the unexpected guests in his bedroom.

"You know, you're a lot of trouble around here, Pops," Evan kidded. "But we're mighty glad to have you back."

"That so?" he asked with a defiant frown. It was a grouchy mood they had often tolerated from him and would gladly tolerate again. "Where have I been?" Grace said, then repeated soberly, "Yeah . . . where *have* I been?" His eyes found Lydia's next. Tears pooled quickly between the two of them. He nodded silently, acknowledging her.

Then he spotted Pauline. She lay in her bed, a Band-Aid across the bridge of her nose, eyes discolored from her impact with the windshield of the land rover. The instant he saw her, Dr. Grace's expression tumbled like a sand castle at high tide.

She lay with a trembling hand covering her mouth, crying silently behind her fingers, engulfed in the miracle of his sudden presence. *He is loosed!* she thought. *He is here! What will he say?*

He reached quickly for Evan's support and stood shakily to his feet, keeping his eyes glued to his daughter. Then he began determinedly shuffling forward on stiffened limbs. Danna grabbed his IV bag from the bedstand and carried it alongside of him.

Pauline wondered, Did he remember the arena? Did he know she had been there with him? Would he love her for what she had done? Would he accept the changes in her now? The decisions she had made without him? She couldn't stop her thoughts from running wildly to every possibility, good and bad, as he closed the gap between them. Reaching the bedside, Dr. Grace stood still, looking down at Pauline as he had done so often when she was a child. She braved a smile at him, and immediately his smile returned, breaking through a mask of guilt and fear on his face. His handsome features seemed to come to life in that smile, like the unfolding of a resurrection plant.

Jilly hurried again to Evan's side, taking his hand. He knelt down, letting her sit across his knees as they watched.

Grace reached down with his right hand, a hand that had been placed on the heads of thousands of the world's sick, lame and dying—and often on the apple of his eye in her tender years. He gently pushed aside the strands of blonde hair straying across Pauline's forehead.

This much is true, she thought, looking up at him, *he has always been a healer*. It suddenly came to her that in all of his life, his undivided concern had only been given to the sick. As a girl she had craved the sore throats and fevers that had brought him to her room. Suffering, pain, grief, weakness—this had been his special province. His landscape. Perhaps the only focus of his life without hidden motives. It was something worth salvaging from the wreck of his ministry.

His fingers brushed the tears from beneath her eyes, affection for her written in every line of his face. He mustered his strength and spoke in a labored voice. A mere ghost of the orator's bass that had rumbled from his chest two weeks ago in the Valley of Hinnom. "How's my baby girl?" he said.

Oh the joy and the pain of it! These words, which had once held the power to make everything right with the world, now twisted her heart in two. She could not go back to being his "baby girl." He was not the same man to her now and never could be again. For the remaining years of his life he would need her far more than she would need him.

AFTER

The confrontation could wait no longer. Simon Grace would have to face his children and the consequences of his reckless decisions. Pauline had gained strength rapidly. Even with her blackened eyes, she felt well enough to get out of bed the day following the board meeting. She went to the executive offices for a couple hours work. Dr. Grace had remained bedfast, but after a couple more days gained enough strength that he began to ask questions: "How is the ministry income? Did our letter go out? How are the hospitals? Would you send Jann by to see me? It is time I get back to work." The answers to those questions seemed absurd to Pauline and Evan. There could be no business as usual. But because their father seemed content to ignore that fact, they had grown privately angry with him. Together they had agreed that Dr. Grace owed answers to the whole world for the recent tragedies of the ministry, and they would make it their business to see that he not escape that responsibility.

As they waited for the right time to confront him, they took the next several days to piece together a "damage control" plan by which to operate the ministry through the transition. Certain allegations were being made about the Matamoros lab by probing reporters for *Texas People*. Other national news organizations were raising new questions about the whereabouts of Dr. Grace during recent weeks. No one knew the full story, nor would they ever, but much more was soon to be revealed. It could not be avoided. While they waited for Sharpey to assemble a new board, Pauline used her interim power to place Evan in Neva Sylvan's vacancy, with a mandate to free all of the Grace Missionary hospitals from Dunamis money and influence.

In that role, Evan first called Max Commagene's office in Mannheim. All of his calls were diverted to a man named Werner Kleburg, a new appointee for the Grace account within Dunamis. He seemed polite, discreetly informed, and accommodating to Evan's proposal to sever their financial link. In fact, he had already been ordered to take steps in that direction. Max Commagene, Evan was told, would not be involved anymore. His full attention had been called to much larger enterprises within Commagene Industries.

To Evan's near shock, Kleburg went on to acknowledge the purchase of *The Seven Sleepers of Antioch* icon and insisted that the final amounts had already been transferred directly to Dr. Grace's account the week before. He faxed a copy of the documents of sale to Evan's office. A subsequent call to the Brownsville Bank confirmed that the transaction was a "done deal." Simon Grace was forty million dollars richer. Inspecting the documents, Evan noticed his father's' signature. Perhaps it had been forged?

Evan dialed international code forty-nine, placing a now-familiar call to Colonel Canaan, who had taken temporary residence in Germany's Frankfurt Marriott, from which he led undercover surveillance of Dunamis and Commagene's several German residences. Evan wanted the colonel's advice about the legality of the icon transaction. Canaan confirmed that Dunamis's Common Market assets were known to be in the billions, and that the documents seemed complete, including Simon Grace's signature.

"The Uriel Mission has not given up," Canaan reassured him. "We will find the tablets and the Patriarch yet. In the meantime, we are making some progress on the facts in your case. We have discovered that the 'Reverse the Curse' letter was paid for in advance by Dunamis. It appears they introduced the weak letter through Alan Lavalle in order to cripple the finances of the ministry. It was not your dad."

"What was in it for them?"

"As you suspected, possibly to slow down internal investigation. We would like to know if your father was in on the details of that plan. That is the only question that remains for us as far as he goes. How much did he know? We are certain that he was completely in control of the 'Tree of Life' letter that went through Dallas WordSmith, but what about the other one?"

"I'll see what I can find out."

Evan went to his father's office to see Pauline, who had taken up her duties from there. As he informed her of this new information her eyes took on a metallic hue and she exploded. "So he signed for forty million! What on earth did he have in mind, Evan?"

He shook his head incredulously.

"Well, it is time to get to the bottom of it. And I mean right now, before he gets strong enough to wriggle out of our grasp. Let's go see that old man."

❖

And so they went. As the limo traveled from the administration building toward the family compound, Pauline gazed out of her window toward the south. The Prayer Steeple faced the square-shouldered medical building across the sixteenth fairway of the golf course. It seemed to her that her entire life was divided like those two buildings: prayer versus medicine, faith versus science, holiness versus sin, light versus darkness, black versus white (at least until lately, when she had been forced to deal with some very difficult shades of gray).

Gray areas, she found, existed in life between people of faith and those without it. Believers became doctors of medicine, but many more unbelievers seemed to excel in that profession. Were their contributions to healing any less than the believing healers? The same question applied in life every which way she turned. Christ claimed to be the way, the truth and the life, but the world was filled with many well-doing nonbelievers. As if they didn't count, the Bible insisted on dividing the world into two opposing kingdoms. Not good and evil, but life and death. Yet that division was not easily discerned. In fact, historically, terrible errors had been made by those who presumed to divide the wheat from the chaff. She shook her head with brain-weariness. The bottom line seemed to be that in many ways Christianity complicated her life. *Why should it be that way?* she wondered.

"Evan," she said, suddenly struck by a dilemma that had become acute for her since Colonel Canaan's recent attentions, "can a Christian and a Jew be . . . can they be romantically linked? Let's not say 'married,' for heaven's sake. Not yet. But I just don't believe in starting a romance for nothing. I'm of a mind to be serious. But in that regard, is it just impossible with Canaan or what? I have to confess, I'm confused. They aren't believers, are they?"

"Well, some are. We serve the same God, Jehovah, Creator of Heaven and earth." He had not really put his thoughts together about the relationship between Jew and Christian before, though he had thought of it often. "We share the Old Testament in common. And then, of course, you've heard of 'Jews for Jesus.'"

"Canaan isn't one of those," she answered quickly.

"Well, have you asked him?"

"It seems presumptuous."

"I don't think so. I think it is probably time you had this whole discussion. Get an understanding between you."

She sighed. "You're right about that." She knew that she could never give her heart to a man who did not first give his heart to the Lord Jesus Christ. That was her total life commitment. But what did that mean to a Jew? Not just to *a* Jew—but to *this* particular Jew who had shared so much adventure with her lately. "I don't know where to begin the discussion."

"You'll find a way." Evan suddenly had an idea, and he chuckled at himself. "Why not begin on common ground? Tell him you are both Jews."

"What?"

"Yes. Tell him you are a faithful follower of a Jewish rabbi named Jesus! See what he says."

She smiled. Of course. She liked that. Jesus had not come to repudiate Judaism but to fulfill it. He followed the Temple customs. He was Messiah. The answer to whether she and Canaan could encourage a romance hinged entirely on his acceptance of Jesus, a Jewish rabbi, as Messiah. She had her place to begin at least. At that moment the limo pulled up to the side entrance of the mansion, and her mind turned to more immediate concerns.

❖

Their father was asleep when they entered the room, which added frustration to Pauline's already simmering anger. Lydia told them that he had been asleep for about an hour, so Pauline gently nudged his shoulder, calling insistently until he woke up. She then brought him a glass of water.

"Daddy, Evan and I need to have a serious talk with you. Can we get you to wake up real good for us?" Her tone of voice was pregnant with trouble.

Grace looked over the top of his water glass, eyes darting back and forth as he sipped. Evan thought he resembled a guilty little boy calculating which rule he had been caught breaking, not wanting to confess any of the others. How odd to see his father this way. Childish. It occurred to him that some forms of childishness remained unchanged throughout a lifetime. Even in his own father.

Pauline paced restlessly. She noticed a nurse attending to medications across the room and turned to Lydia. "I would like you to stay, but would you kindly see the nurse to the door?"

Lydia nodded and hurried to obey.

Crossing her arms, Pauline could not wait a second longer. "Daddy?"

Evan pulled a chair near the bed and sat down, steadily watching his father's face.

"Go ahead. What's on your mind?"

She spun around. "Don't talk to me like that! Don't you dare act impatient with me. Or condescending. I have something to say to you, and don't treat me like I'm your little girl."

His eyes grew pained. She had never spoken up to him this way before. Then he seemed put off by it, dismayed, appealing to Evan, "What is this? What does she mean?"

Evan's own anger rose at his evasive response. "I think she expressed herself quite well, Dad. She is upset with you, and she has a right to be."

Lydia quietly shut the door after the departing nurse.

Pauline began to cry, but her tears were not shameful nor accompanied by helpless sobs or any sign of weakness. It was the strength of her pain and anger toward her father that flowed from her. Feelings now supported by her brother, who understood. In this context her anger might not turn to bitterness; not if it found its proper expression.

"Daddy, do you know that Neva Sylvan is dead?"

He looked guardedly back and forth between them. "No, I did not."

"She committed suicide."

"No!"

Pauline and Evan glanced quickly at one another. Either Dr. Grace was a perfect actor or he was truly shocked. She lowered her voice in light of his surprise and repeated the next list with careful emphasis. "Did you know that Osis, Santesteban, Lester, Sutphen, and Kassabian *all* committed suicide?"

His face seemed to drain of color, and he swayed slightly on the bed. Pauline rushed over to his side, catching him by the arm. "Daddy, are you OK?"

"Suicide?" he asked weakly.

"What does that tell you about them, Daddy?" Pauline asked sternly, shaking her father by the shoulders, refusing to baby his feelings. "They were murderers!" Her aqua eyes blazed fiercely into his. "They were cultists and murderers, and you let them into this ministry! Do you deny that?" At close range she saw the trapped expression deep in his eyes. He was caught, and he knew it. He could not pretend that he had made wise alliances in medical research. "You are responsible in this situation, Daddy. Not only the suicides—but innocent people have died while you've been up there at Nimrut Dag."

"How do you mean?" Gone was the superiority from his voice, the evasiveness of his manner. He looked at Evan searchingly. "Tell me what I need to know. The whole thing."

Evan had no intention of cutting in front of his sister with an answer. That would give the wily old manipulator a way to play the words of one against the other.

"You are going to hear it all, Daddy," Pauline said curtly, standing to her feet again. "But first you are going to give some straight answers to some straight questions. Did you sell the icon to Dunamis?" She turned to watch the way he answered this.

Evan couldn't believe his eyes. The old man looked quickly away from them and grew red in the face. Her question hit close to home. A forty million dollar embarrassment. They glanced knowingly at one another.

He turned again and looked straight at Evan. "Dunamis made the offer when I arrived in Jerusalem. It was a surprise."

"Not to mention a lot of money," Evan prodded.

"It was not only for me. They had lost a doctor at Nimrut Dag and were beginning to believe my preaching—that there were two spiritual kingdoms, not one. It was an opportunity for Jehovah to be tested against the prophets of Baal in this new medical arena. I had invested years toward this day—I just hadn't expected it to come so soon. They were ready for the test. Wanted to see if I could cross over. Surely you know about the medical possibilities of this by now?"

Evan nodded. "We do."

"Well, I had a big problem. Cash flow was critical back here. I couldn't go off and leave it without a guarantee. That's when they made the icon offer, and it gave me the insurance that the ministry, not to mention the two of you, would be taken care of whether I came back or not." After a pause he added, "I believed I would be successful."

Evan wondered if his father really cared about *both* of them in that forty million dollar endowment. He smiled, prepared to push him to the wall to find the truth about the explosion on Alan's yacht. "Of course that's not the only reason you accepted the deal, Dad. You had also authorized a bogus letter to make sure the ministry lost even more money while you were away. Then you could come back and save it. Right?"

Grace stared blankly. "I don't know what you are talking about."

Evan didn't believe him, but wanted to. "'Reverse the Curse'? A letter you wrote in Jerusalem?"

"I didn't write any such a letter. Stiles had a letter ready before we left for Jerusalem. It was called . . . 'Heaven Help Us' as I recall."

Evan was favorably impressed. "Yeah, that's the one alright. You didn't go over Stiles's head and order another letter through Alan while Stiles was still in Jerusalem?"

"I did not." His gaze and his voice remained convincingly steady.

"You didn't wire three hundred thousand in advance to San Diego to see that it happened?"

"I didn't have my hands on that kind of money. No."

"Well, Alan got the money and did exactly that. A 'Reverse the Curse' letter ran instead of 'Heaven Help Us,' and Stiles thought you had given him an end-run."

Dr. Grace shook his head slowly, eyes searching for the meaning to this.

"Oh, come on, Dad," Evan scolded, "you know what that means. You've manipulated enough mail to see the implications." He recomputed the facts quickly in his mind. If indeed his father did not know, the truth was, he had been outdone by Dunamis. It occurred to him that his father might also have had nothing to do with the explosion. "Did you know Alan and Logos Mail handled the icon deal?"

"Alan had nothing to do with the icon deal," Dr. Grace protested. "There was no middleman."

Evan smiled cynically, remembering that Alan had been left out of the recent Dunamis transfers. "True. That turns out to be true, Dad. There is forty million in your personal account, and only the first thirteen million came through Alan's hands. They didn't need him to handle the deal at all. They were using him the same way they used you. Your corruptibility made it all possible."

"The icon money belongs to the ministry, Dad," Pauline added. "Are we agreed? The ministry needs it to clean up this mess."

Grace hid his response, listening intently.

"Daddy?"

Evan held up his hand to Pauline, indicating that it was not yet time for this point to be made.

She nodded with perfect understanding. "Did you call Neva, Dad, ordering delivery of the icon?" She recalled Danna's account of the phone call.

"Neva had nothing to do with it."

"Then Dunamis did that too," Pauline declared. "It is going to be nearly impossible to separate out all of the lies Dunamis injected into this transaction," she said, looking ominously at Evan. "I can see mistrial written all over it, unless we have better lawyers than they do."

Evan nodded absently, combing busily through his thoughts for more evidence. If his father was telling the truth, Dunamis had taken advantage of his signature on the icon deal in order to gain the confidence of Alan Lavalle. Promises of a commission on a "done deal" enticed the materialistic preacher to use his unique position to insert Dunamis's "loser" letter into the Grace Ministries mailing list. After that, Dunamis had intended to take possession of the icon and be done with Lavalle. They had never intended to pay his commission. Evan felt sure of that. All had gone according to plan until Evan had switched the icon case, and then they had revealed their true murderous colors. So, *they* had been the ones to try to impede the investigation, not Simon Grace. He felt somewhat better about his father for this bit of knowledge. "Did you know that ancient cuneiform tablets were in the icon case all these years?"

"Tablets?" Grace's eyes searched the air as his mind raced through his sketchy knowledge of Otto Commagene, Max's uncle who had given the icon to him in the 50s. "What kind of tablets?"

"The original 'Songs of Jubal.' Cuneiform."

Grace showed a sudden insight. "Now I understand. The icon was given to me with the strict instruction that it never be removed from the antiquities case. Perhaps to protect the tablets. Dunamis has paid for the security measures on the icon all these years. They have shown unusual interest in it."

"Did you know about 'The Songs of Jubal'?"

"I know of the manuscripts. Never heard of the tablets."

"Did you know they were anti-Semitic?"

"They are not. I have read the entire text in English. I knew that they were rumored to have been used by Hitler, but Dunamis had nothing to do with that . . ." The trapped look came back into his eyes. "They assured me they were just rumors," he protested in a convictionless voice.

"Right. They turned out to be much more than rumors, Dad. Six Dunamis research doctors have committed suicide. They could not have been your average practitioners, now could they? In fact they were members of the Secret Society of Apostates who kept 'The Songs of Jubal' and the icon. During World War II they committed medical atrocities. That was the original chartering of the Dunamis Foundation. The predecessors of Neva, Sutphen, Osis, and Kassabian worked with Mengele. I've read your notebooks on Nimrut Dag, Dad. And the cavern. You should have suspected all of this. Neva was a Society initiate. Your own medical director. Didn't you even do a simple background check on her? You would have found out that she had not studied to become a doctor—she had been living in Jonestown." Evan noticed that Lydia had gone to a corner of the room where she now remained in silent prayer. He felt glad for her presence there.

Pauline had stopped pacing and watched her father closely. "OK. Enough of Dunamis, Daddy," she said, walking around to face him squarely from the foot of his bed. Her tears had stopped. "Now I want to take up the part that directly involves you and whatever future you may have outside of prison."

His eyes quickly checked Evan's.

"She's right, Dad. There is no guarantee that you will not go to prison in the cleanup of this thing."

"How could you, Daddy," Pauline continued steadily, "use dirty secrets from people's past lives to control them? Your own people?"

At this, Dr. Grace looked sharply down, not with contrition, but scowling to himself. "Now wait a minute. You have never had to carry the kind of responsibility—"

"I wouldn't want it!" she screamed, slapping her hands against the footboard of the bed in distress. "Don't give me another word of excuse!" Evan had never seen her so beside herself.

Grace looked up. He had never known his "baby girl" this way either. Whatever had happened since he had left her in Jerusalem had completely changed her.

She softened, just a little. "Oh, Daddy, you're right and you're wrong," she said earnestly. "I have never had to carry that kind of responsibility. I've had a little taste of it lately, and I have failed too. None of us are clean enough to use that kind of power for long. And none of us are worthy to use it at all in the name of the Lord. That's where everything needs to start—with that realization. I will not let this ministry be run by your personality or your ability to raise money again. Not you or me or anybody. Will you say yes to that, Daddy? Do you understand the heart of what I'm saying?"

He looked away with disgust, as if he deserved to be better spoken to.

"Daddy!" she screamed again, slapping the bed frame.

He turned back slowly, still holding to his expression of offended reserve.

Pauline felt as if she would burst if he did not acknowledge that she was right. No ifs, ands or buts would satisfy her in his answer; it had to be an unqualified yes. To the dismay of her heart he still seemed to be resisting, bowing his will against her. She felt almost as hopeless as she had felt in the arena after commanding the Nephil to go to The Pit, only to have the creature mock her. Only this was her father, not a Nephil she faced. Her love for him was as great as her love for life. If he chose to reject the purity and logic in her request, it would permanently break her heart. She would have no choice but to become his enemy, and that would tear her apart.

Tears suddenly leaped down her cheeks again, and her finger stabbed at him repeatedly as she promised with conviction, "I will send you to prison myself if you do not say yes to me now, Daddy. Say yes to the new board of directors appointed over this ministry by Chester Sharpey! Say yes to the correction measures they will take against you. Say yes to God who demands that you live according to His Law. Say yes to the policemen who may come and put you in irons!" She wept silently for a moment, biting her lower lip. "Say yes to Evan, who is taking the hospitals from Dunamis! Say yes to the truth, and only to the truth, that you will write in your letters from now on! No more manipulation. You will be held accountable by me, Daddy, and by Evan, if not by anyone else."

She said no more, but waited, watching his eyes for a sign of submission that would allow her to be his daughter once again. Her stomach knotted and groaned within her, fearing the stubbornness of his mind, feeling that she had touched a dark, forbidden monster in the soul of the man. If his heart bowed before God Almighty, then surely he would say yes to her now. But she did not know him that well. She did not know what he would choose, and she was terribly afraid.

Meanwhile, Lydia had bent double in her chair across the room. She could no longer suppress the prayer of her spirit. It forced itself between her lips in a near-silent moan. Grace tilted his head in her direction, recognizing the sound of her travail, then cast his eyes downward once again. He seemed like a man poised between truth and manipulation, humility and pride, forgiveness and the fires of a most severe correction.

Evan sat calmly in his chair watching. His part was over. Now he simply wondered what kind of father had sired him. Did the Spirit of Christ dwell in this man? Or had he been a user from the beginning? Had he gone astray by the errors of a feeling heart, or had he built a life on the cold purposes of an apostate mind? *Who was Simon Grace?*

The preacher looked up, directly at Pauline. He started to speak, then stopped, cleared his throat and began again. "I have sinned against God and done this evil in His sight," he said, paraphrasing a Psalm she had read repeatedly to him during his coma. Then he added the confession of the prodigal, "I am not worthy to be called a son." His voice caught with emotion.

Pauline sobbed aloud with joy.

Dr. Grace nodded and smiled at her and continued to speak. "Yes, Pauline, I will say yes to everything you have asked, even though it hurts me more than you can know to think you would send me to jail, my baby g—" He struggled, forcing himself to continue, "—my daughter. My very blessed daughter. And of course I will accept Evangel." He glanced acknowledgingly toward Evan. "I will even accept the board and their recommendations."

Pauline came to his side and embraced him, kissing him. He brushed tears from her cheek.

"Daddy?" she said, earnestly seeking the soul in his eyes. "Daddy, I love you. I have to know something . . ." She paused, afraid to ask, afraid not to. "Did you see me over there . . . on the other side?" She waited breathlessly to know the truth. She did not want him to humor her in any way with his answer.

His eyes darkened with a faraway memory, and he nodded almost imperceptibly. "I did see you, sweetheart."

Evan still found it difficult to accept that such a thing was possible—two people meeting in the netherworld. If so, it could only be real between the two of them, and he planned to live the rest of

his life with feet planted squarely on *terra firma*. Then he remembered something. "That's funny," he interrupted, rubbing the ache
in his broken arm. "I remember when she came to, I was hanging
upside-down there in the cave and she was calling for Mama. Did
either of you see Mama over there?"

Father and daughter turned to look at him, then looked inquiringly back at one another. They slowly shook their heads no.

"Then what were you screaming 'Mama' for?" Evan asked,
looking curiously at his sister.

Lydia had stopped praying. She too watched and listened
intently.

Pauline collected her fading memories of the trip through the
Tree and into the Sides of the North. The arena, the angel, her
father. "Daddy was trying to tell me something just as I came
back," she recalled, turning to him. "Daddy, what was it? Do you
remember?"

He was watching her with an odd twinkle in his eye. "I was trying to tell you the name of the Nephil," he said.

A chill ran over her body, recalling the evil creature playing its
evil game: "What's my name?" "The name of the Nephil," she murmured. "Daddy, did I set you free to be able to speak its name?
After I took off the metal gag?"

He paused thoughtfully, then nodded. There was obviously
more to tell about it. "It was the key," he said simply.

"The key. Then what was the name? 'Mama'?"

"Mama had nothing to do with it," he replied. "The name of
the Nephil was . . . Mammon."

In the deep and thoughtful silence that followed, each one in
the room knew the part of the truth pertaining to their own experience. Money, filthy lucre, greed, the lust for riches, "the root of
all evil." Mammon had not only a modern kingdom, but an idol
on Nimrut Dag named in his honor: Fortune, the patron of
Dunamis. He also had a living Apostate Patriarch. He was a netherworld giant who ruled in an arena dedicated to his name.
Mammon. Evidently human souls could become trapped by
Mammon while still living—preachers not exempted—and they
could be ruled by his hand in the afterlife, perhaps forever. Unless
they were set free. Christ had said, "How hard it will be for the
wealthy to enter the Kingdom of God."

Lydia understood the nature of the Nephil's birth. Evan understood that he had smelled Mammon's foul breath from the moment he heard of his father's disappearance.

Pauline turned to look at her brother now with a deeper appreciation than ever before. He had followed the trail of money from the very start. "Evangel, you were so right," she said.

He shook his head modestly. He would not accept praise that didn't rightfully belong to him. "Half right," he said. "At best."

She smiled appreciatively and turned back around. "That's why we need Evan around here, Daddy. Do you know that? I've asked him to stay."

Her father's expression darkened, and his voice took on a gruffness and a bit of distance. "Sweetheart, it seems you are becoming quite the preacher around here yourself, and I don't want to take anything away from you, but in Jerusalem . . . who did I tell you to call if you got in trouble?"

She was taken aback, then understood and laughed aloud, recalling his disconcerting words: "Call Evan." How differently she felt about her brother now.

The three of them faced more difficulty ahead than she could ever have imagined a few weeks ago, but Pauline was sure they were more ready to face it than ever before in their lives. In her heart she breathed a sigh of thanksgiving for an answered prayer—perhaps a more important prayer in the Presence than any other—they were a family again.